Chapel Noir

An Irene Adler Novel

Carole Nelson Douglas

A TOM DOHERTY ASSOCIATES BOOK
NEW YORK

CHAPEL NOIR: AN IRENE ADLER NOVEL

Maps by Darla Tagrin

A Forge Book
Published by Tom Doherty Associates, LLC
175 Fifth Avenue
New York, NY 10010

www.tor.com

Forge® is a registered trademark of Tom Doherty Associates, LLC.

ISBN: 0-765-34347-9
Library of Congress Catalog Card Number: 2001040151

First edition: October 2001
First mass market edition: September 2002

Printed in the United States of America
0 9 8 7 6 5 4 3 2 1

Grateful acknowledgment is made to the following for permission to reprint material:

Belford, Barbara. *Bram Stoker*. Copyright © 1996 by Alfred A. Knopf. Reprinted by permission of Alfred A. Knopf.

Harsin, Jill. *Policing Prostitution in Nineteenty-Century Paris*. Copyright © 1985 by Princeton University Press. Reprinted by permission of Princeton University Press.

Hovey, Tamara. *Paris Underground*. Copyright © 1991 by Tamara Hovey. Reprinted by permission of Orchard Books/Scholastic, Inc.

Jakubowski, Maxim and Braund, Nathan. *The Mammoth Book of Jack the Ripper*. Copyright © 1999 by Constable & Robinson, London. Reprinted by permission of Constable & Robinson.

Schwartz, Vanessa R. *Spectacular Realities: Early Mass Culture in Fin-de-Siècle Paris*. Copyright © 1997 by The Regents of the University of California. Reprinted by permission of the University of California Press.

For Claire Eddy,
with many thanks for her eagle editorial eye,
and for her scholarly approach
to the art of making books

Acknowledgments

The author owes much to the invaluable assistance of Delphine Kresge-Cingal, a professor at the University of Amiens, France, and her associate, Thierry Melan, founder of a French Sherlockian research organization, the *Centre de Recherches Holmésiennes et Victoriennes* (http://www.crhv.org).

Thanks to the modern wonders of e-mail and the World Wide Web, both sources researched Paris then and now, forwarding images of vintage Paris street maps and scenes.

Delphine also read the novel in manuscript, offering encouragement, research information, and explaining the fine points of French language and usage.

Where these have not been followed, it is due to English usage traditions with French words, or because the author needed to take a little literary license with the facts in what is ultimately a work of fiction.

Delphine and Thierry were tireless detectives on the trail of particular street names and facts, and performed tenaciously enough to impress Sherlock Holmes himself.

I also thank them for an honorary membership in the *Centre de Recherches Holmésiennes et Victoriennes*. I'm very glad that, at the end of *Good Night, Mr. Holmes*, I moved Irene Adler from London to Paris, where she has been so welcomed, and where her books are being reprinted.

Also most helpful were Barbara Peters of The Poisoned Pen bookstore in Scottsdale, Arizona, and "Ripperologist" August Paul Aleksy Jr., of Centuries & Sleuths Bookstore in Forest Park, Illinois. I thank them both profoundly.

—Carole Nelson Douglas

Contents

. . . she has a soul of steel. The face of the most beautiful of women and the mind of the most resolute of men.

—THE KING OF BOHEMIA, "A SCANDAL IN BOHEMIA"

Editor's Note

The release of this volume is extremely satisfying. Discreet chiding in academic circles has for some time labeled me an outlaw editor. My "crime"? Allowing several years to pass before presenting this fifth installment of the Penelope Huxleigh diaries, which record the life of the only woman to outwit Sherlock Holmes, the late Irene Adler of revered and enduring memory. Even my publisher and the public have joined in the general clamor for more.

Rumors abound that the publication delay proves that the content of all the Huxleigh diaries is confabulated, that I am simply slow in carrying on the masquerade.

As is usual with clamor and rumors, nothing could be farther from the facts. The reason for delay is the astounding nature of the following testaments that I have spent so many years verifying.

In addition, I encountered among the Huxleigh material yet another document from a completely, shall I say, alien source? This yellow-bound journal or casebook apparently had been seized, or perhaps, more innocently, had fallen into the hands of the principals mentioned in the diary. It was written in a language other than English so I had to find a circumspect translator familiar with nineteenth-century usages who was willing to sign a letter of utter silence on the source and contents of this account.

Let my critics know that I am working feverishly to complete work on the next and companion volume even as this one goes forth to meet its public.

*—Fiona Witherspoon, Ph.D., A.I.A.**
April 2000

*Advocates of Irene Adler

Cast of Continuing Characters

Irene Adler Norton: an American abroad and a diva/detective who is the only woman to outwit Sherlock Holmes in "A Scandal in Bohemia," reintroduced as the protagonist of her own adventures in the novel, *Good Night, Mr. Holmes*

Sherlock Holmes: the London consulting detective with a global reputation for feats of deduction

Wilhelm Gottsreich Sigismond von Ormstein, King of Bohemia: the Crown Prince who courted Irene years before, then feared she might disrupt his forthcoming royal marriage. He hired Sherlock Holmes to recover a photograph of Irene and the Prince together, but she escaped, promising never to use the photo against the King. They crossed swords again in *Another Scandal in Bohemia* (formerly *Irene's Last Waltz*)

Godfrey Norton: the British barrister who married Irene just before they escaped to Paris to elude Holmes and the King of Bohemia

Penelope "Nell" Huxleigh: the orphaned British parson's daughter Irene rescued from poverty in London in 1881, a former governess and "typewriter girl" who lived with Irene and worked for Godfrey before the pair were married, and who now resides with them in Paris

Quentin Stanhope: the uncle of Nell's former charges when she worked as a London governess; now a British agent in eastern Europe and the Mideast, he reappeared in *A Soul of Steel* (formerly *Irene at Large*)

John H. Watson, M.D.: British medical man and Sherlock Holmes's sometimes roommate and frequent companion in crime-solving

Inspector François le Villard: a Paris detective and admirer of the English detective who has translated Holmes's monographs into French and worked with Irene Adler Norton in *The Adventuress* (formerly *Good Morning, Irene*)

Baron Alphonse de Rothschild, head of the international banking family's most powerful branch and of the finest intelligence network in Europe, frequent employer of Irene, Godfrey, and Nell in various capacities, especially in *Another Scandal in Bohemia.*

Chapel Noir

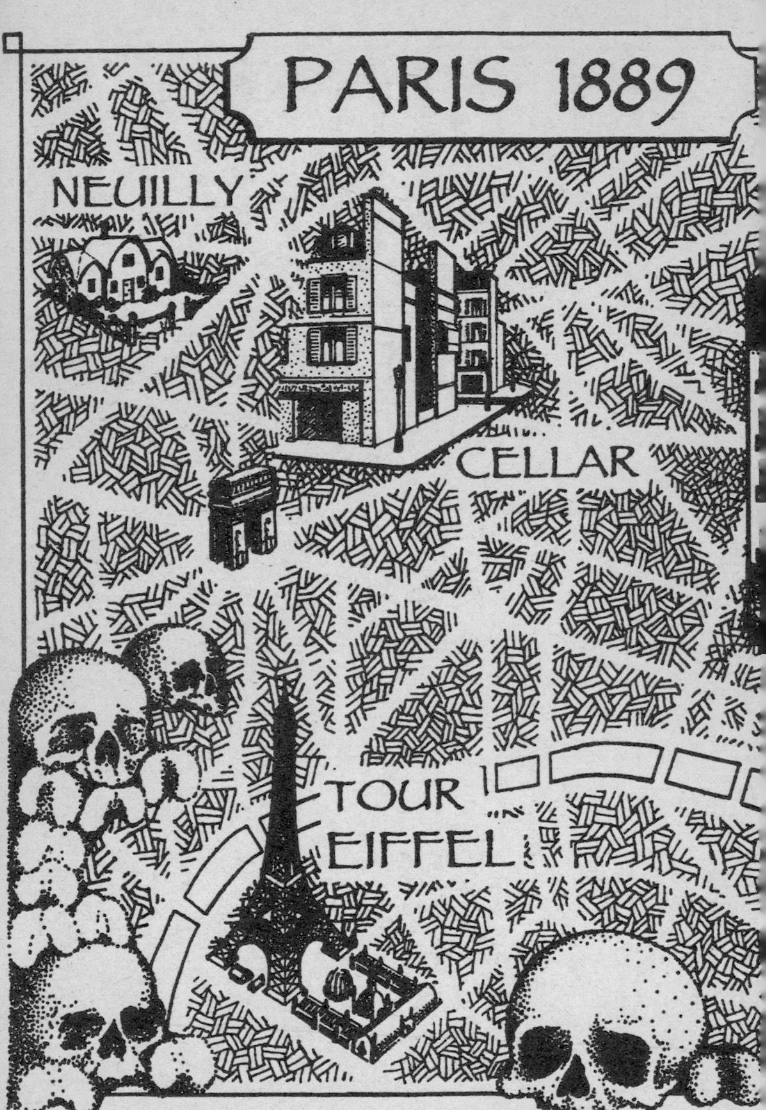

PARIS 1889
NEUILLY
CELLAR
TOUR
EIFFEL

MUSÉE GRÉVIN
MAISON DE RENDEZVOUS
MORGUE

Prelude

Little gleams of light . . . seem to come from tiny hut windows in the forest. "Driver, can't we stop a minute at one of those huts, where the lights are?" "Lights! They're wolves."

—K. MARSDEN

FROM A YELLOW BOOK

He is hungry tonight.

He came home, such as it is, exhausted, confused, clad in a rough shirt other than he had worn on leaving. I insisted he wash his hands. (This is one habit he resists). The wash water swirled with a pink, pulpy substance he could not explain.

He is a wanderer, as am I. Homeless and free, like a wolf in the woods, a hawk in the air.

Sometimes I think he is a god and I am a devil.

Sometimes he is a devil and I am a god.

Which will win, good or evil?

Who will win, God or Devil?

I love this awkward language that yet plays a bit of unholy fun: subtract an "o" from "good" and you have a god. Subtract a "d" from "good," add it to "evil," and you have a devil.

Another game of words: an Englishman, surely one of God's most contradictory creations (or the devil's) would like this. God backwards, in English of course—and to an Englishman there is no other country, no other ambition, no other arrogance—spells "dog."

So, another game of words: in the place of god or devil, let us put master and beast.

So I am his master.

So he will be my beast.

And which of us is most god or devil? He, she. You, me. Good or evil? Writing in a language not one's own permits all. Living in a land not one's own excuses all. Having no god destroys the devil, so we cannot have that.

This I record, whatever bestiality it celebrates, whatever gods and angels fall, whatever devils triumph.

This I have chosen as my experiment. And one last question. Which is stronger, life or death?

The answer is not as obvious as all the civilized world likes to think.

1.
Somewhere in Paris

I often have this strange and moving dream of an unknown woman. . . .
—PAUL VERLAINE, *MON RÊVE FAMILIER*, 1866

FROM A JOURNAL

Saturday, May 18, 1889.

I must be strong and record my impressions before they fade.

Yet . . . no wonder my penmanship resembles the thin, palsied scrawl of a very old lady, though I am not yet twenty-five. My hand shakes despite myself, as my body shivers despite the snapping flames I sit so near.

I had hoped that my unconventional life thus far had prepared me to face disagreeable things, things that those who lead more circumscribed lives might call distasteful, even bizarre. Brutal. Shocking.

But this . . . where to begin?

With the beginning, I tell myself now. I take pride in not being the green girl I am taken for by the blind old eyes all around me. Buck up, my dear childish self! You are a mistress of deceit, and besides, the world will need to know the truth. Someday.

How odd it is that when one is assaulted by the unendurable that the mind fastens on the irrelevant.

So I stood alone and undiscovered on that horrible threshold and elected to notice that the center of the chamber was occupied by the most bizarre piece of furniture I had ever seen. A sort of barber's chair by way of Versailles.

Barber's chair. The phrase puts me in mind of Sweeney Todd, the murderous "demon" barber of Fleet Street in London, the city which I last visited before this one.

And, of course, thoughts of the barbarous Sweeney Todd made the rivulets of drying blood encrusting the chair's brocade into something more than . . . distant and gruesome embroidery.

Having forced my mind to admit what my eyes had already seen and repudiated by looking elsewhere, I forced my gaze to the figures that occupied the bloody appliance.

My first thoughts are unforgettable, and so unlike me, who has seen much unpleasantness from an early age:

I will not swoon.

I will not vomit.

I will not go mad.

I WILL NOT!

2.

Somewhere in France

Never go to France unless you know the lingo,
If you do like me, you will repent, by jingo.
—THOMAS HOOD, 1839

A secret is a stone. You pick one up and think, *Oh, this is not so heavy. And it's rather interesting, isn't it?*

So you walk along carrying it for a little while. And you find it heavier. Yet you dare not just drop it anywhere, for simply anyone to find, so you walk with it for a long distance, for a long time. Then you find that you cannot let it go no matter how much you wish to. And you realize at length that it weighs the world.

We all carry secrets we have picked up almost unwittingly. Almost, but not quite unwittingly. Some are mere pebbles. Others true loadstones.

All weigh more than they are worth.

I recently have found myself weighing one of my secret stones, the heaviest I have ever carried. I turn it over, examine it, consider passing it on to another. A secret shared has wings and becomes a confidence. And sometimes unwanted confidences can become insupportable stones for another.

And so I walk on alone.

Nothing is more soothing to the female soul than a quiet evening of needlework, if I do say so myself.

This thought came to me as I crocheted a charming cover for the tabletop bell by which we summon our maid-of-all-work, Sophie. I do not know why a bell should require a crocheted cover, save that it would keep the dust off of it. Somewhat.

Irene was reading a book, a French novel, I am afraid, on the chaise longue across the room. She would have been pleased that I thought she looked almost as decadent as Sarah Bernhardt in one of her swooning portraits.

On his perch near the antique grand piano by the window Casanova was currently torn between gnawing a half-devoured grape and his own scaly foot. (I cannot choose which is the more loathsome occupation myself.) Occasionally, the parrot would croak out a word, but we two humans managed to remain silent and engrossed in our peaceful occupations.

This evening in Neuilly-sur-Seine, not far beyond the gaslit mists of Paris, felt so unlike the hectic London days when Irene and I had shared quarters in the Saffron Hill district.

Ever since I met Irene Adler eight years ago my peace of mind has been sorely tested. I don't know if we so much "met" as that she selected me as suitable for salvage. As I recently looked through my diaries for those days I could sniff an attitude of despair lifting off the yellowing pages like the smoky miasma that perfumes crowded London streets. Paris is airier, and therefore far less comforting than dear olde London towne. That portion of my diary sits on the table beside me.

> By night, when gaslights glitter through the fog and the cobblestones gleam like bootblack, London seems a landscape glimpsed in some *Arabian Nights* tale. By day the effect is more commonplace, as the city streets throng with omnibuses, hansom cabs, and pedestrians.
>
> Yet that daily, daylit London can intimidate even more than its dark nocturnal side; at least a respectable young woman like myself found it so in the spring of 1881. I trudged the streets of London town, wondering how I came to be adrift on this tide of strangers, my few belongings tumbled into the carpetbag at my side. I was alone and friendless and—for the first time in my four-and-twenty years—homeless and hungry.

So there I was, much younger and quite lost, carrying not secret stones, but a laden satchel containing all my unworldly worldly belongings. A street urchin made to run off with it, for my numb fingers were no obstacle. Suddenly Irene was descending on us, not like the goddess of peace the name meant to the ancients, but like Diana on the hunt, an angry goddess. She drove off the small thief (after filling his grimy paws with coppers) and took me in hand and to tea (which, it turned out, she could as ill afford as I).

From the first it became evident to me that Irene Adler was a fraud. Perhaps I should put it more gently. She was an aspiring opera singer who survived on her wits and some private inquiry commissions stemming from her work with the Pinkerton detective agency before she had forsaken America for England.

The fine copper-colored silk gown and bonnet that so impressed me that day proved to be resurrected street market scavengings. From such remnants she configured an eclectic wardrobe to suit whatever persona she needed for this audition or that inquiry.

My savior was not only in need herself, but was a human chameleon who recognized none of polite society's boundaries. None! And that included outings in gentleman's dress on occasion! Although she admirably spurned the aspiring actress's easiest ladder to fame and fortune—the sponsorship of wealthy noblemen willing to trade pounds and jewels for a woman's favors—in less personal matters of morality she practiced an alarming flexibility. I can best sum up her outlook in that ancient legal catchphrase and popular children's chant: "finders keepers."

It was clear from the outset that she needed me as moral compass. Certainly her hardheaded survival skills were useful to a gently reared spinster who found governess work vanishing and employment as a shopgirl too brutal for words.

We shared rooms in the Saffron Hill Italian district while I went to school to master the mechanical beast that was invading offices throughout London. I became one of the newly named typewriter-girls, and the first female such person employed in the Inns of Court when one Godfrey Norton, barrister, dared to hire one of the new breed. . . .

Godfrey. My jaunt through the past had completely predated his arrival on our domestic front of two, and felt so pleasant for that reason, that a stab of guilt for my present contentment caused me to jab the crochet hook into my forefinger.

"Oh, botheration!"

"What is it, Nell?" Irene inquired.

I was hardly about to confess that I had just realized that I did not miss Godfrey, her husband and my former employer, a man who was the closest thing to a brother I had ever had or was ever likely to have in this vale of woes.

"My crochet hook has taken it upon itself to admonish me for inattention. It's nothing, really. Not even a drop of blood."

"Then we shall hope that you do not fall into a hundred-year slumber until Prince Charming comes."

"Why Prince Charming would be interested in such an immobile girl as Sleeping Beauty, I cannot imagine." When one catches oneself being selfish, it is always best to make rapid public amends. "I was just thinking about missing Godfrey," I said piously. (I had indeed been thinking about missing him, only that I did *not*, which is a fine point that Irene need hardly be told.)

She sighed and let her finger mark the place in her novel while she dropped it to her lap. "His journey has just begun. He will be gone a good deal longer."

"It is most inconvenient that the Rothschilds feel they can call upon Godfrey so often with so little notice."

"Inconvenient," Irene agreed with a rueful smile, "but highly lucrative. And Godfrey enjoys the challenges of foreign missions."

As the lamplight flickered beside her, illuminating her face with some of the flattering glow thrown by theatrical footlights, I reflected that she looked not a day older than when we had met eight years earlier. I have no idea how time has treated my features. I have never been a beauty, and no one notices such things about me, including me.

But Irene, now just past thirty, had been blessed with more virtues than one woman should claim. The fairy godmothers had flocked around her cradle, wherever in the wilds of America it had rocked, and left her infant self endowed with intelligence, a peerless singing voice, an indomitable will, and, of course and most obviously, beauty. Luckily, Irene also had inherited some few flaws that it was most useful for me to point out, and one was about to show itself.

"This country life is so dull, Nell!" she burst out, hurling the inoffensive novel to the floor. (Actually, I suspect it was a rather offensive novel, having been written by that shocking George Sand woman, and the floor was probably too good a place for it.) "I do not know what I will do with myself while Godfrey is in Prague all these weeks."

"Surely you would not wish to encounter the King of Bohemia again?"

"Godfrey may wish to forestall such an encounter. I am more adventurous."

"Exactly why he is selected for these diplomatic missions

over yourself. I am sure Baron Alphonse is well informed as to your past Bohemian escapades."

"Escapades!" she mocked, even as her tone celebrated the word. "I believe that our mild entanglements in Prague are remembered only by ourselves. I do agree, Nell, that Godfrey deserves the Rothschilds' recognition of his abilities, which far exceed the usual skills of being a barrister. There are times, you know, when I am quite content to play the proud helpmeet."

"Play! Exactly. All life to you is a series of roles to be played. If you are the bored and abandoned wife at the moment, I suggest a retreat to your former occupation."

"I am not as I was formerly, an unmarried woman. I do not know even what I would call myself if I sang in public again. Irene Adler has died in more than a few newspapers and some people's imaginations. Can she be resurrected?"

"Why not sing as Irene Norton?"

"She is a stranger. She has no reputation. No history."

I thought. For all Irene's force of will, when it came to her own interest she could be as indecisive as any ordinary mortal. Much of the confidence of the artistic soul is purely armor.

"What of that lady violinist?"

"Which 'lady violinist'?"

"She has two last names, hyphenated. The first is something feudal, and the second is Indian, East Indian."

Irene frowned with blank alarm, as if she thought me demented. Finally, her expression cleared.

"Norman-Nèruda. Feudal-Indian, really, Nell! You are so quintessentially British! I believe her maiden name was Wilhelmine Nèruda, but she married a Swede named Norman. If I followed in her footsteps, I would be Irene Norton-Adler."

This time I frowned. "You follow in no one's footsteps, Irene. You would be Irene Adler-Norton."

There came a long pause while her mind played with this new incarnation. Irene could never resist recasting herself in new roles. Or other people.

I nodded toward the parrot. "There is the piano and your vocal exercises."

"Yes—" Her face, suddenly pensive, rested on her bent elbow and clasped fist, a hoydenish posture I should never tolerate in one of my charges, though it had been years since I had seen employment as a governess. Still, the corrective instinct, once encouraged, is ingrained. I managed to hold my tongue.

"But what is the use, Nell, no matter what I call myself?" Irene demanded, agitated again. "My scales only show how far my range and tone have degraded. One cannot dabble at operatic singing, Nell. One must be always in rehearsal, always performing. The voice must be kept in constant condition, or it soon sours."

"You sound as sweet as ever to me."

"That is because you have no ear for music."

"Most people do not. You are far too exacting of yourself. Why not do as Godfrey has suggested, and seek a new career in stage acting? That would not require the ceaseless practice that opera does."

"I cannot believe *you* encourage such an immoral occupation."

"I have mellowed. And you are married now," I added pointedly. "Madam Adler-Norton."

"Still, even if it now basks in your acceptance, the stage is a demanding mistress. And Paris has its supreme actress in Sarah Bernhardt. I am not so rash as to set up in competition to her."

"You are an American. The French find your kind fascinating for some reason. And you are British-trained for the stage. Even the Divine Sarah could hardly compete with that. In addition, you are much prettier than she."

"Heavens! You praise my art, my American birth, my looks. That is sure to be bad for me, Nell."

"I don't doubt it, but you seem to need cheering up. I know! Why don't you read Godfrey's latest letter aloud while I crochet? It would be an excellent vocal exercise for you, and I do so enjoy it."

"His letters, or my reading them?"

"Both. Now, if you find any little passages that are . . . personal, you may simply omit them. I am impressed by Godfrey's narrative style. He is most descriptive for a barrister. It shall seem as if he is in the room with us while you read. Please do."

She obliged by plucking the fat envelope from the table beside her, the unwholesome fictions of Monsieur/Madame Sand forgotten on the figured Turkish carpet, as all such enterprises should be.

"I've only read it once myself," she murmured, casting an odd look at me from under the raven wings of her eyebrows. "I might stumble over the handwriting."

"Poor Godfrey! Writing on a train can be a most challenging task. I know this from experience. Yet he has been a faithful correspondent—a letter sent back from the first day's journey already—and deserves a formal hearing."

An enigmatic smile quirked Irene's lips as she regarded the letter like an actress a script. "I shall skip the greeting; it is no doubt too flowery for your ears."

"Godfrey flowery? You do intrigue me."

Irene shook the parchment sheets to loosen the folds, then began.

"My . . . dear."

I noticed that her eyes had dropped halfway down the first sheet by the time she finally pronounced the word "dear."

"You are right: an exceptionally florid beginning for a barrister," I murmured to my crochet egg.

"It is his first letter to me since we have married," Irene murmured back.

"If it is too personal, I certainly don't wish to hear it."

"No." Irene waved a graceful hand. I detected a certain wicked glint in her golden eyes. (Yes, they are indeed literally gold in certain lights. One fairy godmother had given her brown eyes such a warm hue that Midas would envy them at times.) Irene cleared her throat imperiously for my attention: she was now committed to presenting the letter as a stage reading.

"My dear," she repeated, launching herself fully upon the task. "Although I have traveled this route before, I find it even more fascinating a second time. Perhaps solitude makes a more observant, though melancholy, traveling companion."

"Nicely put. That solitude bit."

Irene looked up from the letter to nod at my interruption.

For the next few minutes I was treated to an excellent description of the mountainous terrain and meadows punctuated with cows that I had seen myself during my solitary rail trip to Bohemia en route to Irene's rescue years before.

Godfrey's narration was so vivid I could close my eyes and envision the very scenes he described.

Unfortunately, my mind also relived Irene's Bohemian escapade (however much I would like to forget it), which fortunately predated Godfrey, and which resulted in the King of Bohemia pursuing her and me to London. There he engaged a renowned consulting detective to pry from Irene's possession a photograph of herself and the King together. This was a remembrance of the days when he had been merely a Crown Prince and she a prima donna. She was also a brash American who assumed that an enamored European king, albeit minor, would deign to marry a beautiful, talented, intelligent, and spirited diva of absolutely no means and no family history that she has ever shared with anyone, including me!

In this instance she was the innocent and I the sophisticate, but I cannot say I relished the exchange of roles.

For one thing, it brought a man far more formidable than the hugely handsome King of Bohemia into our lives: the consulting detective Sherlock Holmes.

Of course, this Holmes was astute in one respect: he never liked the King of Bohemia. When the King began mourning "what a Queen she would have made" and bemoaning how it was "a pity Irene was not on his level," Sherlock Holmes was wise and sly enough to answer that, from "what I have seen of the lady, she seems, indeed, to be on a very different level to Your Majesty."

These words are emblazoned on my mind, for I witnessed the exchange in disguise when the two men came to Irene's residence to wrest the photograph from her and found the house empty. Those words bring me a reluctant, but no less warm glow for that fact. Much as I despise the source of such high praise for Irene, I must admit that Mr. Holmes was detective enough to get that one incontrovertible fact, at least, precisely right.

"Nell! Are you listening?" I was startled from my reverie as Irene, actress that she was, darted me a sharp glance to see how I was appreciating her rendition of Godfrey's words.

"Yes, of course. Wonderful," I murmured. "Please go on."

"I must say," Godfrey obediently said through the medium of Irene's fluid voice, "that without conversation or company to distract me I find myself strangely mesmerized by the countryside.

"Perhaps it is our steady but serpentine upward progress toward the dazzling white peaks tinted rosy by the westering sun.

"One feels like a Lilliputian mounting an assault on some sleeping Gulliver's body, yet the soft roll of mountain meadows outside my window is far more fecund than bone and sinew beneath the soft skin of earth."

"Why that is almost like Mr. Tennyson," I commented, crocheting apace.

There is nothing so cozy as a domestic scene warm with lamplight and the murmur of someone reading aloud. I sighed in sheer content.

"Our train," Godfrey went on through the offices of Irene, "has only eleven passenger cars, but a hunter's green engine trimmed with a great many gilt curlicues.

"This industrious machine leans into the task of leading its train of attendants up the mountain like a bull into an attack on a toreador: mechanical head down until the horns, or cowcatcher in this case, brush the tracks; mighty lungs (or firebox) huffing and puffing until billows of steam waft past the passenger windows. We hear its labored breathing (chug-chug) and our excitement cannot help but mount as we feel our vehicle pull upward, upward, into the Alps.

"As we sense ourselves pushed back into our plush upholstered seats, we pant as if we, too, were exerting ourselves to the maximum. Every muscle tenses, and still we rise higher and higher with the train, at an angle growing ever more vertical until we seem to be set on piercing the sky—"

"Goodness," I interrupted. "I remember some steep grades

when I made my solitary way to Bohemia to rescue you from that faithless King, but nothing so strenuous as Godfrey describes. My heart is quite pounding from the tension."

"Yes," Irene murmured, her eyes fixed upon the page. "Perhaps my reading is overdramatic."

"That is always a possibility," I admitted, "but don't stop now. It sounds as if that poor train and all its passengers could quite tip over backwards on the mountaintop."

She continued.

> Yet we have now driven into the snow-shawled uplands, a shining white expanse that looks as cool and soft as eiderdown, encouraging the engine's Herculean effort to reach the summit. From the window we can see the setting sun casting a rosy glimmer over the swelling snowfields.
>
> Our engine strains as if to outrun the setting sun, a steel ramrod determined to drill through the imperious mountain blushing in the last rays of daylight.
>
> Clouds of steam, or perhaps the cooler clouds caught on the mountain's peak, rush by our windows. All we can hear is the monotonous, fierce throb of pistons.
>
> Our upward motion seems to have slowed nevertheless, as if we are poised upon a precipice with no guarantee of summoning sufficient force to tip the balance and break through to the other side.
>
> And then the long, lonely battering ram of steel plunges into the last barrier: a tunnel through the Alpine rock and snow. Darkness encases us as the train's whistle shrieks its triumph. We go roaring deep into the hidden darkness of solid stone, suddenly level and gathering speed, suddenly plunging down faster and faster.
>
> The burnished whiteness of the snow and steam as we emerge on the other side seems like a glimpse of paradise, another world. A strangely satisfying peace descends upon the passengers with the setting of the sun as true twilight steals upon us from the dark, wooded valleys below.
>
> Strain is past, and we feel free to doze in our uphol-

stered seats, our foreheads nodding against the cold window glass, our eyes immune to the magnificent scenery dimming like a stage setting before us.

We have climbed the mountain and made it ours, and all else is nothing.

In the stillness that followed Irene's last declaration, I caught my breath. I saw that I had not been crocheting for some time.

"Well," I said, "I do not know whether to cry *Bravo* or *Brava*. Quite a stirring passage. Thrilling one might say. I feel quite exhausted."

"I as well," Irene admitted, staring into the moth-wings of flame beating in the small parlor fireplace. "Performance is so taxing."

"I had no idea riding a train to a mountaintop could be so enthralling, although I have been there myself."

"By yourself," Irene added.

I nodded.

"And not by yourself."

"What do you mean?"

"I mean that you made a return journey in the company of Quentin Stanhope. Did you not notice then the thrilling aspects of railway mountaineering?"

"Ah, not in the manner Godfrey describes. Perhaps such a reaction is only for the solitary. When one has someone to talk to—"

"Quite," said Irene, fanning herself with Godfrey's letter. Her face looked quite flushed in the firelight.

"Is there not more of the letter to read?"

She glanced at the last page. "Oddly, no. Obviously, the journey has released Godfrey's powers of . . . description."

"They do say that travel is broadening."

"Yes, they do." She glanced at me. "I was sure you would approve, Nell."

3.

Nell and the Night Visitors

"A Monsieur le Villon of the Paris police, I believe, speaks highly of your amazing deductive abilities."
"Monsieur le Villard," Mr. Holmes corrected me.
I bridled a bit, then showed confusion. "I beg your pardon?"
"Is the French connection you speak of Monsieur le Villard, not le Villon?"
"Yes, you are right! These French names are so similar."

—CAROLE NELSON DOUGLAS, *THE ADVENTURESS*

At night the countryside is darker than death and quieter than a confession. One becomes aware that one's cottage is an artificial island in a great dark sea of tossing fields and whatever chooses to prowl them.

A fierce pounding at midnight on a thick oak-wood cottage door sounds like blunderbusses exploding under the casement windows.

I sat up in bed, heart galloping like a coach-and-four.

The moon was dark and so was the piece of night framed by my unshuttered window.

The booming began again. Our simple cottage seemed under siege.

A third bout of thunder forced my feet onto the chill bedside rug. I fumbled for the lucifers and lit my candle while my feet probed the dark for slippers to fill.

A flash of light under my door made me seize my dressing gown and fight my arms into its commodious sleeves.

Footsteps on the stairs!

Were we being invaded?

I tossed my long braid over my back so it should not catch fire in the candle flame, picked up the icy pewter holder, contemplating using it as a weapon, and rushed into the passage.

All I glimpsed was Irene's waist-length hair rippling like a chestnut brown river against her scarlet-brocade dressing gown. She vanished into the puddle of lamplight that preceded her down the stairs.

Heedless as a child, I scurried downstairs in her wake, feeling no fear now but for her.

She was already at the wide front door, wrestling one-handed with the latch. "Nell! Good. Hold this."

I was now the Lady with the Lamp, only I held my candlestick in the other hand.

Irene attacked the latch again.

"We dare not admit anyone, Irene. It could be robbers. It likely *is* robbers."

"Robbers don't knock."

"Ruffians then, with unthinkable designs. Sophie sleeps at her own cottage tonight. We are two women alone."

"Not quite alone." Irene smiled grimly and lifted the handle of the small pistol from her dressing gown pocket.

Even as she pushed the hard latch over, and I opened my mouth to voice another objection, the knocks sounded again, virtually driving the door open.

Irene snatched the oil lamp from my hand and stepped back, lifting the fluttering light to reveal our visitors.

As I feared: strange men. Two of them.

Even Irene recoiled from the dark, overcoated forms filling our doorway like the night made incarnate.

Her trusty little pistol, I reflected, had looked a bit too little. I searched the hallway for handy cudgels. Only the umbrella stand, alas, and Irene stood between me and its contents.

"Madame. Mademoiselle," one man said, nodding rather than bowing.

As I suspected! They were French. Worse and worse. And they knew that one of us was married, the other unwed. They had been studying us.

"You are alone?" the stranger inquired, looking past us.

What did he think? That we entertained visitors at half past-whatever in the morning? Only the Frenchman!

Irene had retreated as far as she intended and withdrew the pistol from her pocket.

"Madame Norton," the speaker rebuked, at last doffing his slouch-brimmed hat.

"Inspector le Villard," she returned, also returning the pistol to her pocket. "You look a thorough villain in that hat and coat. Why didn't you announce yourself at once? Come in, then."

I clutched my dressing gown close.

"We apologize for intruding at such an hour," the French policeman went on in his execrably accented English. "It is not our wish, but there is no help for it. When the Great demand, the mice must scramble."

"Oh, you are not a mouse," Irene answered, laughing. "Nor am I." She turned to see me cowering behind her. "Nell, hurry upstairs and dress while I settle our visitors in the parlor. Their business is obviously too urgent for the formalities."

I started up the steps, grateful to creep out of their sight in my shocking state of disattire. On the other hand, I was most anxious to hear what had brought the French police inspector and his companion to our country door at such an indecent hour.

Irene, as usual, was right: one of us must be properly garbed and able to attend to the situation with dignity. I rushed upstairs to don my petticoats and corset in the almost-dark, lace my boots askew and misbutton my gown.

The flickering candlelight kept time with my shivers as I dressed in the chill bedchamber, my icy fingers mismanaging every stage.

At last I was reasonably clothed and hurried downstairs.

Irene had lit the two oil lamps in the parlor. The man with Inspector le Villard hunched over the charred logs in the fireplace, coaxing flames from the remnants of the woodbox.

Irene's pistol lay openly on the small table beside her chair, as I might leave a crochet needle in plain sight.

None of my implements was in view, however, for Inspector le Villard had set his dripping hat atop my worktable and had taken my chair.

I was forced to perch like a parrot on a tapestry-upholstered stool beside Irene's chair.

"You understand that I am entirely against this," François le Villard had been saying when I entered the room. He had utterly ignored my entrance and did not quite look at Irene. The inspector was a dandified individual much given to waxed facial growths, yet I was pleased to see that he possessed enough gentlemanly instinct to dislike addressing a woman in her dressing gown.

Irene had few qualms about being so addressed. No doubt it was a result of her many years on the stage. Actors and singers are always being seen half-dressed both offstage and on. It quite destroys their sense of propriety.

My reaction to the scene could not be farther from her mind. Her fingers were tapping the tabletop near the pistol. When she was abstracted or impatient her fingers often mimed playing some mute piece of music.

"You have fully stated every objection you could to coming here, being here, and remaining here, Inspector," Irene noted. "Now that your objections to your duty are done, what is the nub of the matter? Which Great Personage has forced you to such an unpleasant task? Or is it a name that dare not be spoken?"

While le Villard hesitated, Irene glanced at me. "I suppose we should offer you some refreshment."

"No!" Le Villard nearly shouted the word. "There is no time. You must accompany me into Paris at once. This matter is better understood when it is seen rather than heard."

The man at the fireplace stood and began to speak rapid French.

As he talked, Irene leaned forward, then sat up straighter, and then straighter still, like a puppet being drawn to attention by an unseen force. She was virtually at parade attention, and I could not say why.

Oh, how my head aches to hear a foreign language rattled off like a laundry list! Irene knew French like an Englishwoman's maid in London, but I! Only the caught crumb of a familiar word here and there hinted at some meaning.

Le Villard sat in my chair with his head and eyes cast down. The words *"abbot noir"* were bandied back and forth by the strange man and Irene more than once. Whatever he said drew her face into a mask of troubled disbelief.

This nondescript man who accompanied Inspector le Villard was no servant, as I had first thought, but his superior.

"I must go," Irene murmured to herself and only incidentally to me. She stood, shaken out of her strange paralysis. "I must dress."

The men exchanged impatient glances.

"Four minutes, gentlemen," she said sternly, reading their concern. "If you wish to clock me—"

She was clattering up the stairs like a racehorse before she finished her sentence.

Inspector le Villard did withdraw a gold timepiece from the vest beneath his sopping cloak and dry inner coat. He clicked the lid open.

I moved to Irene's chair, but the unnamed man did not sit, not even on the vacant chaise longue by the now-crackling fire.

Casanova, under his cage cover for the night, cackled eerily, startling both men.

"The parrot," I said.

"Le perroquet," the inspector repeated to his superior.

They nodded gravely.

A loud clatter in the hall announced Irene's return, booted and . . . as I had feared, dressed in men's clothing.

The inspector leaped to his feet as I did to mine.

"The time?" Irene demanded.

"Four minutes, Madame," he admitted.

She came to the table to swoop the pistol into her frock coat pocket.

She had twisted her hair atop her head into an burnt brown froth all more charming for its carelessness. She was not attempting actually to impersonate a man in this ensemble, although on occasion I had seen her carry off that guise uncannily well. Her attire now was a mere matter of speed, not deception, or so I thought at the time. Even I had to admit in my secret soul that this feminine interpretation of male dress, such as Sarah Bernhardt wore when sculpting in her art studio, had its charms. La Bernhardt affected pale colors, like the American author Mark Twain, but Irene wore black: dainty louis-heeled boots and fine wool trousers and jacket, softened only by an ivory-silk ascot at the throat.

Inspector le Villard spoke with some consternation. "You are aware, Madame, that you could be arrested for wearing such articles in the public streets?"

"Really? The escort of yourself and the Prefect of Police himself, I pray, will prevent me from having my mission stopped for a trifle. I believe that this garb will serve us all better at the scene of the crime. Shall we go and find out?" She turned to me. "Nell, please do not wait up. This might take hours."

"I certainly do not intend to 'wait up,' " I said stoutly. "I will accompany you, of course."

Even the man who did not speak English grasped my evident intentions. Had the situation not been so tense, it would have been amusing to watch the Frenchmen's reaction, which was now far more appalled than it had been at the first sight of Irene's unconventional attire.

They spoke at once, in French, to each other, then to Irene, and finally to me. They ordered, they pleaded. They almost wept with the intensity of their argument, as Frenchmen can when sufficiently stirred.

I imagine that the burden of all of it was that my presence was not required.

Or so Irene translated the jabber to me.

I swept into the passage. That is one of the many advantages of female dress: one can sweep. And one who sweeps has the advantage. I had learned that years ago from Irene, who was unsurpassed in the art of both sweeping and imposing her will on others.

"Nonsense," I said, eyeing all three with my sternest expression. "Irene, your accompanying these two men, even though one is known to you, alone . . . at night . . . on who-knows-what errand, is completely improper. I must accompany you. Explain it to them."

Irene, looking amused, did. They remonstrated some more, and more loudly, simultaneously spewing both French and English at me so that I could understand neither.

"If there is need for speed," I told Inspector le Villard, "you would do better arguing with me in the carriage on the way to Paris."

Incredulous, they looked at Irene.

She shrugged, a very Gallic shrug. "She is English," she said, as if that explained everything.

Perhaps it did.

4.

NOT SO SWEET A HOME . . .

It has been thus enjoined to the maîtresses de maison only to receive those whose physical appearance suggest that they have reached at least their seventeenth year. . . .

—CIRCULAR, 1842

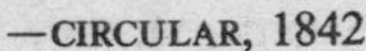

Irene and I were shortly facing each other across the divide of leather-upholstered carriage seats while the driver cracked his whip above the poor horses' withers until our four-wheeler careened down the dark country road like a runaway beer wagon.

Bands of light from the carriage lamps streaked across our faces, and there was no talk during this jolting journey, not until the cobblestones of Paris came under our steeds' hooves, and mist-filtered rays of gaslight streamed into the open carriage windows like skimmed moonlight.

I could smell the river and the evening damp, the incense of wood fires, the faint odor of manure.

At last Irene began conversing with our escorts in French,

soft-spoken, probing. They answered shortly, almost gruffly. She turned to me.

"A ghastly crime of some sort has been committed. We are not to know the details because I am needed as a translator. They do not wish foreknowledge to taint my role. A young American girl was apparently a witness. It is she I will be questioning."

"Inspector le Villard speaks English passably enough to interrogate an American witness."

"You think so, Nell? His superior does not, and in such a case I agree with him. A woman will win her confidence much sooner."

I lifted an eyebrow at her attire.

"If this crime is as brutal as I have been led to believe, my mode of dress will not even catch the poor child's attention."

"She is a child? Then it was well I came along. An English governess can handle a child like none other."

"As you say."

I always worried when Irene did not disagree with me.

"You did bring your notebook and pencil, Nell?"

"I am never without it. And I brought something else."

"Oh?"

I leaned close to whisper into her ear, which was more accessible than usual with her hair pinned up. "My chatelaine. Did you not notice its ostentatious—and noisy—presence at my belt?"

Irene smothered another quirk of her lips. I suspect she had less faith in the powers of my chatelaine—a gift of sterling silver trinkets from Godfrey—than I did. But to me it served the same function as her little pistol, and I felt quite naked without it. What an exaggerated expression! I, of course, never felt naked at all; nor should any decent woman.

Our vehicle had drawn up behind a grand building, one of the magnificent *hôtels* of Paris, I perceived as Irene helped me dismount the high carriage. In Paris, *hôtels* had been the palatial city dwellings of noble families for centuries, and only had turned to other ownership and uses in our new industrial age. I do not know why the French must confuse the issue and call buildings *"hôtels"* that are not meant for public accommodation.

I lifted my skirts to keep them from sweeping up soot, mist, and other less discreet flotsam of the city streets. We soon were bustled into the maze of rear service rooms that support the massive façades of these grandiose erections.

A man in a rumpled suit awaited us in the ill-lit pantry. The inspector snatched a lit oil lamp from a crude table and led us onward by its light.

Soon we were coiling up a narrow rear staircase that reeked of the sweat of many workmen's brows and . . . oh, garlic and coal and other noxious domestic scents that are banished from the front rooms.

My attention was fixed on not stumbling over my hems on the narrow, turning steps. The unintroduced Frenchman behind me seized my elbow quite firmly to pilot me upward without mishap.

At length we came to the third floor, where we were led down a hallway that went up three or four steps here, and down four or five steps there, until we finally entered a passage wide enough for us four to walk abreast.

It soon transpired that the three walked abreast, and I rustled behind. They were conferring in French again, whispered words I would have had trouble translating even had I been close enough to hear well. Again much mention of the mysterious *"Abbot Noir."*

Irene's operatic background had made her a mistress of languages. I had noticed during my brief career as a governess that those who excel at musical matters also have a numerical and language aptitude, although I cannot say that Irene had any head for numbers at all. Unless they be on bills of exchange.

At a closed door both men took up posts on either side. The inspector flourished it open for us.

Irene entered at once. I would have hesitated, but feared that if I did, the awful man would shut the door in my face, and I was determined not to remain alone in a passage with two Frenchmen if I could help it.

So I swept after her, into the most unusual chamber I have

ever entered in my life. And having visited Madame Sarah's menagerie of peacock feathers, tiger skins, serpents, and panthers on the Boulevard Péreire, I had some experience of unusual chambers.

I was struck first by the warmth and light, only then realizing how uncomfortable our journey here had been.

Figured Aubusson carpets floated like islands on a blue-marble tile floor. Their soft colors of rose, aqua, and gold ran into each other as in a woven watercolor. The furnishings were as luxurious as the floor coverings. The room was filled with tapestried chairs and sofas, every arm and leg carved and gilded until the furniture seemed to be wearing court costumes trimmed with gold lace. A crystal chandelier dripped candlelight onto strings of crystals as precious as Marie Antoinette's famed Zone of Diamonds (which Irene and Godfrey and I had rescued from historical obscurity, a tale which the world at large unfortunately knows not).

Already in those early days of our association I was picking up secret stones, usually in Irene's service, for there is no doubt she rescued me from worse dangers of the street than mere urchins. She was convinced that this Godfrey Norton had knowledge of a missing jewel of Queen Marie Antoinette she was hunting for the American jeweler, Mr. Tiffany. I was to spy upon Mr. Norton as well as spin his script into print.

Suffice it to say that by the end of the affair Mr. Tiffany had purchased the French queen's lost jewels from Irene for a king's ransom, Irene and Godfrey were wed, and we all three had moved to France, with my two housemates then considered dead!

So here I was, in Paris, the gay and sinful heart of France, staring at Marie Antoinette's partners in crimes against the people: portraits of pale-complected, fashionably over-upholstered, red-nosed French aristocrats of eras gone by. This powdered-wig company literally paved the walls, all encased in lacy frills of gilt frames like so many Valentine's Day offerings.

Amid all this . . . well, the French do sometimes have the perfect word for it; after all, they invented excess . . . amid all this *frou-frou* I finally detected a living, contemporary soul.

She sat alone in the very middle of a long, tapestry-covered Louis XIV sofa with as many gilt legs as a centipede that had wandered through a gold-leaf workshop.

I was struck by large, deep-set eyes in an oval face furnished with a pleasing generosity of chin and brow. With her dark hair done up in a far more mannered fashion than Irene's and her girlish figure corseted into a sweet pink evening gown low of neck and almost nonexistent of sleeve, she yet looked as fresh-faced and dewy as any English lass of eighteen. My own former charge, dear Allegra Turnpenny—

Of course Irene had to step into this picture of dewy innocence in her dark man's suit and shatter it.

"My name is Irene Adler-Norton," she said in that businesslike American way she usually employed with older men of position and power. The greater the difference in Irene's station and that of those whom she addressed, the less deferential she became. One would think this would turn her betters against her, but it never did. Indeed, they seemed to relish it as a welcome curiosity. There is no doubt that her years upon the stage gave her a formidable advantage in understanding, and manipulating, human nature. "And this is my friend, Penelope Huxleigh," she continued, brisk but gentle. "We are here to help."

All the while Irene was moving into the luxurious scene, a dark, trousered figure from a melodrama almost, save for her flagrantly female face and head of rampant hair.

She sat on a chair at right angles to the sofa the girl occupied, so I was forced to take the matching chair a full ten feet away.

"Although I have lived in London, Miss Huxleigh and I now live near Paris. And, of course, I lived in America for many years before I came to Europe."

I had never heard Irene chatter so, or reveal so many details of our lives, history, and geography to a total stranger.

Then I saw that although the girl was the very picture of composure, so still that she might have been sitting for Mr. Whistler, the folded hands on her silken lap were white-knuckled, and her pleasant features had frozen into an expression of such rigid control it almost reminded me of a classical masque of tragedy.

A decanter of some dark liquor sat on a silver tray surrounded by short-stemmed crystal glasses. One was half-full. I suspected it was untouched, because the French, extravagant race, are adamant about not filling spirit glasses full in order to let the liquors inside "breathe" and no doubt perform other tricks to seduce the unwary.

The girl seemed not to notice Irene's odd manner of dress, or even what she said.

"What is your name?" Irene asked in the most kindly tone possible.

The girl glanced at her for the first time, the look of a startled doe upon her face. "Name? Ah . . ."

"I am called *I-reen-ee* here abroad, but of course I was simply *I-reen* in the States. Miss Huxleigh has always been Penelope. Until she met me and I began calling her 'Nell.' So what are you called, pray?"

Again, Irene's chatter gave the girl time to gather her wits, which were apparently in flight. "They call me *Rose* here," she said at last, as if not quite believing her own statement.

I spoke for the first time, in an encouraging way. "Rose. A lovely name. Very English."

The blue-gray eyes feinted in my direction for the first time. "That's how the French translate my name. At home . . . it really is . . . Pink."

"Pink?" I repeated, taken aback by such an inappropriate appellation.

"Pink," Irene said approvingly. "A pink is as lovely a flower as a rose, Nell, although it is more often home-grown." She smiled at the girl. "It suits you. Now then, Pink, you must realize that the reason we two are here and not the French gentlemen of the Sûreté, is that they believe that you would testify more easily to one who spoke your language, to another American, to a woman."

The girl (I cannot call her Pink!) took a breath so deep it seemed to threaten her corset strings with breaking.

"You must excuse me. I have never seen anything so horrendous in my life."

"It is not a very long life," Irene pointed out.

"I am nineteen!"

This was declared as a challenge.

"With whom do you stay in Paris?" Irene went on.

"No one. I am on my own." Her youthful indignation collapsed. "I stay here."

"And what is this place?"

That question engaged our young miss's full attention. She eyed the Old World richness, plucked at the bejeweled tissue of her skirt as if surprised that she was wearing it, and took another breath.

"It is a *maison de tolérance*."

Those words struck a chill into my soul. I knew enough French to recognize the oft-employed word for "house" that is as familiar as the word *"chez"* for the same meaning in English. And I understood the word *tolérance* in either English or French. Indeed, it was likely spelled the same in both languages and thus spelled out the odious situation for me. We were in what the French call a brothel. Oh, a very elegant brothel for the use of only the most blue-blooded, wealthy, and well-known roués, but a brothel nevertheless.

Irene did not blink at this revelation. "Have you had some of the brandy yet?" She nodded at the libation.

The girl shook her head.

"It was meant medicinally. I think you should sip it. Nell, can you—?"

By now I had realized that the young woman was in shock, as who would not be to find oneself unexpectedly in a brothel, however opulent?

I slipped quietly to the sofa and sat beside her. Lifting the delicate glass like a medicine vial, I brought it to her lips.

"You must try some. I know it will taste strong and nasty, but you will feel better for it."

The girl glanced at me, then obeyed. After a tiny sip, her hand reached up to take the glass stem. I felt the tremor as its custody transferred from my hand to her own, but at least she had released a measure of that paralytic grip she kept upon herself.

As I returned to my chair I noticed that Irene was nodding approvingly at me.

"Not too much," she advised the girl. "You want to clear your head, not cloud your memory. Now. We have been told nothing of what is wrong here. We rely on you."

The brandy appeared to have been a hair too effective. "Pink" shook her charming head as if awakening from a bad dream. "Why are you here?" she demanded. "You cannot be from the police. They do not let women do that sort of thing on the Continent."

"And they do in the United States?" I demanded myself, surprised.

"Of course they do, Nell." Irene did not glance at me. She was still concentrating on the girl. "I was an agent for the Pinkertons when I lived in America, and also in England, for a time."

The girl clutched at the familiar word. "A Pinkerton. They have sent a Pinkerton to a Pink? How crazy, but then this whole place is crazy . . . of course, it doesn't help that I am just learning the language."

Pink laughed so hard she sputtered into the brandy glass, then coughed violently, until her eyes watered and she hiccoughed.

I recognize incipient hysterics when I see them and rose to go to her, but Irene shook her head at me.

"Is that why you're wearing man's dress?" Pink asked Irene through her tears and hiccoughs. "I feel like Alice in Wonderland. If you were a White Rabbit instead of a lady Pinkerton in man's dress . . . I'm sorry. I'm not usually such a fool. But it was pretty dreadful. The most awful thing a body could ever see. Quite retchingly dreadful."

By now I was not anxious to know the details Irene had been sent to ferret out.

"Tell me," Irene said, sitting back in the chair to draw her elegant cigarette case from one pocket and a matchbox from another.

The letter *I* worked large in diamonds shone like a heavenly constellation against the glorious blue-enamel case as Irene removed a thin brown cigar. The case was a priceless

Fabergé creation, but seeing it always made me shudder. It reminded me of the two people I most detested in the world: Sable, the Russian spy who had given this poison-armed trinket to Irene, and Sherlock Holmes, who had discerned and disarmed the lethal gift while we had watched. That Irene should use this object, and even treasure it, struck me as foolhardy beyond belief.

Pink watched her light the slender cigar in one hand by a lucifer from the other with wide eyes. "Does that taste good, really? I would like to try."

"So you shall." Irene leaned forward to extend the small dark cylinder to her. "Just . . . sip."

That poor young thing put the smoking thing between her dainty lips and drew a shallow breath. Soon she was coughing again, while I cast Irene a disapproving look.

"It takes practice," Irene said, retrieving the tiny cigar and drawing thoughtfully on it until she was able to exhale a thin stream of smoke. "Now that your mind has contemplated other matters, perhaps it can return to the dreadful recent past with an objective eye."

Pink, clutching my handkerchief to her mouth, nodded. "I pride myself on an objective eye, Mrs. Norton, is it?" She straightened on her sofa cushion, posture alone drawing her spine taut as a bowstring.

Her hands no longer trembled.

"I have found murdered women in this house, two stories below. I was the first to find them, and to alert the inhabitants. I'm afraid I screamed."

"You are sure they were murdered?" Irene asked.

Pink regarded her blankly, then spoke.

"They were more than murdered." Pink tossed back a great swallow of the brandy. Her voice came clear and sharp, precise yet angry. "They were butchered like carcasses one sees hanging in Les Halles, the great open marketplace of Paris. I only recognized them for women from the shreds of clothing clinging to . . . what was left."

As suddenly as this, I knew. I had solved a petty mystery that had been niggling at me all night: the French phrase *"Abbot Noir."* The Black Abbot in English.

I had felt foolishly reassured that a churchman was involved in the matter, even though he be Roman Catholic and the hue of his habit be black. But the inspector and Irene had not been speaking of my mythical head monk at all. Not *"Abbot Noir,"* but *"abattoir,"* a word I did know even if I did not expect to hear it spoken in polite society.

Abattoir.

The French word for slaughterhouse.

5.

The Abbot Noir

The disorders of the room had, as usual, been suffered to exist.

—EDGAR ALLAN POE, "THE MURDERS IN THE RUE MORGUE"

Not very much later, the girl's brandy glass was empty, and Irene's slender cigar had shriveled into a pyramid of silver ashes impaled by a dark dead stub in one of the empty crystal goblets.

Much as I deplore the stench and the mess of the smoking ritual and much as I abhor spiritous liquors, I had to admit that these masculine vices had put raw emotion at a distance.

"Stay here," Irene told Miss Pink, who was much calmed for having unburdened herself of her dread cargo of horror. As for me, had someone offered, I would have indulged in a glass of the contents of the decanter, and I only drink spirits under severe duress.

We left the room. The men guarding either side of the door leaped to confront us, their Gallic faces so eager for news they resembled agitated poodles.

It would have been laughable had not we heard such grim tidings.

Irene wasted no time on preliminaries. "This was her first day . . . night at the house. She did not know, or even recognize, the dead women. I understand that is quite understandable." Both men nodded, dropping their eyes. "Apparently there has been an atrocity on a scale of 'The Murders in the Rue Morgue.' You know the story?"

Inspector le Villard nodded. "I am a student of the methods of foreign detectives, as you know, especially Miss Huxleigh's countryman."

I shuddered for the first time that evening to hear a reference to *the* man, that all-too-ubiquitous consulting detective, Holmes.

"Even fictional detectives?" Irene asked.

"Mr. Poe's setting was Parisian, and the investigator was French. C. Auguste Dupin," he said as if savoring Napoleonic brandy. "You are right to invoke that long-ago tale. It is the closest thing to what has happened here, except for—"

"Yes," Irene said. "I must see the murder scene. Miss Huxleigh can remain here with Mademoiselle Rose."

"No!" For once the inspector objected before I could. "The scene is not fit for female sensibilities. You cannot see it."

"If you wish me to elicit every shred of testimony from her, I must see what she saw. I must know what questions to ask. In such cases, with the shock, she may have seen more than she realizes."

"That is true, but now that you have heard of the grotesquerie of it . . . I would not ask even my gendarmes to face such a scene, were it not necessary."

"Commendable, but I am not one of your gendarmes."

"You were not brought here for such viewing."

"I was brought here, and now I ask what will help me perform the service you requested. Nay, demanded. You and your anonymous Great One."

The inspector sighed and slapped the damp felt hat in his hands against his leg.

The shadowy superior murmured a torrent of French.

After some discussion between them, le Villard turned back

to Irene. "You may go, but only because we must answer to your . . . sponsor. I will not be responsible for any hysteria."

"There will be no hysteria."

"Indeed not," I interjected. "For I will go along."

The Frenchmen began blathering again, hysterically.

Even Irene turned to me in disbelief.

I explained myself to Irene. "I have seen the body on Bram Stoker's dining-room table, I have been to the death chamber of the Paris Morgue with you, remember? I cannot allow you to confront such perfidy alone, or not alone, I should say. I owe it to Godfrey that you do not go off unsuitably chaperoned."

She was not fooled by my invoking the proprieties, eternal pretext in my limited arsenal of argument. She laid a hand on my arm.

"I will be all right, Nell."

"I know you will, for I will be there with you." Then I added, "It would be cruel to keep me in the dark, when even that child has seen the truth, and survived."

"Not without brandy afterward."

"I will have brandy afterward if necessary."

Irene's further arguments never passed her lips. She knew that if I was willing to take spirits, I was serious indeed.

The inspector's lively features had frozen into disapproving resignation. "Your presence was requested by an Eminent Personage. We must allow you to pursue actions you will deeply regret. I hope you will not try to misplace the blame."

Irene glanced at me. "I never misplace blame."

I inhaled as deeply as Miss Pink had a few minutes earlier. I must be prepared to face what I had demanded to see. I had no doubts it would be a vision of Hell.

The Frenchmen, stiff with disapproval and with funereal step, led us down the back stairs to the first floor. Their dark figures, etched into murky relief against the rays of the lamp they carried, looked as misshapen as latter-day Quasimodos. I began to wonder if they had changed into monsters once their backs were turned upon us. The narrow stair, the sound of our footsteps as regular as the pounding of coffin nails . . . in truth, the mention of the American fantasist Edgar Allan Poe, whose horrific stories I had read during my Shropshire days when ghost stories were my only entertainment, all combined to heighten my natural dread at facing death, and death in a particularly revolting form.

Still. I was a country parson's daughter, and had seen much in my tending of the ill young and old in the parish that would surprise a dweller in large cities, where much ugliness is swept away into institutions.

On the first story we were led again to the wide passage. A rich flocked wallpaper of oriental design glinted gold back from the walls as our guiding lamp passed. Dragons writhed in the flickering twilight, and roofs like piled hats seem to shimmer with worms instead of tiles.

By the time we came to the painted and gilded door where two gendarmes stood at attention, my hands were cold and clasped before me. Just like . . . Pink's, I realized, and I had seen nothing yet.

"The first to see has the least to fear," Irene whispered in my ear.

I noticed that her face was pale, her features drawn into the same falsely serene control I had seen on Pink's young face.

The man who had never identified himself nodded to the guards. One swept open a door with military precision, never glancing inside.

The stench that rushed out to greet us was unfortunately familiar, though stronger than any I had encountered before. A charnel-house reek of unfettered blood and bowel.

All six of us recoiled involuntarily from that awful odor.

Grim-faced, Inspector le Villard held up the lamp. "It is not too late to retreat."

Irene's answer was to take the heavy light from him and step inside the door.

I followed, fumbling with both hands in my pocket for my silver talisman and one of the many objects that ornamented it.

"We are on the banks of the river Seine again, Nell," Irene muttered.

I knew instantly what she meant, seeing again the sopping dead body of the sailor, reeking of death and damp. We were to breathe through our mouths.

Yet the notion of taking that fetid overwhelming scent into our lungs . . . I thrust my find to Irene. A slender glass vial capped in silver on both ends.

"Rub the perforated end on your nostrils."

She recoiled from the strong scent that assailed her. I answered her confused look.

"Smelling salts. You should not be able to detect any other odor for some minutes."

By then she had inhaled as deeply as a Regency dandy ingesting snuff, and I did the same. I noticed the Frenchmen behind us exchanging rueful glances, and turned to offer them a medicinal whiff. But men are foolishly fearful of being thought womanly, and they refused my remedy with terse headshakes.

The salts had not only driven all other odors from my nostrils, they had cleared my senses and stiffened my spine. I was now free to join Irene in gazing on the scene Pink had stumbled into.

I remembered most clearly the strange barber's chair she had mentioned. The lamp abetted us by picking out the swirls of gilt wood that defined its outré shape.

Gold winked from elsewhere in the chamber. It was as richly overdecorated as the room upstairs.

Irene had lowered her gaze to the floor and was studying the wood parquet visible between the Savonnerie carpets scattered before the furniture. An unusual black background to the florid French designs gave the chamber a properly sober note, and made a dramatic canvas for the even more elaborate furniture.

And what strange furniture it was, even for Paris! A dressing table with a towering rococo mirror. A chaise longue. Some upholstered chairs and small tables. The room was accoutered like a bedchamber in every respect . . . except that there was no bed.

I may not know much of worldly matters, being a spinster, yet even I knew that it was most unlikely that a brothel, however elevated its clients, was not likely to have a bedroom without a bed.

"Have you taken photographs?" Irene asked the men lurking in the doorway still open behind us.

"This is not a scene to commemorate, Madame."

"You will rely on memory, then, and notes?"

"We will photograph the bodies at the morgue, when the full extent of the wounds can be shown."

I was abstracting my notebook and pencil from my other pocket as they spoke. The activity kept me from observing the gruesome centerpiece of the room.

"If you will leave us," Irene was saying, as I drew the items from the folds of my skirt.

"Impossible!" Inspector le Villard said.

"It is quite possible," she rejoined, "and necessary if we wish to examine the scene without supernumeraries present."

He jerked as if avoiding a dash of cold water at being called a spear-carrier on a stage where he was accustomed to being in utter charge.

"The First Gentleman of Europe who insisted on our assistance would want us to have all the facts," Irene continued. "We can best assemble them if left to ourselves."

Although I was not sure who the First Gentleman of Europe might be, Inspector le Villard was sufficiently impressed to pale. "This is outrageous, Madame! This scene is not fit for females to see, and to leave you alone with such carnage—!"

"Apparently it is fit for females to be the object of such carnage. I assure you that Miss Huxleigh and I will neither swoon nor disturb the scene."

A brave speech, but I noticed that Irene's complexion looked a trifle green and felt in my pocket for the smelling salts.

The other man murmured to the inspector, and they withdrew, not without muttered French imprecations on Inspector le Villard's part.

As soon as the door closed silently behind them, Irene turned to me.

She met the uplifted vial in my hand with surprise, then a quick sigh of relief. We both inhaled mightily at the tiny perforated ending.

"No photographs!" she objected to our absent guides. "Of course not. They do not wish to implicate the aristocrat who was expecting to dally with these ladies."

"Ladies? Bodies? Plural? How can you tell?" I glanced sidelong at the contorted piece of furniture piled with contorted limbs, clothing, and bloody bits of things it was best not to identify.

Young Pink had done well to compare the scene to Les Halles. I had walked past hung carcasses of plucked fowl and disassembled pigs. In Shropshire, sheep country, the young parson's daughter had also tended the old parishioners besieged by gangrene and bedsores. I could survive facing this. If I did not look too closely.

Irene pointed to the odd piece of furniture, which reminded me of a patten, those tall platform shoes worn by medieval women to keep their skirts from the offal on the streets.

It truly beggars my descriptive powers. Pink's "barber chair from Versailles" it was, a strangely sinuous affair, perhaps purchased at some goblin market. Every surface snaked into the other in white-wood tendrils edged with gilt. Two arms lifted from its upholstered top, but curved backwards, like no chair arms I had ever seen.

At the front of both bottom and top surface bronze metal brackets protruded at each curved corner.

Around and through and within this tangle of wood and upholstered brocade and metal prongs draped a quantity of silken fabric revealing the hint of a vastly distorted body, actually *bodies*, behind and beneath it all.

Irene's face was grimmer than I had ever seen it as I lifted my eyes from my jotted-down description of the scene.

"You see the lower bronze stirrups, on the floor-level upholstery?"

"Yes, but stirrups? This is a kind of rocking horse? As in a child's schoolroom?"

"Not child's play, this." Irene eyed me worriedly, then without a word dropped to her knees on the costly Savonnerie carpet.

"Irene!"

"I must examine the trail of disturbances before the whole French prefecture arrives and tramples the carpeting like a herd of Indian elephants."

"You expected to be making such a close inspection," I noted in surprise, surveying the indignity of her hands-and-knees position concealed by the trousers and coat-skirt of men's dress. "Why?"

"You remember the poisoned cigarette case in Prague?"

"Of course. A 'gift' from that Russian woman."

"You remember how Mr. Holmes examined it, as if it were the veriest mote in God's eye?"

"That man does believe he *is* God's eye," I agreed. "Most impious."

"But *I* saw even as he saw. I am used to looking at the stage *en scène. En masse*. As an overpopulated picture framed by the proscenium arch that separates it from the audience. Full of power and glory, yes. But crowded. He looks at the scene as a scientist, through the microscope of his eye. He looks for the telling minutiae. So must we here. Look. Come down on your knees. You can see the footprints in the black background of the carpeting, as you can see fingerprints on black-velvet skirts, if only you get on a level where the light casts the past into a trail."

I complied. "It is no difficulty getting on my knees at such a scene, Irene. Prayers are needed here, if anywhere."

"While you are praying, Nell, could you see if that chatelaine of yours bears a quizzing glass."

"Quizzing?"

"A magnifying lens!"

"I do not think so . . ." There we were, prostrate in the presence of vicious death, hardly daring to breathe and yet splitting hairs and carpet fibers. "My pince-nez, however, has magnifying properties."

"Bless your farsighted eyes! And hand me the spectacles."

Irene barely glanced at my face as I removed my spectacles

from the bodice locket that held them at the ready. She took them blindly.

"Ah!" she said a moment later, holding my pince-nez to her eyes like a mask.

"What is it?

"I don't know. But it is something. Do you have in that bottomless pocket of yours some . . . container? And a pincer of some kind? I see a few crumbs worth preserving. They do not seem native to this room and its purpose."

"Container? Other than my pocket itself—"

"That will not do. These tiny crumbs would crush to powder."

I thought furiously. It is my role in lifc to be useful if not decorative, and a dereliction in utility is most humiliating. "I know! My, ah, my ah . . . etui!"

"You are sneezing from the carpet dust?"

Startled, it suddenly struck mc that a word familiar to me would sound not like a word at all to Irene. Despite our grim situation, I found a nervous giggle bubbling in my throat. "An etui is not a sneeze, Irene," I objected. "It is just the thing you asked for."

"Forgive me, but an *etwee* is not from any vocabulary I have heard of," she complained. "Pray tell me what it is, if it is indeed a 'what' and not an inarticulate wheeze."

Despite her tart impatience, so unlike Irene, by now the laughter was threatening to choke me, so unlike me. I was ashamed, but helpless. "I'm sorry. I can't. I can't—" Now I did indeed sound as if I were about to sneeze.

Irene's fingers clenched on my upper arm. "Hold tight," she rather harshly advised me.

By now tears were blurring my eyes and streaming down my cheeks.

"Hush," she whispered. "We promised no hysterics."

"But I'm not," I was able to choke out. "Having hysterics. I'm laughing, though I don't know why."

Her voice was low and urgent. "That is a form of hysteria, if you don't contain it."

I gazed at her, seeing only through a wavy pane of glassy tears. "I don't know why I would laugh in such a grim circumstance," I managed to get out on a wavery sigh of words and whisper.

"Because our circumstances are ludicrous, Nell." She allowed herself to sink onto her hip, after glancing carefully around at the carpet. "We are searching for needles we don't know are there in a haystack of rococo furnishings, on our hands and knees, in the presence of crude death."

"I cannot tell whether I am laughing or crying now," I complained, wiping my cheeks with the heels of my hands, which were impressed with the costly whorls of the Aubusson carpet.

Irene regarded me carefully, and somewhat wearily. "Why do you suppose the Greek masks of comedy and tragedy are always shown paired, tilted together like a pair of gossiping neighbors? When I was performing at La Scala in Milan, I encountered a composer, Ruggiero Leoncavallo, who was working on an aria by Pagliacci, the tragic clown. It is a virtuoso exercise in despairing laughter."

I shook my head. What did opera have to do with my unforgivable behavior?

Irene took my wrists in her hands and pulled my fingers from my face, as one might demand the attention of a petulant child, save I was not petulant, but mortified.

"Nell, laughter and tears sit side by side in the chamber of the heart, as any actor can tell you. And any tenor who will someday sing Pagliacci can tell you that the same contraction of air and muscle that produces sobs produces laughter. The brilliance of Pagliacci's aria is its interplay of forced hilarity and unsurvivable despair."

Having settled to a discreet hiccough during her lecture on the finer points of stage performance, I finally nodded, relieved that the irresistible urge to giggle had sunk beneath an exhausted melancholy much more appropriate to the situation.

"Now. What is this object by any other name? Besides a rose?" Irene smiled slightly.

I recognized the Shakespearean allusion. Strangely, all this stagecraft talk had given me a sense of distance from the terrible scene in which we played such ludicrous parts.

"My needle case," I said with sobriety. "Here." I drew the

long, narrow, enameled case from the chatelaine. I removed the needles, lancing them into temporary lodging in my skirt's sturdy twill fabric until the case was empty. "It's meant to hold needles and bodkins and toothpicks, but may serve for other things. Will this do?"

"Admirably!" Irene pronounced, inspecting it through her—my—spectacles. "And the pincers?"

I extended the small sterling silver tweezers. "I use these for picking up threads and beads."

"Excellent." In a moment she had bent to pluck some vague brownish yellow crumbs from the carpet. She dropped them into the enameled needle case.

She paused to eye me. "How are you doing now?"

"Doing? That is such an American expression. I am not doing at all. I am pretending to be in another place at another task, breathing other air. Will that do?"

"It will," she said. "That is also a clue as to how our Mr. Holmes performs his miracles of detection in the face of human iniquity. He looks close, not far, dear Nell, and spares himself much anguish."

"We are looking through a microscope then?"

"Yes. As a physician or a botanist. We look small, so that the large does not overwhelm us. Yes?"

"Yes." I crawled forward behind her on my elbows and knees. "It is most undignified."

"So should we be in the presence of such indignities to the human body and soul. Does this not remind you of something other than the fictions of Edgar Allan Poe about the rue Morgue?"

"Oh yes, Irene." I found my voice quivering and cast a quick glance at the heavens, which in this room was a painted ceiling of naked cherubs and naked ladies, a pairing I shall never understand. "Despite the distance in location and in time, I find this scene most distressingly reminiscent of the depredations performed in London just last autumn."

Irene rose to her knees, reminding me of some rearing centaur in her unnatural man's garb. Her hastily piled locks seemed to writhe in the wavering lamplight like the Medusa's snaky tendrils.

"Jacques the Ripper appears to have turned his ghastly attentions on Paris."

"It does not make sense," I objected.

"But it does make for murder," she said. "And politics. And a most brutal puzzle."

6.

Frère Jacques, Dormez-Vous?

Well, I say, December's here already and January, February and March are waiting for us and I'm one of those plants which can't stand the cold of winter. Would you like to see my legs? Then they say, Come along in. And indoors it's so snug and warm that one immediately wants to strip to one's chemise and stay like that. A fortnight later one's so completely forgotten the draughty street-corners up our way that the mere sight of a wet overcoat is enough to astonish us.

—LA BELLE OTÉRO, *MY DAYS AND NIGHTS*

After our inspection of the death chamber, we were taken to another grand chamber and there sat down to wait. Inspector le Villard seemed much surprised by our composure.

Again ensconced in a grand but empty room, I occupied myself making sketches of the footprints on the scene in my tiny silver-encased notepad.

"Four sets," I noted. "Some dainty slipper impressions. A large man-size imprint, but narrowed with dandified daintiness at toe and heel. A massive imprint as undefined as a bottle side. And many man-size boot prints, uniform in shape if not in size."

Irene nodded as she studied my sketches over my shoulder. "The ladies, the police in their uniform boots, and two men, one well shod and one ill shod."

"What would an ill-shod man be doing in such a room in such a place?"

"An excellent question, Nell. We shall have to see if a doctor was called previously, but I doubt it. Officialdom will only fully invade the scene now that our Eminent Personage is well away from the carnage."

Her last word suddenly took my mind and eye from microscopic distance to the enlarged view of everyday reality. I felt my stomach and my senses spinning.

The only remedy was to resume my close-work. I began to wonder if this was why fancywork attracted me.

I attempted a far more challenging artistic task: to draw an approximation of the barber's chair.

Irene inspected my efforts. "Very good."

"What is this thing?"

Her lips pursed as she eyed me. "You have held up very well, Nell."

"You always manage to say 'well, Nell,' as if you were declaiming 'how now, brown cow.' "

Her laugh was weary. "Guilty. I have underestimated you, I admit. But then, you were not reared in America, and are unused to uncivil atrocities."

"Ah. The Red Indians, you mean."

"Ah, the White Devils, I mean."

"Is that not an English play by Webster?"

"You have me there, Nell, as usual. No, what I mean is that because you have not been exposed to the incivilities of life that I and Pink have—"

"That chit!"

Irene eyed me until I blushed. "She is most forward," I said.

"Perhaps she has had need to be." Her look was so abstracted that she spoke to herself more than me. "*He*, of course would make a thorough job of it. It is not enough to see signs if you cannot read them."

I did not ask who "*he*, of course" was. "We have the contents of my needle case," I said in consolation, removing it from my pocket.

"Which are teasingly familiar to me, but not in this form." She frowned as she took the slender enamel container to a white-marble table topped by a great-globed lamp.

Sitting beside the table, she shook a pale brown fragment onto the glaring marble.

"A crumb, as you said," I suggested as I followed her to the impromptu specimen table. "But why would anyone have eaten in there?"

"A crumb could have been picked up on a boot or shoe and have dropped off in the murder chamber."

"Then it could have dropped off the footwear of those poor women."

I fought the memory of their feet, one of the few recognizable portions of their anatomy, clad in rumpled silken hose and embroidered satin shoes. Cinderella shoes. And then I remembered the Grimm fairy tale about the girl whose blood-red shoes would not come off until she had danced to her death.

Irene lifted my spectacles to her face again, peering at the single crumb as through a lorgnette. "Not bread, though brown and crumbly. Yet it reminds me of something. Ah, well." Her smallest fingernail prodded the mote back into the Oriental needle case, which I could finally think of again by its proper name, etui. It was shocking to think that my humble case had carried a grain of evidence from a scene of such chaos.

"The police are right about one thing," Irene said.

I waited.

"They will not know what really happened here until they examine the bodies at the morgue."

"You don't believe that we—?"

"Should view the remains? The police would not let us, and even our anonymous . . . er, client, would not be interested in our opinion of that."

Irene straightened and absently turned down the lamp, an economy we practiced at Neuilly because the oil for them must be hauled in by the barrel.

Here, in this palace of luxurious decadence, I believe her gesture was an instinctive effort to soften the bright light and harsh shadows that made every scene seemed etched in the black-and-white cartoon of a sensational newspaper drawing.

"What do you know of the Jack the Ripper murders in London, Nell?" she asked.

I started, guilty. I recalled feeling the same unhappy emotion what now seemed ages ago (and had only been hours ago), when I realized that I relished the notion of Irene and I alone together again.

Indeed we were.

I started guiltily now because last autumn I had suffered from an irresistible curiosity about that string of atrocities in the city we had left in haste only months before. I had such a case of curiosity, in fact, that I devoured any English-language newspapers available. Luckily, Godfrey acquired them regularly for the political and legal news. Naturally, after seeing the lurid sketches of the Whitechapel horrors, my jaded eyes saw this far-removed death scene as drawn in charcoal on dun-colored paper.

"I ask," Irene said, "because I confess I did not pay them much attention, except to be glad of leaving a capital that was so beset."

"Oh. You do not know much about them." What a rare opportunity. I personally thought that Irene was rarely interested in newspapers unless she was in them. "I could hardly avoid reading of the atrocities. Truly, a madman was abroad. He was so often almost glimpsed, yet still eluded everyone, like some ogre out of a wicked fairy tale, chopping up children, except these women were hardly innocents. No reason for it all but unreasoning savagery. It did not seem at all English."

"No?" Irene's gaze was piercing. "What of Balaclava? Or Maiwand?"

"Well, that was war. Men murdering men, and used to it. Whatever those poor women were, they were defenseless."

"And poor, quite literally." Irene sighed and handed me the etui. "Store this for a while. It is time to revisit Pink. Now that we have seen what she has seen, she will be more forthcoming."

"Why so?"

"Shared shock creates bonds between strangers."

"And why should we want a bond with a girl who is already on the path to perdition?"

Irene leaned close enough to whisper, every word clipped. "Because we might change her path, Nell. Is that not a noble goal?"

"But it would require consorting with a fallen woman."

"And how are they to be kept from falling even more if the righteous will not consort with them?"

"I suppose they won't. But the chance for infection—"

"You are saying that the righteous are weak?"

"No. Only that evil is contagious."

"So," said Irene, "is ignorance. I believe that if we can discover why someone would kill these women in such a fashion, we shall know a great deal more about evil, and righteousness, than we did before."

"Oh, my head is spinning like a compass. We should not be here. We should not be inquiring into these morbid matters: we should not be encouraging a girl of tender years in a life of depravity."

Irene drew back, some of the censorious glint in her eyes dimming. "This place is depraved, I'll grant you that, Nell." Her expression softened as it rested on my troubled expression. "That young woman will be better for sharing her horror. Perhaps this incident will cure her of a life of luxurious vice," she added dryly.

"That is true," I agreed, hastening after her out the door with new heart. "One theory about Jack the Ripper was that he sought to discourage women from taking to the streets."

"An annuity would have perhaps been more persuasive," Irene threw over her shoulder. "I am so relieved that you have some acquaintance with the previous work of this monster."

It was one of those times when I sensed that Irene's words were as double-edged as the most lethal of swords, but I could not say why, nor determine who was the recipient of her highly honed instincts, Jack the Ripper, or I.

⚜ ⚜ ⚜

Pink had not moved. She might have been the portrait she had resembled when I first saw her.

Her head lifted as we entered the room, and I realized that our ammonia-scoured nostrils were failing to detect the new odor of the charnel house that clung to our clothing.

Pink's face hid in her open hands. "You've seen it."

"As much as we can make out," Irene agreed, resuming her former seat.

"Both of you?" Pink asked incredulously, lifting her eyes from her fingertips like a naughty child peeping through them. They queried me.

"Both of us," I said. "It is not necessary to smoke little cigars to face death."

"But it is so much more dramatic," Irene put in, producing one of the objects in question and lighting it. "All of the gentlemen entertaining firing squads do it."

Her motion distracted Pink's attention from me. Really, she was a charming girl, and I could not believe she had been fully corrupted. I sensed of a sudden that Irene's cigar was masking any unkind odors that clung to us.

"You are a most dramatic individual, Madam." Pink regarded Irene almost as intently as Irene was regarding her. "I take it that you and Miss . . . Foxleigh –"

"Huxleigh," I hastened to correct.

"I take it that you both have encountered recently dead people before."

"Recently," Irene agreed, "and not-so-recently dead. Is that not right, Nell?"

"Only twice," I said. "I would have been content to leave it at that."

"Well," said Pink, "you two are certainly good scouts about it. I'm sure that I would have not been so upset if only I'd had a chance to go west instead of east, and had seen the frontier life for myself. I apologize, ladies, for acting like such a fading violet."

I felt like something of a fading violet myself, now that I

had heard the young lady's Americanisms in full flower. And she still seemed such a placid and well-bred girl for a harlot.

"I should worry had you *not* been upset," Irene said. "But why did you go east instead of west, and how did you end up in the trade you follow?" She sounded as if she were interviewing a dressmaker and not a globe-trotting tart.

"I was the thirteenth of my father's fifteen children," she began.

"Good heavens," I cried, "fifteen!"

She went on as if I had not spoken. "My father died when I was just six, and my mother, who had outlived one husband before him, was eventually forced to take another to avoid utter poverty for herself and the six children she had borne my father. Although my father had been a respected judge, he died without a will, and any assets were scattered among the children. My mother left the marriage with some furniture, the horse and carriage, the cow, and one of the dogs, and you will quickly see that most of her 'inheritance' required even more feeding than her six children."

"So you plead poverty for your profession," I suggested in a tone more kindly than critical.

It was not taken thus. Pink's hazel eyes darkened with temper. "I plead nothing, and apologize for nothing." Her gaze returned, mild again, to Irene.

"Within three years of my father's death we had been forced to sell the horse and carriage and cow, and had acquired a stepfather, a Civil War veteran."

"Wonderful," I interjected, eager for a happy—and quick—end to this story. "A soldier is just the sort of upright model for fatherless children. One of my charge's uncles—I was a governess for a brief time—fought in Afghanistan. Quite the dashing hero when he returned."

Pink's utterly emotionless eyes turned on me. "Jack Ford was a mean, drunken lout we suffered for five years. He berated my mother for money, but never brought any home himself, called her names I suppose no Englishwoman wishes to admit exist, and one New Year's Eve when mother and us children went to church against his wishes, he threatened mother with a pistol and instant death."

"Military life does not agree with all men," I put in lamely.

"So," said Irene, "how soon after that did it end?"

"How did you know it would end soon?"

"Because it could not go on without bloody murder otherwise. And if your father had killed your mother, that is where your story would have begun."

Pink shrugged. "Nine months after that New Years' Eve he went berserk again, at dinner. He flung his coffee to the floor—"

(In that I could not condemn the man, but I refrained from saying so.)

"—threw the meat bone at my mother, then drew a loaded pistol from his pocket. My brother Albert and I jumped between them to allow our mother to escape out the front door. The other children followed."

"And you were not even living in the Wild West," I murmured in distress.

Another flat look. "There is nothing wild about Pennsylvania except the turkeys, Miss Huxleigh."

I could not seem to speak without irritating this artlessly immoral young lady, so I subsided.

"It was obviously the end of the marriage," Irene said.

"Right." Pink's cheeks were flushing to match her gown. "Jack Ford nailed the doors and windows shut and went in and out by way of a ladder. When Mother finally got in a week later to get the furniture, the house was a wreck. There was nothing to do but the unthinkable. She sued for divorce."

I gasped. Yes, I had resolved to comment no more, but divorce was a scandal of such proportions that I imagine it even shook this backwater town in Pennsylvania.

Pink looked straight ahead, as if my gasp echoed a legion of them years ago.

"I testified, and so did Alfred."

"How old were you?" Irene asked.

"Old enough. Fourteen. Mother's was one of only fifteen divorce actions in the county that year, and one of only five brought by the wife. The neighbors testified that Jack Ford was usually drunk, never provided for her, swore at and cursed her, threatened her with a loaded gun, had kicked and broken the household furniture, had ‘done violence to her person,’ as they put his beating her. They also testified that she had always washed and ironed his shirts (though I had seen him throw them on the floor when she was done and dirty and throw water on them so she’d have to do them all over again), bought and paid for his underwear out of her own money and was never cross or ugly to him, no matter how he treated her.”

Her tone had become positively corrosive.

“She got the divorce, but the shame of it forced her to leave the town.”

“And you, Pink?” Irene inquired softly.

“I determined to make my own way in the world, and that did not include marrying any man.”

I opened my mouth to point out that she had “married” many men, thanks to her immoral profession, but Irene was giving me such a stern look urging silence that I converted my gesture into a yawn, which Young Pink’s recent lurid testimony of married life in America, guns and all, hardly merited.

No one was paying me the slightest attention after that, anyway.

“A truly sad history,” Irene said soothingly. “Now we know that you have been a fine and brave witness from an early age, tell us exactly what happened, remembering that you need not spare us any impression, any fact. We are all women of the world, after all,” she added most speciously.

“Right. Women of the world.” The phrase seemed to infuse the girl with backbone. “It was like this: I am new to the place, and was taking a . . . stroll to get my bearings.”

“Then you were not expected in that particular chamber?”

“Oh, no. I wasn’t expected to do anything except dress myself up, with the help of the French maid, and make myself available for inspection later. But . . . I am never one to wait well.”

“Nor I,” said Irene.

“Patience,” I put in, “is a supreme virtue.”

Pink eyed me. “Maybe in your line of work, if you have one. Not mine.”

Our return had indeed made her bold.

She resumed her story, directing her words and glances to Irene.

"So I was looking things over, peeking into this room and that to get the lay of the land, when I tried to push open the door to that room."

"Tried?"

"Yes, ma'am! It didn't open at first. The handle was stiff. But I pushed, and I was in like Blackstone the magician."

"Did you determine what kept the door from opening at first?"

"No. I forgot that the moment I took my first breath over the threshold. I am from western Pennsylvania at least, and we have a few barnyards nearby, but I never smelled anything quite like that."

"Except in Les Halles," I murmured.

"Oh. I'll not go there again. Slipping on pig's intestines and all that."

"It is an honest marketplace," I said.

Her cheeks pinked scarlet at my meaning, and I suddenly understood the reason for her nickname.

"I won't be lectured," Miss Pink told me sharply. "I've been on my own for some time now, and do the best I can."

"Have you done it here?" Irene asked. "Yet?"

Pink's cheeks remained cherry red. "None of your business, Missus Adler Norton. I have just been introduced to the house and procedures before that is made formal. I was strolling about to get acquainted with the lay-out. I hadn't reckoned on finding what I found, though at first I couldn't quite make out what was what."

"Were all the lamps still on?"

"Bright as sunshine. If the odor had not warned me . . . but I soon saw the blood, then realized—"

"What did you realize?"

"That he'd done it again. The Ripper. The way those two women were cut up, carved up."

"How good a look did you get?"

"I tiptoed as close as I could without . . . well, getting sick. You can't really see much."

"Thankfully." Irene doused the second little cigar end in the graveyard of the first. "I should like you to come home with us."

"Home?"

Seeing an opportunity to save a soul, I leaped. "The most charming cottage in a village near here, Neuilly. Of course what is considered a cottage in France would be a country manse in England. We have a parrot there, and a cat, even a mongoose. And some . . . snakes." My list trailed off. Miss Pink's hazel eyes were not widening in youthful interest.

"I have seen snakes before, Miss Huxleigh. We had plenty around Crooked Creek."

"Crooked Creek?" I repeated faintly.

"Well, it's no worse than Pondham-on-Rye or dozens of other English hamlets that are named like something you eat rather than live in. Wild western Pennsylvania's the place I hail from, and I am proud of it."

"I am from New Jersey myself," Irene put in, thus sealing the alliance between the Americans. "Tame eastern New Jersey."

"New Jersey? Really? How did you come to live near Paris?"

"If you would join us in our palatial cottage"—here Irene glanced at me a bit sardonically—"I'd have time to tell you."

"Oh, no." Pink's curled head shook firmly. "I went to far too much trouble getting established at this place to leave now."

I made one last plea. "But surely the murders are enough to encourage removal! And you have not even, even—" I could not find a single phrase to decently describe what Pink had not yet committed.

She stood, picked up the brandy glass, and finished its contents in one swallow.

"I am sorry if my temporary shock misled you, Miss Huxleigh, but I am quite a determined sinner and not about to give up my chosen profession. Thanks for the invitation." She glanced to Irene and back to me with a bright, brave smile. "I have work to do here, and am not in the market for 'saving.' "

With that she rustled to the door and left us.

7.

Woman of Mystery

For whole hours at night she lay in bed unable to sleep because of the tirelessness of her imagination, weaving tales and creating heroes and heroines . . .
It was her wont to get the girls of the town together and tell them these stories . . .

—ANONYMOUS

FROM A JOURNAL

I have met the most remarkable woman! She is American, of course. And very beautiful. And was dressed as a man! And smoked the most adorable petite cigars.

The sudden appearance on the scene of this most intriguing apparition has banished my unusual state of suspended animation. Here I had imagined that I wished to see and experience every side of life, no matter how squalid or sordid. Yet discovering the dead women my first night at the *maison de rendezvous* was enough to give me serious pause, despite the poverty, misery, and filth I have experienced elsewhere.

The luxury of the death scene added a sort of operatic decadence to the violence of the slaughter.

It was as if the ghost of brutal death still hovered in that reeking and fashionable room. As if its unseen, hollow, pitiless eyes watched me. And me done up like a French crumpet in a whalebone corset and frou-frou, as ready for crunching as a marzipan cake.

I shiver as I write this. The murderer could still linger in the house. I find myself most puzzled, though the trail has led here and I but followed it.

From the gutters of Whitechapel in London to the boudoirs of brothels in Paris: it hardly seems possible that Jack the Ripper could manage such a leap in place and time and stage setting.

And besides, the wretch is dead.

Or so the London police would have us all believe.

I have not properly "sketched" my new acquaintance and fellow countryman, though. She has the rare sort of face whose beauty is undeniable yet so indefinable that neither men nor women can keep their eyes off of her. I am not considered unappealing, yet would pale beside her, and I cannot precisely say why. I can only imagine how men would react. She seems indifferent to her physical force although I suspect she sometimes hides behind it.

Her companion is another sort. After my recent visit to London, where I soon became fed up with the English whore's attitude of superiority to all other living beings, I am in no mind to suffer this American beauty's typically British familiar. Even the most innocuous of that breed marches to the tune of "Rule, Britannia" and radiates the snobbish certainty that she was put on this earth to set other people straight. This particular domestic martinet is a mousy soul named, of all things, Nell, like the spineless put-upon heroine of a melodrama. Those blessed with great beauty seem to crave the company of the plain. Or perhaps it's the other way around. I wonder what her husband is like. Not the companion's; she is a spinster. "Irene Adler Norton" the cigar-smoking beauty called herself. That implies a husband, though why he would let his wife go off on such gruesome investigations alone is beyond me.

I had heard of these European practices among certain privileged women—tattoos, cigars, naughty lingerie—but never expected to meet such a creature. And she has the ear of the police, has worked for the Pinkertons. Not one to underestimate.

I wonder if she follows the same trail that I do? The companion admitted that they had been in London, but that was many months ago, and is irrelevant.

Or is it?

I cannot believe my luck, dreadful as the state of affairs is. I could not wish to be in more fortuitous circumstances. Not least among these lucky aspects is the fact that police have ended all custom at this *maison de rendezvous* for the time being. For the time being, Thanatos and not Eros is in residence here. Death and not Love.

I admit that, for my purposes, Death is the much more desirable resident.

8.
Call Her Madam

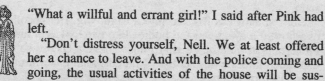

No doubt it gives one a comfortable feeling to wear smart underclothing, pass the laws that suit one and preach endless sermons about virtuous behavior . . . But no sooner have the streetlights been turned low than off they go to pay us a visit.

—AMÉLIE HÉLIE, KNOWN AS CASQUE D'OR

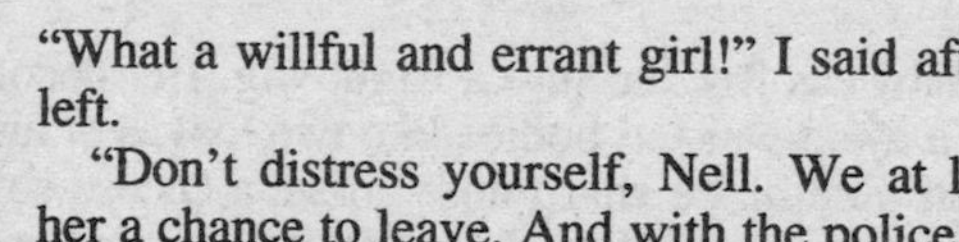

"What a willful and errant girl!" I said after Pink had left.

"Don't distress yourself, Nell. We at least offered her a chance to leave. And with the police coming and going, the usual activities of the house will be suspended for some time."

Irene cast a wistful glance at the brandy decanter. "I am afraid I shall have to interview the madam."

"Madame who?"

"A woman who supervises a house of convenience is a called a madam, Nell."

"Supervises? You seem to imply some sort of order."

"A place like this is also called a disorderly house," she said with a rueful smile.

I was too confused to ask for further enlightenment.

We went into the passage, where a gendarme in his handsome uniform of navy blue stood on guard.

"*Monsieur l'inspecteur*?" Irene asked.

The man led us to the front stairs and then down to the first floor and to a grand salon larger and even more lavishly appointed than the chambers upstairs.

As we entered the opening double doors, we passed a white-veiled bride leaving in the company of a black-robed nun.

Naturally, I stared at their departing backs, a most incongruous pair, but Irene paid them no attention. Or rather, I should say, they did not receive her prolonged attention. Irene's eyes darted over every detail of the room and its occupants, even the departing ones, like emissaries from a crossbow.

I was reminded again of her admonition to "look close" and see small.

That seemed an impossible task in this vast, gilt-hung salon, with elaborate furniture floating like gigantic lily pads on its blue-marble floor.

And this exceedingly large pond had its resident frog: a most unpleasant person sat like the spider in the center of this web of golden threads, stuffed into a gown of obvious green satin.

Her red hair was frizzled into a fright wig. Her decollétage overflowed a wasp-waisted bodice like two loaves of unbaked French bread. She had a sharp nose above a cheese-soft chin that faded into the high collar of fat cushioning her throat like a necklace of fleshy aspic.

Inspector le Villard hastened to this woman's monstrous side and apparently explained who, or what, we were.

Her bead-bright eyes moved like roaches in the suet pudding of her face to study us.

"*Entrez,*" she urged at last. Pudgy, dingy fingers festooned with rings gestured us over the threshold.

I noticed a motley assemblage of persons seated and standing elsewhere in the chamber, including a grown woman in a child's high-waisted cotton frock, her hair in a pigtail and her hands bearing a pail and spade fit for a nursery outing to the seashore.

There was also a wizened elderly man with a terrible squint and some large burly women in house servant's clothes.

Irene crossed the threshold as bid, but waited for the inspector to join her, as he finally did, most reluctantly.

"These are employees of the establishment?" Irene asked in low tones, in English.

"Yes. We have assembled everyone and are almost through with our questioning."

"What of the clients present at the time of the murders?"

Even Inspector le Villard's mustache seemed to blanche at the question. "Clients? There were few. The hour was between dinner and going out for entertainment."

"Where are these few?" Irene asked, implacable.

"Another room. Madame Portiere is willing to answer your inquiries."

"Is she?" Irene advanced on this woman sitting like a sultan in his seraglio, and I suppose she was not much different from one, save that she did not indulge in the favors of the harem.

I followed, feeling more in the presence of evil than I had in the death chamber.

Madame's piggy little eyes beamed at Irene, admiring her form of dress as if it were a particularly sly joke.

"*Brava, Madame. Monsieur*. You would do well in Montmartre in your habit so suave." The glittering swollen hand patted the sky-blue-silk sofa seat beside her.

I cannot describe how badly that bilious green gown and pale blue sofa failed to complement each other.

"It is convenient for the city," Irene agreed, pulling one trouser knee slightly upward as she crossed her legs after sitting. "I imagine the doings upstairs have put quite a crimp in your custom."

The woman's tiny eyes rolled expressively toward the ceiling, as if enlisting heavenly witness to the truth of her next words. I could not imagine that Heaven would wish to witness anything that transpired in this corrupt place.

"The prefect has been quite plain. We are to close until further notice. Meanwhile, our staff is under the question." She nodded to knots of humble persons around the room, each tied around the central figure of an interrogating gendarme.

"Most intolerably inconvenient for a *maison de tolérance*," Irene said, sounding sympathetic. "Although the preferred name is *maison de rendezvous* these days. Let us hope that the culprit is soon caught and your suspension of service ends."

"Huh!" the woman huffed. "He was not caught in London."

"Then you think that the Ripper has relocated to Paris?"

"Who else would commit such atrocity?"

Irene glanced casually around the huge room. "And will they find a suspect among your retainers?"

"I hope not!" the woman snorted.

"Among your clientele then?"

"Certainly not! That is a sure thing. I cater to only the best, the noblest, richest, and most discriminating men in Europe."

I could have taken issue that the best, most noble, and discriminating men in Europe would ever patronize such an establishment, but I knew better than to insert my opinion.

I had been left standing, like a servant. I was simply Nobody, hardly important enough consciously to ignore. It often happened thus. It often happened that being ignored was a great advantage in observing and learning . . . things. And Irene knew that as well as I.

She kept her glance carefully away from me as she questioned the woman in her usual erratic way, leaping from one topic to the other so adroitly that Madame leaked information like a punctured balloon.

Finally, Irene's eyes ceased their constant surveillance of the clots of people in the room and focused on me.

"Nell, I do not see Inspector le Villard in the chamber any longer. Do you suppose you could find him? I have a question or two for him."

Of course, I bustled obediently away. Irene continued to chat with the dreadful woman as if she were a long-lost aunt.

Once in the passage I was at a loss, a state I do not enjoy. I had no idea where the miserable inspector had gone, and imagined that he was only too glad to be rid of us. A series of eggshell cream-painted doors lined the long hallway like ghostly soldiers at attention, the cursive woodwork's gilt details evoking military braid.

All were closed. I was not about to blunder into each one in search of the vanishing policeman.

Perhaps I would overhear some betraying conversation if I merely eavesdropped at each keyhole.

So I moved down the row, crossing from one side of the wide passage to the other, listening for signs of occupancy.

I was singularly unsuccessful.

Why was it that when Irene sent herself upon such a mission, she merely touched the lever of the first closed door and it would spring open like a Fabergé egg, full of lavish surprises?

I seemed fated to plod through life meeting nothing untoward and making no earthshaking discoveries.

It was in this mood that I paused before a door like any other in the endless line. I was startled to hear the frame crack as it opened.

I could not see into the room beyond, for the entire opening was taken up by the massive figure of a man in evening dress, a man of sturdy build whose head must have reached past six feet.

For a moment I thought the King of Bohemia loomed before me. But no, the King was flaxen-haired, and this man would have been called Redbeard had he been a Viking.

I gasped. Not because I had thought it was the King. Not because he was so large and I was so small. Not because his sudden appearance had startled me, and it had.

No, I gasped because I recognized him at last.

"Why," I said before I should embarrass myself and gasp again. "Why, Mr. Stoker. What on earth are you doing here?"

9.
Horrible Imaginings

He was a gentleman on whom I built an absolute trust.
—*MACBETH*

Inspector le Villard popped out from behind Bram Stoker's substantial figure like a puppet in a Punch and Judy show from behind a curtain. I almost expected him to begin hitting Mr. Stoker with a loaf of French bread.

"You recognize this man?" the inspector demanded of me.

I glanced to the person caught between us. Mr. Stoker's face had gone white and was now in the process of suffusing with red. Heretofore, I had not noted such reactions in the visages of grown men, although I was familiar with them on the faces of ten-year-old boys who had been caught with an illegal spoon in the jam jar.

"Of course," I said.

"I do not know you, Madam," Mr. Stoker said swiftly. "No doubt it is considered amusing to the clientele to deal with a woman got up as an English governess, down to her correction devices, but I assure you and anyone else who might inquire that is not my form of diversion."

"I am English, but I am a *Miss,*" I corrected him sternly, "and were I indeed your governess, I would be forced to discipline you for both rudeness and memory loss."

My words made the man only blush further. They seemed to have robbed him of all speech.

"And we have indeed met," I persisted in the name of accuracy. "On more than one occasion."

"Are you employed here?" he began in confusion. "For I honestly do not know you—"

The inspector had no patience for a guessing game. "What matters, sir, is that the lady knows *you*."

"Not intimately, I am afraid," I put in, watching Mr. Stoker's face turn an alarming shade of scarlet, "though all London knows Bram Stoker. A most renowned gentleman of the theater," I informed Inspector le Villard, happy to impress him with British excellence in this area that the Divine Sarah Bernhardt claimed solely for France. "He manages the acclaimed English actor, Sir Henry Irving. Surely you have heard of Irving."

As I spoke, the towering figure of Bram Stoker seemed to shrink like a freshly blooming crocus in a spring windstorm. I imagine the poor man was embarrassed because he did not recognize me, despite the fact that we had met on several occasions during my eight years in London.

I was, for once, blithely unembarrassed. I did not expect to be recalled by persons of fame, fortune, or noble birth, some of whom I had met who combined all three attributes.

In fact, I considered it my duty to educate the French police inspector on Mr. Stoker's importance, for obviously the man was too modest to brandish his achievements like a pedigreed cudgel. We English are entirely too retiring about our virtues, and I was determined that no honor pertaining to Mr. Stoker go unburnished by my praise.

"In addition, I have it from confidential sources that Mr. Stoker is something of an aspiring author—not that many are not aspiring authors these days"—I added, thinking of a doctor of my (thankfully) very slight acquaintance—"but he has far more hope of attaining publication, given his deep knowledge of theatrical plays."

His own mother could not have waxed more proud and pleased. I had no doubt the man would thank me profusely when he finally remembered who I was.

Le Villard, at least, was all bows and gratitude. "Many thanks, Mademoiselle Huxleigh. I was completely ignorant of our friend's accomplishments and history. You see, I had the odd notion that he is one of the few men large enough to have committed the atrocities you and the admirable Madame Norton have had the recent misfortune to view."

"Mr. Stoker!? Why ever would you think so?"

"Perhaps," Inspector le Villard noted with another unnecessary bow to me, "because he has been using quite another name at *Chez* Homicide. A Mr. Adam Eden, according to the information he gave Madame Portiere."

I gazed at Bram Stoker. His high color had faded during the length of my helpful introduction until his skin was paper white again, which made his red hair and beard resemble flames eating away at the edges of his face.

I realized what I had done, and could feel myself pale in turn.

Inspector le Villard turned to smile pleasantly at Mr. Stoker. "And you say you do not know the lady? She appears to know a great deal about you, *monsieur*."

"Indeed," I said hastily. "A man of such wide renown would of course wish to travel in anonymity. It is not at all remarkable that Mr. Stoker would use another name on the Continent."

"Or in a *maison de rendezvous*," the inspector murmured. "Believe me, Mademoiselle Huxleigh, we Paris police are quite accustomed to that particular habit of the English, who are noted for peculiar habits to begin with."

His words brought the blushes to my cheeks now, for there was only one answer to my heartfelt surprise and the question I had burst out with on first encountering Mr. Bram Stoker. Why on earth was he here? Why, to patronize the facilities.

I could no longer gaze up at him with innocent eyes, so kept them down, facing the floor.

It was then that I noticed that, despite his height and girth, Mr. Stoker had feet of a refined size. His shoe toes were polished into obsidian mirrors, and they narrowed elegantly toward the ends, as I am sure the heels also did.

This was, of course, the very impression that I had so carefully sketched in my notebook, along with a notation of length and width made most painstakingly with the tiny retractable tape measure on my chatelaine.

I was most curious what the tape measure would reveal if

I cast myself at Mr. Stoker's feet in apology and managed a surreptitious measuring.

Of course I could not do anything so undignified, more's the pity.

Oh dear.

10.
Carried Away

Being in a touring company provided abundant opportunity for dalliances, but Stoker must have been discreet—or uninvolved—to have left no whiff of gossip.

—BARBARA BELFORD, *BRAM STOKER*

When Irene and I left the *maison de rendezvous,* we found not the serviceable carriage that had conveyed us here, but a gleaming black equipage drawn by four perfectly matched and caparisoned black horses.

I gasped and drew back. In my state of guilt and repentance, it seemed to me a funeral conveyance.

Irene's hand on my cloaked forearm bade me be calm. "Our night is not over, I'm afraid. We are to meet our sponsor."

"Our sponsor?"

"He who has called us into this brutal farrago."

"You still do not know who it is?"

"Quite the contrary. I have always known who it was. What I have not known was why he feels the need to have his own agents on the scene."

A footman in white wig and satin breeches required my hand in mounting the step into the carriage.

I was loath to give such a fop custody of my person, but

there was no graceful way to refuse, so I was shortly boosted into the brocade-upholstered interior, and Irene soon after me.

"He must be used to aiding far more portly ladies than we, Nell," Irene muttered. "I was fairly catapulted in. Too many dowager duchesses, I wager."

"Oh, Irene, I am so mortified!"

"That Bram Stoker did not recognize you? It was merely a matter of context."

"Oh, I know that men do not remark upon me when you are around. That is quite all right with me. I am not mortified that he did not recognize me by myself, but because I utterly betrayed his anonymity and played directly into the hands of the French inspector. Mr. Stoker could not have killed those poor women."

"I fear that he could have, if you speak of possibility. He is of such superior size that he seems one of the few feasible suspects for such a double murder."

"Then so is the King of Bohemia!"

"The King of Bohemia is not here in Paris."

"Oh? Are you so sure? The King traveled under a pseudonym before, as when he pursued you all the way to England. He is a king and can do what he pleases. Why would he not be in Paris, visiting a *maison de tolérance*? I do detest that phrase. It make these establishments sound merely accommodating, rather than utterly immoral."

"The utterly immoral always is the most accommodating, Nell," Irene said with a smile. She pushed her fingers into her extravagant hair, stretching her neck like a cat contemplating licking its cravat. "I would have dressed differently had I known I was to visit a baron as well as a brothel tonight."

"A baron. Then this is the Rothschild coach?"

"The coat of arms on the doors is covered with bombazine, but that is like putting a cheesecloth over a Michelangelo sculpture. I ran my fingers over the carving as we entered. There is no doubt."

"Oh. I am not dressed to pay a call on a baron either."

"But you are conventionally dressed. I don't believe Baron Rothschild is acquainted with my many methods." She laughed. "Perhaps he should be. And don't fret yourself over

Bram Stoker, Nell. Many an innocent man, so to speak, has used a false name in a place such as that. It does show that he is capable of shame, yes? And may be worth saving."

"That is true, and somewhat consoling. But I do not understand why so many people that I know, or that *you* know, fall into the category of 'worth saving.' "

"It is a wicked world, Nell, and we investigate the dark side of it. What else is worth the investigating? And . . . I fear you are a born bloodhound, with a nose for wrongdoing. Else you would not have such a familiarity with the Whitechapel horrors. I am not sure how that was possible."

"Well. Godfrey. The English papers. It was . . . inescapable."

"How fortunate. Dear Godfrey. Suddenly I am glad that he is far away and well out of this."

"You think Godfrey more in need of protection from this monstrous act than I myself?"

She shrugged. "Men take gruesome acts personally. We women are used to our monthlies and childbirth and attendant pain. All of these are little deaths. Also other . . . matters. Men presume that they are not subject to such inconveniences as violence to their persons."

"I cannot say what men presume, having known so few of them."

"You are advancing fast, Nell. Bram Stoker in the hallway indeed. He is merely the smallest fish, or the net would not have detained him. I am interested in the leviathans that have been let go."

11.
Rue Royale

To us, who for twenty years have been crying out that if the Rothschild family isn't dressed in ghetto yellow, we Christians soon will be.

—EDMUND DE GONCOURT

"Why such secrecy?" I asked Irene. "We have met openly with our baronial 'sponsor' before."

"I apologize. I have been imprecise, as your question so elegantly points out. Obviously, we have more than one sponsor, hence the secrecy. One of our sponsors we have met before: Baron Alphonse de Rothschild. The other, I believe, only I have previously met."

"Yet you know who it is? How?"

"By paying close attention to one key portion of the newspapers—though you berate me for ignoring the press in general—the society pages. Apparently I would have been better off ignoring the comings and goings of polite Parisian society and paying more note to the hackings of the London homicidal maniac of last autumn."

"*Touché*, as they say in swordplay, but I am merely a needlewoman. If my knowledge of the London atrocities proves a boon, I will be only too happy."

"And so it already has." Irene eyed the finely appointed interior of the carriage. "Not a place where I can deposit an ash."

"Surely we are not on our way to Ferriéres at this hour?"

"Heavens no. We will visit the town house of Baron de

Rothschild, I believe, on the rue de Saint-Florentin, which is very near."

I could not quite stifle a yawn. "At least we are to remain in Paris. I could not have survived a journey of such length as Ferriéres."

Irene leaned her head against the tufted brocade that lined the vehicle. Small oil lamps illuminated the interior, making it seem as if we sheltered in the nook of some cozy inn.

"We will not be home before daylight," she predicted, drawing a pocket watch from the inside of her jacket to consult it by the jiggling lamplight.

Arriving past one in the morning at even a great house is a hurried, chill affair.

When the carriage stopped, the footman assisted us out and into the custody of another footman, who escorted us up some broad stairs and through tall gilded doors into an echoing entry dominated by a curving marble staircase befitting the Louvre, on which more footmen stood, bearing lamps. All wore the embroidered livery of the eighteenth century, and I felt like a fairy princess entering a fairy castle, deserted except for the mute, enchanted manservants who swarmed the place like ants at a picnic.

Because Irene was attired in man's clothing and I wore my sturdy checked coat-dress, we had no outer garments to offer the surfeit of willing hands around us, which seemed to be such a disappointment that half their number melted away in an instant.

A butler approached us and, after the hesitation of a fraction of a second, bowed to Irene. "Madame Norton?" He frowned at me. Butlers always did. Fortunately, I was not often in their presence.

"My companion is Miss Huxleigh," Irene said.

"A companion was not expected."

"The unexpected is always more interesting."

The man hesitated again. Although he cultivated the lofty impersonality expected of the best butlers, I saw that he was a man nearing sixty. The harsh night lamps picked out pockets of fatigue in his impassive features.

My presence seemed to present a quandary, but at last his eyelids flicked shut in resignation.

"Follow me," he said, turning away.

Actually we followed him as he followed the sole remaining footman, who carried the lamp.

Quite a procession we made, our footsteps echoing over the marble floors, our order a martial single file, with me bringing up the rear.

We skirted the cascade of stairs, I peering up its shadowy heights a little wistfully, and followed our guides down the dark and silent hall, our feet muffled on thick Turkish carpet at last.

The smell of warmed oil and lemon wax became a kind of incense as we moved deeper into the house as if approaching a sanctuary.

At a pair of magnificent marquetry doors the butler paused, and the footman held up his lamp.

The butler opened a polished brass latch and preceded us into the room beyond.

"Madame Norton and Mademoiselle Huxleigh," he intoned in perfect English.

Irene preceded me within. I breathed a happy sigh. I could not possibly get into trouble treading along behind her train. Or her bootheels, rather.

The chamber was huge and shadowed. Only the pools of light around the sofa tables illuminated anything, and the massive fireplace fairly pulsed with fresh flames.

Bits of gilt twinkled in the shadows like faint stars in a moonless sky . . . book bindings and picture frames, no doubt.

But we were not here to gaze on literary treasures or on the oil-painted faces of forebears.

Our focus was on the neat man in sober black standing near the fireplace.

I had seen—met, I suppose, though the better description would be "had been presented to"—Baron Alphonse de Rothschild. The French branch of the international banking house of Rothschild was its most wealthy and influential.

And Baron de Rothschild looked every inch of what those two words implied, except that there were not very many inches of him. He was a neat, mild individual, with a snowy mustache and side whiskers the size of Cupid's wings that distracted one from his sharp and ever-watchful gaze.

"My dear Mrs. Norton," he addressed Irene in English, lifting one white eyebrow. "You wear bohemian dress tonight."

A tone of surprise, even of slight dismay, could not quite be concealed.

"It was necessary." Irene managed to glide forward in her man's dress like a lady wearing the latest intricacies of a Worth gown. "The site. The situation."

The Baron looked away as if so doing would spare him the details of what we had seen.

I was amazed. We were two women of no station or wealth whatsoever, yet this man of incomparable power was not willing to face what we had. Perhaps that is what wealth and power buys one: the ability to look aside.

"Miss Huxleigh." He nodded at me, who had hastened after Irene like an acolyte, astounded to be noted and even more so to be addressed.

"Sir," I said in acknowledgment. I did not know how I should address a French Baron, and did not wish to learn.

Even within a few steps of the Baron, we were lost in that massive, high-ceilinged room, marooned on a desert island defined by a few wavering lamps.

I suddenly realized that no servant had lingered. How odd.

"Did you interview the witnesses?" the Baron asked Irene.

She nodded, but corrected him. "Witness. The young American lady."

The Baron started, then brushed a nervous finger over his mustache. "I was interested in your estimation of the scene, and of the young American lady. Please be seated." He indicated a sofa covered with what seemed to be down-filled cushions upholstered in the fabric of the Bayeux Tapestry.

"Miss Huxleigh may sit down," Irene said with a quick smile. "In fact, I suggest that she does so, and you also, Baron. I am too . . . restless to sit. I think better on my feet."

"Ah. You thrive on crisis then. So do I, Madame Norton." His amused glance caught mine, and he nodded to the sofa while seating himself in a kingly chair with gilded arms and legs.

I did as indicated, but longingly eyed the fire twenty feet away, and especially the massive pair of wing chairs before it, fit for a giant. My toes were chill in their hard leather boot toes. I should feel like Alice in Wonderland sitting in one of those huge chairs, my feet swinging toward the cheerful flames a full foot from the floor. . . .

"You have heard about the brutality of the scene?" Irene was asking the Baron.

He nodded gravely. "Was it as bad as they said?"

"Perhaps worse, but the true extent of the barbarism will not be evident until all is stripped bare in the Paris Morgue."

"I would not," said the Baron slowly, "have sent even as formidable a woman as yourself to such a scene, but—"

Irene waved a too-dismissive hand. I agreed wholeheartedly with the Baron. "What did you wish to know most?"

"The American mademoiselle. She was not involved?"

"Only as an innocent bystander. She is new to the establishment and apparently blundered into the death chamber."

"Poor child."

I could not tell whether the Baron was commenting on Pink's happening on the death scene or on her being new to the establishment. The Rothschild family was just that: many generations of intermixed family business and marriage, risen from the meanest poverty to the most luxurious wealth. As a good Christian I had been taught that the Jews had slain Him whose Name named my faith, but since I had become only very slightly acquainted with the Baron de Rothschild, I had come to see the offense as historic rather than personal. And one thing I could say for the Rothschilds: they were not known as profligate.

Irene did not comment on his sympathetic murmur, but instead paused in her pacing before him. "What is the question you really wish answered?"

He responded just as quickly as she had challenged. "Could this be the work of the man London called Jack the Ripper?"

She nodded, slowly. "It could. Although there are several objections to such a theory."

He seemed not to hear her qualification, but ran a harassing hand into the thinning white hair at his temples, as if we were not there.

"This is very bad. You know the tendency in London to place the blame on 'foreigners,' always a code word for Jews?"

Irene, less familiar with London nuances than I, could not nod, but I could, and did. The motion caught the Baron's quick eye.

"Yes, you see it, too, do you not, Mademoiselle Huxleigh?"

I did not, but was not about to admit it, so I again nodded soberly.

Irene looked betwixt us two, an expression of exasperation vying with one of amusement on her face. She waited. I always marveled that even when caught at a loss, she managed to turn a situation to her advantage.

Her silence encouraged the Baron to further voice his fears.

"Very bad," he repeated. "The pogroms in Russia these last years. The accusations in London last autumn. And now, if the poison has moved to Paris . . . I speak not only of the poison of murder, but of the venom of slander."

He had spoken long enough for Irene's quick mind to overtake her own ignorance of the events last autumn in London.

"You fear some massive retaliation against the Jews."

"It takes a pin dropping to start some minor retaliation. These frightening, vicious deaths could cause a conflagration."

"Only two deaths in Paris, so far."

"So far. Yet I would be pleased if you would continue to investigate this matter."

"If there are links to the London killings, I am at a disadvantage. I know little of the events, since we were traveling on the far-flung edges of the Continent."

The Baron shook his head with an amused smile. "I will have the London branch of the family supply all newspaper and police reports by messenger. They should be in your hands within two days."

"Through official channels?"

"Through whatever channels best suffice. If information is all you require, ask and you shall have it."

"What of the police reports here in Paris?"

The Baron paused to stroke a forefinger through his silky side whiskers. "Those may require more finesse."

"You do not trust the Paris police."

"It is rather the opposite. The Paris police do not trust me, or any Rothschild. They have kept massive dossiers on me and my family for decades. And the climate has grown even more intemperate of late: the gossip, the lies, the hatred. The city throngs with newspapers of all stripes, with the anti-Semitic journals everywhere. We thought the Russian situation was severe, but I fear that Paris is burning for its own kind of pogrom. We Jews are too successful."

This was the first tang of bitterness I had ever heard in the Baron's voice.

"As I was at La Scala in Milan," Irene noted wryly, putting her hands into her jacket pockets as if feeling for the presence of her revolver, "when the sopranos put ground glass in my rouge pot."

"No!" He looked up, both appalled and surprised by the petty acts among opera singers.

"Success is always a cause for suspicion and resentment in the untalented."

We were silent—I was certainly not going to speak out of turn.

"It is not just Jews who are successful," the Baron said quietly. "Or suspect."

"Indeed." Irene turned toward the fireplace and the high-backed chairs I had so coveted. "I think perhaps His Royal Highness could join our conversation now, instead of merely eavesdropping."

12.

Family Resemblance

Many times subsequently I had the pleasure of meeting him, and I found less of the airs of office about him than I have many times seen displayed by third-rate officials, even in our own dearly beloved and highly-spoken of democratic republic.

—WILLIAM F. CODY, A.K.A. BUFFALO BILL

A bemused chuckle issued from beyond the right wing chair facing the fire, sounding uncannily like an apologetic throat-clearing as well.

Then a figure rose from the shelter of the chair like a ghost in a Sheridan Le Fanu story.

No ghost he, but a man to whom the word "portly" would be a compliment. I had seldom seen such a fat man, except in the newspapers.

While I stared, the familiar features took undeniable shape: the heavy-lidded, sleepy eyes, both amiable and arrogant; the neatly trimmed mustache and the beard whitening at the corners of his obscured mouth.

One feature was decidedly not familiar. The Prince of Wales was balding quite markedly. I realized with shock that I was seeing him in intimate circumstances common only to family and friends, not to the public. It also occurred to me that all the photos published of him had been made out of doors, when His Royal Highness wore a dignified top hat or a jaunty yachting cap or sportsman's cloth cap. Hence I deduced that the Prince was vain as well as in line for the throne, although perhaps the latter fact accounted for the first.

He was staring dumbly at Irene and squinting those already

half-shut eyes. "You look like what the photographers call a negative of Sarah Bernhardt in her pale-trousered sculpting ensemble. So you are the formidable Madam Norton. I have met you before, have I not? I never forget a pretty face, even when it is later presented to me above a gentleman's frock coat."

She approached him, hand extended.

The Prince of Wales was one man she did not force an American-style handshake upon. Instead, he took her limp offered hand while she executed as pretty a curtsy as I have ever seen done, though performed by a woman in trousers.

"It was many years ago," Irene said. "How kind of Your Royal Highness to remember."

"Ah. I do not remember where or when, though."

"Luckily, Your Highness, I could never forget."

His sleepy eyes fluttered at this flattery. "I trust so." He leaned as close as his great bulk would permit, and she honored him with the details.

"It was dinner at William Gilbert's house, Sir, when I was singing in *Iolanthe: The Peer and the Peri.* Mr. Gilbert enjoyed inviting the ladies of the chorus for a brush with greatness."

I hoped only I had noticed that Irene had not specified if the greatness to be so brushed with was that of William Gilbert, the renowned librettist, or of the Prince of Wales. "Bertie," of course, would leap to the conclusion Irene wished him to swallow like the Queen's pet Pomeranian diving through a hoop for a bit of the dinner roast. Perhaps royalty did not eat roast, on second thought, but I was certain that the Queen's Pomeranian, and her eldest son and heir, both leaped on her command.

For a moment I envied Americans their wild, ungoverned state.

Irene was showing no sign of being a republican rather than a royalist now though, as she smiled at the Prince.

"I *do* remember you." His pudgy forefinger tapped possessively on the soft silk ascot at Irene's throat. Only I saw her stiffen. "Quite a forward miss, as I recall. Insisted on a private audience."

"Which Your Royal Highness so kindly granted."

His walrus eyes began to twinkle. "I remember every moment of it. And now you are married?"

"Indeed," Irene said. "And now I am permitted to meet Your Royal Highness again, and to hope to do you some small service in repayment for the favor of a royal audience so long ago."

"Tut, my dear. It is I who owe you a royal favor for sharing your beauty with the world. Do you still perform? I mean, er, sing, was it?"

"Alas no, Sir. I am now kept busy with private inquiries. As you may imagine, the great have need of protection."

"Imagine nothing! I am plagued by the Paris police, who follow me everywhere, or everywhere they can. But you were a clever girl, I recall. Was there not some unpleasantness involving a peer of the realm and a chorus girl?"

"An unpleasant murder, Your Royal Highness, as there is here."

The reminder pushed him away from her as from a bad omen. "Yes. Again. That was a trifling affair, that operetta instance. We were able to hush it up. This—"

"This is too gruesome to hush up," Irene agreed.

"And how did you know that I was here?"

"At the Baron's residence? In the chair? In Paris?"

"Any or all of it?"

"I knew you were in Paris to inaugurate the Eiffel Tower at the opening ceremony; the papers were full of it. From there it was but a skip and jump to guessing the extreme concern you would feel over the terrible murders that occurred so near to Your Royal Highness's . . . neighborhood. How may I be of service, other than interviewing the American girl who discovered the atrocity?"

"You have heard what the Baron fears," the Prince said, sounding like a prince concerned with issues larger than his own interests for the first time.

"Yes, but I was not in London during last autumn's Whitechapel events. Does Your Royal Highness also fear that fresh murders will raise fresh fury against the Jews?"

"I do." He spun away from us to pace to the fireplace, then

turned and addressed us as a group. I was amazed to see those lazy eyes pass over me as well as the Baron and Irene. It was as if he addressed an audience.

"I am sure you know that I am not held in the public's highest regard—oh, they are *fond* of me," he hastened to say, as if any one of us had argued with him, "but I am merely tolerated. They love my mother and admire my wife. *I* am tolerated. 'Good old Bertie.' " His massive shoulders shrugged. "I enjoy good food, good company, good gaming, good sailing, good hunting, good friends, good cigars, good women."

Irene waited politely, as must all who wait upon a prince, but I was possessed of an unexpressed restlessness I could only quench by pushing a hand into my pocket and squeezing my fingers shut on the many sharp angles of my chatelaine.

No wonder the Prince of Wales was merely "tolerated" by his subjects, as he put it! He was a careless pleasure-seeker, and that was all.

"I am criticized for my love of foreign climes," he went on, "Paris, Vienna, Baden-Baden, Marienbad. I am as liable to associate with jockeys as with Jews, commoners as with nobility. These are modern times, Madam, and I move with them."

You move with the money, I heard a wicked voice I did not know I possessed answering him. And who had more money than the Rothschilds? Of course, Irene and Godfrey and I had benefited from their patronage ourselves, but we worked for it.

And, of course, the Jews whom the public turned on from time to time included both the wealthy and the powerless. I had to admire Baron Alphonse for responding to attacks on the most humble and helpless of his kind.

Apparently, he had also won the sympathy of the Prince of Wales, not an insignificant achievement.

"Sir," the Baron said now, "do not doubt that my family is most grateful for your support."

"And I for yours," the Prince said, chuckling again. "You rascally bankers know you have rescued the crowned heads of Europe from fiscal and political ruin time and again. Not to mention that you offer such splendid hunting and cigars at Ferriéres."

The Baron shrugged modestly. I realized that I was hearing of affairs the public and even the journalists never dream of eavesdropping upon.

Irene, however, grew visibly impatient with this mutual self-congratulation, though it involved a baron and a prince. I recalled that she never had been very intimidated by princes, not even when they resided in Bohemia.

"Sirs," she said, "if you wish to avoid an eruption of anti-Jewish sentiment, this killer must be stopped before the public suspects Jack the Ripper is at work again. He must be caught and identified."

"Well said, and not easily done," the Baron noted.

Irene fixed Bertie with a stern eye equal to any maternal glare. Having been an opera diva did have its uses. "Your Royal Highness." In just such a tone would I as governess have addressed a naughty baronet of eight. "Is it not true that you were present in the *maison de rendezvous* at the time of the murders, that you were the caller the two now-dead ladies were expecting, instead of Jack the Ripper?"

"Oh dear God, yes." Bertie whispered the words, then stumbled toward the fire, sitting heavily in the wing chair.

Irene followed him like a Queen's prosecutor at the bench.

"But you were entertained elsewhere in the house at the time."

"Yes." He looked up at her with the meekness of the found-out. "Who told you—?"

"No one told me. It was obvious from the moment I entered the house that the first business had been to remove and conceal the presence of a person of high rank. I merely imagined the highest rank I could and arrived at you."

He blinked. "P-p-poor girls. So y-y-young and pretty. Vivacious, both of them. Charming."

I thought I saw him shiver, despite the roaring fire.

Irene glanced at Baron Alphonse, who, along with me, had followed her pursuit of the Prince's testimony.

"Baron, you were the first informed."

"His Royal Highness had dined with me before departing

for the house. My driver was still at the back stables when the Prince fled."

"I did not flee, my dear Alphonse," Bertie said, his gaze still fixed on the flames. "I retreated in good order."

"You did the right thing."

"And you," Irene asked the Baron, "then sent for me to question of the young woman, Pink, who discovered the dead women instead of the Prince?" She eyed the distraught heir apparent. "Or *after* the Prince?"

"I saw nothing, thank God. From what I have heard, I salute you, Madam, if you have witnessed what I have heard described. I could not have . . . tolerated it. So charming, so fresh. Ah!"

"There is something else," Irene said, her expression sharpening. As usual when she wanted incisive answers, she looked to the Baron de Rothschild.

He nodded slowly. "In London. Lately. There have been rumors."

"Rumors that make the Prince's nearness to the scene even more dangerous?"

"Yes. These are false and devious untruths, that my race has had aimed at it for centuries. Only now, it fixes on the Prince of Wales, perhaps for his friendliness to our family and our welfare." The Baron's thin lips thinned further. "Nothing must be said of these matters outside this room, and I hold your companion to that charge also." The Baron glanced at the Prince, then lowered his eyes and his voice and told us two women the dreadful truth.

"The latest rumor is that the royal family is tangled in the Ripper horror. They whisper of Prince Eddy in that regard."

Before I could murmur "Prince Eddy," Irene had seized upon the news and made it hers.

"Prince Eddy. The heir of the heir to the throne."

I glanced at the Prince of Wales, confused. He was muttering brokenly to himself, "Just a 'dear, good, simple boy,' as Mother said."

I confess that I did not much follow the doings of royalty, however stoutly I upheld Queen Victoria and the Succession, no matter how weak its links.

That had been before I had personally met the Prince of Wales, however. If he was the example, what could have that "dear, good, simple boy" his son been up to?

Both men gazed at Irene, their faces corroded with worry as she spoke what they could barely face.

Apparently it was "like father, like son," and Prince Eddy was now reputed to be as much of a lady-killer as his sire. Perhaps even more so.

13.

Rogue Royale

The very air of Paris seemed to encourage license. Foreign celebrities passing through the capital hastened to pay their respects to the most notorious filles en renom.

—JOANNA RICHARDSON, *THE COURTESANS*

The birds were trilling in the hedges as we were driven back to Neuilly.

Irene had taken the combs out of her piled hair one by one as the dawn brightened the glittering leaves of the tall poplar trees. With the locks rippling to her shoulders, she looked no older than dear Allegra Turnpenny when I had tucked her into bed on Berkeley Square more than a decade ago.

I wished that I could tuck myself into bed this morning, into such fresh, innocent sheets as young Allegra had slept in, but my mind churned with the sights, sounds, and smells of our dreadful evening in Paris.

Irene bent forward, leaning her elbows on her trousered knees and her face in her hands. Her fingers massaged her temples and forehead.

"I shouldn't doubt you had the headache," I observed, "after all we have seen tonight."

"It's what we didn't see that haunts me, Nell."

"Jack the Ripper?"

"No one has seen him, at least knowingly, except his victims."

I agreed. "We are like those poor people of Whitechapel, or the constables, who stumbled upon the bloody deeds just after they had been committed. Would you really care to catch the killer in the act?"

"If that were the only way to catch him, and in such cases as these, I fear that is so." She sat up, energetic again. "Nell, you have read about the exploits of this monster. How does this Paris case differ from the London murders?"

"Several instances," I said promptly. I am much better dealing with the dimensions of a thing than its deeper meaning. "The violence was committed indoors, unlike every London murder but the last, the slaughter of Mary Jane Kelly. And that poor creature was set upon in her tiny room; this outrage took place in a large room within a vast, occupied building, with people all around."

"Who heard or saw nothing but the result."

"So it was in the case of Mary Jane Kelly. A neighbor thought she heard her call 'Murder!' once, but did nothing about it."

"At least those neighbors were willing to testify. It is in the interest of every resident of the *maison* to conceal the details of these killings. Certainly no one would breathe a syllable of the Prince's presence."

"That is one thing I don't understand, Irene."

"Only one?"

I refused to be drawn into a defense of my assertion. "It is the Prince. He was to . . . call upon two of the women at once."

"Yes, Nell."

"Two? At once?"

"Yes, Nell."

"I had heard a rumor that he was most gallant with the ladies—"

"He is a rake, Nell. You know what a rake is?"

"Yes. Of course." I could feel my cheeks warming. "Hell-fire Club. The kind of person that Queen Victoria has dedicated her life to eradicating from the realm."

"To no great effect. Her uncles, son, and grandson are notorious examples of the species."

"A rake . . . goes with a lot of women."

Irene flared a wrist toward the open window of the carriage and the chitter of bird life. "As many as birds in the bushes."

"Is that not rather . . . greedy?"

"The Prince of Wales is a greedy boy."

"And I didn't understand your conversation with him. It seemed to have an unwholesome undertone. I cannot comprehend you, Irene! You were absolutely fanatic about preserving your reputation in connection with the King of Bohemia, but you seem to be on far too intimate terms with the Prince of Wales. What, pray, is the difference?"

Irene smiled, her face looking drawn for a moment. "The difference is that the King of Bohemia is in Prague and Bertie is in London, and often in Paris."

"I don't understand—"

"The King of Bohemia, like all princelings, felt himself entitled to a mistress. He erred in assuming that I would settle for such a compromised position. *A* mistress, Nell. He was not a rake, merely a privileged man exercising his royal prerogative.

"Bertie, for all his boyishness, his vanity, and his actually admirable tolerance of classes of people his royal forebears would have nothing to do with, including Jews and opera singers, is a rake. He never rests in his quest for female conquests. They are not even conquests. Every female whom his eye falls upon is his for a night, be she street doxy, dairyman's or duke's wife. It is simply so."

"Not you! But he spoke in that odious way, as if—"

"He believes that he, we, have . . . *hmmmm*."

"No! Not . . . *hmmmm*?"

"He believes it so because I want him to believe it so."

"Why?! That is madness, Irene. You would not compromise yourself for a very real alliance with the King of Bohemia, however unsanctioned. Yet for this Prince of Wales—"

"For this Prince of Wales I needed to devise a stratagem that feeds his vanity and his appetite without costing my virtue. You remember how years ago the Prince overheard a murder on Sir William Gilbert's newly installed telephone device that connected sound from the very stage wings to his home?"

"Yes. You had been invited to sup there with some of the other operetta singers. I was not able to accompany you, and now much regret that. You realized that the Prince had heard a conversation important to the murder of a chorus singer by her titled lover and used Mesmerism, which you had learned in the States, where they apparently teach anything to anyone, to pry the pertinent information from the future King. I can't say I approve of Mesmerizing an heir apparent, but—"

"I instructed Bertie to forget what I had learned through him, and added one notion that would be with him forever after the spell was over."

"One notion? Global accord?"

"No. I led him to believe that he had consummated his wishes in connection with me, but that we had agreed to nevermore meet in that fashion."

"Irene! You let him believe that he had *had* his way with you? Why?"

"Because he cannot resist using his princely power to seduce any woman who catches his eye. I let him think I was already conquered territory; hence he can leave me alone for so long as we both shall live. That is the way of princes."

"But your reputation. The Baron must certainly think—"

"If the Baron thinks that, he thinks no more of it than that the Prince has consorted with Sarah Bernhardt, or regularly visits the Princess de Sagan."

"Or pairs of nameless women in a *maison de rendezvous,*" I added with a shudder, and not at the recent deaths, but at the more recent revelations of debauchery.

"In many *maisons de rendezvous,* Nell. Albert Edward is not choosy. Chambermaid or countess. Or opera singer. It is all the same to him."

"How can you abide being misjudged?"

"This method saves me the future effort of repulsing a man who will be King. It is nudge, nudge, wink, wink, and over with. I do not doubt that many a woman favored with a nocturnal call from the Prince would wish she had my method."

"And what do their husbands say, if they have them?"

"Many do. But the husband's hands are tied. It is a privilege to have one's wife coveted by a future king."

"Nonsense! And what of Godfrey? If he should hear of this?"

"He will not, and if he did, he will understand my strategy."

"He would not stand still for it."

"No, but the damage is done, the seed is planted, the Prince is deceived. I was younger then, and it seemed a practical solution, particularly if I was ever to encounter the Prince again. And you see, Nell? It was only the Baron and yourself who heard the Prince's implications. Neither of you will think the less of me for it, for both of you will recognize my deception for what it is."

"Even the Baron?"

"Do you not think that he has politely and quietly conceded much for the friendship of the Prince? Perhaps even his beautiful and spirited English wife, Leonora?"

"His wife the Baroness? *He* is one of complaisant husbands that strew Bertie's trail?"

"Rumor is not always credible, so I seldom bother believing it. You must understand, Nell, that wealthy men mark their achievement in life by what things belonging to other men they have taken: businesses, wagers, horses, women. And these aristocratic wives have been traded on the marriage market like thoroughbred horses on the race circuit. They have little to do but bear heirs and dress well. I think they relish these Society skirmishes in infidelity, gossip, and subterfuge. It relieves the boredom. Remember Alice Heine, the American banking heiress who has a French duke and a Monacan prince to her credit so far, as well as less well known gentlemen not suitable for matrimony. So no, I don't doubt that the Baron has conceded much for the freedom the Prince's friendship gives to him and those he cares about, which includes the far-flung members of both his large and international immediate family, and the many million members of his race. So have I, too, conceded a little to the Great Game of Western Europe. The future King of England is a mighty man indeed."

" 'The future King of England is a mighty man indeed.' That sounds like a patter line from a Gilbert and Sullivan operetta."

"It does," Irene said, laughing with delight, repeating the phrase in a perfect English accent. "Amazing how my time in the chorus has made its mark upon my diction."

"It is pleasant to hear you speak with proper diction, even if I do not like the tune you sing: that the Prince's power is absolute, and that we must, like all good subjects of Empire, bow to even a debaucher."

She said nothing in reply. I was silent, too, listening to the Baron de Rothschild's silken springs barely rustle as we hurtled over deeply rutted roads.

If they could keep so many serious secrets, so could I.

⚜ ⚜ ⚜

Our maid Sophie was much discommoded that we arrived home just as she was arising to tend to us. She is a tall, rawboned woman whose approval of us has somehow become more paramount than our approval of her work. Given Sophie's irritation, and the fact that it is very hard to keep satisfactory servants in the country, especially in a small establishment such as ours, Irene and I allowed her to serve us breakfast and pretended to go about our day as usual.

I then tended to the menagerie of beasts I had accidentally acquired through the years, mainly from the fact that no one else would have them.

There was the parrot, Casanova, who had been trained to talk by a foul-mouthed master, and had survived yet another master—this one murdered—to require a new owner. I was elected. There was the huge black Persian cat, Lucifer, also never named by me. Irene had presented him to me on my arriving in Paris to join her and Godfrey safely across the

Channel from *the* man, whom only I had reason to know she had more dire need than anyone suspected to stay well away from. There was Messalina, named after the barbaric empress, a lithe mongoose we had inherited during our pursuit of the cobra-bearing would-be assassins of Dr. Watson, and dear to me for having a connection to Quentin Stanhope, of whom I shall not speak of more, here. And there were the snakes acquired as well in an outré manner.

Luckily, the bird and the snakes were restricted in movement, at least some of the time.

So I made my morning rounds and saw that all were fed and had clean quarters and were not engaged in eating each other, or seeking to avoid being eaten by each other.

Although I do believe that they were all evenly matched and hence unlikely to harm any but the unwary human.

I intended to see that the unwary human was not I.

While Sophie bustled about the rooms, scrubbing and dusting and sighing, I pretended to do needlework, and Irene pretended to read and play scales.

Finally, Sophie left us a cold supper and departed for her room to mend linens.

Irene and I took one look at the repast: chicken, and retired upstairs before the sun set to our respective featherbeds.

Once again I awoke in the utter dark of a French countryside, as far from Shropshire as I could ever have imagined myself to be, to the sound of strife.

I heard not thunderous rapping on our broad safe door, but cries and whimpers, almost of an abused child. The governess in me started up, hurling myself out of bed. The shock of cold boards on my bare feet woke me fully, and I fumbled for the candleholder. Not to light it, but to seize it as a weapon.

A louder cry made me launch myself at the dark, hunting for remembered objects and distances, smashing into the doorjamb, then lumbering down the hall, rubbing painful elbows with the rough stucco surfaces.

The sounds were coming from Irene and Godfrey's bedroom.

I ran facefirst into the closed door, then flailed to find the handle. I must have sounded like a small herd of elephants to the room's occupants, but the gasps and cries continued despite my clumsy arrival.

At last the cold iron of the doorknob turned with one desperate wrench, and I felt the door swing wide.

The muted sounds paused. Then Irene screamed, a spine-chilling, heart-stopping aria of a scream not ten feet from where I stood.

I threw myself in the direction of the bed to arrive and find the linens in an uprising. Had the robbers I feared the previous night come in fact now?

A form from the dark met me as if demon-possessed.

I was determined not to be overpowered. We lurched back and forth in the bed linens. I had no time to speculate on who—or what—I fought. I heard its labored breath, and my own. Something sharp cracked on my forearm, and I could not repress a cry of distress.

The bedclothes grew still of a sudden.

"Nell?" Irene's voice asked, husky.

"Irene!"

"*You* are the attacker?" she demanded.

"*You* are the housebreaker?"

"We need some light," she decreed firmly, as God must have on the First Day.

I felt the mattress shift as she knocked over what sounded like a great many things on the nightstand.

At last a match scraped into a spark and then a candlewick tremored into flame with a pungent scent of sulphur.

We sat staring at each other over a tangled welter of bedclothes.

"Only you?" I was amazed.

"Only you!" she replied, with a relieved laugh. I noticed that her face was the same pale shade of ecru as the sheeting. And her laugh contained what even she would define as far too much tremolo.

"Why did you cry out?" I asked.

Irene's face took on an expression I had never seen on it before. Sheepish, we would say in Shropshire.

"I, ah . . . it was a nightmare, Nell."

"A nightmare! You never had nightmares in all the years we shared rooms in Saffron Hill."

Irene pushed the feather pillows into a mound against the old wooden headboard, drew up her knees until her bed shirt's ruffles covered her bare toes, and nodded.

"That's true. But I had never seen Jack the Ripper's work during all those years in Saffron Hill."

I mounded the remaining pillows (she and Godfrey favored a great many for some reason) into my arms and collapsed upon them, feeling like a girl again, or at least a young governess who'd come in to quiet a charge's nighttime frights.

"It was a dreadful scene, that is true," I agreed, "but we were spared the worst by the confusing tangle of the clothing."

"It did not spawn nightmares for you?"

"No. Not yet. I do not understand, Irene. You are ever so much more adventuresome than I am, yet I have never seen you so upset. We have seen corpses before."

My blunt term made her shudder, then shiver. She drew the coverlet that was half on the floor close around her shoulders and almost up to her nose.

"It is my cursed theatrical imagination, Nell. Usually it works for me. No matter how . . . terrible and distasteful the scene, I pretend it is *Otello*, or *Lucia di Lammermoor* or *La Traviata*, so I am but a poor performer who frets my hour in the presence of whatever horror we have encountered. And the two drowned men we saw were victims of natural elements, even if one was deliberately held underwater. This was a scene of carnage incarnate. Yes, the dress was disarranged, but in such a way that I could guess at the unthinkable excess of the wounds."

"So it is always a play to you: murder and crime?"

"No. I did not say that. Only that my part in it, my role as observer, feels as it would on a stage. I must play it to the hilt. Oh, dreadful metaphor! I can stave off full realization of what has happened because I see myself as playacting, do you understand, Nell? Tonight, when I slept, in my dreams, I was no longer playacting." She bit her lip. "And I deeply regret leaving Pink in that place."

"So do I! And not because of the poor dead women! I do not believe in ghosts, Irene, although I enjoy reading about them, but I do believe in sin, and that house of death is also a house of iniquity."

Irene did not seem to be listening to me, but rather watching me with cautious wonder. "You are not . . . disturbed by what we saw last night?"

"Of course I am. Deeply. Imagine! Bram Stoker in that place of infamy. And the Prince of Wales, not only there, but possessed of the odious notion that you . . . that he . . . that the unthinkable—Yes, I was most distressed and had great trouble falling asleep. I must have spent half an hour twisting and turning until my linens make this tumult look like nothing."

Irene said nothing for a moment, then smiled. "I wish our fender from Saffron Hill were here, and we could cook some tea and toast some scones."

"Tea and scones are in the pantry far below," I pointed out. "And neither of us is wearing bed slippers."

"There is a decanter of brandy by the window seat."

I stared in that dim direction. "*I* am not going to ice my feet again in search of spiritous liquors."

"Oh," Irene said, huddling under the coverlet and looking no more ready than I to leave the warmth our bodies had won from the bedclothes. "Perhaps I had the nightmare because Godfrey is gone."

"Indeed. We are undefended in this drafty cottage. I almost wish we lived in Paris proper, and you can see how strongly I must feel to make such a despicable weakness known."

"Indeed, Paris seems custom-made for the despicably weak," Irene said with the old sly tone I recognized and took for her returning equanimity. She sobered instantly. "This is a bad business, Nell. Far worse than anything we have ever been drawn into before."

"Why do you think I got no rest for half an hour upon retiring? I know that."

"I should not have allowed you into this affair." Her face

and body twisted in uncharacteristic expression of an emotion I had never detected in her before: guilt.

"And who are you to 'allow' me or not allow me anything?"

"Now you would have me be condescending as well as overprotective. But I know far more of the ways of the world than you do, and would like to keep it that way."

"So I am sure that I would prefer it, save that I deplore being ignorant, even if it is better for me, and I do see that it might be. How I wish I had never known that the Prince of Wales has been allowed to assume, to presume, to dare to think that you have succumbed to His Royal Lowness like apparently scores of women before you!"

"I was young when that choice was thrust upon me. I would not do it now. But you understand that it was the lesser of two evils at the time."

"Your reputation—"

"Reputation can be falsely tarnished. At least in this case I did it myself. And I know it to be a falsehood. Before a Rothschild ever became a baron, the family reputation was impugned again and again. It still is."

"Not by anything so distorting as your imagined alliance with the Prince of Wales!"

"No? What of the rumor that Baron Alphonse had a child out of wedlock by a mistress?"

"I suppose it could be true."

"And that he sent mother and child packing, until they were forced into a brothel, then he came and knowingly patronized his own virginal daughter?"

"Baron Alphonse! I have some judge of character, Christian or not, and that certainly would be impossible. What a vile and twisted lie—"

"So you see what a minor deception my trick on Bertie was? He is a benign sort of tyrant, your Prince of Wales. If you allow him his self-deceptions, he will underwrite your own."

"But it is corrupt! All society is corrupt."

"Yes!" Irene trumpeted the single word like a professor well pleased with a student's hard-won correct answer. "That is what I had hoped to spare you, but you will not let me."

A silence fell between us.

"I am not having nightmares," I said finally.

She was silent in turn, then sighed as if from the bottom of her soul.

"Not . . . yet."

14.

Gypsy Fortune

He makes love in the same wild way that he drinks, all is a sensual quest for some elusive transcendence. All his appetites demand excess, even his love for the eerie Gypsy music that makes violins wail like wolves mating with banshees . . .

—NOTE TO MYSELF

FROM A YELLOW BOOK

I went among the Gypsies tonight.

The campsite reeked of dog dung and old piss, spilled wine, smoke and sausages, but the music and laughter were a symphony for my soul.

Paris, London, Rome, Vienna, Warsaw, Prague, St. Petersburg . . . they have their palaces and dynasties, theaters and opera houses and museums, their universities and government ministries, but those grand and glorious buildings and the pretenses of the people who haunt them are all so many houses of cards.

The old Gypsy, Tasarla, lays out her dirty pack of tarot, telling me my latest fortune. The tarot cards are worn to faint images. She seems to recognize each card by touch as much as sight. I cross her seamed palm (with the lifeline that curls around the mount of her thumb into the bracelet lines of the wrist and across the back of her hand) with foreign silver until she deals the cards again and again, giving me the amusement of an array of various fortunes.

Some are dire, some triumphant, all are ambiguous and oddly apropos.

To the people in the great cities and palaces, the Gypsies are a distant, stinking mist at the vast, unknown rim of the civilized world, where peasants toil to supply the wood and wheat that make the glittering cities go.

Most of the world is raw land ruled by rawer emotions, but the great in their cities seldom see that. Although I have walked on their marble floors and Aubusson carpets, I am never more alive than here, my feet on a carpet of dead leaves, my chair not gilded but a pile of tattered Turkey rugs.

The Gypsies drift at the edges of the great cities and settle like fog on the wastes between the towns, selling their inferior crafts and moving on before the mendacity is discovered, telling their mysterious fortunes, dancing and drinking around their campfires, to the music of fiddles and wolves.

They are an unholy lot of beggars too proud to beg and thieves too accomplished to bother stealing real riches.

The young girls wear their gold and grime like ornaments of equal value, and are given in marriage among themselves in childhood, reaching a man's hands and first blood at the same time. The Gypsies give their women to men from the cities or towns at the drop of a copper, but as usual the exchange is always in their favor, and the favors given are short and unfulfilling.

He is here, of course, prodigiously drunk.

Although, with time, I have come to move among the Gypsies as I please (and as long as I pay sufficiently), a rare honor for a non-Romany, he pays nothing.

Like a young wolf he strides into their campground, pissing where he pleases.

His strange, savage vitality fascinates the Romany as much as it does me.

He brings his own brew, the potent liquor of a land even

wilder than the imagination, and his intoxication never brings him to his knees, only to more fascinating excesses.

When the fire flares high and the violins wail like wolves, he is dancing in their midst. His clumsy boots both seem to break the ground and break free of the ground. Gypsies dance like demons, but he is the very Devil himself. I have seen the mad, swirling tarantella of southern Italy and the whirling dervishes of Afghanistan. They cannot compare. Frenzy. Fever. Inhuman energy. He dances alone, and the violinists are sawing their arms off, sweltering in sweat, on their knees, silencing one by one.

And still he dances. When at last he drops of exhaustion, the girls run to pour water down his throat. He soon submits them to his gropings and, having assembled his harem of the night, calls for more wine and more women.

He never pays for his pleasures, but takes them, and the Gypsies let him, even celebrating his violations of the laws of all decent society and their own ancient, cruel, and pragmatic code.

While Tasarla lays down a Hanged Man for me, for instance, he is lying like a sultan on a pile of rugs, his gathered pants disarranged, his huge hands tangling in the bodice laces of three nubile Gypsy girls in turn, exposing their breasts like a housewife weighing apples on a market stand and buying none.

He is barely twenty, but like all men must have younger women, even if they are twelve.

Yet I have seen him come behind some Gypsy matron of forty tending the campfire, embracing her with clumsy possession, groping under her many layers of coarse skirts. The men laugh, the violins screech and whine approval, the gold coins the women wear chitter with excitement.

Even I find myself excited by his audacity, by the extremes to which the liquor will lead him, by watching him.

The Gypsies are feral, abiding by their own mystical and clannish rules, mystical and savage. It is hard to study savagery without being taken with it. Civilization, I have found in my travels, is merely the velvet glove over the steel fist that all mankind aspires to.

I have not yet decided how to use him, but there will be a way.

15.

In the Pink

Inmates rose very late in the morning . . . They spent the days . . . talking, singing, playing the piano and reading. (Parent-Duchâtelet . . . expecting to find them engrossed in pornography . . . was surprised to discover that they preferred light romances.) After an early supper, they prepared themselves to appear in the salon for an evening of comings and goings.

—JILL HARSIN, *POLICING PROSTITUTION IN 19TH CENTURY PARIS*

The note from Paris lay crinkled on my worktable.

Irene had cast it there when she went to raid the household funds for a gratuity for the messenger who had brought it.

I assumed the gawking horseman left well paid. The journey from Paris was long enough to be worth a pretty price.

I read the alien handwriting as best I could.

Madam! You are needed here at the maison, *but must arrive discreetly. I should be called away on some pretext I confess I can't think of at the moment. There is something still most mysterious in this house! Hurry!*

Your "American cousin," Pink

"You would think you were reading a French novel, Nell, so gingerly do you handle that note," Irene said, reentering the parlor.

I dropped it as if the ink had leprosy. It was not addressed to me, after all. "It was on my worktable."

"What does she say?"

"You know it is from Miss Pink Whatever-Her-Real-Name-Is?"

"The melodrama is purely American. I just interviewed the messenger-swain. She cast it down at his feet, wrapped in a silk handkerchief, from a window. The laundryman's slow son was so eager to play the knight-errant he borrowed a nag from his father's pair and plodded all the way here sans saddle. A veritable Don Quixote—tall, lank, and quite deluded by his lady fair's favor. I paid him a sou for his pains, and he will indeed have them tomorrow."

"The minx! No doubt she flirted outrageously with the poor lad to gain his attention. A boy of that class surely cannot be aware of what sort of house she lives in."

"Nell, his father does the place's laundry. Such assiduous changing of the sheets must be a sure sign of suspicion even for the laundryman's *horses*."

"Oh," I said, not sure why this was a clue, but aware that I should not admit this. "So we are to run off to Paris at the beck and call of an immoral snip?"

Irene picked up the note and studied it. "We are to run off to Paris to see what she has discovered in the house that the police have not."

"That was why you did not argue with her determination to stay on in the brothel!"

"She was not going to leave in any event. I had hoped that she would wish to consult us if she learned anything. We are, after all, 'cousins.' "

"I am not a cousin to anyone, and certainly not to any Americans," I said hastily, if not quite accurately. "She is most presumptuous, but I begin to see that this is a national trait. We will go at once, I suppose."

"Perhaps you wish to abstain—"

"I might wish it," I said loftily, "but duty requires that I go. You are far too gullible in the case of this American girl. She is not even a decade our junior, after all, and obviously far too well acquainted with the ways of the world for her age."

"Two little nannies fresh from school are we," Irene said-sang with an open grin at her Gilbertian paraphrase, making a demure curtsy, "and that is how we shall revisit the house."

Although Irene was fond of tormenting me by visiting articles of clothing from her many wardrobes upon me when necessary, in this instance she enjoyed rummaging through my humble assortment.

"Seal brown, gray camel's-hair, copper-colored jersey, dark blue silk . . . ah, black file and sadly out of style. This will do for me. You had better wear the camel's-hair. Simple cuffs and collars will finish the ensembles, and untrimmed bonnets."

With this she stripped two of my best bonnets of their paltry ribbons and feathers.

We stood before the looking glass inset into my wardrobe door, side by side, an hour later. My walking skirts were a trifle short on Irene, but it only added to her air of humble circumstances. Indeed, I was most impressed by her transformation. It is one thing to spring forth as a peacock, which Irene often did as if to the feathered train born. It is quite another to play common sparrow. I was surprised by how utterly a modest demeanor dampened the native fire and heat of her performer's persona.

"Here we stand," she crowed pathetically. "Two poor but respectable women—perhaps caretakers of an inconvenient infant?—wishing to discuss what no one in the house wishes to acknowledge with the new young woman in residence.

"We shall be shunned, Nell," Irene predicted triumphantly as she studied our images, "like temperance workers in a tavern, and therefore we will be ignored and allowed to go about whatever surreptitious business we wish."

"Why are you so sure our business will be surreptitious?"

"Because Pink would not need our help otherwise."

"Abominable name. Can we not find another more suitable for her?"

Irene smiled as she pulled my borrowed bonnet brim onto her hair-bare forehead like a dark, louring cloud. She reminded me of a deranged Covent Garden flower seller. "Why should we? It is almost the only true thing about herself that young woman has told us."

Only the fact that our loyal coachman André drove us into the city and lurked around the corner to whisk us back to the security of the country allowed me to participate in this mad masquerade.

I suppose it wasn't much of a masquerade, but Irene had been right, and I had suspected as much from my own history: dress drably enough, and no one will notice you. Particularly at a bordello. It was a bit chagrining that my everyday wardrobe was so suitable for such an assignment.

We knocked humbly at the service door, literally balancing on the worn stone stoop. When a harridan-faced woman jerked open the door Irene stuttered out her business in perfect if apparently low-class French. (In my opinion, everything French is inferior to everything English, but I admit that I adhere to very high standards.)

I did recognize a request for "young *mademoiselle* Rose."

What can one make of a language without a word that precisely conveys the concept of "pink," as opposed to red or rose-colored? Not much, if you ask me. In English, please.

We were allowed inside to wait. Our antechamber was a redolent pantry, chiefly supplied with garlic and onions, to judge by my nose. Various glass jars housed hideous objects of uncertain origin that seemed suitable for erecting a Frankenstein's monster. Pickled mushrooms for ears? Ginger root for nose? Leeks for . . . whatever. Witches' warts?

Irene looked truly drab in the smoky lamplight. I cannot say what it was—some slump of her shoulders, the dampening of her hair and all expression—but for the first time in her life she seemed quite unattractive.

Miss Pink suddenly burst through the door, wearing her signature shade and a suspiciously high color in her face that could only come from a rabbit's foot that had severed all acquaintance with the rabbit to become a rouge applicator. *Rouge*! Why not bow to a French translation of her English-American name as Red? Unfortunately, it was what one would call a cancan dancer in Montmartre, and quite unsuitable.

Pink frowned at us for half a minute, then gasped. "Well, aren't you two the dowdy Doras! My land! All right, ladies, as they say in vaudeville. I will pretend to be all upset at some indiscretion, and you two will steer me into the outer hall and through that nasty little wooden door beyond the pantry and down the stairs. It's dark and it's dank, but I've a candle hidden at the bottom, if somebody has a match—oh, of course Madam Norton. You would. Then we're set." She grinned like a mischievous child.

I admit to a sentimental fondness for even grown-up girls who remind me of my former charges. Such a dainty, pretty young thing. Such a dreadful place and profession she was in. Such a miserable way of using the King's English! Except it was the Queen's now. And except she was no subject of any king or queen, more's the pity.

Miss Pink then commenced to shriek and wail as if we had brought her tidings of her grandmama's death. Naturally, when irritated eyes rounded on our tragic threesome, we were forced to take Miss Pink by her furbelowed arms and escort her beyond the hearing of civilized ears.

The moment the cellar door swung shut behind us Miss Pink ceased howling. Irene made up for this lapse by producing affective mewlings as we stuttered down the stone stairs in the dark, all clinging to the damp stone walls intermittently softened by moss or . . . slime.

It is amazing that we did not break our necks on those rough steps. At the bottom a scratch and flare of light showed Irene keeping good her promise.

Pink, looking like a furbelowed imp in the match-flare, produced the candle.

In a moment a flickering light led us onward.

"What have you found?" Irene asked, all business.

"Something very strange, and very frightening."

"Good," said Irene. "I should not like to go through this masquerade with nothing to show for it. Perhaps you could prepare us a trifle."

"This is the wine cellar," Pink obliged. "I'm told it's one of the finest in Paris. Only the sommelier comes down here, and only once in a while. The wines for immediate use are kept upstairs for expected guests in far more elegant surroundings, but this is where the vast majority of them are stored."

As she spoke, I felt a cool, damp brush of air on my cheek.

Irene lifted the candle. Its light limned the low arches of an ancient cellar with arcs of highlight against the utter dark beyond.

Great wooden kegs lined the stones. Bottles dotted walls of wooden racks. I sensed great age, and an almost funereal calm, as if these liquors had been entombed here, deep within the cool, chalk and oyster-shell-rich earth.

Although I have no liking for spirits, I felt the presence of another, personified spirit here: the soul of France itself, which had amassed lifetimes of the vintner's arts that passeth the comings and goings of generations and noble families and revolutions and the Rights of Man and the number of falling stars in a millennium.

"Here." Pink vanished into the dark beyond Irene's candle glow. "I found it here."

I glanced at the floor, scarred by the pickaxes that had roughed it out from stone and dirt. I remembered that many monasteries distilled rare liquors, that hooded monks might pass in ghostly array among these bottles and kegs of their hidden brewing . . .

Irene's boot toe scraped the stone in a wide arc. "Shattered glass. Someone could not wait to decant some of these wines."

I looked down horrified to see dark burgundy stains on the floor.

"Wine, Nell. Merely wine."

Under another broad arch we went, into a niche of sorts.

Pink had squatted on her heels like a child inspecting tadpoles in a murky pond. "Here, Mrs. Norton, Miss Huxleigh!"

Irene and I stood over her, our candle casting a surprisingly wide circle of illumination.

Dollops of wax . . . red and black and gold candle wax blotted the stone floor like so many careless signet seals.

I saw some crude marks, as if stone had scraped stone bone-bare. I saw—

"Ah!" Irene lifted a pale crumbly object between her forefinger and thumb like a snippet of flesh. "Your etui, Nell?"

I had not neglected to bring my chatelaine, and brought it jangling into the candlelight.

Miss Pink frowned at my racket, but when I elevated another tiny crumb pincered from the etui beside the larger piece Irene held, her ingenuous features gaped in amazement.

"What is that?" she asked.

"A remnant from the murder room," Irene said. "And this is the motherlode"—she glanced at Pink with a familiarity that left me completely in the dark—"from which this ore has been mined, or I miss my guess."

"Oh, yes indeed," said Miss Pink, beaming. "Isn't this place strange? So oddly sinister? As if someone awful had passed through here but moments before us?"

I was loath to agree with her, but then a faint breeze stirred a loosened filament of hair along my cheek, and I shuddered.

"I do think," said Miss Pink contemplatively, "that it connects with the sewers of Paris. Isn't that absolutely wonderful?"

16.
Jacques the Ripper

The earth below the city was not the firm clay known across the Channel in England. It was a baffling honeycomb of abandoned stone quarries, of age-old river deposits . . . of a seeping blanket of water that turned dirt hopelessly to slush.

—TAMARA HOVEY, *PARIS UNDERGROUND*

Even Irene Norton, née Adler, was not about to wade into the sewers of Paris wearing my best walking skirt, thank the Lord.

We stood on the lip of a greater darkness than currently surrounded us, staring into the candle reflections on a glassy black expanse of water which did not ripple so much as tremble in an invisible, insensible wind.

"We are not equipped to explore this channel," Irene said regretfully, "but I am not ready to loose the police on so promising a path without more knowledge of my own. You will remain here a while longer," she told Pink. "See if anyone of the household, or a visitor, shows any interest in this wine cellar."

She had led us back to the main cellar.

My nose, fresh from the dank, sour air of the underground water, detected the musky scent of spilled wine here now.

Irene began a circuit of the walls of wine kegs and bottles, her toe pointing out more shards of dark green glass, a jagged bottleneck even, scattered corks.

"An unauthorized wine-tasting, I think. I believe the events that led to the deaths above began here."

"Jack the Ripper came by way of the sewers? Perhaps that explains his quick escapes in Whitechapel," I said.

"The Paris sewers are far vaster and traversable than those of London," Irene objected. "Perhaps it does explain this attack upon women in a luxurious house. The sewers are the great levelers that underlie all Paris. A highway for the aspiring murderer."

"Thanks a lot," Pink said. "I will sleep like a Latter-Day Saint on that thought, Mrs. N."

"You might as well call me Irene," she answered.

I took a deep, indignant breath.

"And Miss Huxleigh would much prefer that you called her Nell," Irene said, neatly forestalling me from expressing my true preferences.

"I would," I interjected into this conference of girlish confidences, "prefer a Christian name to call you by."

I caught Miss Pink's eye, and held it.

Her lashes fluttered like a butterfly's in a net, but my years as a governess had given me an authority less obvious than Irene's stage presence, but no less commanding.

"Elizabeth," the girl muttered, as if ashamed.

"A fine name, Elizabeth, with many splendid diminutives . . . Eliza, Beth, Bess, even that American derivative 'Betsy,' if you prefer and don't mind sounding like the ragman's horse—"

"I prefer 'Pink,' " she insisted despite my generous suggestions, "but you may call me Elizabeth if you must."

Frankly, I was loath to call a girl of ill repute by the name of England's revered Virgin Queen, but it was either that or Pink.

I remembered Irene's remark that the nickname "Pink" was the only true thing our companion had told us about herself. I wondered if Elizabeth was also true, or merely another lie.

I could not understand why Irene was drawing this mere witness into our orbit, and on a first-name basis now, really! However sad Pink's personal history, it did not mean she had to misbehave in the present. I feared that their common American background was creating an instant and false sense of intimacy that was unearned. At least Irene was not totally taken in by the girl, and that cheered my spirits a trifle.

What also cheered my spirits quite a bit was leaving Elizabeth, Bertie, and Jacques the Ripper behind in Paris as we returned to the peace of Neuilly-sur-Seine and the French countryside.

We crept into bed late, as we had recently, and I didn't awaken until the linnets were serenading the shutters.

I lay abed, watching threads of sunlight creep across the wide wooden floorboards.

I am not a lazy person, but this morning I relished all things about our life outside the city and its compromises and corruptions.

Even the unauthorized presence of Lucifer sprawled by the wall, also watching the sunlight edge across the floor, could not dampen my good cheer.

Suddenly the huge furry cat leaped and trapped something between his paws. A dust mote? Sunlight? Or a skittering vermin visible only to that predatory eye? If it was the latter, Lucifer was welcome to it. The fewer skittering vermin on my floor the better.

Naturally, the thought of skittering vermin brought my mind where it was not wont to wander: back to the *maison de rendezvous,* the horror in its strange bedchamber, and the musty mysteries of its wine cellars.

I was deeply suspicious of the young American courtesan who had "happened" to discover the death scene, despite the easy artlessness of her gown and manner, like a debutante among the dissolute. I recalled the creatures we had brushed past, the women attired as the epitome of innocence, a nun and a bride, walking and giggling together. I shuddered to imagine how such an establishment could turn good upon its heels into evil. How would a girl christened "Elizabeth" come to be known as Pink? It wasn't in the least likely, so perhaps Irene was correct, and it was simply true. The unlikeliest things had a nasty habit of being true, including the fact that the Prince of Wales was the worst sort of wastrel.

Like any good Englishwoman, I tried to honor what was best and brightest about my betters. Now I had discovered that the First of them was the Worst of them. I still did not wish to speculate upon the precise nature of any immoral acts that were going on—or were about to go on—at the *maison,* but might have to reconsider Jack the Ripper as a force for good insomuch as he had interrupted evildoing on a grand scale.

Then my mind skittered, like the doomed bug that Lucifer still harried by the window, to the only compromising position I had ever found myself in: alone with Quentin Stanhope during days of solitary rail journeying across most of Europe to France. The situation had been highly improper, of course, but despite that I had not been immune to the tender and delicious thrill that ran beneath our everyday talk and mutual courtesies. Indeed, we had really begun to know each other on that journey, so much so that parting was something of a shock, to me, at least. I would not dare to think that a man who lived and worked on the Queen's secret commission at the long, ever-unraveling selvage edge of Empire in the dangerous East would in the slightest miss a parson's daughter who had briefly been governess to his sister's children.

I sat up in bed, as if gripped by a conscious nightmare. Godfrey! Thinking of Quentin had brought his dear, familiar face and voice into my thoughts. . . .

He had first entered our lives like a thunderbolt, storming our Saffron Hill lodgings in London because he had detected Irene's interest in his late father's possible possession of Marie Antoinette's lost Zone of Diamonds. Like Sherlock Holmes was to do later, and repeatedly, he had accused her of meddling, a charge she took then no more gracefully than she does now. And, after all, she has accepted private inquiry commissions for as long as she has pursued an operatic career, so who can say which is the prime, and which the secondary, pursuit?

At any rate, I eavesdropped on Godfrey's splendid tirade, all in defense of his family honor and especially his wronged mother. No wonder he was a barrister. Godfrey is most impressive in high dudgeon. And, of course, he was even more handsome when so animated.

When I went (Irene would say I was sent) into the Temple to work with him as a typewriter-girl, I came to know Godfrey as the considerate and temperate gentleman any woman would be proud to call brother.

Of course he was a barrister, and I an orphaned parson's daughter, and I would never think of him in any other role. I must admit that when circumstances brought him back into Irene's hunt for the Zone, and they actually worked in concert, I had no idea that events would take such a rapid turn and that Irene should feel no constraint whatsoever in regarding Godfrey as other than a brother! I am afraid it is her American upbringing, but I couldn't really object, though I was most surprised that their sudden trip to Paris in pursuit of the Zone had led to other sudden alterations in our heretofore simple and separate relationships.

I am a little vague about when it happened, or what happened, but by the time Sherlock Holmes was hot on Irene's trail at the behest of the King of Bohemia, Godfrey was firmly established in Irene's heart. They wed and fled, although neither the King nor the detective ever knew anything of the Zone of Diamonds.

I was left to close down the establishment in the Serpentine Mews in St. John's Wood. Imagine my surprise on visiting the newlyweds in Neuilly, the village near Paris where they had settled to avoid further pursuit, when they insisted I join their household. I tried to demur, but they were intractable.

I am not ungrateful for my continued presence in the Norton household, even if it must be in exile in France. There is no creature as alone in the world as an orphaned spinster, and I do all I can to make myself useful, whether it is wanted or not. I am assured that an unrelated spinster is more than any pair of newlyweds might want on the premises, but neither Irene or Godfrey has for an instant made me feel unwelcome.

Yet what should I do if my stable domestic arrangement with Mr. and Mrs. Godfrey Norton were upset by the near and present danger of Mr. Sherlock Holmes? (Whom, I admit to my secret self, Irene finds fascinating in his way, though purely as a deductive force, I am sure.)

And there is where my heaviest secret stone lies, at the bottom of a well of unwanted knowledge, obtained by rank and shameless subterfuge.

For the events involving the King of Bohemia's pursuit of Irene to London brought her to the attention of another Englishman, the detective's friend and associate, a medical man named Watson, who, I had later learned to my secret horror, harbored literary aspirations.

This discovery has left me to trudge on alone with my most worrisome stone. Yet the horrifying words I read many months ago will not let me turn the page in my mind that has lain full open since I skimmed the private papers in Dr. Watson's desk and found the dreadful truth, or the truth as he believes he knows it.

My intentions were always honorable . . . well, as honorable as acquiring access to the doctor's office under false pretenses could be. I went there to help save his life, and ended up risking my peace of mind.

I had come across a manuscript in his desk, a work clearly intended for future publication, in which he committed to paper Sherlock Holmes's side of the Bohemian affair. (My own, and accurate, recounting of the full and true circumstances of the case remains entombed in the privacy of my diary, and shall stay there so long as I live.)

But this Watson person, this physician with obviously far too much time upon his hands, has written his own muddled account of the events and will no doubt seek publication, for no one is more persistent than a person with one perfectly good vocation who aspires to distinguish himself in another.

At least the benighted doctor had the sense to describe Irene as deceased, although during the unfortunate erratic encounters between her and the detective Holmes after the Bohemian events it would have become clear even to a man not renowned for much perception that Irene Adler was far from dead. (And at least this Holmes had the wisdom not to enlighten his friend the doctor as to Irene's remarkable state of preservation.)

No, it was not the doctor's secret recounting of this incident from his own nearsighted point of view that had disturbed me.

It was especially the truth he spoke from that point of view. The words are scribed upon my soul: *To Sherlock Holmes she is always* the *woman. In his eyes she eclipses and predominates the whole of her sex.*

As her friend and companion, I cannot deny that Irene is indeed remarkable . . . but I shudder to think that this odious man, an avowed opium-fiend from the doctor's own account, should fasten his attention and admiration on my friend, who is now another man's wife. Indeed, this impossible Holmes person even witnessed their wedding in disguise as part of his investigation! Has the man no shame?

The doctor did write that it was not "any emotion akin to love" this Holmes creature felt for Irene, that "love" was alien to the man's "cold, precise" mind. I was not surprised to read that he "never spoke of the softer passions, save with a gibe and a sneer." I have since had occasion to observe this Sherlock Holmes more closely, and he is indeed very full of himself and the "reasoning machine" of his mind.

I was also pleased by the doctor's closing comments, to the effect that Mr. Holmes had "used to make merry over the cleverness of women, but I have not heard him do it of late. And when he speaks of Irene Adler, or when he refers to her photograph, it is always under the honorable title of *the* woman."

If Irene has taught him a lesson, good! Now all he need do is keep his distance and subvert his doctor friend's attempts at publication, and we shall all be allowed to live out our lives in the peace, quiet, and anonymity we so richly deserve.

I, for one, sincerely hope that no unpleasant "problems"—as both Irene and Mr. Holmes seem to refer to these annoying mysteries of life which are really the police's business and no one else's—lurk in our futures. Such a course could even reconcile me to living in France.

But despite all these assertions, Dr. Watson is precise on one fact: "there was but one woman to him, and that woman was the late Irene Adler, of dubious and questionable memory."

That is another irritation: how dare he slander her memory, even though she is not dead! The fool has no notion that she, and I, and Godfrey, and my former charges' uncle, Quentin Stanhope, moved Heaven and Earth to save this miserable medical man's life! All too successfully, unfortunately! Apparently our efforts were successful so that he could survive to write more such drivel. And so that my . . . so that *dear* Quentin was forced to engage in a mortal duel with a master spy and heavy-game hunter named Moran.

But I will not allow myself to become exercised, much as it is my right. I never told my companions of the doctor's unpublished manuscript (may it forever remain so!), which is not of a quality or interest that will appeal to a publisher or a reader.

What would Godfrey say, or do, to know another man harbored such inappropriate feelings toward his bride?

What unsuitable pride might the fact that the world's greatest detective considers her the world's most admirable woman do to Irene's already healthy sense of self-esteem, which I am daily devoted to urging to a more realistic level?

Of course it is some consolation that Dr. John H. Watson, however much he may be in the detective's confidence, still did not know the whole story. In that fact I see a glimmer of relief, for obviously there are some stones which even Mr. Sherlock Holmes carries that he will not confide to his nearest companion, and Dr. Watson admits in his narrative that this Holmes man is far from the most sociable of beings.

Yet I am also disturbed to be the only one to know aspects of the affair that Mr. Holmes has kept to himself, as another less rigorously logical man might preserve a rose fallen from a woman's bouquet. . . .

And according to Dr. Watson's account, Mr. Holmes did keep the photograph of herself Irene had left for the King of Bohemia. It was the only additional reward he wanted, having already refused an emerald ring . . . Most worrisome.

If only I dared share my concerns with Godfrey. I owe him fierce allegiance. Godfrey, especially, perhaps because of our prior working relationship, has always been aware of my best interests and has even taken my part when Irene has been particularly . . . Irene-ish.

My eyes had blurred and my nose was congested. Godfrey was a prince among men! An amusing companion, a tireless adviser, a strong and sagacious man whose existence was a blessing to all womankind.

How could I have ever thought just a few days ago that I was enjoying a return to the days of Irene and my solely female domesticity? If I missed Quentin as much as I did when I allowed myself to think of him, imagine how Irene must feel the loss of her husband! I had been utterly and foolishly selfish, and the realization lacerated my conscience like a cat-o'-nine-tails.

While I struggled with these questions, Lucifer encountered no such fits of conscience. He pounced full weight upon whatever he wrestled, and vanished under the bed to finish the battle.

An advancing snatch of aria warned me that Irene was up, energetic, and about to roust me from my peaceful bed.

The door swung open, and her figure filled it, looking as pert as a barmaid in a German opera, a tray between her extended arms.

"Breakfast?" I deduced, pushing myself upright in the bed linens in such a way that I was able to discreetly wipe away any unshed tears of repentance. "In bed? For me?"

"Indeed. You have slept a full twelve hours, as well you deserved. Do not move, but let me place this on the bed. There! The teapot is not only heavy, but full of boiling water fresh from the woodstove."

I eyed the bounty on the tray. Hot porridge with currants and fresh cream, steaming bacon, slices of lemon for tea like sunny smiles of citrus, snowy napkin . . . I was, of course, highly suspicious.

"You are in good, high spirits," I noted.

"Here." Irene pounced like Lucifer on an object atop my bed table. "Don your spectacles so you can fully appreciate this repast."

"I only need them for close work and reading," I pointed

out. "I suspect my table manners are adept enough that I don't need them to eat."

"Of course not. But"—Irene patted the pocket of the most unlikely apron she wore (she never wore aprons)—"there is a new letter from Godfrey."

"A cause for celebration, yes, but hardly for breakfast in bed. Sophie must not be pleased to be usurped by you, even if you are the mistress of the house."

"Sophie needs a small domestic insurrection now and then. She is entirely too domineering. And there is something else in the post . . ." She paused.

"And?"

"An urgent summons to Paris."

"Again?"

"I will dress while you eat, and then return to see you dressed. Meanwhile, you can entertain yourself with Godfrey's letter. I have read it, and he is in full descriptive cry. Adieu."

With that she was gone, leaving me chewing like a cow on my cud in amazement and distress.

Of course I gulped the whole, hot, and steaming mess down as quickly as I could, glancing at Godfrey's many pages with regret. She had obviously left me with the most innocuous document while keeping the provocative summons to herself. Thus would she lure me on my way to Paris again, saving the news for the moment when I was safely fed, clothed, and tucked into the carriage.

At least, I reflected as I swished horribly hot tea around in my mouth hoping it would cool, she was presuming upon my accompanying her. Given the notorious characters who awaited her in Paris, I would have it no other way.

17.

La Tour Awful

Ridicule . . . only ever kills the weak and the false. The tower has continued to scribe the ever-changing sky with its gold-tipped silhouette and to hold its lacework calculus erect like a desire . . .

—SCULPTOR RAYMOND DUCHAMP-VILLON

Among the many interesting and useful sights in London is the Time Signal Ball near Trafalgar Square, a six-foot-diameter zinc ball that drops ten feet at one o'clock every day. This is not only a visual landmark, but a most practical device, against which all may set their timepieces according to the world standard of Greenwich Mean Time, also an English invention.

In Paris, in the year of Our Lord and incidentally of *l'Exposition universelle de 1889*, there is, alas, the Eiffel Tower.

There, in a nutshell, you have the difference between the two capitals, the two countries, the two nationalities. What is useful and interesting in London is useless and overpowering in Paris.

To my mind, the construction now rising from the Champ de Mars along the Seine is a modern Tower of Babel. Befitting the god of war who names its location, and the Red Planet, this iron giant has been painted crimson. At least it has not been painted pink! Never has so much overweening pride in the form of twisted metal stretched an ugly fist to Heaven, gold-tipped penultimate finger notwithstanding.

For once I am not alone in my disdain of this French landmark, but am joined by a committee of outraged French artists and persons of importance. I cannot imagine what future generations will make of it, though surely it will be torn down by then. My fellow thinkers have used such apt phrases of description as "barbarous mass" and "factory chimney." I particularly liked "foul and bolt-encrusted pile of sheet metal."

Despite myself, I am learning to read French, if not to speak it fluently. I do particularly well with words which the French have borrowed from the English, such as "*exposition universelle*." Of course the French must ever be contrary. They do not pronounce it properly and add a fancy finale to the "universal."

But I can now translate enough French to have informed Irene and Godfrey some months ago that the committee managing the competition for the signature building of the exposition had found Mr. Eiffel's design "more appropriate to the barbarism of America, where good taste was still not very developed."

Irene had remained unperturbed. "Exactly why America thrives, my dear. And we did have the good taste to accept the Statue of Liberty from the French. I understand that an earlier plan for the Paris exposition landmark, since this year is also the centenary of the French Revolution, was a three-hundred-meter-high guillotine. So I see no reason why they should blame us for Eiffel's imaginings, which they ultimately accepted anyway, when they had originally intended a monument to organized slaughter."

Indeed they had embraced bad taste, for here Gustave Eiffel's tower stood, complete, the towering symbol of *l'Exposition universelle* that would continue drawing millions of gawkers to the Champ de Mars until early November.

Whatever my opinion of this ungainly structure, it certainly is something to steer by, as old-time sailors used the Pole Star. Three hundred meters high (I will forever envision a matching guillotine of that height, thanks to Irene's unwelcome information), it is the world's tallest structure—it exceeds the highest cathedral spire—a show of mechanical modern hubris overstepping hand-hewn medieval piety.

When our carriage stopped, Irene and I could not help

sticking our bonneted heads out the open windows and gaping like peasants. The tower loomed over us like a gigantic red tack upholding the gray baize of the overcast Parisian skies, gaudy as a Chinese pagoda built for a Cyclops.

From its very top, a lightning rod almost too tiny to see, the French tricolor fluttered in the upper winds.

Though the tallest sight, the tower was not the only excess strewing the vast area. Domes, minarets, tents, huts, pagodas, and colonnades created a global village on the Esplanade des Invalides adjacent to the tower grounds. Behind and beyond and above it all loomed a massive domed pavilion backed by smokestacks flying pennants of smudge. The exposition celebrated, after all, industrial achievement, and industry is a thing of drudgery, machines, and smoke.

It was only a moment after taking dazed stock of the scene thronging with workmen that I noticed the uniformed gendarmes infesting the parklands.

Alas, the gendarmes also noticed us at the same time.

Three immediately approached our coachman and ordered him to decamp to a nearby street.

Irene, today attired in full Parisian splendor (that is to say a Worth walking suit in plum scalloped faille decorated with falls of jet beads and the newly fashionable broad-brimmed velvet hat supporting a flotilla of plumes instead of the modest bonnet that tied so sweetly under the chin like a child's cap), burst forth from the carriage like Athena from her father Zeus's forehead, and was as prepared to give any surrounding males a god-sized headache.

She cast the names of princes and financiers as pearls before swine, but only achieved a result when the lowly syllables "le Villard" passed her lips.

At that, our warders became our escort and we were soon threading our way amongst pieces of construction for the surrounding pavilions to an area a bit distant from the exposition grounds. I kept my parasol open and sheltering me from any view of the stiff and awkward mass towering above us. Irene kept hers closed and used it as a walking stick and pointer.

It was also quite a novelty that I would feel encouraged to

spy Inspector le Villard's mustachioed face under its round-crowned hat, but so I was.

He was most apologetic for our brusque greeting by the gendarmes, as well he should be, and nervously smoothed his curling mustache.

Soon he was escorting us down some dim stairs into the bowels of an excavation. If I was not pleased to contemplate the tower itself, I was even less enthralled to visit some sewerlike delving in its vicinity.

At a narrow, low portal, the inspector paused to light an oil lamp.

"I am sorry, Madame, Mademoiselle," he said in English at last. "I must advise you that an appalling sight awaits us beyond this point. Also, the ventilation is not as generous as at the *maison de rendezvous*. I would not conscience escorting ladies onto such a scene, but since you, on your own insistence, witnessed the atrocity of the other evening, your opinion of this site would be of use, if you are willing."

While Irene assured the inspector of our complete willingness, I was busy delving in my skirt pocket for my chatelaine, and particularly the vinaigrette. This time I was prepared: I had dosed two linen handkerchiefs with the contents of the vial. I handed one to Irene. The other I clapped to my own nostrils.

Despite the breathtaking effect of my improvised mask, not only did I still detect the fetid scent of stale water and long-unturned earth, but an odd metallic tang that was quite unpleasant, which I attributed to the surrounding ironwork.

I heard the distant tick of a clock, then realized how unlikely that was. Perhaps in the empty, dark passage I was hearing the second hand moving on the watch pinned to my bodice; certainly I could almost hear my heart beating.

Deeper we went on inclined ground, the lamp casting watery lights on the rough but solid soil. The place had the close, subterranean feel of a crypt, and I was all too sure that it in fact had been turned to just such service, and only recently.

Irene had been surprisingly silent. No doubt she much lamented the encumbrances of her woman's dress in this rude area meant for workmen. No doubt that Inspector le Villard much regretted our submersion in this raw atmosphere.

Then the tang that pierced the handkerchief pressed to my nose became more than metallic . . . it became the reek of a great quantity of fresh blood. My mind did an unwelcome quadrille. I felt I was standing on the other evening's elegant threshold again, confronting inelegant death.

The inspector's lamp revealed a natural rotunda in the stone tunnel ahead, and I was startled to see . . . bones. Leg bones and arm bones piled like a library wall of parchment scrolls, with rows of jawless skulls interspersed in the shape of a cross, a design both reverent and macabre. I had braced myself to confront fresh death, not the stale toothpicks of *La Mort*'s last dinner in Paris.

"This is part of the catacombs then, Inspector?" Irene asked, her voice muffled by my handkerchief.

Catacombs! Of course.

"Paris is underlaid not only by our famous sewers," he said in English, "but by hundreds of kilometers of granite quarries first cut by the Romans. Just before the Revolution, the church and the police prevailed upon the inspector general of the quarries to move the bones into the catacombs. Paris was growing beyond the once-rural cemeteries, which were contaminated by poor burials and mass graves. People grew ill, and some churchyards' ground level had risen ten to twenty feet from the volume of human remains."

I inhaled deeply and pointedly into my handkerchief to let the inspector know that I did not appreciate such lurid detail.

He cleared his throat. "Most of the cemetery bones were moved into the catacombs south of the Seine. This site was unknown until the Tower workmen found it recently, but more undiscovered sites no doubt remain, housing nameless bones. However, the latest addition here is unfortunately all too fleshly." His lamplight swept over the floor and a pale pile of rags that lay heaped there.

This was coarse fabric, sailcloth as might be used under painters' scaffolds, I thought at first. Irene took a deep breath next to me, pressing my makeshift barrier to her face. I realized that I was seeing a tumble of common linen petticoats.

"Another woman?" Irene asked.

"Another slaughter," the inspector said somberly.

"Who?"

"We can only speculate. Perhaps a bread-seller, perhaps a prostitute."

Irene lifted the smelling-salts compress away from her face.

I moved involuntarily to stop her, aware of the foul mélange of odors she invited to invade her lungs.

She inhaled so deliberately I saw the arch of her nostrils flare, like a hound's.

"Irene! The odor must be hellish in this closed-in place."

"It is. Like a battleground, I suppose. Blood and . . . guts. A certain rank dankness. And—" She stooped to the floor, gesturing the inspector's light to a spot near her feet.

Her fingers, bare now of gloves, swept through a dark puddle.

I drew back, thinking of blood, and cringed to see her ruddy fingertips in the lamplight.

"Wine," she said. "Red wine." Her fingers swept the stones again, then came to her face as she sought to identify what was on them. "And something stronger."

"Madame must not play the bloodhound," the inspector said, as repulsed as I to see her crouching in such a ruinous place. "We will bring in the dogs shortly."

"Really?" Irene stood, wiping her fingertips on my fresh and freshly supplied handkerchief. "Bloodhounds are a dramatic touch, Inspector, but I doubt they will do much good. I should send for a sommelier myself."

With that she turned, clapped the handkerchief to her nose and mouth again, and led us out of that dreadful place.

"A sommelier?" I challenged her when we had reached the open air and were now being roundly ignored. "That is a wine-waiter. I grant you that the French are very serious about their wines, but how could you suggest such a ridiculous thing?"

"Because it is not ridiculous. I should very much like to know if the wine that was spilled here at the foot of *La Tour*

Eiffel is of the same vintage as that stored and smashed in the cellar of the *maison de rendezvous*."

Before I could digest this unappetizing idea, Inspector le Villard caught up with us, looking harried.

"Now that you have seen this, your presence is requested at the Hotel Bristol," he said without so much as a bow. "Can your coachman take you there? It is in rue Faubourg-Saint-Honoré."

"Both I and my coachman are familiar with the rue Faubourg-Saint-Honoré," Irene said. "We are expected no matter the hour?"

"No matter the hour," the inspector repeated grimly. "This is an affair well beyond the bounds of the usual channels. I am sorry, Madame, Mademoiselle, that you should be subjected to such sights, but we are all pawns in the hands of higher powers."

With a brisk bow of farewell, he returned to the lantern-bearing gendarmes clustered at the entrance to the death chamber.

A wagon-lit waited nearby, its heavily harnessed pair of horses standing with their weight on three legs, heads bowed as if in sorrow.

"She will soon join her more elegant sisters lying on cold stone beds at the Paris Morgue," Irene said in a somber tone.

"And whom will we join at the Hotel Bristol?"

"It is the favorite hostelry of the Prince of Wales when he is in Paris."

I raised my eyebrows, though no one took note of the gesture. I was about as eager to take another meeting with Bertie as I was actually to encounter Jack the Ripper.

⚜ ⚜ ⚜

The Hotel Bristol was, of course, fit to house a prince, even an English prince.

A discreetly elegant façade of gray stone opened into a lobby carpeted like a Monet water lily painting: those costly carpets known as Savonneries were woven in misty hues of blue and green that seemed too delicately tinted to dishonor by stepping upon.

Marble pillars and floors should have made the vast place echo, but the thick, exquisite carpets, the even more exquisite rustle of silks and velvets and finest wool broadcloth, the hushed tones of the people who passed at a stately pace made everything seem muffled in great clouds of the fine silk net that is called Illusion.

I am not sure if a footman or an equerry met us in the hotel lobby. Whatever his position, he was awaiting us, recognized us as we entered the vast space, and intercepted us before we took four steps into the marble-paved interior.

Or rather, he recognized Irene.

He bowed so profoundly that I could almost hear his heels click.

"Madame Norton, I am to take you and your companion immediately upstairs for lunch."

His great height and lance-straight spine reminded me of Prince Willie, now King of Bohemia, and I suspected the man was German. Despite his military bearing and manner, he was dressed in a good-quality frock coat that did not look out of place in the imposing lobby.

I wish I could have said the same for my ensemble, though I seldom allow myself to be troubled by notions of not dressing well enough for my surroundings. Simple, useful clothing will pass muster anywhere. And if I am taken for a nanny, or a duenna, or, in this case, as a lady's companion, that is not so very different from my past and present role in life.

I saw with some dread that we were to be conducted to our place of assignation in an elevated car. Although this was a fine and decent apparatus that went directly up and down, and not on an angle like the two terrifying, steam-driven, inclined American Otis elevators on the Eiffel Tower, rather like mechanical dragons to my mind, I found myself hesitating over the dark space between the solid if polished ground of the lobby and the varnished wooden floor of this mobile box.

"Ladies," our escort urged from behind us. This was one

instance where male courtesy forced women to take the first risk.

Irene, of course, had scampered over the gap like a cat leaping a puddle. I followed, feeling more uneasy than I had at either of our body-viewing expeditions. Imagine my emotions when a collapsible metal-mesh grating closed us off from the multitude in the lobby. In instants we lofted upward, causing such an uncustomary flutter in my innards that I crushed my doctored handkerchief to my mouth and feigned a polite cough, all the while inhaling heady fumes that made my eyes water and my senses clear.

Upon our arrival in an upper hall cushioned with a thick runner of Turkey carpet, our escort led us to a pair of double doors, painted and gilded on every cursive surface.

I was not surprised by the richness of our surroundings, not even when we were ushered into a reception area that would have done a London town house proud.

And to think that this was only in Paris.

Fine oil paintings stacked two and three high on the lofty walls allowed portraits of aristocrats to gaze across to country-estate scenes. The gilt frames jousted with the array of costly trinkets on the marble-topped tables dotting the room, beside enough upholstered sofas and chairs to accommodate a regiment.

On one of those seats sat a common laborer who did not know enough to rise when we entered the room. Instead, he showed a mostly toothless grin and nodded with revolting familiarity.

Irene's head was tilted to examine a particularly large and fine portrait of a family in eighteenth-century garb.

"Irene, there is a strange man in the room," I whispered under the velvet brim above her right ear.

"I know. He was the first thing I noticed."

"And should have been the last! What is such a low fellow doing here?"

"Could he be a witness, do you think? Why else are we here, if not to testify to what we have seen in the past two days?"

"Testify? Surely we have seen nothing worth testifying to.

And surely they could have had this fellow come by the servants' stairs."

"I did not wish to stare when we entered, Nell. Perhaps you could describe him to me and I could determine what he is doing here from his appearance."

"So *I* am to stare, then?"

"You know you stare so subtly. And your powers of description have much benefited from the exercise of keeping a diary."

That was true, so I fussed with the handkerchief, played with my chatelaine, consulted my lapel watch and otherwise made many useless movements that conveyed I was doing everything but observing our fellow loiterer.

He seemed ill at ease, as well should anyone sitting in those worn, homespun clothes upon the exquisite petit-point upholstery.

"A typical French street peddler or laborer," I told Irene in a swift aside, as we made our way around the chamber, she studying the oil portraits, I creating a word portrait of our unlikely companion.

"Workman's boots, scuffed and cut. A stiff-crowned cap. Rough trousers. One of those silly short jackets that should be on sailors."

"And his features and peculiarities?" she asked, sotto voce. An opera singer can execute a sotto voce that is as soft as falling snow.

I was forced actually to regard the man's face.

"A French nose."

"Which is?"

"Large."

"Ah. Like an English nose."

I was too busy doing my duty to object. "Bony, raw hands. His are kneading his knees."

"Perhaps they trouble him."

"Or he is nervous to be in such fine surroundings."

"Anything more to his face than a nose?"

"Clean-shaven save for an untidy, unduly thick mustache, but then a workman cannot afford the meticulous upkeep of facial adornments. Of course one cannot see his mouth. The ears are . . . ears."

"Age?"

"Perhaps fifty. His eyebrows are liberally sprinkled with white, and the mustache is milk-pale in the middle, though what hair I can see is dark. That is so odd, Irene. Why is men's facial hair so often at odds with the hair on their heads?"

She shrugged, but before she could answer, the sound of a door cracking open made us turn to face the room. The far door stood ajar, our guide in it. He nodded to the workman, who sprang up and vanished through the door without a word.

"Irene!"

"Yes, Nell?"

"That, that . . . ill-kempt individual was allowed in before we were."

"Yes, Nell."

"And we are to wait?"

"Yes, Nell, but not for long."

"I cannot see why even so debased a person as a royal rake would invite a common French workmen into his presence before two respectable English ladies."

"You forget that I am neither English nor respectable."

"You would be, if you had been born in England and had never gone on the stage. This is outrageous. Is this how Bertie treats a . . . an imagined paramour? He has no manners, not to mention morals."

"True, but we are not waiting for Bertie. What time does your clever little watch say?"

Irene was not about to insert a pin into her silken Worth bodice, no matter how useful it was to know the time.

"It is eleven minutes after 1:00 P.M."

"*Hmmm*. And our humble workman has been absent for about three minutes. I believe we will be received in another six minutes' time, give or take thirty seconds. Shall we sit down?"

"No. I shall pace the chamber until we are allowed the same easy entrée as a . . . ditchdigger."

With that I took several furious turns around the room

while Irene watched me from the very same chair in which the miserable fellow had lounged but minutes before.

Hence it was that my back was to the door when I heard it crack open again.

"Please come in," said a voice in perfect English, though a bit high-pitched and more than somewhat complacent. "I am delighted that two such noted ladies have consented to lunch with me."

It was as if a rasp had been drawn over my teeth. I recognized the voice instantly. We were being entertained by *the* man.

Irene rose slowly, as if finally hearing a long-awaited cue that called her onstage. So had I seen her advance to a duel with swords against a man in Monaco. I suspected the weapons in this forthcoming duel would be much more subtle, if not less capable of wounding.

"Thank you, Mr. Holmes," she said. "I thought you would never ask."

18.

An Unappetizing Menu

You know my opinion of that sad string of events, Watson. The Whitechapel Ripper is likely no more than a disenchanted ticket-taker seeking a bit of attention.

—CAROLE NELSON DOUGLAS, *ANOTHER SCANDAL IN BOHEMIA*

While my imagination had peopled the chamber behind our host with ogres and opium addicts, we found instead a small receiving room that had been furnished with a square table set for three.

On the spotless napery lay a deceptively simple and

wholesome repast, mostly cold, it is true, but filling nevertheless. There was not a slab of goose-liver pâté, or tripe, or any other foreign "delicacies" in sight.

It did indeed seem odd to sit down to lunch with Sherlock Holmes, although I imagine even the pope in Rome ate lunch. Not even Irene knew of the unwanted yet intimate glimpse I had gained of the man and his habits—and of his particular and peculiar and dangerous romantic notions—during a less forthright encounter with the papers of his physician friend, Dr. John H. Watson, who apparently fancied himself a Boswell to a Johnson.

Since those written revelations so accidentally read, I took on a new and secret role: human hedge between Irene and this strange man who was all too fascinated by her. Although that was a common state among men who had but to meet her once, I was wise enough to realize that Mr. Sherlock Holmes was not a common man. And his purported dismissal of women in general did not ease my fears one iota. Irene had never been a woman in general.

Were it not for his formidable reputation as a solver of puzzles, I should not give the fellow a second thought. I had mostly seen him out of doors, either in some foolish disguise or else accompanied by hat and cane and appearing confident and insufferably certain. Our encounters were too many for my taste: his abrupt appearance years ago in Godfrey's chambers at the Temple, quizzing me about this and that while Godfrey was out. He learned nothing. The second, the sweet occasion during my first foray into disguise at Irene's hands, when I had opened the door to Briony Lodge to him, his doctor friend, and the King of Bohemia, only to announce the nest empty and Irene fled. A later occasion: him broaching Irene and me at breakfast on the terrace of the Hotel de Paris in Monaco, arrogantly warning her off a case she had all but solved. Perhaps the most dramatic circumstance had been in Irene's dressing room at the National Theater of Prague, when he had saved her from that devil dancer Tatyana's venomous parting gift. And then there had been our memorable foray in disguise into the heart of Baker Street itself. That masquerade had strung gray hairs through my coiffure that could not be rinsed out!

Indoors and hatless, he seemed am unprepossessing sort: rather scholarly though taut-strung, like catgut on a violin, perhaps five-and-thirty years old I should say, in the prime of life but past first youth: tall, thin, his clean-shaven face free of any distraction from the sharp hawklike nose and the sharper gray eyes. In the broadest sense, a description of Sherlock Holmes and one of Godfrey Norton would be similar, but the fine points made all the difference. Godfrey was both far better-looking and much more genial-natured than the consulting detective, although all three—Mr. Holmes, Godfrey, and Irene—possessed the apparent supreme self-confidence of those used to expressing themselves or their opinions in public. I say "apparent" because those who express themselves in public are often surprisingly shy when it comes to other matters. Irene was correct about the "armor" many people affect to hide their true worries and fears.

But I was used to no such thing as supreme self-confidence, I reflected sadly as, despite the sights of the morning, we all fell to our meal of artichoke soup and potted crab with gusto but without any loss of manners.

I could not help remarking aloud on our shameless conversion from horror to gluttony.

"The hunt sharpens appetite in some people," Mr. Holmes said at once. "Perhaps because it gives so little time for satisfying it. When I am truly on the trail, I cannot eat at all." He turned his lofty attention to Irene. "How did you know that I was the laborer?"

"Because I knew that you were in Paris."

"And how did you know that?"

"If the Prince of Wales was worried enough to summon me from Neuilly to Paris at midnight, he certainly would have wired London for the aid of the famous Sherlock Holmes."

"Why? I had nothing to do with the Ripper investigations in London."

Irene ignored this statement and began demurely deshelling an egg, skepticism screaming from every gesture as well as her long silence.

"It is true," I put in meekly. "The newspapers never mentioned his participation. Not once."

Irene's skeptical glance met mine. "Now that is a telling omission, and the key to the real story."

"Which is?" Mr. Holmes asked before I could. A rude man from start to finish.

"Whatever is least reported is most true," Irene declared. "At least that is my experience of the police and the newspapers when matters are most extreme. If you somehow managed to avoid involvement in the most sensational murders in the world, I cannot believe that you would avoid involvement in a similar case when your country's heir apparent had the ill luck to be at the scene of the slaughter."

"As Watson has said time and again, Madam Norton, when you explain yourself conclusions prove a very simple matter indeed. Mere common sense."

"I don't think so. I have never found sense to be very common. I hope, by the way, that you will find room on your watch chain for the sou I gave you yesterday, though it is not so grand as the sovereign I offered you on my wedding day."

"Ha!" His bark of delight, or laughter, was so abrupt that I nearly swallowed a bite of food the wrong way and was forced to drink a great deal of the luncheon wine I had determined to avoid.

He slapped his napkin to the tablecloth, though he had eaten very little. "You see through me, Madam, like no other."

"Oh, it was masterfully done, my dear Mr. Holmes, but I was expecting you. Though not so near my own cottage stoop. Why did you come all the way to Neuilly?"

"You came to my doorstep in disguise to wish me 'Good night' once, Madam. I sought to return the favor by coming to wish you 'Good morning.' "

"Hmmm." Irene did not seem very convinced.

Mr. Holmes lifted his watch to display the chain. A gold sovereign twinkled there like a morning sun. Beside it dangled the cold bronze moon of a well-used French sou.

"Had I been able to fly like a gull across the Channel, instead of taking the boat train to Calais and rail again to

Paris, you would never have been exposed to what you saw in the *maison de rendezvous*."

His words were both an apology, and a dismissal.

"But we saw what we saw. Have you?"

His head was quick to shake. "No. The Sûreté had cleared the house with its famous dispatch. It hardly matters. They had trampled the site so thoroughly by then that no mote of evidence could remain, although I spent hours on my hands and knees examining the carpeting and was able to find some small shreds, signifying not very much, I daresay."

He savored the wine with the ease of a Frenchman. I added the charge of "dipsomaniac" to my lengthening list of Holmesian vices. It went very well with "opium addict."

"Then you are not interested in our observations of the death scenes?" Irene persisted.

"I am sure that you noticed some of what I did: that precise timing or luck was needed in the house of ill repute; that the killer had some influence over the victims; that they must have been killed quickly and damaged afterward, also quickly. Quite like the Whitechapel Ripper, I grant you, but also quite unlike him. The second killing by the Eiffel Tower smacks more of Saucy Jack, but already these matters have diverged too much from the Whitechapel murders to be considered part of that sequence, if it is indeed a sequence."

"You doubt the Whitechapel horrors are the work of Jack the Ripper?" I was startled into asking.

That quick, piercing gaze, as searing as a hot iron, focused on me and me alone. Oh, dear.

"Apparently you do not, Miss . . . ?"

"Huxleigh."

"The typewriter-girl in the Temple," he said with narrowed, amused eyes, remembering our first, unpleasant encounter. "Quite the watchdog for the absent barrister."

"I am always proud to serve as watchdog for my friends."

"No doubt why the bulldog is the British mascot," he murmured, my unspoken challenge not lost on him. "But you are convinced of the existence of the Ripper?"

"It is a given, sir. Any informed person—"

"Has read too many newspapers too uncritically. I assure

you, Miss Huxleigh, I could make a convincing case that any of two dozen persons were the Whitechapel Ripper, from street sweeper to tree surgeon to prime minister."

"Why do you doubt the Ripper's existence?" Irene asked.

Those gimlet eyes returned to her, and I was momentarily relieved to escape their gaze, though I had resolved to sacrifice myself for Irene's sake.

She, however, had that hazy acceding look she wore when winning a game of chess with Godfrey or dealing with an operatic director who wanted her to sing a role a certain way. She looked quite amenable in an intelligent way, but was growing as stubborn as Satan beneath the affability.

"I do not believe in frightening horses in the street or ladies at luncheon," Mr. Holmes noted, "but, since you insist, I will only note other events of the year of 1888 in the working-class sections of London. You realize, of course, that the Ripper's supposed victims were all middle-aged women of the lowest orders? Is there anyone who does not recognize that quintet of names: Mary Ann Nichols, Annie Chapman, Elizabeth Stride, Catharine Eddowes, and Mary Jane Kelly? They are as famous as wives of the Henry VIII."

"They also are as dead," Irene muttered in a stage aside.

"Ha! Why is there not an opera on that subject? You could play all the wives admirably."

For a moment her composure shattered. "That is a rather brilliant idea, Mr. Holmes."

"Then I hope you will act upon it and leave investigating these poor women's deaths to those who must delve into the lowest impulses of man. I have investigated many criminous matters, but that a voice such as yours should be silenced from the stage is the greatest crime I have ever encountered."

I have seldom—nay, never—seen Irene at a loss for words, but she was tongue-tied then. In fact, her eyes brightened suspiciously, and I leaped into the chasm of silence.

"It takes constant practice to maintain a fine voice, Mr. Holmes, and such a discipline allows for very little life of any normal sort."

"A life of 'any normal sort' is very little indeed, Miss Huxleigh," he replied abruptly. He, too, seemed suddenly stricken in some strange way. "You and Dr. Watson!" He sounded rueful and also a trifle envious.

I hastened to change a subject that was becoming unsettling to us all.

"I do not understand your earlier point, Mr. Holmes. Each of the women you named was murdered within proximity of the others, in similar and too-loathsome-to-mention ways, within a period of time ranging over two and a half months. And then there were the letters signed 'Jack the Ripper' taking credit for the crimes. He even predicted two of the murders before they happened."

"Indeed." The eagle eyes were back on me and the topic of murder most foul rather than Irene and her wounded singing career. "You are suspiciously well-read on this subject, Miss Huxleigh."

"It was a sensation worldwide, after all. And . . . it was news of home," I added lamely.

"There was other news of home that did not draw worldwide attention, also in the year 1888."

He glanced once at the tabletop as if to assure himself that we had eaten and drunk our fill. Then the long fingers on his right hand flared, and his left hand began ticking them off, starting with the small finger.

"In February of that year a thirty-eight-year old widow of Spitalfields was stabbed in the nether region by an unknown man wielding a clasp knife.

"In March a thirty-nine-year-old woman was stabbed twice in the throat by an unknown man with a clasp knife. In April a forty-five-year-old widow of Spitalfields was . . . unspeakably attacked by an unknown man. In August, a thirty-nine-year-old hawker of Spitalfields who hawked herself as well as her wares was stabbed thirty-nine times in Whitechapel. And on August 31, Mary Ann Nichols's mutilated body was found in Bucks Row, Whitechapel."

He had reached his thumb and flared his left hand to continue the count. "Then: Annie Chapman, Elizabeth Stride, Catharine Eddowes, and Mary Jane Kelly, the roll call of the so-called Ripper."

His little finger remained upright after he had ticked off

the victims. "Mary Jane Kelly is buried on the twelfth of November. And in December, Rose Mylett, described as 'a drunkard,' is found dead, though unmutilated. A murder verdict is brought in."

Irene bestirred herself. "You are saying that many murders as vile as the Ripper's have occurred in Whitechapel before and after his reign, and still will."

"What is remarkable about the Ripper case is the public furor, not the victims of the crime, nor even the acts of violence. I assure you that did I wish to solve sensational crimes rather than interesting ones, I could be in the papers every fortnight with a new atrocity."

"You would not be involved in solving these crimes at all, were it not for Queen and country," Irene observed with some surprise.

The man sighed, then glanced to us both. "Would you object if I smoked?"

"Not at all," said Irene, "if you do not object if I smoke."

I added "nicotine fiend" to my list of *the* man's vices.

We had removed ourselves to the antechamber, where the smoke of my companions could lose itself among the plaster-and-gilt ceiling cherubs, who no doubt wondered why they had won a place in Heaven only to inhale the fumes of Hell.

"Dr. Watson is not in France," Irene noted as she and her host directed companionable streams of smoke toward the ceiling.

I was not deceived. The duel was continuing on different ground, but the feints were as fierce. I would rather see her jousting with the dreadful detective than conjoining with him.

"No, as he was not in Whitechapel. I could not allow him to enter an arena where one with his skills was so suspect. All this twaddle about Jack the Ripper having medical skills—"

"He does not?"

"The work was mere butchery, Madam. Even butchery may show a certain order. But you would find it incomprehensible how many respectable persons were suspected of being the Ripper during the height of the fever."

"Perhaps," I said, "but the public suspects were usually of the lower orders."

"Sacrificial lambs," Irene said. "So the mighty were not immune from suspicion, despite the Whitechapel setting?"

"The mighty have been known to lower themselves." He shook his head impatiently as he drew on his pipe. "This is a most sordid affair, ladies. I cannot discuss it freely with you. Count yourself fortunate that you have matters other than the revolting excesses of madmen to occupy you."

"And your ultimate message is . . . besides luncheon, of course, and the pleasure of your company?" Irene asked in a silken tone I knew enough to avoid like a honed razor edge.

"That your loyalty has been welcome to His Royal Highness. That I am here now, and you are not needed. That this subject matter is not suitable for ladies. That I have the case in hand, and your services are no longer useful. That your Prince appreciates your subjecting yourselves to much unpleasantness. And that you are free to resume your pursuits innocent of the tawdry details of brutality and murder."

"Thank you." Irene stood, crushing her small cigar in a crystal dish. "I do appreciate knowing my place in the scheme of things. I wish you luck in hunting this new, not-Ripper, and am happy to have given a sou, however humble, to the cause."

Oh, my. *The* man may have been a nine days' wonder in solving murderous conundrums, but he knew nothing of the fury of a woman scorned. When Irene Adler applied the word "humble" to herself . . . well, the shoe was about to slip on the other's foot before he could say . . .

"Thank you, and farewell." *The* man stood, bowed to us both, dismissed us.

I found myself sharing Irene's outrage. We had not asked to be drawn into these atrocities, but we had suffered and seen more than gently reared women should, and no thanks, however princely or glib, could restore what had been lost in us.

Irene glided to the door, remembering at the last moment

to pause to let our host open it for us, to release us.

He hesitated, almost urbane for a moment. I thought he would take her hand and kiss it.

But he didn't, and we sallied out together, as we usually did, moving down the hall until we were out of sight, then taking a deep, mutual breath.

"What an astounding meeting, Nell. At least we learned more from him than he did from us."

"We did?"

"Indeed. Well."

"We certainly have been sent on our way. It would have been more gracious if the Prince had tended his gratitude and farewell in person."

"Oh, it is not the Prince who has brushed us off."

I was pleased to note a rising note of fury in her tone. "Not the Prince?"

"And not the Rothschilds."

"The Baron was decidedly absent."

"As we will be. Apparently."

"Apparently? We are going home to Neuilly?"

"Of course. And then we are moving to a Paris hotel."

"Moving to Paris?" I was dismayed. "Why?"

"If Jack the Ripper is in Paris, so must we be."

"But Sherlock Holmes said there was no Jack the Ripper."

"Sherlock Holmes is about to learn a lesson. From Jack the Ripper. And from me."

19.

A Movable Feast

Paris is the most volatile of cities. It is also—in ways that reveal themselves slowly—one of the most reclusive.

—ROSAMOND BERNIER

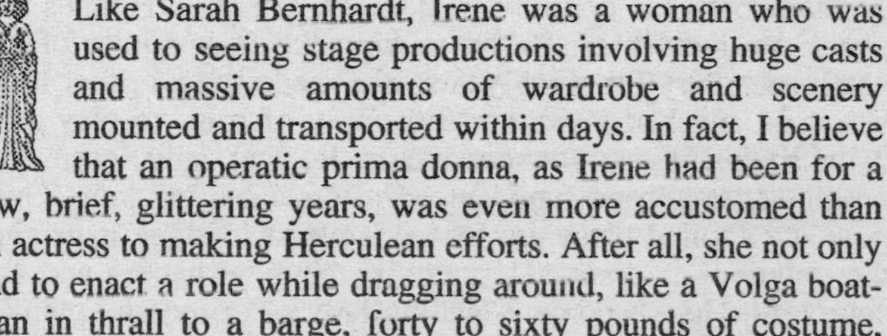

Like Sarah Bernhardt, Irene was a woman who was used to seeing stage productions involving huge casts and massive amounts of wardrobe and scenery mounted and transported within days. In fact, I believe that an operatic prima donna, as Irene had been for a few, brief, glittering years, was even more accustomed than an actress to making Herculean efforts. After all, she not only had to enact a role while dragging around, like a Volga boatman in thrall to a barge, forty to sixty pounds of costume, she also had to trill like a nightingale while doing it.

In other words, actress or opera singer, these were women who were used to moving mountains, and whatever puny humans happened to inhabit them.

A simple project such as relocating two women from a rural village to the nearby heart of Paris in one day was but a trifle to Irene. She was in one of those moods that would brook no opposition. I could have more easily turned a twenty-two-stone Brunhilde away from an imminent stage entrance as persuade Irene to another course of action.

Godfrey, perhaps, would have had some influence, but there was no time to wire him, and he likely had not even reached Prague as yet.

On first observing Irene's wholesale thirst for swift action, one might think it was directed by a certain autocratic self-absorption.

But I had come to see, through my years with Irene and my accompanying observance of the demands of stage productions, that the case was quite the opposite. The leading actor, or the prima donna, is the engine upon which the entire great enterprise of imagination and art made concrete depends. The weight of the entire cast's employment, as well as the responsibility for doing due honor to the maestros whose words and music are presented, falls on the performer. Only a confident, courageous, and deeply committed person would dare set foot on the boards with so much at stake. Uncertainty and hesitation are death onstage. Once the curtain has opened, there is nowhere to hide.

And so it was with Irene in life as well. Her enforced retirement from the opera, in which Mr. Sherlock Holmes had played an incidental role by making the false rumor of her death necessary for some years, had made the world at large her stage and had given her a panoply of roles to play on a daily basis: playwright, conductor, leading lady, costumer, prompter, stagehand, and, on occasion, cleaning lady. Only now she applied these arts and this effort to stage-managing the solution of dramas written in the newspapers and the courts. She had become a leading lady of crime and punishment.

Like all leading ladies, she had her eccentricities. Thank God she did not sleep in her own traveling coffin, as La Bernhardt did. But Irene did travel like a one-woman Shakespearean company, with an enormous quantity of costumes. André was to make many return trips with our baggage once we were settled in our hotel. (Sophie was indulging in a grand pout at being left behind, but was secretly glad to sleep at her own cottage for a few days.)

I must admit that the sense of embarking on a great and possibly dangerous journey entranced even as settled a soul as I. It was like taking a carriage to the opening of a new and mysterious play, without quite knowing whether it would be tragedy or comedy of manners. Or perhaps a bit of both.

As much as my upbringing and inclinations might encourage dragging my feet to resist being swept away by the grand illusions before us, my wayward heart would beat a bit faster as I went stumbling after Irene en route to one of her great enterprises.

The village of Neuilly was only a few miles from the Champs-Elysées, that avenue along which all Paris—the *tout Paris* of legend—drives to see and be seen. In the carriage en route Irene was forced to sit still long enough to explain herself.

"I much appreciate your readiness to do what must be repugnant to you, Nell," she said. "There is no time to be lost. Sherlock Holmes may be clever, but he is most unsuited to find the killer he has been charged with stopping. No wonder the Ripper escaped London unscathed and uncaught."

"You were sufficiently astute to outwit this so-called consulting detective in London, and elsewhere later. I am sure the man's reputation is exaggerated. And I have never found him suited for much."

She regarded me quizzically. "I know you are loyal to me to a fault, Nell, but I have never held his assignment for the King of Bohemia against Mr. Holmes. It was always clear that he saw through Willie from the first. In that regard, he was a good deal cleverer than I."

"You were a woman misled by your heart."

"By my hubris, I fear, but you are kind to call it heart." She shook her bonneted head, for she had dressed in the height of convention, no doubt to soothe my misgivings about our unconventional decamping to Paris. "I admit I was dazzled by Willie's obvious enamourment. I did learn that one's heart may most yearn after what is worst for it, and that a most unlikely man may be far more worthy of regard than the more obvious candidates."

"Godfrey was never unlikely, Irene. You just did not like him at first."

"I did not trust him at first, solely because of his late father's connection to that bit of skullduggery involving Marie Antoinette. In this I was unfairly judgmental. Would that Mr. Holmes had learned such a lesson of the heart as I have. Unfortunately, he is supremely untutored in that regard, and it makes him a most unreliable investigator of these particular crimes. If I do not take a hand in it, more women will die in this unthinkable manner."

"I agree that Mr. Holmes is not likely to solve these fiendish crimes, but why do you think so?"

She eyed me cautiously. "I am bothered, Nell, at having to involve you, though it is at your own insistence. These are the ugliest, most inhuman murders one could imagine occurring on our planet. Unless one recognizes, and admits, that this inhumanity is a part of human nature, one will never see the murderer were he to cross the square ahead of one. This is not Mr. Poe's 'Murders in the Rue Morgue,' alas. No great ape can take the blame or absolve the hand of man in these slaughters, both here in Paris and in London earlier. These murders bear the mark of the beast, and he is all too human."

"I do admit that I would do a great deal that is against my nature to see you show up that Baker Street detective once more, but why is he so handicapped, in your opinion?"

"He is not a woman."

"And a woman—?"

"Would understand immediately that these crimes strike to the heart of womanhood."

"Oh." Since I *was* a woman, I was not about to admit that I didn't understand her point. "Of course."

"And you saw today . . . he makes the same arrogant error he made when first we encountered one another. He dismisses my observations, and yours, as insignificant. He has no wish to know what we may have seen and what we think."

"He also dismisses the observations of the Paris police."

"He dismisses. No doubt his experience of the police, and his inexperience with women, have given him some cause for finding them both unreliable. Yet his experiences with me should have prevented him from making the same mistake of underestimating me twice."

"Now who is sounding like a prima donna?"

She shrugged, then laughed. She has the most musical, unfettered laugh of anyone I have ever heard. It is like a Pied Piper's fluting, and so effective with men, women, and children that I imagine even rats would follow Irene's laughter into the mouth of the King of Cats. Which is probably Lucifer in disguise.

For a moment I fretted about our menagerie left to Sophie's untender mercies. The worst thing about having servants is that they invariably end up feeling superior to those they serve. Perhaps that is because they see far too much of them.

"There is at least one purpose for our removal to Paris that you are bound to approve, Nell," Irene said at last, breaking a companionable silence.

"And what is that?"

"To get Pink out of that bordello."

"Wonderful! I shall endeavor with all my heart to help her see the error of her ways."

"That is not exactly what I had in mind for her, but your approach will be equally interesting, I am sure, Nell."

⚜ ⚜ ⚜

Irene insisted on going alone to retrieve Pink, or Elizabeth, I should say. My first step toward reform would be the elimination of that infantile nickname.

I objected strenuously to Irene's going there unescorted, but she argued that she would be accompanied home by Pink. Two women alone was also improper, unless in the most public and expected of places, but propriety was always the last thing Irene troubled herself about.

I remained puzzled and deeply hurt that she would care to burden us with a stranger during a time when we were confronting crime on a level unprecedented in touching the both highest and lowest levels of society.

Pink, I concluded, fell somewhere in the middle of that social ladder. Perhaps I should have been worried about having a fallen woman in our midst, but the governess in me actually relished the idea of enlightening the girl. She had a bright mind, was very well mannered for an American, and seemed far more likely to respond to my advice than Irene ever was. A rather odd fallen woman actually, but I suppose the establishments that catered to aristocrats preferred to offer girls of the middling classes to their clients, odious as the thought was.

Poor Pink. That terrible family life! What chance had the poor girl had? And then I recalled Irene's comments that Pink was sharing only the tip of the truth about herself with us . . . *Pink*!

I had been blind! Of course. Pink. From America. As Irene had been, years before. And, as Irene had been, also a *Pinkerton* private inquiry agent! Could a young woman be both a trollop and a detective? I suppose it would be a useful combination of . . . pursuits. Think of the state secrets such an agent could learn, the commercial dealings!

Then how should I treat her? I must not betray her secret. All must seem as before. I remained hurt that Irene did not share this information about Pink with me. Perhaps she felt that I would give away Pink's true assignment. I would show that such a concern was needless! I would treat Pink as purely the foreign *fille de joie* she appeared to be.

Irene had chosen a hotel on the rue de Rivoli central to the various sections of Paris, which are called *arrondissements*. The Hotel du Louvre was nothing to sniff at, and we had a large suite with a receiving room and dining room separating two bedchambers as well as a sleeping alcove off the dining room. I was not sure where Pink would sleep.

We had no maid, but Irene and I were used to playing maidservant to each other. She had always been far too American to accept the waiting-on that the profession of prima donna offered her. She rarely used dressers during performances, unless absolutely necessary. Since her marriage to Godfrey she had more played the maid to me than vice versa, as he apparently took over such tasks as corset-string tightening and loosening, which is so difficult to do on one's own. I imagine that masculine strength was better suited to this troublesome task, and then ceased to imagine more lest I imagine too much.

I shall never forget my reunion with Quentin Stanhope on the train from Prague to Paris, and how when I swooned at penetrating his disguise at last, he made short work of my confining corset strings in a manner I am still not fully sure of to this day, save that it was quite improper and strangely thrilling.

Indeed, all of the events that I became involved in through Irene and her sideline of private inquiry agent were usually quite improper and strangely thrilling.

I had never met such a pack of scoundrels and murderers and wicked women until after I was "rescued" from starving on the streets by Irene Adler! Now one of these fallen women was about to be imported into our very midst. This girl seemed fairly fresh and innocent, but I suppose that could be a pose. I cannot say I relished her close company, but could hardly object to a "rescue" attempt when I myself had benefited from one.

While Irene was gone I occupied myself with copying my sketches of the footprints in the carpet from the miniature chatelaine notebook onto pieces of the sketching paper I use to lay out designs for my needlework projects. I must admit I took an intense pleasure in translating my measurements into a life-size representation of the impressions. Imagine! I might be looking at the sole of Jack the Ripper!

In truth, I enjoyed my role as recording artist for Irene's problems almost as much as I relish my role as diarist, though no one will ever read my homely narratives. I suppose there might be some interest in the more lurid aspects of our investigations, but I certainly would never countenance the publication of what is so private to me and of such little interest to the world in general.

I can only hope that John H. Watson, M.D., is similarly sensible and discreet.

The time fairly flew, and then Irene made her entrance in the open door of our apartments, the American girl beside her, along with a porter with yet more baggage. I was pleased to see, however, that Miss Pink traveled with only one trunk.

Miss Pink (I must remember to call her Elizabeth even in my thoughts) wasted no time on renewed acquaintance, but came rushing to the desk at which I worked.

"Well, here I am, persuaded by this silver-tongued diva to accept free room and board with no need of accepting other, more intimate offers, and given an opportunity to develop my skills for other marketplaces than *maisons de tolérance*. I see Miss Huxleigh has been as busy as a bookmaker! I am told that I am to apprentice you in the useful arts. What wonderful work! Imagine: those faint impressions we saw on the nap of a carpet are now laid out as clearly as a footstep in hot tar. You could do illustrations for the daily newspapers."

"Oh, no. My poor drawings are for private viewing only. And what journal would care to print representations of something so ugly as boot prints?"

"Why, the *Police Gazette*," said she, drawing up a chair and sitting down beside me without being invited, an American habit, I take it. "If only you and Missus Norton had been crawling around Whitechapel, they would have paid you royally for all these footprints . . . this one looks like my best satin slipper with the Louis XIII heel."

With that the girl ran to unbuckle and unlock her steamer trunk and began tossing out articles of clothing until she emerged triumphant, rather like Prince Charming, with a single slipper except that hers was fashioned of silk and not glass.

She galloped back to the desk and set the filthy sole down on my drawing. It fit the outline to a T-strap.

"Call me Cinderella!" she crowed (and indeed, her voice lilted into the raucous range of Casanova in full cry). "That is very good work, Miss Huxleigh! It shows that your other drawings are liable to be tip-top, too."

"Tip-top?"

"Perfect. Splendid, as they say in Blighty. That was my last stop, you know, and I learned a thing or two about that nasty Ripper. I'm sure I can help you pursue the fiend now that he's moved on to Paris."

"My dear girl, we are here to help *you*."

"Then we are all of one mind. We will work together. I hear that you have met with Sherlock Holmes. I would give anything to meet him. He is all the talk of New York. And I hear that you take notes. So do I!"

"Indeed. I rather thought your line of work was less . . . practical."

"Oh, anything a girl may do to stay alive and independent

is practical, Miss Huxleigh. I admit I don't let much stop me. If I am overbearing, you must let me know."

Where would I begin?

"Dinner," Irene said from the door to her bedroom, "would be a good idea." She had shed her coat and bonnet. "I think we three may patronize the hotel dining room without causing scandal. We can also be served in this chamber, but perhaps should celebrate our alliance with a public outing."

Alliance? Is that how one would describe good works?

I was beginning to wish that we had got on better with Sherlock Holmes.

20. Wild Oats

Some would see only the surface: an ungoverned, filthy boy, sexually crude and personally licentious, precocious only in sinning, sneering, and thumbing his "snot-nose" at a wiser world.

—NOTE TO MYSELF

FROM A YELLOW BOOK

He is resisting my efforts to accompany him on his nightly outings.

I have given him his lead for long enough, first in London, now here. It is time that I am initiated into his secret ways.

I was forced to point out that he depends upon me for everything: food, drink, clothes. Especially drink.

His capacity is the stuff of legend. I must remind myself that he is still so young, though his rough features and unkempt hair, his amazing lust for everything sensual—and "sensual" is too elegant a word, perhaps "the sensational" is better—his every instinct is the opposite of culture, of civilization.

When I look at him, I feel that I am on the fringe of some borderland inhabited by Huns and Vandals. Or Vikings. Those whose reputation for pillage and rapine still goes unsurpassed. I look into his simple, savagely compelling eyes and think of Nero the crucifier, Genghis Khan the conqueror, Vlad the Impaler, Torquemada the torturer, Ivan the Terrible.

Oh, he is magnificent. There is nothing of which he is not capable, which means that he can be a great and powerful force in the world of tomorrow, if properly trained. If properly harnessed and disciplined.

But he is like those fierce northern pack dogs with the pale blue eyes and the strength many times their size. He runs for himself and no one else. He runs for the fire of running, the fire of breathing the icy air, the raw alcohol fumes, for the lust of hunting and mounting and rending.

And yet this magnificent animal nature is fettered. Is tied to hundreds of years of simpering self-doubt and guilt. Christianity and that broken god on the cross have much to answer for.

The contradiction is tearing him apart, as it rends all who meet and have doings with him.

I must be careful.

I must go where he goes, see what he does.

I must be very careful with my beast, my master, my beast.

My cipher in light and dark, good and evil, life and death.

My creature, my butcher boy.

My key to the future of empire, and everything that goes with it.

21.

The Women of Whitechapel

Every man is a moon and has a dark side which he never shows to anybody.

—MARK TWAIN

"The most puzzling aspect of these Parisian crimes," Irene said the next morning as we studied my portraits of footprints, "is the great variance between the scenes of the crimes."

She glanced at me and Elizabeth.

"You two have absorbed far more from the sensational press about these atrocities in London. I can't imagine what I was thinking of, to ignore the entire sequence of events."

"I can do more than imagine, Irene; I can tell you. You were busy hobnobbing with that Bernhardt woman and driving out with Godfrey to visit Maison Worth in the rue de Rivoli."

What I intended to be a roll call of idleness Elizabeth took for a list of honor.

"Bernhardt! Worth! Rue de Rivoli! You have seen Paris, Mrs. Norton! Oh, can we not go see these wonders?"

"You are to call me Irene, remember, and we cannot go anywhere amusing until this matter of the transplanted Ripper is settled."

"Of course," Elizabeth murmured contritely. "I forgot myself."

"You do not want to do that again," Irene said sardonically. "There is so much of you to forget."

At that Elizabeth lived up to her nickname and blushed bright pink.

"I do not have a sensational cast of mind," Irene mused regretfully. "Perhaps I have absorbed my quota of sensationalism through the medium of opera plots. That really is a very good idea, you know."

"What!" I admit that I was a bit exasperated by now.

"The creation of a cantata, or a closet opera, based on the lives and wives of Henry VIII, with me singing all the female roles. I would need a sophisticated composer, and a fine, fat basso for a partner."

"You would have to lose your head twice."

"Singing angelically, of course, to the bitter end, over and over. Perhaps it could be combined with the legend of Bluebeard," she speculated, "for an additional French flavor."

In fact I was glad to hear her reconsidering a performing career. A compact "portmanteau" piece that could be performed anywhere with a minimum of cast, costume, and stage setting would be most convenient to her current life. That this fortuitous notion emanated from Sherlock Holmes was incidental, I told myself, though my teeth ground at the thought for some reason. Perhaps it was at finding myself thinking in a French expression: *portmanteau.*

Was I possibly becoming . . . Continental?

"I have some notes myself," Elizabeth said, producing a blank-page book filled with a strange combination of handwriting and cryptic symbols.

"It's my own system, Miss Huxleigh," she said as she noticed me noticing her script.

This cryptic form of shorthand only confirmed my suspicion that Elizabeth was among us because she was a Pinkerton agent. Why did Irene not trust me with this intelligence? Of course, when it came to the London depredations of Jack the Ripper Irene was facing a condition she relished less than all others: ignorance.

"You write shorthand?" I asked Elizabeth quite pointedly.

"Not quite shorthand," Elizabeth said, rushing on. "Anyway, there were suspects aplenty for the role of Jacky-boy, most of them low-class persons from the slums. From the start, though, there was some notion that the Ripper might be a step up in class from his victims. They all went meek as lambs to the slaughter, and sad as their lots were and drunk as most of them were, they were wise enough to know a rum dude from a legitimate client."

She stared for a moment at her own writings as if they were an alien transcript, then went on.

"Mary Ann Nichols," she said slowly, as if naming the dead repeated the crime in a way.

"The first Whitechapel victim," I prompted her, sometimes known as "Polly" Nichols. After all, I read the newspapers at the time as well.

Elizabeth straightened and resumed her brisk report, eyes on her summary. She reminded me a bit of Sherlock Holmes at his most officious.

"Her husband had an affair with the midwife who delivered their fifth child."

I couldn't help gasping at the cruel betrayal.

"He kept the children and paid her an allowance of five shillings a week until he learned she had become a prostitute. She liked to drink. Needed to, would better describe it. She was a small woman, just over five feet tall, of forty-three years."

Irene noted, "You are well informed."

I couldn't tell if it was a straightforward comment, or a gibe. Did she know Elizabeth's real role, or not? The uncertainty was maddening, yet I did not dare ask her on so little evidence. Nor did I wish to know that I was being kept ignorant with Irene's complicity.

"The London newspapers erupted with information about the Ripper's victims," Elizabeth said. "I have always thought that information was the answer to all life's problems, but am no longer so sure. Anyway, on August 30 last, Mary Ann was drunk and hadn't four pennies for a doss house, though she'd tried for a bed. She had high spirits, though, and a 'jolly bonnet.'

"At 2:30 A.M. she was even drunker and told a woman friend she'd be off the streets soon. Within an hour and forty minutes, a carman found her dead in Bucks Row. Her throat was cut, and her abdomen had been slashed until the intestines showed.

"Dark Annie Chapman," she went on in a monotone that sounded like a dirge, "was even smaller than Mary Ann—barely five feet—and older, forty-seven. She'd had three children: a daughter lost to meningitis at twelve, a son sent to a crippled children's home, and another daughter sent to an institution in France."

I shook my head at these serial tragedies, but Irene stiffened at mention of France.

"Her husband gave her a weekly allowance of ten shillings until he died in '86. Then she turned to drink and doss houses and the streets. She was seen alive, with a man, at 5:30 A.M. on September 8. At 5:45 her body was discovered by a carman living at 29 Hanbury Street, her throat cut and her skirt bunched above her knees. The intestines had been drawn from her slashed abdomen and placed over her right shoulder. Like . . . ribbons. Her stomach lay above her left shoulder, and her womb was completely missing."

"These were the first internal injuries," Irene observed.

I nodded.

"Elizabeth"—our own Elizabeth faltered at the name—"Long Liz, she was called. Long Liz Stride, though she was only five-foot-two. She was Sweden-born, forty-four, and had married an Englishman named Stride, who died in '84, four years before her. She later claimed that her husband and children had died during the famous steamer collision of the *Princess Alice* with the *Bywell Castle* in the Thames, in which six hundred-some people lost their lives."

"A steamer collision," Irene mused. "I suppose she sought sympathy."

"But she was not believed, and rightly so. She was seen many times on the night of September 29, often embracing a man variously described, but once he was said to be well dressed in a cutaway coat."

"A cutaway coat," I pointed out, as few of the Ripper suspects were that well garbed.

"Indeed. She was found at 1:00 A.M. on Berner Street, throat cut, but she wasn't mutilated. Catharine Eddowes, who was found forty-five minutes later, was not so lucky. She was forty-six and just five feet tall. She was arrested for drunkenness the night of September 27, but let go at 1:00 A.M. the next morning. She gave the false name of Mary *Ann* Kelly to the jailer. He released her *at the very moment* that Elizabeth Stride's body was being discovered. She was found forty-five minutes later, throat cut, skirt bunched at her waist, her bowels pouring from her body."

I couldn't help wincing at Elizabeth's cut-and-dried description, which read as if taken from a police report, void of the horrified expressions that found their way into the press accounts.

"The Ripper was interrupted earlier," Irene suggested, "but made up for it later with a vengeance."

"So the police concluded," Elizabeth said. "This was the same night the anti-Semitic scrawl was found about 3:00 A.M. in Goulson Street. 'The Juwes are the men That Will not be Blamed for nothing.' At least that is what the message was rumored to be. Sir Charles Warren ordered the graffiti removed within two and a half hours."

"He feared an uprising against the Jews?"

"Perhaps. Jews was reportedly spelled 'Juwes,' which is an unlikely spelling, even by the ignorant. Those who hate people for their race generally learn to spell the hated syllables, if nothing else. Perhaps the message had nothing to do with Jewish matters.

"He cut her face. Eddowes's." Elizabeth's voice shook for the first time. "Catharine's. He slit her eyelids and sliced off the tip of her nose. What was done elsewhere was not reported in the press, but I have heard that this was the most thorough mutilation yet."

"An odd sort of distinction," Irene observed, "as if taking a body apart was an escalating achievement."

"The most thorough dissection until Mary Jane Kelly, that is," I put in. "The real Mary Jane Kelly."

Irene immediately fastened on my distinction. "One almost identical first name and a single surname attached to two different women, both victims of the same killer. Merely coincidence?"

"I don't know," Elizabeth said. "The newspapers and the public throve on the details of the deaths. I found myself dwelling on the sad lives of these women rather than their brutal deaths."

"And the 'real' Mary Jane Kelly?"

"Used the name of Marie Jeanette Kelly sometimes," Elizabeth said. "She claimed a fine gentleman client had taken her to Paris last year."

Irene frowned at that. The word "Paris" in any Ripper context alarmed her like a siren in the street.

"Her first husband died in an ironworks explosion," Elizabeth went on. "The man she lived with in Whitechapel, Joseph Barnett, didn't want her to be a prostitute, but they were thirty shillings behind on their rent of a few square feet in Miller's Court, a one-room hovel, and he was out of work. What else was she to do?

"Marie Jeanette, or Mary Jane, was fair, blond and blue-eyed, and only twenty-five years old." Elizabeth's voice trembled as if she saw this young woman in her mind's eye, as if her youthfulness touched the American girl. "A lissome girl of five-foot-seven, she would have stood taller than most reported Ripper suspects, save for the one tallish man seen with Liz Stride.

"Two people heard the cry of 'Murder!' from the area near her room about 4:00 A.M., but she was seen in the neighborhood by several witnesses between 8:00 and 10:00 A.M. The landlord's agent, coming for the delinquent rent, peered through the room's window at 10:45 A.M. and ran screaming from what he described as 'more the work of a devil than of a man.'

"Mary Jane Kelly had been flayed, mutilated, disemboweled, and dismembered."

We were all silent for some time, imagining that tiny room splashed with blood and guts.

"They didn't suffer," Irene said at last. "There is that."

Elizabeth paled, then burst into impassioned speech. "How can anyone know what those women suffered, even before Jack the Ripper? Those poor creatures just needed a couple pence for a bed for the night. Cribs, they called them—miserable, filthy cots in a row at a doss house. They were mostly widows and wives who'd been turned out, or who'd left brutes of husbands. They didn't deserve to draw Jack the Ripper for a final client and a final crib."

I was silent, remembering my few but desperate hours of homelessness after I'd been unfairly dismissed from my clerking position in London years before. If I had not met Irene . . . or if Irene had not seen my plight and chosen to rescue me. Yet the notion of these women selling themselves remained repugnant to me.

"Client!" I repeated the word with disdain. "You make their downfalls sound like an accident in a respectable business."

"Respectable, no," Elizabeth said, "but unavoidable, given their circumstances. Saucy Jack had no right to be 'down on whores,' if it was indeed the killer who penned those notes to the newspapers. Why or how was he any better?"

"Why do you think," put in Irene, "that the Ripper *didn't* write to the newspapers?"

"It stands to reason," Pink said firmly. "Cranks are always writing newspapers claiming this and that. In the States, anyway." She blinked rapidly and looked down at her notes.

"That is an interesting point," Irene continued, "because if the 'Jack' letters are false, then most assumptions about the Ripper may be false as well." She sat back and eyed us both as if we were students and she the governess. "So. Summarize all that you have read of the Ripper."

We both spoke at once, hesitated, glanced at each other, and spoke in tandem again.

At last order prevailed, and I started a fresh list of our joint conclusions.

⚜ ⚜ ⚜

A little before noon, a knock sounded on our door.

I started as if with guilt, for who would know how to find us at our new lodgings? Unless that Baker Street man . . .

While I imagined the worst, Irene rose to answer the door.

A snub-nosed boy in short jacket and beret stood there, in grinning possession of a note.

"He will come at once," he caroled in French so simple even I could understand it.

Irene drew a coin purse from her skirt pocket, from which she plucked a gleaming coin for the lad's open but dingy palm. "Well done; swiftly, too," she told him before bidding him adieu and shutting the door. At least he was too short to be Sherlock Holmes in disguise.

"Who is coming at once?" I asked as she glanced at the note's contents and nodded in satisfaction.

"Bram Stoker."

I sat silent. Once that name and that personage had stood for all that was stable and admirable in the flighty circle of actors, artists, and writers Irene had moved among during her early days in London before her operatic performing career took wing. Now I regarded it with shock and a certain bitterness.

She had immediately perceived my reaction and argued against it.

"Who better would I consult on the Wives of Henry VIII project than the consummate manager of Henry Irving, who is the consummate English actor of the age? We are fortunate to have made his acquaintance so long ago, Nell."

I said nothing.

She glanced at Elizabeth. "Between Nell's issues of last autumn's London newspapers, which she had the foresight to tuck among the trunks of clothes I removed from Neuilly to this hotel yesterday, and the forwarded Rothschild documents, I think you have sufficient material to take to my room for study. You may remain to meet Mr. Stoker, but I have theatrical business to discuss with him, so it is best that we confer privately."

"That's all right," Elizabeth said. "I don't mind being left out. Mr. Stoker is a frequent visitor to America when Mr. Irving is on tour, and I had lots of opportunity to read of him there. Besides, I do so enjoy rummaging through these illustrated crime gazettes. They are such shockers, and so shockingly inaccurate. It's like reading a dime novel."

She promptly began removing our piles of Ripper documentation to Irene's bedchamber.

"Irene," I said when Elizabeth was safely absent, "I really do not wish to meet Mr. Stoker again. As you may imagine, our encounter at the *maison de rendezvous* was exceedingly embarrassing to us both."

"That is why another meeting would be so instructive, Nell. You can't think that I only wish to consult him about a vocal presentation, although he is an ideal expert? I wish to know the why and wherefore of his presence at the murder scene."

"I do not! He has a young wife, one of the three most beautiful women in London, according to that *Punch* cartoonist, George du Maurier, and a sweet young son of only seven or eight. I cannot imagine what such a man, with such a fine reputation and family, would be doing in that kind of establishment."

"Oh, you can imagine only too well, which is why you were upset. Yet we were there for innocent reasons. Perhaps Bram was, too."

"I do hope so, but I fear not."

Irene nodded, approvingly. "You begin to suspect the ways of the world. They are often disappointing."

"This has been a most disappointing sequence of events. I am told that all the people I have met are habitually immoral, and that even my closest friend has found it more expedient to pretend to be! So that everyone who is not bad in a wicked world must feign to be so to preserve what goodness is left! It is insanity!"

Irene had the grace to look a trifle sheepish. "We are traveling in society, Nell, and society is often hypocritical. Wealth and power always corrupt."

"Bram Stoker is not wealthy and not particularly powerful," I retorted. "And . . . I have always liked him."

Irene exchanged chairs to sit close to me and give my shoulders a bracing hug. "You may still like him, Nell! Bram is one of the most likeable men in London, after all, and I daresay Paris, too! Remember the Testament warns us, 'Judge not, lest ye be judged.' "

Irene quoting Scripture was just one step up from Lucifer the cat doing so. I laughed, shakily. "But how can one judge how not to be judgmental when those famed in fortune and men's eyes lead secret lives that betray their wives and encourage every woman they meet to compromise herself, or at best, merely pretend to!"

"Not every man, Nell. The Prince of Wales is an acknowledged rake. After all, what else has been left for him to do? His mother seems likely to live into her hundreds, yet allows him no role in government."

"You make excuses for him."

"Because every one of us has reason for what we do, bad or good."

"Even Jack the Ripper?"

"Even Jack the Ripper."

"It is like solving a crime then, to detect the circumstances that turn a man mad."

"Indeed. As for Bram, you will remember that I told you years ago that I found the fair Florence a trifle chilly. No doubt Bram has, too."

When I frowned, she continued in an undertone that promised confidences, "Many women marry, produce a child or two, then no longer fulfill the marital role. You do comprehend, Nell?"

I had to think about it. "Florence Stoker—"

"—may likely be one of those. Henry Irving keeps her genial husband absorbed all hours of the day and night with his theatrical enterprise. Florence must rely for male escort on a man less taxed by work, William Gilbert."

"No! Gilbert is the womanizing cad who hosted the dinner party with all the D'Oyley Cart female chorus singers present for the Prince of Wales . . . where you mesmerized Bertie into falsely believing that he had indeed had his way with you!"

Irene nodded. "I doubt that the relationship between Gilbert and Florence is of that sort. She would not wish it, for one thing."

"Then why does he bother?"

"Gilbert keeps up his reputation as a ladies' man by being seen with a handsome woman on his arm. Florence gets out and about as she would not if she waited for her husband to ever be free of an evening, and can bask in her beauty being praised without having to deal with men who wish to possess her. It is an ideal arrangement."

"And Mr. Stoker?"

Irene smiled enigmatically. "That is the real mystery, now that he has been discovered in a Paris brothel. Was he merely caught by happenstance? It is his role to go everywhere, to associate with the high-and-mighty so as to lobby in Irving's behalf. Or has he turned to seeking elsewhere what his wife won't give him? I admit that I am not sure of the facts in his case. If Florence is a wife in name only, as I suspect, he would be free to seek satisfaction elsewhere without worrying about bringing dread diseases home, although such contamination is always a risk for the adventurous."

"As well it should be! Really, Irene, I cannot believe that we are talking about people we know in this vulgar way. I don't wish to think about it."

"Then don't. But you must understand that most people wear armor of a sort, sometimes many different suits of it. In different places and at different times, they behave as different people. None of them are solely what role they play on any one occasion."

"But you are talking about theatrical people, like that odious popinjay Oscar Wilde. Oh! Don't tell me that he is deserting his lovely wife Constance for other women?"

An unreadable expression crossed Irene's fair countenance. "No, I think it is safe to say that Oscar is not unfaithful with other women."

"Amazing! That one so puffed up with himself, so artificial should actually be faithful to his wife!"

"You are reacting to the armor that Oscar has carefully shaped and donned to protect himself because he is too sensitive. Then there is Sherlock Holmes."

"Him! He is too arrogant to adopt a pose."

"So he thinks, but he does. Man of Logic. Man Who Stands Alone. Man Who Does Not Need Woman. At least I believe that I can guarantee that you will not find Sherlock Holmes in a *maison de tolérance*, Nell. Unless he is in disguise and in the pursuit of a criminal."

"Is everyone a fraud then? I am not!"

"Why, Nell, you have several roles you rotate regularly."

"Roles? What roles?"

"Parson's Daughter." Irene mimed simpering rectitude so aptly that I laughed despite myself. "Indignant Governess." Again, her expression and attitude became both humble and proud at once, like the heroine of a melodrama, and utterly amusing. "Innocent Spinster." She lifted a pair of invisible spectacles to her blinking eyelashes. While I laughed, she added, "or is that . . . Ignorant Spinster."

As my face sobered, trying to decide whether to show offense, she added, "and I am Prima Donna. Woman of the World. Frustrated Artiste. Married Woman. Adventuress. Solver of Enigmas."

"Is there anyone we know then, who is not encased in false fronts?"

My question had truly given her pause. For a moment she gazed blankly at the far wall. Then she smiled like the Mona Lisa and turned that fabled expression of enigmatic satisfaction on me.

"Why, yes, Nell. There is one."

"Who?"

"Godfrey," she said simply, opening her hands to show the emptiness of any other answer. "Godfrey."

While I sat stunned at the undeniable truth of her choice, Elizabeth returned to the room, and I was forced to subside into my role of Ignorant Spinster. Irene was right; roles did prove useful.

22.

The Judgment of Paris

By all accounts, Florence was an enchanting hostess and made a comfortable home for her husband and his friends, when they were there. In every way, she was a social asset. By Victorian standards the marriage, although lacking passion, was successful.

—BARBARA BELFORD, *BRAM STOKER*

Within ten minutes another knock sounded at our door. As Irene swept it open, I saw Mr. Stoker's tall, imposing figure, his red beard and mustache immaculately trimmed, and his gray eyes serious.

Given his usual energetic yet amiable nature, he seemed rather dampened. I suspected he dreaded this meeting as much as I did, whatever pretext Irene had put upon it.

In fact, as he crossed the threshold he glanced from her to Elizabeth to me, and I sensed something I had never glimpsed in him before, reticence, and also a strange excitement.

"Such a bevy of beautiful ladies." He tried to boom out the greeting in his old hearty manner, as he doffed his hat like Sir Francis Drake for Queen Elizabeth. He was ever gallant with the female sex, though his gentlemanly attentions could never be taken awry for forwardness.

Now as he glanced around at us, I understood that his bonhomie might be a pose, and he might be intimidated by us, that we three exercised a certain classical power over him, like muses or furies.

I studied us from his point of view. Irene was of course exquisite in a pale blue silk skirt surmounted by a frilly breakfast jacket of pale pique edged in lace scallops and tied extravagantly at the neck, waist, and wrists by royal blue satin ribbons. Elizabeth, I realized, was a remarkably pretty girl and certainly knew how to gown herself to remind gentlemen of that fact by wearing a rosewood and cream-plaid wool gown with a broad girlish sash at the waist. A wide white collar at the neck and deep cuffs on the sleeves added a casual air. Perhaps even I had been elevated to a higher level of attractiveness by the showier surrounding flowers. My day gown was of saffron-colored jersey trimmed with neat pleats, innumerable tiny buttons, and copper-colored cord at neck, waist, and bodice.

At any rate, Mr. Stoker blushed and bowed as if he had never spent half his life in the company of glamorous women of the theater.

Perhaps my "catching" him in the bordello two evenings ago had made him too conscious of the presence of any kind of women, even respectable women such as ourselves. Mostly. He must not have encountered Miss Pink at the place, for he treated her with the courtesy a well-bred girl deserved.

Yet there was an undeniable nervousness in his manner, and he seemed to tilt like a top first to one of us, then another, as if we all were at once equally irresistible and intimidating.

How strange to see such a man of the world off-balance. I could now understand why Irene insisted on my presence while banishing Elizabeth, who excused herself and departed the room even as I entertained the thought. I, like she, had met him years ago, when he was closer to thirty than to forty and he was not yet the world traveler and raconteur. We would be able to judge any change in his manner or personality.

A new thought hit me like a hod carrier's barrow: as a theatrical manager Bram Stoker kept late and unaccountable hours. Could he be a candidate for the work of the Whitechapel Ripper? If he was a worthy suspect here—and the Paris police apparently thought he was—he would be a suspect there, however unlikely.

I sat at the large round table that had so recently supported pages of lurid drawings and speculations, where Mr. Stoker had so recently advanced to take my hand while avoiding my eyes. I remembered Mr. Holmes's comment that suspicion of the Ripper murders had emigrated into the middle and even to the upper classes. I also recalled his reluctance to let his physician friend join the hunt for fear he would be mistaken for the hunted simply because he had surgical skills. If even Sherlock Holmes felt incapable of defending his closest associate from the taint of suspicion, the net must have been flung far wider than the public had heard.

And if *any*one could be the Ripper, then *every*one was suspect.

"That is an inspired idea, Irene!"

Bram, impresario that he was, had forgotten all recent awkwardness in his enthusiasm.

He sat on the edge of the petite French chair, Irene's big basso perched on Miss Muffet's tuffet, as his large hands smacked his knees with enthusiasm. "It would travel anywhere, such a production, and you would, of course, change gowns with each queen, so it would be quite a fashion parade, which the ladies like. And, in your case, the gentlemen could not help but like it as well. The key is the composer. English, naturally. Perhaps even Sullivan. He fidgets to escape the confines of ditties. Such an enterprise would go over very well in America. Your being a native returning from triumph in Europe would sell newspapers like candy. I heartily endorse the idea, and will do all I can to encourage and promote it."

"I am delighted, and grateful," Irene said, "but I cannot begin immediately. First I must investigate a small matter for an eminent client here in Paris."

"You still supplement your income with private inquiry assignments? I thought you had married a successful barrister and had retired from both stage and cloak-and-dagger work."

"Once a singer, always a singer," Irene said lightly, forbearing to add that Godfrey was a successful barrister on foreign soil only because he undertook delicate assignments involving matters that crossed borders and involved bankers and bureaucrats and aristocrats.

"I am worried," she added, "on your behalf, Bram."

Mr. Stoker's transparent expression quickly sobered into concern as she went on.

"You seem to have stepped awry of the Paris police the other night. Have their suspicions lessened?"

"Who knows?" he said uneasily, rising to pace to the window that overlooked the street, hands in his trouser pockets. "I came to Paris with Florence. She prizes the few shopping expeditions we can take together, since I am so often abroad by myself . . . with the Lyceum company of course, which is hardly by myself. She will never accompany me across the Atlantic again, not after she and Noel nearly perished in the tragedy of the steamship *Victoria* sinking. That was almost two years ago near Dieppe on her way to Paris, but she will brave the Channel and the North Sea. She has returned with Noel to Ireland. Of course I have my sister Matilde to visit here in Paris. She married a Frenchman, you know."

"No, I did not," Irene said. "No wonder you and Florence visit the City of Light so often."

"And Amsterdam and Nuremberg, too. Florence is an urban butterfly, though, and not fond of my walking tours. Those I must take on my own."

"Yes, that is right. You are quite an inveterate walker."

I recognized that Irene wished me to note down this fact, and so I did. People were used to seeing me taking notes, and used to ignoring me in Irene's presence. I recognized from long experience that Irene's most idle observations were quite the opposite.

She continued her subtle interrogation of our mutual friend, Mr. Bram Stoker.

"You must have been marooned in London last year, dear Bram, with that monumental production of *Macbeth* to stage. I hear that Irving was astounding in the role, that he portrayed the Thane of Cawdor not as an ambitious warrior, but as a craven killer. Quite a bold reinterpretation, but what else does one expect from the inventive Irving? So there you all were, cast and company, shackled to the dread Scottish play in London while Jack the Ripper, another craven killer, stalked Whitechapel."

"We hardly had time to be aware of that Whitechapel business. The play opened December 29, on the very cusp of the New Year. It cost sixty-six thousand pounds and almost a year of unremitting effort."

The sum was staggering, but Irene instantly fixed on another figure. "The twenty-ninth," she murmured, eyeing me.

Thanks to our morning of study, I recalled that the final murder attributed to Jack the Ripper occurred November 12. Bram Stoker would have been in London throughout the entire run of the Ripper's starring role on the dark stage of Whitechapel's narrow, disreputable streets. I jotted down a note to reexamine the times of the murders with the letting out of the Lyceum Theatre in mind, suppressing a small shudder of distaste. I hated suspecting someone we knew.

Irene eyed Mr. Stoker over the rim of her Meissen teacup. She had sent down for a tea table while we awaited Mr. Stoker, and now we all desultorily nibbled at tiny French appetizers and pastries. I thought guiltily of Elizabeth, sconeless in Irene's bedchamber, but it did not prevent me from trying another delicate sugared cake.

"And did the Scottish play bring any noteworthy disasters?" Irene asked.

Even such a theatrical dunce as I knew that uncanny woes so plagued various productions of *Macbeth* through the centuries that superstitious actors refused to even pronounce the name of the play backstage or in public during a run.

"Not the slightest," he said quickly, ever the proud theatrical manager, "other than a dismissive review from George Bernard Shaw, but then what would one expect from that professional curmudgeon?

"And even Shaw had to praise the scenery of our new painter, Joseph Harker. We had traveled to Scotland to research the play, and I intend to return there on a walking tour."

"Yes," said Irene with a smile. "That is your preferred method of solitary travel."

"The theatrical life puts me in the midst of what is essentially controlled pandemonium. I relish occasional solitude and exercise amid those lonely heaths and rugged headlands. Harker's gloomy set paintings of blackened Scottish castles and battlements and labyrinthine passages superbly evoked the realities of the scene. I helped him lease studio space at Her Majesty's Theatre, and Irving is set upon using him again. No, the play was an enormous, spectacular success, a fine choice to follow *Faust*. The research has even inspired me to move from writing my short tales to something a bit longer. I am finishing my first novel."

"A novel! Shall we see anything of Jack the Ripper in it?"

"Oh, my dear lady, no. I confess myself more inspired by Irving's masterful enactment of *Macbeth* than any real-life bloodshed. But there will be treasure and true love, villainy and much of the ancient superstitions of my native Ireland, and perhaps a bit of bloodshed. The public much relishes that. You may know of my latest weird tale, *The Squaw*, which features a crude American, an iron maiden, and a vengeful mother cat."

"I would not want to cross any of those," Irene said with a mock shudder, "a quintessentially crude American, a death-dealing medieval torture device, or a vengeful mother of any species. *The Squaw*. Such an American title. It sounds like something Buffalo Bill might write."

"Quite a splendid fellow. I met him on a transatlantic voyage. I entertained the passengers with a reading or two, and he read their minds."

"Buffalo Bill did a mind-reading act?" Irene was astounded into a fusillade of laughter. "It is not my impression of his expertise."

"Oh, his Wild West Show has made him an international showman. There is nothing he would do that would surprise me. Even sophisticated Paris has become enchanted with the sharpshooters and the trick riders and your Red Indians, but that is just so much showmanship, and idealizes a past fast fading. Your America is not the wilderness we Europeans and British like to think."

"No. Wilderness is fast becoming hard to find. Even those

wilds of Scotland in *Macbeth.* Perhaps the last wilderness is in our own hearts and minds."

"Truly said."

A silence followed, during which I could hear the clockwork mechanism of Irene's mind changing gears.

"I hope that we did not embarrass you with the Paris police the other night," she said, leaning forward confidentially.

"You certainly testified to my worthiness as a citizen." He glanced deferentially at me, the first time in my life anyone had done so. "Especially Miss Huxleigh. I am so dreadfully sorry to have failed to recognize you. The setting was so, so—"

"Foreign," Irene finished for him.

Mr. Stoker pushed away the delicate plate that had held the enormous quantity of sweetmeats he had consumed during our conversation. Lunch was long delayed, but he did not dare in courtesy leave until Irene released him, and she would not release him until she had wrung him of every morsel of information he had to give.

He was wise enough to sense he owed us an explanation for his presence at the house of accommodation, and wise enough to wish to avoid giving one unless forced.

"And seeing you there—" he mentioned, managing to sound as if he did not intentionally point the finger he was pointing. At us.

"I still have highly placed clients of my private inquiry work," Irene said with a frank smile. "Such clients might be concerned to have one of their own on such a scene by happenstance, as you yourself were."

He nodded soberly. "Happenstance makes cowards of us all," he paraphrased the Bard. "I, too, have eminent associates, and at times it is necessary to accompany them to . . . unsavory settings."

I breathed a sigh of relief. He implied his presence was an unpleasant accompaniment to his work. Perhaps he had even been with the Prince of Wales's party, but I dared not ask.

Nor did Irene.

Instead, she smiled with wry amusement. "Oh, yes. I recall the story being told that when you accompany Henry Irving to Paris, your first call is upon the Paris Morgue. Apparently he is much taken with the quaint French custom of dressing up the dead and putting them on display as an identifying technique."

"True. He finds the morgue the most entertaining attraction in Paris. The vast majority of the dead are not shown clothed. On the contrary. But when a child is found, or someone who might be more recognizable dressed, they are attired and propped up in chairs like living persons. Irving does not care about the costuming, or the lack of it. He is fascinated by the expressions frozen on the faces of the dead, and says that one can read an entire character from them. Afterward we go to the courts to study the expressions of the accused. He claims he can tell the guilty from the innocent." Mr. Stoker seemed pleased that the subject had moved, quite literally, from the *maison de rendezvous* to the morgue. I cannot say which I thought the more unwholesome place.

Mr. Stoker did not share my reservations. "The Paris Morgue is endlessly fascinating, like the best theatrical play, although its actors have stopped moving. Irving says it is better than a wax museum."

"And it speaks to the bloodthirstiness of the population at large," Irene mused, "nothing new to Paris or the Mob. Only a century ago Parisians were busy beheading their aristocracy. I believe that is how Madame Tussaud of Baker Street got her start as a girl, taking wax impressions of detached royal heads. The French seem far too civil to have been so savage, but then I suppose we all do."

"Seem civil? Or be savage?"

"Both, my dear Bram. Speaking of which, could you accompany Nell and me to the Paris Morgue for a viewing?"

"You wish to join the corpse parade?"

"No, we wish to see the bodies of the other night's victims."

"They will not be on display. The police know their names and are not eager to make news of these deaths public. I can introduce you to a bureaucrat or two . . . but Irene, our conversation today has ranged from creating a musical evening with the six long-dead wives of Henry VIII to visiting the dead bodies of Parisian courtesans. You seem in as blood-thirsty a mood as any Paris mob."

"Not I, but someone else. I believe that Jack the Ripper has crossed the Channel, just as we have."

His face did not so much as pale, as set like plaster. "You think so?"

"And Sherlock Holmes thinks so as well."

She knew nothing of the sort, of course, but was merely brandishing the man's name for shock value.

And it was worth much in that marketplace. This time Mr. Stoker paled visibly. "Sherlock Holmes, the consulting detective, is here? In Paris?"

Irene nodded, watching carefully and not minding if he noticed her vigilance.

"I never believed that the police might be serious in detaining me. I took it for some terribly awkward mistake."

"Perhaps it is, but the Paris police are far less likely than the London police to make 'terribly awkward' mistakes."

His eyes had widened at that "perhaps" and stayed agape.

Suddenly he ran his hands over his face. "This is dreadful. Much as it distresses me that you two ladies know of my presence in that place, if anyone else—"

"Florence," Irene was only too happy to prompt him.

"Oh, God. Florence. I beseech you—!"

"Of course, Bram." Irene leaned across the table, tapped one of his clenched fists. "I promise that I will bend all of my efforts to absolve you of any suspicion and therefore of any public embarrassment. Luckily, I am known to Inspector le Villard, who is in charge of the case. And also to Sherlock Holmes."

"Thank God!"

"Now, you must help me to help you."

"How?"

"As you are doing. Telling me things. Things you might not wish to tell me or any other."

His fist withdrew, but she clenched her own hand over it with a strength and purpose not often encountered in women.

"Sherlock Holmes is not going to solve the riddle of the Ripper," she pronounced like a doctor making a considered diagnosis. "He is a born bachelor dedicated to cerebral pursuits. What is a supreme advantage in the dismantling of a tangle of illogical events that leads to crimes of greed and vengeance is useless in deciphering a crime like these repeated Ripper slaughters. Sherlock Holmes would never be found in a house of pleasure; therefore, he will never untangle the frightening thread between pleasure and pain. And that is how these murders are sewn together.

"You are a man of the world, Bram. Further, you are a man of imagination and artistic sensibility. You know I speak the truth."

"I do not know you," he whispered, struck by her air of command and certainty.

"Men do not generally know women," she answered. "And vice versa. At least not under the strictures of our hypocritical society. But I must know what you know, and you must not be afraid to tell me."

Perhaps she had Mesmerized him, but I think only by her frankness. Certainly he was in her intellectual thrall.

Then those gentle gray eyes looked at mine as at a child's he was about to disappoint with the news that there was no Santa Claus.

"Miss Huxleigh," he began, not addressing me, but reminding Irene of my presence.

"She is my right hand. You are correct that she does not deserve to know what you can reveal, but it is necessary. And you do know what I mean, don't you? You do know that these mutilated women are not the work of a monster, but of a man, and that such brutality is not unprecedented."

He withdrew a handkerchief to wipe his brow, shielding his eyes from both of us. I put pencil tip to paper, preparing to write for my life, hoping that what I heard would not paralyze my hand.

"There was discussion at the Beefsteak Room—"

Irene's glance engaged my gaze as swiftly as a sword. "The postplay dining room at the Lyceum Theatre, where Irving's admirers congregate for celebratory dinners. All men, of course, who probably exchange tales of exploits at *maisons de rendezvous* near and far."

"How did you know?" Mr. Stoker asked.

"I am a woman of imagination and artistic sensibility," she said, smiling tightly. "Did anyone ever bring up the Whitechapel horrors and the Ripper?"

"Not directly, no. We are, ah . . . isolated from daily events there, that is the entire point. There was some discussion of a decadent writer, though. Shocked us all to the core. A German."

I scribbled as quickly as I could. I had spent so much time among the decadent French that a shocking German was a refreshing change of nationality.

"Piece of filthy philosophy. Richard von Krafft-Ebing wrote it. *Psychopathia Sexualis*. I really cannot go any farther. Read it if you must. But it discussed the need to inflict pain as pleasure. Surely the Ripper is merely mad. Demented. Imagining demons and slaying them. Excavating dead bodies as a mole might a pile of dirt."

"As gruesome as the murders and mutilations of women in Whitechapel were," Irene said slowly, "I believe that we will find that the atrocities now occurring in Paris are worse. And the only place that we will confirm my fear and conclusion is at the Paris Morgue.

"That is our next step." She stood. "Thank you for coming, Bram. Tomorrow should do for our outing. We will meet you at the morgue building behind Notre Dame cathedral at 11:00 A.M."

He nodded nervously, bowed, then collected his hat and stick from the table by the door and left without a farewell.

I had never before seen a man so anxious to leave Irene's presence.

As soon as he left, I tsked, for I was sorely disappointed in him. "These noteworthies meet at this Beefsteak Room to boast of encounters in foreign brothels."

"Think what Sir Richard Burton could contribute to such a topic," Irene said.

I found myself blushing, for mention of this daring British adventurer in foreign lands reminded me of my acquaintanceship with another Briton undercover expert, Quentin Stanhope, and I certainly did not wish to think of Quentin in terms of his acquaintance with exotic foreign brothels.

"I am shocked, nevertheless," I said. "These men whose names you and Mr. Stoker mention are the leading figures of our time, many knights of the realm, like Sir Richard Burton."

"I know better knights of the realm. And one of them is Godfrey, a knight, a prince, a king where the true lists of honor among men are read."

"Hear, hear!" I seconded.

"And it is not just wealthy and well-known patrons of brothels who should be ashamed. Those men clients in Whitechapel in all humanity should be *giving* their few pence to these women in a spirit of charity instead of extracting such tawdry exchange. I tell you, Nell, that we ourselves have more in common with the Whitechapel women than the men of the Beefsteak Room. Whether in Whitechapel or in Whitehall, the contempt these men have for these women is bottomless. And in Whitehall, at least, it is returned by the women. How different is Lillie Langtry from Liz Stride, save that she is admired for her corruption and has made some real money for her efforts? Three outrageously wealthy admirers driven into bankruptcy indeed. But this topic drives me to giving long speeches, and that doesn't work well on the stage, so why should it play any better in real life." She frowned at me. "Did you write down that name, Nell?"

"Ah . . . Langtry?"

"No. The one Bram mentioned. Krafft-Ebing. If this book is as . . . unpleasant as he hints, it may be hard to obtain. At least I read German, thank the linguistic demands of opera for that. We must visit the booksellers' stalls on the Left Bank as soon as possible, which will be tomorrow, before we meet Bram."

From Lillie Langtry and English prostitution to this German Krafft-Ebing and the Paris Morgue: I was in the mood for a good English air-clearing, head-clearing walk, but not in the decadent direction Irene so obviously intended.

23.

Deadlier than the Male

Many a young and sensitive creature . . . begs her father, husband or brother to take her to the morgue and although she lingers on the threshold a bit, and looks whiter than usual, she always finds nerve enough to enter and go through the ordeal.

—*THE LONDON MORNING ADVERTISER*

"I do not understand why we require Bram Stoker's company later," I said, as Irene and I crossed the bridge leading from Notre Dame on the Île de la Cité to the Rive Gauche, or Left Bank.

It was a cool morning. Mist hovered over the Seine like the breath of a river god, but pale sunlight brushed the tops of the chestnut trees.

"We have visited the Paris Morgue before, on our own," I added.

"I wish to see his reaction to the public viewing," Irene said, rustling along at a rapid pace.

Before we left our hotel, she had considered not wearing her usual women's dress, but concluded that since so many females attended the public viewing, the conventional was the less eye-catching attire. So her usual pale breakfast jacket had been replaced by a fitted cloak of golden brown silk grosgrain material, with figured brown velvet on pale blue satin forming the bodice, sleeves, and skirt revers. With our demure bonnets, rather than the extravagantly brimmed hats that were blooming like spring peonies on the heads of fashionable

Frenchwomen, we looked as respectable as Salvation Army ladies.

"But he has seen the display many times before," I said, "in the company of Henry Irving."

"Yes, he has seen it before, but not 'after' the murders in the rue des Moulins or 'after' the murder at the Eiffel Tower. The courtesans' identities are known, so their corpses will not be displayed, but the tower body will be on a slab, I am sure of it."

"A dead body is a dead body," I found myself saying with shocking callousness. "And if Mr. Stoker is already so familiar with corpses in the French form, I do not see why his reaction today should be any different than on any previous day. . . . Oh."

Irene stopped to confront my too-late conclusion.

"It is thought," I continued, "that a murderer cannot resist viewing his handiwork?"

"Especially when it is so conveniently laid out for him. There is virtually no risk, unless the victim's friends and family know him, and I am certain that the Ripper did not know any of his victims. The French authorities have allowed these exhibitions for almost a hundred years on the theory that every citizen should do his duty and help identify the unknown dead. They also subscribe to the notion that in cases of foul play the killer will be unable to resist joining the passing throng."

"Passing throng? How many sensation-seeking souls visit the morgue each day?"

"Hundreds, possibly thousands, depending on how sensational the deaths of those on exhibit are. The man who killed and cut his mistress in two before throwing the separate packages into the Seine, for instance, produced a swelling in visitors. Luckily, the police have kept these murders from the hands of the press so far, so the crowds will be smaller, and a suspicious party is likelier to stand out."

I walked alongside Irene on the uneven cobblestones. Ahead of us stretched the makeshift booths of the booksellers who had made this site famous for decades, and perhaps centuries. Behind us loomed that gray man-made mountain topped by gargoyles and flying buttresses, a stone spiderweb of the medieval mason's art and a palace of Roman Catholicism with all its lurid history and superstitions. Notre Dame. And between these two points, just in view as the apex of a triangle at the isle's far end, squatted the trilevel roofs of the Paris Morgue, holding not incense and Romanish ceremony, but the reek of decay and unseemly display.

This part of Paris reminded me of my more recent second visit to Prague, where Godfrey and I had explored the ancient streets of the Old Town in search of a legend made flesh, another monster that had terrified a city's entire populace. We had found him, too, and he was not what we had thought him to be. How many monsters ever were?

Such dark thoughts made me loath to delve into the musty corpses of untold volumes on open display and sale in the rows of stands before us. What monsters might we unearth while hunting a title whose very Latin mystery made it seem vile: *Psychopathia Sexualis*?

This was not a place and pursuit for the countrified likes of a Shropshire parson's daughter.

"You could perhaps make do with Mr. Stoker as an escort at the morgue," I suggested, as Irene moved into the first stand and tilted her bonneted head to read the faded gilt titles of book after book. "I am superfluous."

"Of course you are not!" She turned, one heavy volume already open in her gloved hands. "It is not just Bram's reaction I wish to gauge, but there may be other attendees who have a personal interest in the tower corpse. Then, too, I hope that we will be permitted to view the bodies from the bordello eventually, after we part with Bram."

"Is that necessary?" I asked faintly. "They are already identified, after all."

"But the nature of their death and wounds has only been determined during an autopsy." She put down the book, much disappointing the old, hairy, and pungent individual who operated the book stand.

Taking my elbow, she steered me to the walk along the river.

"You remember that it was by this very river that we saw

the body of the sailor drawn from the water?"

"I do. He was in a most unpleasant state of . . . disrepair."

"Yet had we not seen him, and not visited the body in the morgue later, we would never have known of the odd tattoo that was the key to all the events both murderous and mysterious that came after."

"That is true."

"And you must admit that we did a great deal of good by untangling that puzzle." She smiled in a way that I could only describe as conspiratorial. "You must also admit that you have learned much of Jack the Ripper through the newspapers, far more than I, and are an invaluable expert on those awful events of last autumn in London—"

I would have spoken to deny my interest and expertise, but she tightened her grip on my elbow and went on.

"A side of you I have never before seen, this secret taste for grue. And you must also admit that, years ago, when we first became associated, how you much desired to view Lillie Langtry for yourself despite much disapproving of her, in fact that your eagerness to see her was in direct proportion to your extreme disapproval of her."

"Well—"

"As you should also admit that the most improper circumstance of Quentin Stanhope's surprise escort on the long rail trip back to Paris from Prague last year was also the most welcome impropriety of your life, of which you will not tell even your dearest friend the smallest detail."

"Tell you!" I tried to wrest my elbow from her grip, but she had seized me as if I was the long-ago urchin who had sought to rob a parson's daughter. So would Fagin imprison an escaping Oliver Twist who had not surrendered all that day's beggings. "I . . . I—" I managed to twist myself free and took a firm stand. "There is nothing to tell, Irene. Nothing that you would find of any interest. It was a most . . . conventional journey. Trains, stations, endless countryside."

"Nothing? What did you talk of during all those 'conventional' days?"

"Talk of? I . . . don't remember. Exactly. And even if I did, it would be none of your business!"

"Aha! Don't remember indeed. You remember enough to plead forgetfulness. As Godfrey would say in court, I rest my case. Nell, I am not exaggerating when I say that Sherlock Holmes, for all his wiles and his astounding deductive ability, is more at sea in these affairs than you and I. Only we can stop this fiend, though it will require us to face matters that will give us nightmares for years to come. I admit that I have the edge in suspecting the wickedness of the world, but I know that you are up to whatever this murderous fiend may force us to confront. And"—she dropped her custody of my arm—"I cannot face it alone."

I would have gasped at this last admission, had I not been holding my breath through her monologue. Irene's eyes were intent upon mine, and clearer than Russian amber.

"We can go forward and cross swords with this monster who kills women in such monstrous ways, or we can retreat and leave it to the gendarmes and Sherlock Holmes, as women always have before us."

I clasped my gloved hands. It was one thing to pore over the crime sketches in the illustrated papers. It was another to confront death face to cadaverous face. I recalled Irene's nightmare, the first in my experience. She was putting the decision in my hands. It was not too late to withdraw. We could meet Bram Stoker, stroll through the macabre display as thousands did each week, then return to Neuilly to eat quiche and feed Casanova grapes.

Or we could delve into unholy books and bloody murder.

And perhaps save lives.

My fingers sought the comfort of the chatelaine in my skirt pocket, tightening on the trivial assemblage of feminine tools as if they were the keys to the kingdom, as if I were a Papist clutching my superstitious rosary beads. For the first time I saw that it was all a matter of faith, and a matter of who or what in which one put one's faith.

Since she had rescued me eight years before from the London streets, I had always put my faith in Irene. Now we were in Paris, and she was putting her faith in me.

I nodded. Grimly.

And I would so love to outwit Sherlock Holmes. Personally.

24.

Morgue Le Fey

When the slabs are empty and there is no show to see, they are apt to complain that death allowed itself an intermission that day, without thinking of their good pleasure.

—VICTOR FOURNEL

If anything would have encouraged me to reconsider my rash decision, it was the severe disapproval the booksellers exhibited on hearing the title *Psychopathia Sexualis*.

For the first time in my life, I regretted that I had learned no Latin, although I realized that the word *sexualis* had unsavory overtones that made the word *psychopathia* even more mysterious and sinister.

Finally, one of these ancients deigned to excavate a musty cardboard box at his feet. He plucked the offending volume from it like a *Bürgermeister* of Hamlin producing a dead rat.

The book itself was in surprisingly fine condition, considering the decrepit bookseller and stock.

Irene pounced on it, then read a random section. She frowned and turned a page, then another, her frown deepening.

My misgivings were immense. "Are you having difficulty reading it?" I asked.

"Yes," she said, abruptly shutting the book with a clap like small thunder. She paid a few sous for it and tucked it tight under her arm.

"I thought you could read German well."

"The typeface is one of those maddeningly intricate Germanic fonts, like reading *The Book of Kells*. I will peruse it later," she decreed. "Now, Nell, what does your lapel watch read? Heavens! Almost eleven. We must hurry across the Pont de l'Archevêché to the morgue."

As if anyone living would rush to visit the morgue.

My heart lifted to see children at play in the lovely gardens of the quai. French children are quite charming, possessed of somber, intelligent faces even in frivolous moments. English nannies were quite as much the fashion here as French maids were in London, and I breathed a sigh of pure nostalgia as we passed through the budding flowers, and the flowering buds of French family life.

I would carry this enchanting picture with me as we plunged into the hurly-burly brutality of the Paris Morgue.

Luckily, our escort was a giant of a man, and we both spotted him pacing before the main building at the same instant. But it was the building that made the deepest impression, as it had before.

The Paris Morgue was, like the French flag and the French national motto, based on a trefoil.

I knew from previous experience that the door through which the bodies came was at the rear, near the river.

The public came to pay its calls on death from the front.

And this I had never confronted. This façade was as straightforward as death: a main building and two wings in miniature of itself, each with a Greek pediment. Heavy frontal pillars reminded one of cemetery markers at military attention, and above them on the main building were inscribed the words "*Liberté, Egalité, Fraternité.*" A quantity of narrow chimneys poked up from the side building roofs like rifles on parade.

The French Revolutionary motto struck me as particularly appropriate for a holding place of the dead, for where does any of us find perfect liberty, equality, and brotherhood, save in death?

Of course the French tricolor fluttered in the wind at the center of it all.

I have been known to harbor an English prejudice or two against things French. Yet I must say that it is particularly

French, and specifically Parisian, to elevate death to the level of an exposition. On the one end of the river Seine, the Gypsy carnival of *l'Exposition universelle* transpired on the Champ de Mars under the pierced shadow of the Eiffel Tower. On this end of the river Seine, behind the Gothic bulwark of Notre Dame cathedral, this modest low building erected on a principal of three, like the Trinity, acted as mortuary, mausoleum, and public spectacle for *le tout Paris*.

The City of Light could be very dark indeed at times.

Bram Stoker spied us and hurried forward, tipping his hat as he arrived.

The crowds were quite astounding. Except for the occasional horse-drawn omnibus—high affairs with glittering wheels, the back ones much larger than the front, and curved stairs at the rear leading to the second level; how only two or three beasts could pull such dozens of passengers I have no idea—the people came on foot, though one glimpsed the sole hansom cab or bicycle among the throng.

One sees workmen in crude corduroy trousers and loose, Gypsy-like blouses. Gendarmes in taut blue jackets spangled with brass buttons in military rows. Old women carting baskets as ladies tote reticules. Children in short pants and full short skirts, charming as pastels in Montmartre. And respectable women, young girls even, dragging along reluctant male escorts as if their fathers, brothers, husbands were as good as tickets to the opera or ballet in serving as entrée to this macabre display.

"I don't know what to expect," I murmured once we three had exchanged greetings.

Mr. Stoker cleared his throat. "I have never viewed the dead with female companions. Florence, of course . . ."

Irene picked up his unspoken thought. "I recall that the drowned man you rescued in the Thames and carried home to Cheney Walk in Chelsea upset her."

"Drowned. Dead, despite my brother Thornley's best efforts to revive him. I'll never forget my brother's working over the poor sopping wretch on our dining-room table . . . Florence never forgave the dining-room table for serving as hospital bed and then, plainly, a bier. She wanted to move, and soon after we did."

"It is handy to have a brother who is a doctor," Irene commented, eyeing me significantly.

The man's words came back to haunt me: "I could not allow him to enter an arena where one with his skills was so suspect."

If Sherlock Holmes's physician friend was in danger of suspicion in Whitechapel, what about the physician brother of a gigantic man who kept ungodly hours and possibly patronized French brothels?

Could Bram Stoker have learned enough of surgery from his brother to perform the crude explorations committed upon the dead prostitutes?

And were we about to explore the Paris Morgue with the very man who had perpetrated these internationally infamous slaughters?

I saw that no matter what we saw on our visit to the morgue, the most important observation I could make would be of the behavior of our eminent guide to the horrors within.

The crowd radiated the air of a holiday expedition. I heard English chattered among the French, and saw many girls as pink-cheeked as our new acquaintance Elizabeth. Thank God that she was not with us today! Despite any sordid scenes she had seen in the *maison de rendezvous* and finally on its gruesome *siège d'amour*, this virtual zoo of death was something no young woman should experience willingly. Bram Stoker stood behind us, a hearty wall of vested English tweed I was glad to have as buttress, while we shuffled our way into the main chamber.

Five rows of people were shepherded along the glass barrier that bisected the room as neatly as a surgeon's scalpel making an incision, save this was an architectural division.

Bram . . . I mean, Mr. Stoker, had shepherded us in his own

imposing way, and we were the among the "fortunate" few who could pass with our noses right up against the glass.

I glimpsed a green curtain pulled open its full width at both extremities, and in between . . . ah, it seems an affront to commit a description of what I saw to handwriting on a page: two rows of twelve stone slabs, each surmounted by a body, naked save for a bit of loincloth.

The shock of such a sight is impossible to impart. I felt as if dashed with ice water, then consumed by fire. Was my heart beating? So strongly that it felt as if savage hands were drumming upon my skin. A roaring in my ears turned every word of French or English around me into Hungarian. My feet seemed unconnected to the floor, and my head seemed to bounce against the high ceiling.

Such nudity had only been glimpsed in paintings before, and then I had quickly glanced away. I cannot say whether the male or female form was more shocking, save that they both were white as paper. And so still. Some looked as though they could wake and walk in the next minute. Some looked as though only the undertaker's art held flesh and bone together.

And yet . . . the face and form of death was so fascinating, so horrifying, that I could not take my eyes off of them. What separated them from me? Besides glass? Minutes? More likely hours. Then days. Not long before they had stood upright, clothed, had breathed, laughed, cried, cursed. Then died. And now they lay for all to see, nothing protecting them, no one standing between them and curious strangers.

It was blasphemy to gaze upon them. It was cowardice to look away.

Irene's gloved hand squeezed my elbow.

I glanced into her eyes, so bright and animated, and read their message.

I turned my head to look up at Bram Stoker.

His face was ablaze with a look of unholy wonder, as if he read a book that had never been written before.

⚜ ⚜ ⚜

"Thank you, Bram," Irene said when we had run the gantlet of the dead. We stood on the walk outside again, and she was adjusting her gloves.

People jostled us. I smelled wet corduroy and garlic, lavender cologne. And baby's breath.

"This is all you require of me?" he asked, confused.

"Yes. Nell and I will visit Notre Dame before we meet our coachman, who will return us to our hotel. I am sure you have other sights to see."

"Yes." He sighed, frowned. "I hope this was of use to you."

"Oh, new experiences are always of use to the observant." She cocked her head like a robin inspecting a worm.

He sensed the perception behind the gesture, but not the reason for it, and shook his ruddy head. He was such a gentle bear of a man. I shuddered to think of the expression I had surprised upon his features. And yet, how did the Prince of Wales look when he demanded a woman's virtue, or he swept her from the presence of her husband? How many demons shelter inside the most respectable of us? Inside myself?

I sighed, too, as he left us.

"It is always more instructive," Irene commented dreamily, "to watch the quick than the dead." She eyed me sharply. "And how are you?"

"Shaken. I have never seen bodies so stripped of dignity. Even the most lurid sketches of the Ripper's victims were somehow less awful. Perhaps it's the lack of clothing."

"Clothing. I cannot tell you how vital clothing is, Nell. It is our carapace, our shell. I am an actress, a singer. I am considered frivolous. Yet I can tell you that costume is the shield of the soul. There, that old peddler woman. Rusty, tattered bonnet, moth-eaten shawl, clumsy shoes, and dragging skirt. She wears her heart upon her sleeve, and also her occupation and place in life. In an instant we discern her station, her history. We decide to buy a rag or two, merely in charity. We decide to ignore her, to pass her by, to forget where she may sleep tonight. Still she walks on, pushing her cart. An artist may paint her into a masterpiece, a tiny black blur in the lower right-hand corner. Or he may do a portrait and make her immortal. Anything can happen to a living creature in clothes. But dead, naked. We are abandoned. Nothing but what other people choose to give us for an epitaph. A victim. A lost soul. An unidentified body. I think that is why people come here. Oh, they think it is for curiosity, for callow sensation, but it is to remind themselves that they live, and that motion is the illusion of life and clothes are what separates them from the helplessness of death.

"Speaking of clothes, did you notice the tall, mustachioed policeman near the only figure that was covered by a sheet from ankle to chin?"

"No. But I did notice that shrouded corpse. What can be the reason for such an attack of modesty on the part of the officials?"

"Modesty, nothing. That was the young woman from the Eiffel Tower."

"Amazing! I could not see well enough in that dreary light to recognize her face."

"Neither could I. I know it is she because the sheet covers the severe injuries visited upon her by the killer. The Paris police are thorough, but they are not crude. Though they will exhibit bodies past the point of decaying, and even the modern wonders of refrigeration cannot delay mortal dissolution forever, they take care to disguise the outward signs. Nor do they reveal the brutalities done to these bodies."

"Ah. So they stationed a gendarme near the corpse to watch for a possible visit from a murderer."

"No, they did not. But Sherlock Holmes did."

"I am amazed that the Paris police would listen to even Sherlock Holmes in this matter."

"They did not, which is why he has to do it himself."

I whirled to face the exterior window, through which I could glimpse shadowy forms in motion and the visored cap of the gendarme's striking form. I took in the parallel glint of his uniform buttons and the hilt of the dashing short sword at his side.

"It cannot be."

"I think it is."

"And did he spy us?"

"Most certainly. And our companion as well."

"Do you think he spied someone else truly suspicious?"

She shrugged. "That I cannot say. How irritating that I cannot don my own disguise and follow him, but he would be gone before I could change personas and return. I am afraid that we must follow more conventional methods in this case, Nell. I will think on what to do about Mr. Sherlock Holmes."

"I am relieved to hear you relinquish these games of dress-up and subterfuge. I fear that they are more useful for confusing your friends than confounding your enemies."

"That may be," Irene said, taking my arm companionably. "Now let us stroll along the river to the cathedral. I wish to hear my footsteps echo in that sublime space, and to think of the mighty chords of music that have lifted to that stone vault over the centuries."

"I would never discourage you from entering a church, even if it be Romanish."

"And the religious environs will be a good antidote to the mortal ruins we have just seen," she added.

25.

Dancing with the Dead

Within his wild, indulgent soul, one senses a certain pure energy beneath the coarseness, saint and sinner in primal battle, Michael and Lucifer entoiled in one body, disguised as a whirling dervish.

—NOTE TO MYSELF

FROM A YELLOW BOOK

His pale eyes shine with that odd compelling light they get at times.

At such moments one forgets his less-than-humble origins, his brutish manners, even his slovenly clothing and speech.

He will take me, he says, to the ceremony. To the holy of holies in his bizarre world.

And then I remember how much of a boy he is, although he has lived as a man since he was fifteen. He has boasted of his drinking bouts then, his thefts, his village parlor tricks, his womanizing. He veers from pride in his sins to paroxysms of penitence. He has also mentioned headaches so severe they seemed to swell his brain.

It is as if two opposite persons occupy his body and mind, each striving for the upper hand. His primitive, often childlike religiosity he owes to his peasant upbringing. His lust for life, and for lust, he owes to his physical and mental stamina, more than I have ever encountered in any human, and the Ghurka of India and the whirling dervishes of Afghanistan are tireless.

I feel he will be a man of importance in some place and

time, should events fall rightly for him. The only question is will he be an influence for good or for ill? And who is to say which is which? I have danced both sides of that line so many times in my own life that the demarcation has become irrevocably blurred.

His potential fascinates me.

We speak the same language, though his usages are blunt and inelegant. We share a mother tongue, and little else.

Now that he has agreed to allow me to share in his most secret ways, he bubbles over with excitement.

I must wear a monk's robe.

A hooded cloak will do, I suggest.

No. A monk's robe only. I accede and send Charles out to procure one. I will not ask how. I never do. It suits me that my wishes are always obeyed and I do not know exactly how.

He tells me that I must hide myself and stay hidden, no matter what happens.

This has the autocratic feel of an old fairy tale, as if I would turn to stone if I disobeyed his slightest instruction, so I agree solemnly, swearing on the rough wooden crucifix he produces for the purpose, though I get a sliver in my palm that will prove almost impossible to remove later and will fester for some time.

I have gold and silver and amethyst and malachite and rock crystal crucifixes, that I have collected on my travels, but they are curiosities, and of some value, that is all. I am long past crucifixes.

But not past crucifixions.

He is as nervous as a bride, dressing in his soiled peasant blouse and loose trousers as if they were wedding regalia. I have offered him new clothing, but he is in love with his own smell, like a beast.

He adores the excesses that seep through the folds of his crude clothes.

It is a pity I am a fastidious person. Perhaps I would understand him better were I able to sink to his animal level.

But I am master, and he is beast, and we both satisfy each other enormously on our separate levels.

He makes me kneel and pray before we depart at 10:00 P.M. He pushes my hands together in the traditional steeple of prayer, wraps the tin rosary beads around them like bonds.

He swears me to the monk's robe. Swears me to silent observance, like a monk. Laughs, and then swears me to chastity and obedience.

"Poverty?" I ask.

He shakes his unkempt head. Only chastity and obedience, and only for tonight.

I admit my heart pounds. I find acceding to his wild demands a novelty. I am not used to agreeing to anyone else's wishes. I find his staring, caressing, careless pale eyes invincible. I find the impending promise of his total lack of control exciting beyond all my previous manipulations.

I am used to lurking and watching, to setting events in motion.

The events tonight, I know, will have nothing to do with what I want or wish or arrange. They will be madly random. They will be mad.

I am very excited.

He sees the anticipation in my eyes and laughs, ripping the rosary beads from my hands as if freeing me from bonds.

He is young, ignorant, crude, and no doubt crazy.

And yet he feels my equal.

What a fascinating beast.

And he is mine, as everyone else is his.

We walk. A long way. I trail him in my Gothic monk's robe.

The cobblestones are damp, and he takes the obscure ways, through narrow streets. I smell the river, moist and moribund. I smell frying sausages and the fetid gutters. I smell the damp wool of my heavy robe, the hood literally weighing my head down in a modest—holy?—position of submission, like a beast of burden.

I will be as mute as a beast tonight, no matter what happens. I swear this to myself, the only god I recognize.

My palm throbs. The sliver from the crucifix has proven stubborn, painful. I am such a good monk, I even abuse myself for the cause, for the unholy exultation in being a humble observer of life's mysteries.

When I see the wall of Notre Dame ahead of us I pause. Here I go, bowed over like Quasimodo, clothed in scratchy Holy Mother Church wool, like a walking scapular, following my Caliban of Christianity under the shadow of the most holy cathedral in Christendom . . . or fair France, at least.

For a moment my religious childhood resurrects itself. I fear bands of avenging angels come to strike the impious down . . . but those were the fairy tales, as I have often found out in later life, and the reality is the evil that men do, not the gods or angels who would stop them from evil. These are the myths.

He tugs on my deep sleeve, pulls me against a squat tangle of buildings in front of the louring church. We are alone in the universe, and his breath stinks of stale beer.

"You will say nothing from now on. When I push you back, you will stay there."

"What is this place?"

"They call this something in this city." He spits out the word "city" as if it were cursed. "In my land, we burrowed into the heartless ground below, to hold our ceremonies. Here we must make our own burrows, and we have.

"Below and hidden is our chapel," he goes on, "that we have made with our own hands and hearts." He jerks his rough-shaven chin at the towers behind us. "It is older than that whited sepulchre of stone and rich incense and corruption. Below we make our own cathedral, we call down our own God. And He comes. You will see."

I follow him into the ancient erection of stone and sour wood.

He moves through a decrepit door, and I follow. My robe catches on splinters as possessive as the grasping hands of beggars. I have never given alms.

I hear the wool shriek as I pull it free again and again, and then . . . cool underground air. We are stumbling down rough stone steps.

There is no light. I follow him by smell.

Amazing! I am used to civilized odors, and here I am tracking him like a hound. I almost laugh out loud, save he has enjoined silence.

My self has shrunk into an avid witness inside this irritating cocoon of itchy wool. I know not where I am or what will happen when we arrive there. It is delicious! What a find my winter werewolf is! If only Tiger could see me now, piercing such wilderness at the heart and soul of that most civilized of cities, *Paris, mon amour*.

I must keep myself from laughing like a hyena scenting prey.

The dark and the closeness and the mystery are intoxicating.

The steps end, and I pause.

He grabs my sleeve, pulls me forward a few steps, then thrusts me into a niche of rock.

Stones shift, tumble, and click as brittle as castanets at my feet.

"Stay!" his harsh whisper orders. "You are a statue. You are a saint. Saint . . . Eyebright."

The fact that I watch has excited him as much as it has me.

There are words for this in forbidden books, but I prefer to read the great hidebound Book of Life and Death.

I hear a bottle break, glass scattering like tinkling chimes.

A match flares in the blackness. Candle wax takes fire and melts into a holy odor. Holy order.

I am back again in the chapels of my childhood, dark-visaged madonnas seeming to change expression in a hundred dancing candle flames.

Dancing. There will be dancing.

I hear the shuffle of crude wooden soles along the path he and I have trod.

Matches spit sulphur, and flare. A Milky Way of thick, misshapen candles reveals a grotto.

I look down. The stones at my feet are skulls and leg bones.

I am crammed into an ossuary. Into a niche in an ancient catacomb. My feet trample Roman bones. No wonder he laughed and named me a saint.

I stand on the remnants of another time, deep enough into the sarcophagus of earth that I shall not be seen except as a shadow of the dead.

Around me, they assemble from who knows where? Gypsies, wanderers, peasant nomads, thousands of miles from home, from the crude bunkers dug deep into the soil of the home villages that he has told me of.

Here the earth has been moved centuries before. Here they nestle into an ancient amphitheater, a chapel where gods Roman and Christian have been worshiped in whatever way suits.

A strange sour odor of raw power fills the space.

By the many ill-smelling candles I can see that each man has brought a bottle. Bottles of all sizes and colors, crude bottles of pottery. My beast has been busy. He has jammed a tin grater into an ancient wooden pillar holding back the stone like a tree.

The men crowd around to scrape off the wax sealing their bottles on the grater edge.

And what men! Bearded and barefoot, many of them, like beasts. Clothed in shreds of denim trousers and torn shirts, their skin showing through like filthy parchment, strange shoes tied to some of their feet with mere strings.

They mob the grater, scraping their bottle tops at it, rutting stags. Red wax seals the bottles and soon coats the grater like coagulating blood.

Then one man pulls his bottle away, strikes the bottom with a single mighty blow as if he were slapping a newborn into squalling life.

A cork shoots out like a bullet, hitting the low rock ceiling.

The man's head is already tilted straight back as pure liquid fire slakes his throat and a strangely narcotic, sickly-sweet smell fills the rocky grotto.

I must grasp at the stone and bones to keep myself from swooning.

Somehow, in the excitement of opening the bottles, I had

failed to notice that women had entered the dark chapel under Notre Dame.

They wear white, which they must have donned after entering the narrow shaft into the crypt.

These are gowns with wide sleeves, almost Druidic, although these people are mountains removed from the Druids of Ireland. Colored girdles wrap their waists, and, as they circle and dance, right to left, singing, I feel as if I am watching some subterranean reflection of my beloved *ballet Russe*. There is meaning in their motion.

The men have squatted on their heels in a circle against the crudely piled stones. They drink, slap their knees, huskily cheer the dancers on.

The virginal white gowns snap back and forth as the women gyrate faster. One moment I am watching nuns, the next, nymphs. One instant vestal virgins, the next, temple prostitutes.

The men at the edges are suffering the same subdivision of the mind and perceptions.

They rise, twine amongst the whirling women, tearing off their shirts to lash them into greater speed and spinning and frenzy with fabric whips. Their heads tip up to their rampant bottles like babies' mouths to their mothers' breasts.

The air grows steamy with breath and body heat. I suffocate within my monk's robe, but dare not shed it.

The candlelight warms the women's glistening faces, which glow with fever spots.

The men dance freely among them now, my protégé everywhere, every woman's eyes and hands upon him as if he were the center of the universe.

There is no denying the frantic ecstasy of the dance. Voices lift in strange syllables. Men and women begin trembling, falling down.

On the rock-strewn floor they writhe like snakes, and like snakes bare limbs emerge . . . arms, legs, the male organ. And merge. Speaking in tongues has become speaking with tongues. They fall upon each other like wolves. It is a Roman orgy as Romans had never the imagination to mount. The air reeks with the scent of sin and salvation, liquor and burning beeswax. Ecstasy sensual and religious.

I stand in my hidden niche, behind my veil of wet wool, unseen, unsensed, untouched.

This is a dance both greater and more debased than the Gypsies'. It is a ballet of the primitive soul. The meaningless syllables echo off the bones of dead martyrs. One man stands aloof from the rest.

But he watches with fevered eyes and suddenly rips apart his trousers at the crotch.

Gaping wounds make a mask of tragedy where his sexual organs should be.

"Ecce homo!" someone cries in badly accented Latin, only one of the Babel of languages I have heard snatches of during this mad ceremony.

Behold the man. Behold the *un*manned, I think as I view the castratus. I cannot help shuddering.

The sight of his mutilation and pride in it spurs the congregation to further orgiastic fever. I hear the snap of a whip and close my eyes.

I had thought nothing was too much for me, but I have been proven wrong.

My beast has outdone himself, and me.

Anything is possible.

I grit my teeth against the sounds, the moans, the blood, the reeking fluids of all kinds, the excess, the insanity, the power, the glory.

I will wait until all is done and my beast comes to lead me home.

Then I may let myself do with him what I will.

Or not.

I am still the master, even if I only rule madness.

26.

La Mort Double

Women were the foremost in pushing to the front.
— THE LONDON MORNING ADVERTISER

FROM A JOURNAL

Luckily, I sleep very lightly.

When I heard a creak in the main room, I rose from my bed and crept out, drawing the privacy curtains gently open so that the rings didn't scrape the rods.

Imagine my fright to glimpse a dark-trousered figure moving stealthily through the chamber in the dim light from the windows.

Though we had retired early upon Irene's suggestion, I had been restless and far from ready for sleep. The report she and Nell made on the Paris Morgue drove me to distraction and frustration. How unkind of them to exclude me from such a fascinating expedition! No amount of Nell's bemoaning the dreadful pathos of the scene could quench my curiosity. I was beginning to regret joining them, and was ready to bolt. I am used to being on my own. I am used to leading, rather than following.

Now I might have to take the lead in confronting a burglar, with no weapon to hand but my own wits.

Usually I relied upon those innocuous modern accessories which the wise woman realizes are also her best defense: an umbrella and a hatpin.

One may walk the streets in any quarter of the world so

accoutered and be ready for all that circumstance and the minds of evil men may throw at her.

Alas, one's nightclothes do not call for either accessory, so my mind rummaged wildly for a domestic equivalent. The only item that sprang to mind, and hand, was a bronze lamp on a nearby end table.

This I seized, prepared to do battle, and accidentally disturbed some knickknack on the table beside it, causing a sharp scrape across the marble top.

The figure became a statue. While my eyes were still trying to realign its position in the room, a leather-gloved hand tightened like a manacle around my wrist that held the lamp.

"*Shhh!*" a voice ordered my ear. "You will wake Nell."

The hand that had custody of my wrist reversed my direction and dragged me back into the privacy of my sleeping alcove. Once there, the unlit lamp was removed from my grip and placed atop a bureau.

My curtains were not drawn so tight as those in the outer room so I could plainly recognize Irene Adler Norton despite the men's dress she wore.

"Mrs. Norton! Irene."

She moved to draw the curtains behind us shut, then put her arms akimbo on her hips to regard me as a French nanny might a misbehaving child or an errant poodle.

"What am I to do with you, Miss Pink?" she demanded.

"Where are you going?" I demanded back in the same urgent, hushed tone.

"None of your business."

"I'm afraid it is, now that I've caught you sneaking out of your own rooms at some dreadful hour."

"It is only eleven o'clock."

"Where are you going?"

"Perhaps I have an assignation."

"Not to hear Nell tell of your devotion to the devilishly attractive yet sainted Godfrey. I am most eager to meet such a paradox."

"When did you have occasion to hear of Godfrey?"

"When I spared a moment to listen to your friend, who is not a bit shy in praising her associates and damning mine."

"Really." Silence stepped between us. Finally, she said, "You are not who you pretend to be."

"I suppose so. But you often masquerade as who you are not. What is the difference?"

"The difference is that I have worked as a private inquiry agent, and you have not."

"No, I have not done that. Yet."

"Nell was right to call you a minx."

"I accept the title with pride."

"You will keep silent about this evening's expedition."

"Yes. If I also go."

She breathed out an expletive that was muffled by her vocal intensity. I believe it was French. "You have no idea where I go, to do what."

"That is why it will be a terrific adventure."

"I am not taking Nell, who has accompanied me into a crypt beneath Prague and into the presence of two drowned men. Why should I take you?"

"Because I have found you out and must be silenced?" I inquired innocently. I can still produce a girlish tone. It is my third most effective weapon.

"An impudent minx."

"Thank you."

"You are not dressed for it."

"Tell me what to wear?"

"Your darkest, most nondescript clothing. Something in which you could pass as Nell."

"I have just the thing in wool plaid, a very muted charcoal-and-tan plaid."

"Very well. Be fast about it."

She left me then, for the other room, leaving me to hook myself into my corsets and boots unaided. My fingers flew through the arduous tasks, while my heart beat with triumph. I was sure that Irene Adler Norton was going somewhere that no decent woman would visit at this hour. And she had planned to go *alone*. What a woman!

Were there more like her, my job would be so much easier.

I slipped into the outer chamber, where she awaited me at the door. I noticed then that the curtains had been pulled and pinned closed, to keep the light at bay. She had planned this expedition down to the smallest detail.

Except for my restless mind and keen ears.

Once we were in the hotel passage she led me to the rear servants' stairs.

"Soften your steps," she advised me sternly.

Indeed, the servants' stairs were uncarpeted, so we tiptoed down their endless turns like naughty children. At last we exited into the night, onto damp cobblestones and into a cool mist.

"Where are we going?" I dared to ask when we were a distance from the hotel and I saw her raise a cane to hail a cab on the main boulevard.

With her high top hat and muffling scarf, not to mention movements that were uncannily masculine, we had suddenly become a Parisian couple on the way home from the theater or opera or ballet.

"Someplace your bloodthirsty American soul will treasure," she answered gruffly, in a voice alarmingly male. "The Paris Morgue."

I allowed her to assist me into the hesitating hansom, my heart pounding like a debutante's. The Paris Morgue. Was there ever such a thrilling destination for a not-so-innocent American abroad?

My struggles to survive in America had taught me the pointless scrabble to earn a few dollars through hard labor. I used to call myself "little orphan girl," even though my poor widowed mother was alive. In fact, I had supported her from a very young age. During my sojourn as a factory girl, I learned that the only light in such drudgery was the delusion of "catching a mash." Many a working girl met a man on the streetcar and accompanied him to a bar, got drunk, and had a great "fall," only to repeat the pointless recreational round the next weekend. Having no money left one at the mercy of others' charity. I myself almost lost my tonsils for no reason in a hospital charity ward. I enjoyed more comfortable living conditions during a stay in the Magdalen Home for Unfortunate—fallen—Women, but no freedom. In the French *maison*, although some, including Miss Nell, may consider my role sordid, there was not only comfort, but pretty clothes and superb food on top of it. Now that I had been "reformed" by Irene, I slept in a first-class hotel and met famous men. I also was privileged to join the hunt for the kind of beast not merely content to buy women's virtue, but compelled to brutalize their bodies for the mere sin of needing to survive as best their skills and society would let them. I took the atrocities of Jack the Ripper very personally indeed.

Notre Dame was a mountainous silhouette against the electrically lit mists that wafted from the river Seine. Gas and electric lighting now mingled on the Paris streets as the newer form overtook the old. We were set down beside its stone bulk on Irene's command, and walked to the Île de la Cité's end to enter the Paris Morgue by its rear, riverward door.

My escort was as commanding as any man. Mention of an Inspector le Villard's name spurred a bored but officious lemming of a guard to scurry off in search of an even more offensive bureaucrat.

He came, a monocle in one eye, wearing a rusty black suit.

"Madame Norton. They said your visit would be unconventional."

When Irene nodded, he eyed me.

"My secretary, Miss Huxleigh," she said.

On cue, I dug into my skirt pocket to produce the notebook and pencil that are ever my companions, proud that my own natural impulses made me a perfect substitute for the absent Nell. The thought of that worthy but innocent woman's name made me almost chuckle, save that a morgue is not a fit place for chuckles. Hysterical laughter, perhaps, but not chuckles.

The official lifted the eyebrow that was not engaged in scowling to hold the monocle in place.

"I cannot, unfortunately, show you the bodies of the two *filles de joie*."

Filles de joie. Girls of joy. For whom? Not for themselves, certainly.

Irene's expression was hardening into protest when the man spoke further.

"The gendarmes and surgeons had finished their inspections, and we could not hold them from their families and a decent burial any longer. However, the woman from the Eiffel tower is unclaimed, and you may see her. The sight is gruesome," he added, smiling like a sadistic stork.

Irene nodded, looking resigned.

He led us through a series of clammy rooms.

"Electrically powered refrigeration," Irene whispered in my ear, her words icy. Despite the artificial chill, Death's foul breath tainted the air.

Finally, we stopped outside an ajar door. Inside I saw a small bare chamber. Upon a stone slab lay a naked woman.

I had expected to see death. To see naked death.

I had not expected the vicious assault of those conditions on my senses.

The river roared in my ears like an ocean. The floor heaved and swayed beneath my feet. Irene's hand clawed into my forearm, whether to brace me or herself, I cannot say.

Monsieur Bureaucrat melted like paint in my vision and wavered like a raindrop on a pane of glass as he left us to our macabre mission.

"You have influence with the Prefecture," I said, concentrating on the minutiae so the grosser facts of our surroundings should not overwhelm me.

"Not much," she said tightly. Her eyes met mine. "You are a woman of the world."

"Miss Huxleigh, Nell, is rather more unworldly, I think."

"You are right. I cannot subject her to what we will see here. She has more strength than is apparent, but I am unwilling to disillusion her of certain civilities."

"She has an unsuspected taste for the Gothic, you know."

"I know." Irene pushed aside her dark muffler and smiled. "But this is more than Gothic. It would make sense only to a worldly woman, and you are that, are you not?"

"Of course," I said. It was true. I had seen much that most women had never suspected. But I had also done less than one might imagine.

Irene Adler Norton's remarkable brown-gold eyes seemed to burn like the electric lamp outside the primitive chamber as they measured the truth and the misrepresentations that have always been twin aspects of my soul.

"You may wish this revelation, Pink, but I am responsible for your presence. Can you withstand this?"

"I don't know. I can try."

"Honestly said." She took a deep breath, one so deep that I thought it would never end. "The refrigeration process eliminates much that is unpleasant, and therefore real. We will not need Nell's smelling salts here. Would that there were as useful a defense for the sense of sight."

She took my wrist again, gently. "You have some knowledge of Jack the Ripper. I have greater knowledge. I have riffled through an entire chapbook of Jack the Rippers, and anything we may imagine about him and his ghoulish pursuits and ghastly killings is insufficient. I believe the wounds upon these women are fouler than anything anyone might have imagined about Whitechapel, than anyone might suspect.

"We have the privilege to see the truth, to face it, and to try to stop the evil that kills so vilely. I have decided that you can survive what would drive most women mad, and many men. Can you?"

"I . . . don't know."

"The truth, Pink? At last?"

"The truth at last."

I swallowed. I had vowed to see life in all its ugliness. I had given myself up to witness what most people hoped never to meet in even their nightmares. Irene Adler Norton was offering me a new variety of nightmare, and I realized that we both would never be the same if we met it face-to-face.

But what is the use of living, if one cannot face death?

I squared my shoulders, a fruitless gesture, and nodded to the chamber awaiting us. To the naked woman who would never feel the chill of the Paris Morgue's marvelous refrigeration system.

Would that I were not chilled to the bone and the soul myself.

Irene turned to enter the room, and I followed.

Just as I had when I discovered the bodies in the *maison de rendezvous*, I forced myself to study the larger surroundings before I let my eyes dwell on the object of our pity and horror.

The smallness and meanness of the viewing chamber struck me first. An arched ceiling made it seem like a tunnel, or a crypt or a wine cellar, save that the walls and ceiling were whitewashed to a deathly pallor.

The black bar of a wooden rail sat high on one wall, and from a series of iron hooks articles of the victim's dress dangled like clothes on a macabre washline. High-button shoes as well as limp stockings, grimy bloomers, petticoat and apron, striped bodice and mended jacket hung from the long line of hooks. To see one woman's entire habiliment strung out like this was both chilling and pathetic. The mottled brown-red on the bloomers and corset cover looked at first glance like some overblown floral fabric until one realized that blood had been the dye.

There was only the faintest putrid odor. I was glad no man was here to see me shiver from the cold, from the room's centerpiece that finally became the only thing I had not studied.

The body lay on a stone bier, a slab perhaps two feet high from the floor, on its back, a dingy linen cloth draped from shoulders to knees.

Her face was pale, as I had expected. I had not expected it to look so ordinary, to seem so capable of animating in an instant, the eyes opening, the lips parting, vision and breath restored . . . stirring to acknowledge my presence.

She was neither particularly pretty nor plain. Her face was framed by brown hair pulled back without the relief of softening curls.

The dark line at the base of her neck resembled a fine cord from which perhaps some trinket had hung. It took an act of will to see it for the thin chasm between life and death drawn by a fine steel blade.

"Throat cut, as with the Ripper," Irene said.

I realized that she had been studying me as I observed the room and its occupant.

"It looks so . . . clean," I said.

"They have washed away the blood for photographs, no doubt. I wonder how much they washed the face."

"Why?"

"She does not look like a woman of the streets, but rather a laundress or some other toiler. A prostitute would have used cheap paints, and I'd think the morgue authorities would leave them in place if they wished her to be identified."

"You are saying they don't wish her to be identified?"

"I am saying I would like to know if her face was ever painted or not. And men are so strange about such matters. They might have cleaned her face in an attempt to give her the dignity owed the dead, never realizing they were washing away the chief means of recognizing her. If she was a prostitute and if she wore paint."

"What of the . . . wounds."

She nodded at the linen that seemed to dissect the body into a magician's illusion of a sawed-in-half lady: the dead white feet and lower limbs, the bare shoulders, neck, and head.

Who had sawed her unseen in half, and how?

Irene bent over to lift up the top of the linen covering.

I curled my gloved fingers into my palms until I felt a dull fire like invisible reins being wrenched from my grasp.

I heard a strangled moan. Mine. This woman had no breasts, merely gaping holes where slick underlying tissue showed through.

I imagined the medical men and police investigators who had seen these mutilations wincing at the sheer savagery of the wounds, despite their endless exposure to the worst that may be done to the human body.

Still, only a woman could feel such personal devastation at seeing a portion so unique to her sex hacked away.

For some reason my mind went to the corset with its trailing gray laces hung above her head, to the roses of blood blooming along its upper edge, smearing the limp corset cover.

Had she survived these injuries, these items would be an empty mockery of her woman's dress.

Irene's face was frozen into an expression of utter self-control. She glanced at me as if judging my own command of myself, then let the linen down so gently it settled back on the abused body like the mistiest veiling.

Her hand moved to the bottom edge, then her eyes consulted me. Last, she consulted me vocally.

"Are you able to continue?"

"No such choice was given her. Yes."

Her glance was already on the linen she lifted.

This violation of privacy was really too much to bear. I reminded myself that doctors had stood here in this morgue building and done as much, and more. That male attendants had. That we were women and looking on one of our own, for the purpose of preserving others of our own.

Still . . . the linen lifted up, and I moved beside Irene so I saw what she saw.

She captured a deep breath and held it. Held it so long that I wondered if she would ever exhale again. I certainly had seemed to stop breathing altogether. My head grew . . . giddy. The clothing rack was pushing nearer and retreating like a weapon, its few empty hooks seeming to strike at my eyes. Strike my eyes blind from what they had seen . . .

"The injuries appear to be external," Irene said at last, having drawn on her indrawn breath to speak.

I felt my eyelids flutter and dug my gloved fingernails deeper into the flesh of my palms.

"This is very strange, Nell," she went on, her voice sounding hollow in my ears, and then fading.

I was unable to react, not even to her calling me by the wrong name.

Her sudden grasp dug into my elbow. "Don't swoon; there is no place to sit down here, except the slab, no place to lie down, except the floor."

I lowered and shook my head, waved the buzzing phalanx of flies from my ears, grasped hard on to Irene's wrist with one hand.

"Think of the larger picture," she urged me. "What this means. This woman's private parts have been . . . not surgically removed, but hacked off. The rest of the body is untouched, except for some bruising. There are no entrails, no slashing of the eyes. Why has the Ripper changed? The London victims were cut internally. I suspect if we get honest answers about the women on the rue des Moulins, they were treated similarly."

The thought that such terrible mutilations lurked under that bloody froth of lace and silk on the Prince of Wales's *siège d'amour* was almost enough to tip me over into the swoon of the century.

But then I reflected that I was privileged—yes, privileged—to know and confront such things so that perhaps other women in this city would not have to do so. And I took a deep breath, surprised that the thick metallic reek of blood did not dominate the air, that although I felt hideously hot, as if incarcerated in the lowest circle of hell, the room was actually chilly. That the flies had buzzed away, that I still stood upright, and that the linen was falling like a curtain to obscure the dreadful wound.

"Did you expect this?" I asked Irene.

"I expected carnage. Not this. We have been indeed drawn into something unique in the history of inhumanity."

"She *was* killed first, as the Ripper's victims, and carved up later?"

"I am not sure." Irene sounded as troubled as I had ever heard her. "I am not sure of that at all."

If I had been disposed to faint, then is when I would have had full title to the state. But it was too late; I had drawn again upon my eternal resolve that nothing in life, or death, should abash me. I would be permitted no merciful moments of forgetfulness tonight, or ever after.

This is the terrible drawback of wishing to be a woman of the world.

27.

The Skull Beneath the Skin

The horrid fascination which the morgue has for the female mind, both foreign and native, is one of those phenomena which observers note in going through life, but cannot understand.

—*THE LONDON MORNING ADVERTISER*

FROM A JOURNAL

Side by side, we leaned against the wall outside the chamber many minutes later, its cold leaching the warmth from our bodies, unable to move except in our minds.

"So nothing in the London crimes was as horrific as what was done to that woman in there?" Irene asked.

I stirred against the wall, which was as cold and hard as a stone slab. I felt emptied, emotionless, like a vertical corpse, as I considered the hard facts of so many deaths in a not-so-long-ago London.

"There, I did not see for myself. But from what I have heard, the acts were more in the nature of sheer butchery, like some autopsy gone terribly wrong or performed by an ape. This is pure, premeditated defacement and mutilation, and to me even more horrific."

"I was right to spare Nell this, then. Was I right to think that you could better face it?"

"It is not the sheer gore, Irene, but the nature of these attacks. They have become more—"

"More difficult for women to face. Yet the throat is cut in every case."

"In London, at least, it was a mercy cutting. All the butchery took place afterward."

Irene nodded. "Jack the Ripper was a monster, but he performed his most monstrous acts on dead women. Believe it or not, this is not unheard of. If he has truly relocated to Paris, he has grown crueler. I am not a surgeon, but the mutilations performed on this woman, and perhaps the other two, would seem to have been made prior to, or simultaneous with, death."

I bit my lip and took a breath as deep as those Irene had practiced this night to calm her emotions. "While the London Ripper attacked the internal organs, the Paris Ripper has become more superficial. The breasts hacked off, and what was done between their legs . . ."

Irene nodded, as if to stop my description. "The areas violated are so specifically female, sites of both pleasure and pain in a woman, a mother."

"That is it! He attacks the maternal apparatus."

"Or what is most female in a woman, before she becomes a mother, and after. Many of the Whitechapel victims were mothers, but not Mary Jane Kelly?"

"No. You're right."

"She was the youngest, and most attractive??"

"Lordy, yes." My voice broke despite my best efforts. She had been only twenty-five, my own exact age. I gritted my teeth and stuck to what had always saved me from the warm, oozing trap of sentimentality: the cold facts. "The others were missing teeth and showed twenty more years' wear and tear, but still one of them could take pleasure in 'a jolly bonnet,' for all the threadbare desperation of her life. Except for Catharine Eddowes. She sounded almost pretty, with her auburn hair and hazel eyes. She even dressed with style, a black jacket with false fur at collar and cuffs, and a bonnet trimmed with green-and-black velvet and black beads. It sounded much 'jollier' than Mary Ann Nichol's bonnet."

"And yet she was the most savagely attacked thus far, the next-to-last victim before Mary Jane Kelly. And didn't Catharine Eddowes use the name Mary *Ann* Kelly when she was arrested?"

"Yes. She lived with a man named Kelly."

"And an earlier victim was named Mary Ann?"

"The first. Mary Ann Nichols. You think that the killer was confused by the victim's name? That he was searching for a particular woman, and when he found her, his rampage ended?"

"I don't know. Hearing the details of the Ripper's crimes and victims is like listening to a satanic symphony. There are movements and themes, motifs and reprises, but still the Devil is conducting the orchestra, and we must dance to his demented tune."

She pushed herself away from the wall, forcing her backbone to support her on its own. "I have a devil's dictionary back at our hotel that I will share with you. You will learn what I have: that such crimes, such atrocities, are not uncommon, though not commonly made public. Not even the vile Ripper letter talking about eating the victim's kidney. 'It was very good,' I believe he said. Even that has precedent."

She moved down the passage, but I caught her coat sleeve in my hand.

"Mrs. Norton. Irene. You have not asked why or how I know so much of the London crimes."

Her eyes regarded me with almost childlike clarity. "You were banished to your room to study Nell's and the Rothschild newspapers and the police reports, while she and I interviewed Bram Stoker. I assume you are a quick study."

It was a most generous and even disingenuous view of my role. I could not let it stand.

"I went to London. To see the world. And to work in a West End establishment. It was quite nice, actually. I thought that we were a world away from the 'abyss,' which is how Jack London, the American author, described London's East End not long ago. Yet we girls were all . . . riveted by the Whitechapel murders. We were so far away from, so far above those sad East End prostitutes, safe and well clothed, warm and even paid decently, but—"

"You were just as susceptible." She brushed off my hand,

not with distaste but with true disinterest in my role as a professional fallen woman, in even the details of that life which I confessed. "I don't think that Jack the Ripper is so much 'down on whores' as that he knows the rest of the world is, and that therefore they are helpless targets for his inhuman appetites. *Jack l'Eventreur*, the French call him, and now they have him in their midst."

"You believe it is the same man?"

"I believe it is the same mania." She consulted a pocket watch on a chain. "It is late. We must hurry back to the hotel. Soon hansoms will not stop for even respectably clad clients."

With that she wound the scarf over her lower face, donned her top hat, and offered me her arm.

How very odd. I have always considered myself an independent and typically American woman, needing no man's gentlemanly escort. Yet I was very glad to have this particular woman in man's guise accompanying me back to the life and lights of our hotel, especially after what we had seen.

The guard nodded brusquely at us as we departed the morgue.

Outside of the building, we could hear the river Seine lapping at the stone embankments like a huge invisible cat consuming cream.

The towers of Notre Dame snagged fast-flying clouds.

We walked along the Seine, alone with the fog that the river exhaled like fine veiling. Streetlights spangled the distance like stars. Such beauty, such peace ahead of us, and behind us, ruin.

I would have to revisit the *maison* to discover the names, ages, habits, and heights of the dead women. Irene's musical mind was struggling to discern a design in the madness, and I saw now that even the most aberrant acts of human nature must hide some unseen pattern.

Our footsteps pattered like slow-tempo sleet on the stones along the river. Andante, andante.

We spoke not a word. Every four steps, Irene's walking stick would strike the stones. Rather like the triangle in an orchestra, a tiny sound lost in the vastness of the night, yet as regular as rain or a ringing mantel clock.

The shuffle of other shoes came in our train as we neared the pierced, clifflike ramparts of Notre Dame.

"I feel a sudden need for religious observance," Irene whispered. "Quick! Into Holy Mother Church."

She steered me through a side entrance into the grande dame of Gothic cathedrals.

I was not so sure we were seeking shelter. Oh, it was dark inside, save for a tiny red gleam of a vigil light in the distant sanctuary, like a rat's eye in the dark, and the mass of lit candles before the statues of the saints.

Scents of liquid beeswax and charred wicks filled my nostrils, along with the slightly stale yet peppery miasma of incense that had lofted into this soaring nave for more than seven hundred years.

Irene was pulling me down the side aisle.

Our footsteps sounded like tocsins, and behind them came other steps.

She guided me toward the great front entrance, where we slipped through a small door in the massive façade. Ancient but squat outbuildings clustered, an architectural mob, in the open area before the cathedral's front doors.

Irene took my wrist and pulled me toward the shadowy mass.

At that moment a squeal like a pig erupted from the very buildings we ran toward. A sleet of stone fragments blasted my right cheek.

"A bullet," she said in a deep hush, thrusting her cane into my free hand. "It's a sword-stick. Pull the cane top free if you need to use it. Hurry. In here."

She pushed forward on the first bit of wall that collapsed and proved itself a door. We moved into absolute interior darkness.

My gloved hand lifted the decorated cane top and I heard the metallic slither of a blade pulling free of a sheath, a harsh, sharp sound that challenged the darkness and silence all around us.

"Where are we?" I whispered.

"Inside, away from whoever's shooting at us. That's all I know." She prodded me forward into unknown territory.

Our feet and hands and bodies collided with unknown shapes and borders in the dark, but none of them was animate. The smell was dank and musty. Despite our slow, painful progress, we made no racket, although we heard muffled banging at the fringes of the compound.

Still Irene pulled and pushed me forward. A piece of wall gave way again, and I found my boots stuttering down some narrow, swaybacked stone stairs.

Immediately I was struck by two conflicting sensations: the chill breath of an underground draft, and the scent of warm wax. That heavenly odor mixes with the incense that perfumes the wooden pulpits and altarpieces of the great cathedrals of Europe and England and for me embodies the notion of the Old World.

"Hurry," Irene whispered. "This time we may not be too late."

I rushed after her as instructed, not sure that I wished to be in time for what lay ahead.

Then my sense of enterprise banished all dread. This is what I had come to the Old World for: utter immersion in its secrets.

Our boots ground on sand and cinders tracked in from the streets. Others had been here before us. Spirits had not lit those candles.

Not that my sensible American skepticism had ever for a moment believed in spirits. . . .

We were feeling our way through the dark. When an exhalation of even colder air opened before us like a kind of well, we both stopped as if teetering on the edge of an abyss.

I heard the rustle of Irene's clothing, then a scratch as a tiny lucifer flame burst forth like a firework for Lilliputians.

"There! Fetch that candle stub."

I spotted the pale fat cylinder on the damp ground, running to claim it before her match should burn out.

I spun to return to her just as the small light winked out.

The wax in my hand was chillingly . . . warm.

A scratch and flare later I was able to make my way to her; although half-lit, she resembled a melodrama Mephistopheles, the tall top hat adding horned inches to her height.

She held the sputtering match to the curled wick atop the candle stub. It caught fire begrudgingly, as if exhausted from its previous night's work. The result was a feeble fog of light that clung more to us than illuminated anything else.

"Look." Irene began a tour of the roughly circular space into which worn stones tumbled. She bent to hold the light over the uneven earthen floor. "More wax droppings. A great many candles were used here, but they were taken away again."

She moved away, then lifted the candle close to a wall half dirt and half stone bricks, frowning at what she saw.

I came to peer over her shoulder. "Red candle wax? As if someone moved a candle so quickly the liquid wax drops hit the stone."

"Blood," she declared, "but almost lashed toward the wall, as you describe."

"Was someone killed here then?"

"I don't know. I do not smell the great quantity of blood we detected at the bordello. The candle wax and something else outweigh it."

"Wine?"

"No, something more acrid, harsher."

Irene had continued her inspection of the space's perimeter, stepping into the next unknown swath of dark as fearlessly as a soldier marching toward an enemy.

I was glad to let her lead, which was hardly typical of me, but it shows in what thrall her daring spirit held me. This was a woman who could act as well as masquerade as a man.

As she swept the candle lower against the wall, I thrilled to see that her left hand held a pistol. The sight almost made me wish that I had become a Pinkerton, rather than choosing the profession I had fallen back upon.

But circumstances circumscribe all our fates. I was here because of the choices I had made, and I would not now be anywhere else for a mogul's ransom, flying bullets among the flying buttresses or not!

"Broken glass again," she noted, scraping her boot sole over the ground. "But no scent or stain of wine. Oddly disturbing."

"This is not a wine cellar," I pointed out.

Her expression sharpened in the candlelight. "Very good, Pink! The wine only reflects the setting of the first murder, nothing else. It was at hand. And the Eiffel Tower excavation site could have attracted sots who left empty wine bottles. Here . . ."

She moved suddenly close to the wall. I gasped as her candle seemed to illuminate a standing, skeletal figure.

"A tunnel?" I asked.

"A niche." Her voice was hushed with wonder.

I edged nearer. If skeletal guardians did not alarm her, they should not deter me.

Then I saw that the skull, the long leg and arm bones, were jumbled into impossible physiognomies. Were these dry old bones in proper conjunction, we would indeed be facing a monster. But this was a polymorph, a monster formed of many individual's bones.

"This is a catacomb, Pink," Irene said in some wonder. "We may even be gazing upon the jumbled schemata of ancient Romans perhaps, or even more likely, of early Christians. We must be under the cathedral. This must be an ancient crypt upon which it was built."

"Do the authorities not know about this place?"

"Probably not, but someone else does, and has appropriated it for some very strange purpose." Irene suddenly shook the hand holding the candle, sending a sinuous lash of melted wax against the niche wall. The pattern was exactly like the red spray she had identified as blood.

"The candle stub grows too hot to hold," she said. "We must find the exit tunnel and venture into the streets again."

"What of our pursuer?"

"Perhaps he has tired of the chase." She smiled grimly at me over the fading flicker of the candle flame. "Perhaps we shall meet him coming as we are going. We will worry about that when we face it. For now I thank our mysterious pursuer for introducing us to the mysteries of below ground."

She had taken my elbow and steered me unerringly toward the dark mouth of the passage that had led us here.

The candle died just as we reached that uncertain exit.

I heard the stub hit the ground with a hollow sound, as if something living had just had the breath knocked out of it.

"I will go first," Irene whispered in the utter dark. "I have the pistol, after all."

28.

A Werewolf in London

I go into a case to help the ends of justice and the work of the police.

—SHERLOCK HOLMES

I glanced at my companions over breakfast in our common room the next morning.

Both Irene and Elizabeth were bleary-eyed and, what is worse, were uneager to meet my gaze. There is nothing more annoying than aroused suspicions with no evidence to use as a pry bar.

I drummed my fingers on the tablecloth and accepted only muffins although Irene had ordered every hearty English breakfast item, including eggs, bacon, sausage, button mushrooms, baked beans, and something that passed for black pudding, especially in my honor.

"We must advance events," Irene declared while she shared a pot of vile coffee with Elizabeth.

I sipped my tea deliberately.

"Nell, you are just the person to do it."

I sputtered into my Earl Grey. "And how am I to 'advance events'? I am absolutely in the dark regarding these repulsive crimes."

Irene beamed at me over her coffee cup. "Exactly why you

will go to Sherlock Holmes and throw yourself upon his superior intellectual skills."

"I will not! They are not!"

She clapped her hands together, in the thrall of a new idea.

"This is inspired. You will bring all your annotated evidence to the Sage of Baker Street. Except he is residing . . . where? Probably at the Bristol so as to be near the Prince. It is imperative that you distract him while I follow my own line of investigation."

"With Elizabeth?" I asked pointedly.

"Possibly. But the more important assignment will be yours. Only a keen and subtle mind will distract the great detective. Yes, it must be you! Remember, every moment you mislead him, you will be aiding me and these poor dead women. The case darkens. If you had seen the state of the last victim, laid out at the morgue under her concealing sheet. Imagine what the linens hid?"

Irene managed an artistic shudder which echoed an internal horror that was not feigned. Much as my dear friend loved to dramatize situations, the impulse beneath her surface mastery was always serious. And sincere.

I looked into her eyes. Their expression was both quizzical and hopeful.

I folded my napkin and tossed it upon a French croissant of exceptionally flaky crust, redolent of fresh butter. So I must sacrifice my better nature to consort with the consulting detective.

Yet better that *I* spend time in his presence than my poor ignorant friend, usually so perceptive, but now so utterly unaware in what inappropriate regard that man held her.

"I must share my observations with him?" I asked, hoping she would say no.

"But of course. That is the lure. He is quite lost in certain, very key respects, you know."

"I know." I rose from the table. "I hope you realize what an imposition this is. And I hope that you will follow only such paths as Godfrey would approve in your own investigations."

"Of course, Nell. Only what Godfrey would approve." She

lifted a hand to heart, then covered it with her other hand.

The specter of a dimple beside of her not-quite-smiling mouth made me suspect that Godfrey would approve of a great deal that I would not.

I have always loved Dickens's *A Tale of Two Cities,* so perhaps it is no surprise that I found myself in the self-sacrificial role of Sydney Carton, deposited by a horse omnibus at the door of the Hotel Bristol, prepared to surrender myself to Sherlock Holmes.

I mean that solely in the military sense, of course.

And indeed, I chose to imagine myself as Quentin Stanhope, Cobra by code name, engaged on a mission of espionage.

I hesitated, but gave my true name at the reception desk, and was summarily informed that no Sherlock Holmes was a guest there.

Well.

I turned to face the bustling lobby, crowned by glittering chandeliers above and thronged by the cream of society below.

My palms grew clammy and dampened my dark cotton gloves.

What was I to do? Stymied from the outset. What would I tell Irene?

That *the* man was invisible? That I could not find him?

Never.

I marched away from the desk with the gilt pigeonholed temple of numbered guest-room niches looming behind it.

Not wishing to appear at a loss, I swept up the marble stairs to the first floor. There I could gather myself. What an expression, as if I were a length of fabric that would come unraveled if not neatly stitched together. I resolved not to fray no matter the circumstances.

I moved toward the place where the odious elevated car could be caught on the ground floor.

A drawn grating announced that I could submit to its incarceration here as well.

So. I would take it to the floor and to the room where Irene and I had been entertained by the Invisible Mr. Sherlock Holmes not two days ago.

Naturally such a course was most improper.

But. Who was here to see it?

I squared my shoulders and pressed my gloved forefinger on the mother-of-pearl button that summoned the elevator car.

At least it had a uniformed operator who did not look askance at me. Apparently hotels patronized by the Prince of Wales were used to unaccompanied females.

Imagine! I was taken for a fallen woman. What a relief. There is some consolation in not having to live up to oneself.

At the fifth floor I dismounted, if that is the proper expression, and proceeded to the room I remembered.

I was startled to hear unearthly wails and screams coming faintly from beyond the heavy wooden door. When they continued beyond what even the most sorely tried human lungs could sustain, I realized that the sounds were vaguely predictable, and even abominably musical. A bagpipe? No. A violin belabored by one possessed. Although the violin may in the upper registers, under the fingers of a maestro, produce a high, keening beauty that is impossible to deny, it is more often a hoarse, rasping instrument that teeters closely to the screech of a wood saw.

This was the side of the instrument I detected through the muffling services of the door. How I was to compete with the whining instrument in announcing my presence I had no idea.

No bell was provided, so I lifted my parasol handle and rapped as forcefully as I could.

The caterwauling continued. So our black cat Lucifer had sounded on those nights when his lady friends were not in evidence. At last there was a pause in the day's apparent occupation, and, after a welcome silence, I raised my gloved fist high to knock even harder, when the door flew open.

My gesture rapped at empty air, and almost struck the impressive beak God had granted to Mr. Sherlock Holmes, consulting detective.

"Oh! You startled me," I accused.

"You knocked," he riposted.

"I beg your pardon," I breathed in automatic apology.

"And I yours. Miss . . . Huxleigh?"

I had the rare satisfaction of viewing utter stupefaction on the face of the world's wisest detective.

"What on earth are you doing here?" he asked.

"Can't you deduce it?" I asked in return.

My question appeared to revive his usual overweening descriptive prowess.

"I see you have been opportuned to come here," he pronounced crisply. "You were suborned at breakfast, and departed in obedience but in a temper. You almost turned away at the front desk, but after fleeing the lobby for the mezzanine, you decided to continue. You dislike living in France, but then you would dislike living anywhere. Your father was a country parson, but has died. You are farsighted, detest luxury, and me."

"Impressive," I said icily. "May I come in?" I was of course violating every convention, but better I be sacrificed on the altar of impropriety than Irene.

He laughed, once and sharply, standing back from the door. "And you are an emissary from the alarmingly engaging Madam Irene, who no doubt has her higher purpose for both of us lesser beings."

"Really! You admit that you are a lesser being in relation to another?"

"I am the most humble of men, Miss Huxleigh," he said with a smile and bow, "unless I am in the presence of those who do not practice humility."

"Hmmph. That is good. Irene wishes you to be informed of my notes and drawings taken from the murder scene at the *maison de rendezvous*. I can't say that I approve."

"Neither do I," he said promptly. "And you seldom approve of much," he suggested with a raised eyebrow.

"Perhaps you would explain your litany of presumptions about me. Not that they are correct."

He nodded, pulling out a chair by a square card table for me.

"Your reluctance to be here is obvious in your attitude. I apologize that I can offer nothing more concrete than that observation. Sometimes mere observation is so obvious, but no less true for that. There is a bit of relatively fresh scrambled egg on your sleeve, which implies breakfast. Your boot laces are tied low on the ankle rather than being hooked all the way to the top, which I saw when you lifted your skirts to cross the threshold. Both imply haste, which implies temper. Your left sleeve has picked up a bit of streaked penmanship from the hotel register, which means that you visited the reception desk, but left in confusion, no doubt because I am not registered under my name here.

"I notice that your hem has gathered some of the Turkey carpet fibers in the intense colors used on the hotel mezzanine, which implies that you walked up to the mezzanine, which implies distress and also a fear of elevator cars. The fact that all your clothes and accessories are of English manufacture reveals that you dislike living in France, despite having resided here for many months, as I know from my own encounters with your friend Miss Irene Adler in London's Serpentine Mews before the entire household's hasty decampment. If you dislike France, the belle of foreign cities, you would dislike anywhere. Your father was a country parson, evident from the portfolio you carry, a cheap leatherlike affair much favored in the outlands of England. His death is evident in your black gloves, quite unfashionable, except for mourning. I suspect that they are your last, but lifelong concession to his passing. They also are practical and do not show dirt. I notice the impression on the bridge of your rather Roman nose made by a pince-nez, but it is faint, so you are farsighted. Your entire appearance declares your detestation of luxury, and the fact that you wish you had announced yourself on my nose betrays your opinion of me. Any questions? No. Then perhaps you may proceed to your spurious reason for being here."

"I do not dissemble."

"No?" he added. "Are you truly eager to share the contents of your case with me?"

"Not really. But Irene has insisted."

"She is nigh impossible to resist, I imagine."

"Let that idea remain your imagination."

"Indeed it shall. You will find me most resistant to feminine wiles, Miss Huxleigh, not that you have any."

"Ah. At last. An impressive presumption." I laid my portfolio on the table. In fact, it was French-made Moroccan leather, an artist's dossier, and the only luxury I had allowed myself to purchase in the City of Light. It amused me that Sherlock Holmes had so soundly attributed it to my late father. Perhaps he could not imagine a woman purchasing a case for work.

Mr. Holmes undid the ties with his storklike fingers. What an Ichabod Crane of a man he was, ungainly yet secretly aspiring to a woman well beyond his reach. I glanced around, looking for the vile instrument, but saw no sign of a bow or violin. He must have been playing in the bedchamber. I quickly banished both bedchamber and violin from my mind.

At first glance of my sketches he drew back, braced his face on his lean, steepled hands, and lifted an eyebrow.

"*Your* sketch work?"

"Of course. Irene depends upon me."

"So I understand." A smile quirked his thin lips. "As I depend upon Watson."

"The good doctor no doubt means well." Certainly I had him to thank for my insight into the consulting detective's unnatural interest in Irene. "Why is he not here?"

"Have you forgotten my remark that a doctor in Whitechapel would have fallen under instant suspicion?"

"Of course not. I forget nothing, because I write it all down afterward. But, unlike the London constabulary, the French police are not blaming these latest atrocities on someone with surgical skill."

"That is correct." He gazed aside, as if protecting my eyes from what his had seen. "The injuries are not so . . . surgical here. The body organs are not . . . excavated as they were in Whitechapel."

He glanced at me through slitted, wary eyes, like Lucifer. I meant the cat, of course, not the Archangel of Darkness.

"You are aware of the injuries that have been perpetrated here?"

"Of course," I said boldly. If I did not say too much, and listened well, I might leave here knowing more. "Quite distasteful."

His fingers drummed the tablecloth. I was disconcerted to encounter a habit I had thought of as Adlerian in a Sherlockian form. They had nothing in common, these two, but a natural rivalry, as a cat and dog. Naturally Irene was the elegant, pristine, and enigmatic cat, and Mr. Holmes was the slobbering, noisy hound with distasteful personal habits.

"I suppose Watson could have come," he said out of the blue with a trace of wistfulness, "but I had been sworn to secrecy by one so highly placed that even faithful old Watson was not allowed." His look sharpened itself on me like a razor on a strop. "Do you and your operatic adventuress have any idea what eminent personages would be outraged by your meddling in these frightful murders?"

"I am sure not," I admitted, "but we have a highly placed clientele of our own to answer to."

"Really?" He sat forward. "I will soon know whom, although I suspect already. I do not doubt that both our sponsors are concerned for similar, but perhaps not mutually inclusive reasons. Serving the mighty is always a difficult business. They expect loyalty, but are congenitally incapable of giving it, as your friend discovered with the King of Bohemia. So. She still insists in dabbling in private matters rather than sharing her magnificent vocal gifts with the world, does she?"

"She has a long history of private inquiry work, perhaps as long your own, beginning with the Pinkertons in America. That she should be sought out by persons of influence is not unlikely. As for 'dabbling,' is not your own investigative work a personal following rather than any official position? I would dare to say you also are a 'dabbler.' "

"I would much like to see you and good old Watson go head-to-head on this topic, Miss Huxleigh. I am not sure which of you would be the more vigorous in defense of your companion."

"I do not believe that I would ever care to engage in anything you would like to see, Mr. Holmes. As for Irene neglecting her vocal gifts, that is a true profession, almost nigh to a religious vocation, and a very demanding one. The operatic stage would consume all her energy and time, which is no longer possible now that she has been forced to live anonymously for some months, thanks to you and the King of Bohemia!"

"That may be, but she forgave him. Perhaps she can forgive me."

"I doubt it. Certainly I cannot."

He thrust a thumb into his waistcoat pocket as he settled into argument with familiar relish. I had the oddest notion that I was providing him with a favorite exercise. "Is it the events of last spring that have interrupted her operatic career, or her marriage to Godfrey Norton?"

"Godfrey encourages her to continue a stage career! How can you suggest otherwise?"

"He encourages her. Then he is more than a pretty face, I see. No doubt he is a forward-thinking man when it comes to women. To employ a typewriter-girl such as yourself at his office at the Temple, after all, was quite bold for these times."

"My employment was more a tribute to Godfrey's kindness than his boldness, but he is not lacking in manly strength both physical and mental. I have never known a gentleman of such rare qualities: noble, wise, and yes, possessed of such chivalry toward women as only a knight of the Round Table could practice, especially in these latter days."

"Rare indeed to encounter such sterling testimony anywhere other than beside St. Peter's gatepost in Heaven. Given the man's virtues, it is a wonder that you did not yourself marry the gentleman."

"That is an outrageous suggestion, sir! Godfrey would never encourage such a notion, and it is unthinkable that an orphaned parson's daughter should even dream of committing her mind and heart so far above her station."

"Yet a disgraced opera singer was not beneath his station?"

"There is no disgrace in expecting better of people than

they are able to be. With the King you had a man who would have immured Irene away from her profession for his own convenience. With Godfrey, you have a man who encourages her to restitch the shreds of her career."

"Why does she require encouraging? Perhaps she no longer wishes to devote long hours to practice, rehearsal, and performance now that domestic bliss has become her lot. I presume that her hasty marriage has led to domestic bliss."

"Hasty only because of your foul subterfuges on the behalf of that miserable Bohemian royal person! She was denied a proper wedding ceremony, with friends and, er, friends present only because you were harrying her for the photograph of herself and the King. That photograph, I'll have you know, was taken at the *King*'s insistence. She kept it solely as a reminder of her misplaced loyalty. Only his guilty conscience made him fear that she might reveal evidence of their past association to doom his royal wedding to the unfortunate Clotilde."

"She never harbored ill feeling toward the King?"

"Quite the contrary. She was delighted to discover in the nick of time that he would cast aside true sentiment for a loveless aristocratic marriage, that he would further offend all reason by expecting her to enter into an alliance without honor."

"How was such an honorable woman misled by him in the first place?"

"You did not see them together, Mr. Holmes. He was the picture of devotion. Any woman might have expected such attentions to be purely honorable."

"Any woman, yes! But we are talking about a woman of unsurpassing wit, possessed of angelic talent. Why did she for a moment allow herself to be taken in by the then Crown Prince of Bohemia? It is not reasonable."

He was by then sitting forward, interrogating me like a barrister with a prisoner in the box.

I took a deep breath. How cleverly he had goaded and maneuvered me into presenting an apologia for Irene. In my zeal to defend my friend, I had revealed far more about her history and present life than I would wish the likes of Sherlock Holmes to know.

As I stared into his clear, gray eyes, afire with the heat of argument, I realized that I had fallen completely into his trap.

"Reasonable, Mr. Holmes?" I allowed my own temper and vocal tone to cool. "Human beings do not perform according to the syllogisms of logic, although consulting detectives may. If you have to ask these questions, you would never understand the answers. You may have an admirable mind, but you have no heart, so there will be some mysteries that all your reasoning and deduction and investigation will never solve."

He sat back, winded as if he had run a race against an invisible opponent. I could hardly dare think it was I. In fact, I believe that he was engaging Irene in some way, through me, humble substitute though I was. My own breath came irregularly. Odd how mental differences could excite the emotions.

When he spoke again, his voice was sharp, cool, and aloof.

"I agree that we do not speak the same language. Now. Show me your schoolroom sketches, Miss Huxleigh. I gather that you were sent here as a diversion. Then, divert me." His expression implied that very little in life, or even death, did.

"I do not claim to be an artist," I said briskly, "but I try to be at least accurate." I fanned a card hand of five sketches from between the covers of my case. "The murder chamber at the *maison de rendezvous* had a central carpet with an unusual black background. It took tracks very well, almost like fresh soil, Mr. Holmes, so I copied them and then enlarged the original drawings to match the measurements I made."

"Measurements! Tracks! On your knees in that chamber of horrors drawing footprints!" His voice rang with triumph, but his avid gaze was on my poor "schoolroom" drawings. "You are an unexpected form of bloodhound, Miss Huxleigh," he murmured. "As it happens, I consider footprints the keystone to the art of detection, especially if they maybe preserved. I have written a small monograph called 'The Tracing of Footsteps, with some Remarks upon the Uses of Plaster of Paris as a Preserver of Impresses.' Plaster of Paris is really gypsum, as you may or may not know, and great quantities of it underlie the granite that supports the city, which is why it is called plaster of Paris. As for my monograph, le Villard is translating it into French so that the police of this city will also find good use for their Paris plaster. Was it he who directed your attention to the footprints?"

As usual, he had prefaced the question he wanted answered with a great deal of superfluous details, the better to wear down his victims.

"Alas, no," I was happy to say. "Irene herself pointed out that the black background of the rug would take impressions, as black velvet will show fingerprints at the least provocation, which any woman who has worn such a fabric would know instantly."

"Indeed. My experience of black velvet has been confined to curtains, which are made of much sturdier stuff than gowns and far less subject to impressions. I am disappointed that le Villard missed this most interesting element. The fools! The entire Paris Prefecture had trampled that carpet before le Villard could stop them and I arrived from England. I did examine it, but by then it had been trampled into the chaos of a rugby field.

"I am most intrigued to learn what footprints were discernible to a fresh eye on the scene," he added as his long fingers pulled more of my recently disdained sketches into view with the almost-trembling reverence owed to lost Rembrandt studies. "And when did you and your friend set dainty foot on the scene?"

"Within three to five hours, I would think."

His forefinger speared one drawing to the tabletop. "I saw some female boot prints, but this first sketch is the boot of an early official on the scene, I think. Not le Villard. He has studied my methods and knows better than to tread so openly on the surrounding ground. But his hands—and feet, in this instance—were tied. This?" He held up another sketch.

"The first to discover the deaths. A Miss Pink. It is an evening slipper."

"I am familiar with Miss Pink and both her slippers." He sat back, patting his pockets for something. "What do you think of her?"

"I? You wish to know what I think? I thought it was your job to do all the thinking."

"Indeed. But you were there first. I am always interested in the testimony of witnesses. They often see more than they know."

"I know what I saw. Miss Pink is a brash American girl who finds it a lark to lead a scandalous life. She seems to have come from a moderately respectable family, save for a villainous stepfather, so I cannot imagine why she would wish to follow such a sordid course, of her own free will, it seems."

"She is indeed a puzzle, Miss Pink, but her presence on the murder scene is purely coincidental. And this?"

"The workman's boot. I cannot say how, or when it got there. Unless—"

"Unless?"

I hesitated. His energetic interrogation had surprised an unwelcome thought from my mind. I wished to share it only with Irene, but she was off on mysterious errands with Elizabeth. How much had she failed to share with me?

"*Unless*, Miss Huxleigh? Come. You are a moderately acute observer. Such treasures must be shared."

Moderately acute! Schoolroom sketches, indeed! "*Unless*, Mr. Holmes, the piece of furniture upon which the two women died had only *that day* been imported to the chamber, specifically for the er, occasion that was to follow. At least one workman would be needed to install it."

His trespassing fingers crawled under the folder of my case to withdraw my sketch of the exotic two-tier sofa in question.

"A workman or two." He gazed at the article I had so painstakingly sketched. "I confess that I do miss Watson. He would have more personal knowledge of such matters."

I recalled reading the secret text in Dr. Watson's London office months ago, in which this more worldly friend assessed Sherlock Holmes as an inhuman thinking machine, immune to any emotion, even the love between man and woman. Did this also exempt him from the lust that rules so many men? If a man without love for women could still lust, might he not also be able to kill?

"That is to your credit," I found myself saying, to my horror, referring to his admitted ignorance of the bordello world compared to his physician friend. "Not his." How galling to have to approve of anything about Mr. Sherlock Holmes, who already approved of himself so very much.

The look he gave this speech was icy and imperious enough to stop an Attila in mid-gallop. Luckily, I am an English parson's daughter, and less impressionable than a Hun.

"I have been much disappointed in the Prince of Wales, as a result of these events," I said stoutly. "It matters not the high position one occupies, but rather the high ideals with which one pursues life."

"And death," he added, referring to the crimes that had brought us together. "Knowledge, Miss Huxleigh," he went on sternly, "is always superior to ignorance, however obtained. I agree with you, though, that the less one is subject to the intemperate passions, the more completely one may serve such higher ends as science, intellect, and the battle against those evil souls among us who ruin lives and disrupt society and murder if they must."

"Really? You agree with me? And who are these evil souls whom you suspect of being the Ripper?"

"Only on the issue that there are men among us so intent on wreaking evil that they must be stopped, whatever the cost to ourselves." He lifted my sketch of the odious chair. "Even if it means knowing the purpose of this."

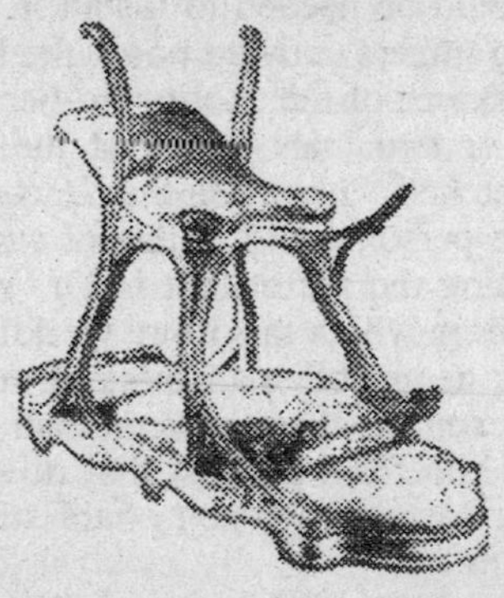

"Quite," I said hastily. Although I did not quite know the purpose of the demonic barber's chair, I was sure it was nasty.

He gazed at my sketch without seeing it, then stood. "I believe you have actually been of some small use. You may tell Madam Irene that I thank you for bringing your sketches."

I stood as well, sweeping my meager offerings back into their container. "I may tell her, and I may not. I am not a flunky. For her, or for you, sir."

"I am sorry. There is no time for amenities." He stood. "And now, if you will excuse me, I have much work to do."

I prepared to leave that suite, despite gathering up my sketches like an art student welcomed with one hand and dismissed with the other by a self-centered maestro, and with the uncomfortable feeling that I may have innocently given him the secret to the Unfinished Symphony.

Then I stopped.

"You have not mentioned suspects, sir. Surely the world's foremost consulting detective must have some suspicions along that line."

"You want suspects, Miss Huxleigh?" He began ushering me toward the door, all the while spewing a macabre patter that would have done credit to a Gilbert and Sullivan operetta, were they working in a ghoulish vein.

"There are more suspects for the murders attributed to this unimaginative butcher who calls himself Jack the Ripper than there are notes in a symphony.

"There are laborers and lunatics. Leather Apron, as one man was described, has been a favorite. He does indeed seem a figure made to inspire the fear of children and readers of sensational newspapers. Then there are the usual suspicious 'foreigners,' in this case Jews and Poles and Russians. Immigrant peasants from eastern Europe flood the East End, irritating the native citizens and bringing with them alien customs that are subject to the worst interpretations. So we have shoemakers and ritual slaughterers among the possibilities. Some suspects have links to America, and Russia. And France.

"Then there are the usual suspects beloved of the police whenever anything explicable transpires of the violently criminal sort: religious zealots against sin in the streets, and recently released lunatics.

"In this case, there is the thrilling possibility that we are dealing with a rogue physician or an otherwise medically linked individual, in other words, with a person of some education and skill, who would not usually be suspected of such crude murders.

"Taking this thrilling supposition further, whispers abound against persons far more elevated than mere doctors, those not only of the aristocracy, but of royal blood."

I tsked, for I liked to think that royal blood deserved its obeisance. Then I thought of Bertie and his table, sofa—what had Irene called it?—*siège d'amour*, and remembered the rumors about his son.

"The royals are not always as admirable as they could be," I admitted with some distaste.

"No doubt you learned that during your association with the King of Bohemia," he put in. "I have had the honor to be called upon by the members of many royal families, Miss Huxleigh, in the course of my cases. Some are admirable, and some are not. In this they are not very much different from the usual run of humanity.

"But back to the identity of the gentleman called the Ripper. I admit that I cannot conceive of why he should dismember so many harmless, hapless creatures of the Whitechapel night. It is as if his acts were made to order for the sensational newspapers. There is no reason but unreason in them, and when I find him I am sure to have in my hands a hopeless lunatic who is as pathctic as his victims.

"But as to which hopeless lunatic . . . the witness's testimony is annoyingly inconsistent. According to their breathless statements, he is a man of forty, just over five feet tall, dark-complected, looking and sounding like a foreigner, and of shabby genteel appearance. Leather Apron himself was a Jewish slipper maker, some four inches over five feet, with dark hair and mustache. After undergoing fierce questioning he proved to have an unbreakable alibi and was released and dismissed as a 'crazy Jew.'

"Then the police called for witnesses to the Whitechapel

presence of a man of thirty-seven, who was seven inches above five feet, with a dark beard, mustache, jacket, vest, trousers, scarf, and hat. And a foreign accent.

"Elizabeth Stride was seen before her death in the company of man of five-foot-five, smartly dressed in a black hat and morning coat, mind you. Less than an hour later, a witness saw her with a man of five-foot-six, dressed as a clerk in a cutaway coat and trousers, middle-aged, stout, and clean-shaven!

"And within half an hour or so, she was seen elsewhere with a man police constables described as eight-and-twenty and five-foot-six with a dark complexion and small mustache. He wore a black diagonal cutaway coat, white collar and tie, a hard felt hat, and carried a newspaper-wrapped parcel."

"Oh, Mr. Holmes! It is so like a scene from *Alice in Wonderland*," I couldn't help remarking. "So sinisterly strange, like the Walrus and Carpenter leading the poor oysters off to being eaten. And the men's descriptions are oddly different, yet so much the same all along."

"It gets curiouser and curiouser yet." His keen gray eyes were actually twinkling. I saw that, like Irene, he appreciated—no, needed—a rapt audience, even of one, to rise to his best level. "Bear with me, Miss Huxleigh."

While he was enjoying confounding me, I was enjoying even more receiving this flood of information to tell Irene. I only hoped I could tally these details with the reports in the papers to provide a better picture.

"The key witness in this case is a man named Israel Schwartz," he went on. "He is lucky not to have been suspected, but his testimony was so intriguing that he escaped the suspicion usually attached to those of his race in Whitechapel. Fifteen minutes after the previous witness, he saw a woman he identified from the corpse as Elizabeth Stride talking to a man in Berner Street. A man five-foot-five, thirty years old, with a fair complexion—"

"Fair!" I cried out.

"Exactly, the first such description. Dark hair, small brown mustache—"

"Brown!"

"Indeed. Full face and broad shoulders. He wore the ubiquitous dark jacket and trousers, and a cap with a peak. He tried to pull the woman down in the street but she escaped, though he threw her to the ground. She screamed several times, but not loudly."

My heart was beating. I was down on the cold, damp ground, the breath knocked out of me so I could only whimper protest.

"While this was happening Schwartz noticed a man standing on the opposite side of the street. This man was five-foot-eleven—"

"A veritable giant," I couldn't help remarking.

Sherlock Holmes frowned at me for interrupting his narrative. He seemed to be forced to relay the incident, as if his own mind had replayed it over and over, like a scene from a play. "The man who had thrown Elizabeth Stride to the ground called out "Lipski" to the taller man across the street. Schwartz thought he was alerting an accomplice to his presence and ran away. But he said no one followed him."

"Oh. It sounds like a melodrama."

"So the papers thought," Holmes said sardonically. "Take into account that about at the same time a dock laborer named James Brown saw a man and woman at Fairclough Street, near Berner. The woman was backed against the wall, the man bent over her, arm raised. This man was five-foot-seven, stout, and wearing a long dark overcoat.

"Fifteen minutes later, Brown reached home to hear cries of 'Police!' and 'Murder!' This was the same time that Louis Diemshutz, a Russian Jew and jewelry salesman, found his faithful pony shying as he directed it into the Berner Street yard. He saw a bundle on the ground, then saw enough to know what he saw. He raced away to alert others. When the police came, she was still warm."

I shuddered. "I remember reading about that gruesome discovery. The pony must have sensed death, and his master was convinced that the murderer was still on the scene as he discovered it. This madman must have a gift for invisibility, or for changing his appearance."

"And witnesses are like clouds that obscure the moon.

Their perceptions shift and so does the image of the murderer. This case has suffered from having many times more suspected killers than victims. The police have never been at a loss for likely suspects."

His face momentarily reflected their level of torment and frustration. Then his expression shifted as he regarded me with some amusement.

"That is enough to keep you writing in your diary for some time. Good day, Miss Huxleigh. Thank you for your most interesting visit. It has been bracing to acquaint you with the whole pilgrim's chorus full of suspects. And then, of course, if you are still hunting the most likely *un*likely suspect, I beg you to remember that there is always your very humble servant, me."

He drew the door shut upon me as I stood gaping in the passage.

29.

Lost Soul

Another mania is his need for movement, motion, the Romany love of traveling. He claims epic journeys by foot in his yet-young life. Even in Paris he may suddenly rise and go, heedless of anything but wandering for hours or days. One feels he could wander for months or years.

—NOTE TO MYSELF

FROM A YELLOW BOOK

He has left the hotel.

I discovered this on waking.

He never liked sleeping under plasterwork.

Frantic, I struck out alone into the Paris morning.

Where would a wolf in human clothing go?

Odd, that this creature so sublimely gifted to protect himself in the most primitive of conditions should be so vulnerable in this most civilized of cities.

Yet I felt this was true, with my very marrow.

I surprised myself. I resembled like an unlikely mother bear whose cub had strayed from the den.

I paced, I searched, I cried to Heaven with gritted fangs. My wandering cub, so strong, so weak. Nothing must hurt him.

I have nothing parental in my soul, which makes this furious panic all the more unlikely.

The business of Paris bustled all around me: concierges were sweeping off stoops and caroling greetings to beggars and breadsellers alike. Horse omnibuses were thronging the streets, pausing to deposit passengers and offal.

Where? *Where*?

Then I knew. I altered course, walked briskly toward the river. Only one site in Paris spoke to his divided soul. Only one site married the sacred and the profane so necessary to his continued existence.

As I walked, I realized that I had finally put my thoughts in tune with the beast. I could never lose him, because at last I was coming to understand him, at last I was beginning to think—no, to feel—like him.

The sense of boundless power was as intoxicating as absinthe, as opium. As insanity.

At last I was as worthy to unleash this beast as to hold him at bay.

30.
Jack L'Eventreur

However, the cerebral anomalies claim the principal interest, since they very frequently lead to the commission of perverse and even criminal acts.

—RICHARD VON KRAFFT-EBING, *PSYCHOPATHIA SEXUALIS*

FROM A JOURNAL

"Here, Pink."

Irene Adler Norton had emerged from her bedchamber with a heavy step and matching expression. Our breakfast table, already cleared by the hotel staff, was bare except for a Belgian lace cloth.

On that elegant surface she laid a volume so slim compared to most that I took it for a book of poetry.

I reached for it, but her hand claimed its closed cover in warning. "This is a dangerous book."

I could only imagine the most lurid possibility. "It contains witchcraft?"

My answer softened her stern expression into a faint smile. "Don't we all wish that life was so simple? That we could encounter Macbeth's three witches and hear our futures foretold? No, this book contains great evil, but nothing that is the least bit supernatural. I almost wish that it was."

At that she drew out a side chair to sit at the table. I examined her face closely.

"Did you send Miss Huxleigh . . . Nell, on an errand so you could show me this book confidentially?"

She hesitated in answering. Her mood held the same sober air of concentration I had noticed last night when, having viewed the anonymous body found near the Eiffel Tower, we stood outside the examining room at the Paris Morgue. This was a woman of unsurpassed vitality and finesse, but in this moment and that one, she was so subdued that I sensed a much deeper vein to her character.

This confused me. I had never before met a woman I so admired, or so wished to be like. Yet at this moment, I realized that I did not know her at all. I wondered if anybody truly did.

And, of course, I was positively itchy with envy. Why wasn't *I* worth diverting to such an enthralling errand as meeting with the renowned and most superior Sherlock Holmes, of attempting to outfox Sherlock Holmes himself? Surely I would be more up to the job than dear but sadly sheltered Miss Penelope Huxleigh! In a strange way I resented Irene's instinct to protect her English friend. On the other hand, I would never have been admitted as easily to the Paris Morgue without Irene's connections, though I would have managed it somehow on my own eventually. I have never failed to cross any barrier, however forbidden.

"Miss Pink," Irene said at last with a sigh, employing the name as a good rider uses a crop on a horse: barely touching the twitchy hide and yet getting a finer performance with that delicate goad than from all the harsh blows such beasts of burden have suffered through human history.

Oh, she is formidable, in ways I can barely yet imagine!

"You recognize the extravagantly vile wounds that were inflicted on that poor woman," she went on, her voice as slow and soft as a lullaby. Again, her unnatural containment warned me that we were in deep waters. "We have been privileged to know the worst, which is denied to most women—for their own good, we are told. Now you must know more, and know worse. We cannot continue without your reading that book. Do you wish to, after what we have seen?"

I am used to rushing into situations and seeking answers, then calculating the consequences afterward. Irene's somber tone and expression made such behavior seem hopelessly shallow.

I reflected. My headlong race toward knowing life in all its beauty and ugliness had brought me to this place and this moment. No doubt it came from being on my own at an early age. Although my wits were quick, there was so little that girls or women were expected or allowed to do once they had lost the protection of a father or a husband. This had forced me to plunge down avenues most women would cringe from. There I discovered an unexpected freedom and the means to support myself without eternal servitude in the factories or shops.

Now I was poised to learn even more of what most women never suspected and far more than many men knew. Did I want to?

Yes. I glanced at the battered and mottled posterboard surface guarded by Irene's graceful fingers. They never fell into a position that did not look as if she was about to execute a Chopin polonaise on a Biedermeier piano.

Pure evil, she said, lay beneath her lightly balanced fingertips. Evil ready to rush through the portal of my eyes and suffuse my mind. I had seen so much, why should I not know more? Not for me the glaring innocence that shrouded Nell's perceptions like a floor-length bridal veil! I reached for the book, and Irene's fingers melted away at my gesture.

A sense of heady power gripped me. Opening the pages as

I pulled the book toward me, I found myself shocked sooner than I had expected to be. This devil's tome was written in German! Like most Americans, I only speak one language. Plain English and lots of it. I glanced up in confusion.

"German is not unlike English," she assured me. "Let the letters and words and imagined sounds wash through your eyes and mind. You will begin to understand words and phrases here and there. Then I will translate, so you understand entirely. It is best to approach evil edgeways, out of the corners of your eyes."

I nodded, and did as she said.

The entries were short, only a paragraph or two or three, or a page or two at most, and numbered. Yet a pattern emerged, even in the runes of a foreign language. As I began to comprehend, I came to appreciate her method of introducing me to the unthinkable. Slowly, she drew her chair nearer, until we sat side by side, elbow to elbow, like fellow students. Her forefinger touched a word. She spoke its English equivalent. The pattern became clearer and clearer. Before I knew it, I understood all.

⚜ ⚜ ⚜

I sat back. My voice came in a hush. "Your grasp of language is magical. Surely you could have . . . eased Nell into this topic?"

"Mentally, yes. In terms of her emotions, no. She is a true spinster. I am a married woman and you . . . you are a woman who has forced herself into the dark side of such matters, for reasons I find vague, but undeniable. We are women of the world."

I lowered my eyes, unwilling to object to her assessment, yet regretting it. "A spinster. It implies a busy but rather benighted creature. Will Nell never be anything more than that?"

"She has already edged well past it, though she doesn't realize it. I believe it will take the proper gentleman to correct the condition. I am not going to force her to confront things that her upbringing and nature have not prepared her for."

"We are all indeed dependent on the proper gentleman still, in this day and age, aren't we? Is that why you married Godfrey?"

Irene shrugged. "Improper gentleman are of no use to anyone but themselves. I once fancied myself as you, Pink, daring to live outside a woman's 'proper' role. My pursuit of an operatic career immediately put me into the shadowed sisterhood of women of the stage. Once everyone thinks the worst of you because you pursue what you are best at, you learn to live without needing the regard of anyone. Except yourself. That is the purest form of freedom. I did not cultivate wealthy sponsors when I sang, and I did not marry Godfrey because the state was respectable."

"Why did you marry then?"

"Because . . . he accepted me not only as I was, but as I will be."

"I doubt any man will ever accept me as I am," I said rather glumly, for I am young enough to still covet glass slippers, even though they would be terribly uncomfortable.

"Perhaps one will," she said, "when you act like yourself."

I frowned at her, tempted to ask what she meant by that, tempted to make my own confession . . . but such frankness was dangerous, given my position. She leaned across the table to pat my hand.

"As for your own path, which you seem dead set upon but not much distraught on taking at the moment, much to Nell's distress, perhaps one must meet many improper gentlemen to recognize a proper one."

I blushed. I can't help it. I have been an unabashed blusher since childhood. I have also loathed this tendency all my life, but it has proven useful despite myself. A woman who cannot blush cannot be underestimated, and being underestimated has been my greatest weapon in a world full of improper gentlemen, and far too few improper gentlewomen.

I shut the book with a thump. "One ghastly thing is clear. Jack the Ripper is no legend. He is a commonplace. A common criminal, God help us. I admit I have glimpsed his shadow before in wife-beaters and confidence men and every manner of low, lecherous man, but never in so murderous a form."

"If he is not singular, something else should be evident."

I thought. I had put a brave face on it, but reading about vicious slaughters still made me quiver deep within, especially when victim after victim was more like me than not. Irene had a point, though, and I'd be damned if I should not prove bright enough to see it.

"If he is not singular," I repeated slowly, as if it were a mathematical theorem, "there is a reason and a pattern to what he does. It is revealed in this casebook. It is that he is . . . not so singular, and therefore—if you know how to look at it—he is predictable."

"*Brava*, Pink! Everyone who has approached Jack the Ripper has elevated him to a unique position: the worst monster the world has ever seen. But he is only the *latest* monster the world has seen. Once we know that, we know that he is not invincible."

"And you think that we two . . . three women, can catch him?"

Her eyes met mine, all banter ended. "I think that we must, for no one else will."

Nell rejoined us an hour later, her key scraping at the door lock like the wild nails of an ejected poodle.

Irene threw me a look and ran to ease the door ajar.

Nell rushed into the room as swiftly as my imaginary poodle. There the resemblance ended, though her bonnet was tied slightly askew and her cheeks were painted, with either fresh air or excitement, to that cherrylike shade that had given me my childhood nickname. Her hands were bare, the mourning gloves she wore having been thrust through the ring on the chatelaine at her waist made for that purpose.

She spoke to neither of us, but bore her leatherette folio to the empty tabletop and let it fall to the surface with a huge, unseemly, un-Nell-like thump.

I had never seen her looking so attractive; she seemed ten years younger, a veritable schoolgirl.

"Oh, Irene, I have been scribbling on the omnibus all the way from the Hotel Bristol, trying to get every syllable down. Luckily my memory is excellent since my days in the Temple with Godfrey."

"Days in the Temple with Godfrey?" I asked, astounded by the phrase.

She paused in detaching the small silver notebook from her chatelaine. "Quick! I require pen, pencil, whatever!" she called almost imperiously, as she extracted her pince-nez from a small silver case on another chatelaine chain.

Irene ran to the desk beside the window while Nell opened the case and began pulling her footprint sketches onto the tabletop.

At last she looked up at me, over the schoolmarmish spectacles. "I was Godfrey's typewriter-girl in the Inner Temple for several months. That was before he had met Irene, to speak of."

"You worked in the Temple?" I could not help sounding impressed. "You must have been one of the first women so employed."

"I was the very first typewriter-girl in the Temple," she answered with precision but no special pride. "That was only because Godfrey had a very forward-looking mind and realized that the typewriter would soon become commonplace. Also, he was the only barrister who would hire me instead of a male clerk."

Irene had gone into her bedchamber in search of writing implements. Nell glanced to see if she had returned, then spoke confidentially. "Irene had her reasons for wishing to know of Godfrey's movements at the time, thinking he was involved with an investigative project of hers."

So this was not the first time Irene had sent Nell to observe someone of whom she wished to know more! And Nell as a spy—? She did not strike me as the sort who would be any good at subterfuge, but perhaps that was the point.

Irene came flying back into the room, her hand clasping a homely bouquet of pencils and pens surrounding an inkwell.

"Wonderful!" Nell glanced at me. "You have the newspaper reports of the crimes at hand?"

Now it was my turn to hasten to my trunk, where I had stored the bulky papers.

When we three had all assembled back at our round table (I was beginning to feel rather like a knight), Nell was already seated and paging through the tiny sheets in her silver-sheathed notebook.

"I take it your expedition to Mr. Holmes's hotel was profitable," Irene said as she watched her friend pull a fresh sheet of paper from her portfolio and begin copying notes from the tiny book.

"Profitable, but I did not dare make a notation in his presence. He chanted this long list of descriptions of men seen with the women killed in Whitechapel. It's clear he knows the facts backward and forward, and many things that have not been passed on in the papers.

"And he said that Ripper suspects had connections with other nations, including France. I was struck by how close, although differing, the various descriptions were. If we can list each suspect's particulars, we may create a portrait that would fit one man."

I was already shaking out the sleazy journals that documented the Whitechapel horrors in the most detail and with the most illustrations. After my visit to the Paris Morgue, the gruesome drawings of the dead women seemed like nursery drawings.

"And—" Nell looked up from her transfer-work, her face aglow with enthusiasm, "his very last words to me were to mention that *he himself had been a suspect*! May still be."

"Sherlock Holmes?" I demanded, unwilling to believe it.

Irene sat down with us, her face lost in speculation. "He would have been seen in the streets in disguise if he were trailing the Ripper. I doubt he would have confessed to you a serious suspicion."

"Ah! How better to mislead me?" Nell demanded. "I am not at all convinced that he is not a wolf in sheep's clothing. Who better to raid the flock than its purported shepherd?"

Even I had realized by then that our Miss Nell harbored a

deep and ruthless prejudice against Sherlock Holmes, for some reason yet obscure to me.

Irene's tolerant laugh expressed her familiarity with this puzzling attitude. "Certainly Sherlock Holmes harbors a certain subtle disdain for women that is common to his gender, yet fortunately uncommon for a man of his relative youth and good health. Sherlock Holmes as the Ripper . . . it would be an international scandal, far too shocking to be true, I fear. Yet the book indicates that men who have no reputation with women at all may be deadlier than the most notorious rake."

"The book, Irene?" Nell asked, looking up from her copy work.

"The German volume I purchased near Notre Dame from the bookseller's stall the other day. I have had time to read a bit of it since then."

Nell's imperious Roman nose wrinkled rather charmingly. "*Psychopathia Sexualis*. Even the Latin title sounds drearily scholarly and pretentious. Why can the title not be in German, like the text?"

"I believe the science of the mind it studies is described in Latin terms so that doctors and scholars worldwide may understand it."

"And only them, of course!" Miss Huxleigh was waxing indignant, an attitude she had mastered many years before meeting me. "What do they say, these international solons, with their secret societies and arcane books and terminologies?"

Irene looked at me, as if to say that my turn under Nell's interrogative scorn had come. She leaned back, her eyes half-closed. I guessed she expected to learn something from our continuing discussion. She was like a general disposing troops and then surveying the battle and their efforts from some lofty hilltop, piecing together a larger picture than the foot soldiers could ever see.

So. How was I to tell an utterly innocent woman some years my senior about the degradations detailed in Mr. Krafft-Ebing's obscure and no doubt rightly vilified book?

"The volume is a study of murderous madmen," I began.

"Oh. You read German?" Nell sounded most miffed. "I

only read English myself." She made it sound totally sufficient for any sensible person.

"Not well, but the book makes some interesting points. It seems that awful as the Whitechapel Ripper's acts are, many men have performed them before. And the point is this: that though these men are utterly, revoltingly mad and capable of insanely brutal acts, most of them move among their fellow creatures very quietly, being the last sort of person you would suspect."

"Like Sherlock Holmes!"

"I would not call him 'quiet.' No, these men are so common as to be unnoticeable. No great intelligence, yet possessed of an awesome cunning when engaged in their mania. They are diffident around women rather than the opposite. Yet when they are compelled to their repugnant crimes, nothing holds them back. Even . . . remember the dreadful letter supposed to be from Jack the Ripper? Telling how he kept and ate one of the women's kidneys?"

"Yes," Nell said with a shudder. "He misspelled the word 'kidney' rather awfully. 'Kidne,' I believe, was the horror. Even a child would not make such a crude mistake."

"Exactly, Nell," Irene put in. "I believe that Pink was not remarking on the Ripper's grammar and spelling, but rather his cannibalism. According to this most interesting book, that is not uncommon among such men."

"But . . . the men in the book must be from *Germany*. There is no connection between the suspects in the Whitechapel killings and that country, only America"—this was pointed out with an accusing look at both of us—"Russia, Poland, and France."

It was plain from Miss Huxleigh's tone that she regarded all four of these nations as barbaric when weighed against the excellencies of the British Empire.

"How interesting," Irene noted ironically. "I have myself sojourned in America, Poland, and France."

"Say," said I, "I must object to your implying that America harbors vicious killers left and right."

"Oh, and what of your savage Red Indians?"

"They are all mostly working for Buffalo Bill nowadays,"

I returned jokingly, "and making a pretty penny at it. But you mustn't believe all those mock chases and shoot-outs in a Wild West Show. That's long past in the United States."

"Did the Indian savages not scalp innocent women and children as well as the white men who fought them? And are they not masters of torture? I have heard tales of that."

"Tales," I began, ready to defend my native land, but Irene Adler Norton sat up suddenly.

"It's true. Not many years ago in America some women on the frontier died horribly at the hands of the Indians." She looked at me. "Suffering wounds not unlike those on the woman in the morgue."

Nell's head was bowed to her list, her lips pursed in schoolroom concentration; otherwise, she might have asked how Irene and I knew the details of those wounds.

I saw that our discussion had delivered the unexpected dividend that Irene was waiting for: an utterly original perspective on the killings that had plagued London and now had apparently immigrated to Paris.

"Bram Stoker," Nell said, writing with intense concentration, "mentioned crossing the Atlantic with Buffalo Bill. I wonder if any Red Indians were on that voyage as well."

Irene was thinking aloud about the present, not the past. "The World Exposition grounds around the Eiffel Tower teem with foreign exhibits. Is there an American Indian display, do you think?"

While Nell visibly racked her brain on this most unexpected topic, Irene leaned toward me to whisper: "We must also consider the shots fired at us near Notre Dame. They missed, of course, but now I wonder if that was the idea. Were they meant to draw us to, or away from the catacombs? Yet that incident merely leads us to a new fact: cowboys and Indians and shooting displays are the heart of Buffalo Bill's Wild West Show. Isn't it in Paris now? When was it in London?"

My breath felt stolen away. No one had dreamed of an American Indian stalking the streets of London and Paris! Yet I had grown up on bloodcurdling tales of Indian depravities against the Wild West settlers, of innocent women and children subjected to the most cruel tortures and atrocities before, and after, death.

True, that era was almost over in America, but could some traveling warrior have gone as mad as the men in Herr Krafft-Ebing's book? How soon we forget the utterly bestial remnants of primitive humanity that survive in our civilized midst despite our best efforts to stamp out such depravities! Simply because the American East was nurturing a seaboard string of major cities to rival European capitals, we could not forget the seething heart of savagery still beating in the American West, in our heartland prairies and western reaches, mostly conquered but still only a generation removed from unparalleled fierceness.

With such possibilities as this, the notion of suspecting someone as civilized as Sherlock Holmes, or Bram Stoker, of being the Ripper became as ludicrous as it should have seemed from the first.

"Bram Stoker," Nell mused coincidentally, "is a most unlikely candidate anyway, despite his presence in the disreputable house where the first Paris murders occurred. Most of the Ripper suspects were well under five-foot-five."

"As were the victims," Irene reminded us. "Except for Mary Jane Kelly, the lady of five-foot-seven who called herself Marie Jeannette at times, and claimed she had been taken to Paris by a gentleman client."

"Kelly," said Nell, assiduously pursuing her confounded list. "There was a suspect named Kelly. He went to France very shortly after Mary Jane's death, and the police were most interested in his movements. He was an upholsterer by trade, but had fallen into lamentable work and personal habits." She looked up from her list at last, to our stunned faces.

"What? *What!?*"

Penelope Huxleigh may have been the most annoyingly innocent woman left in France, and perhaps on the planet, but she was not, in the end, stupid.

"Oh," she said finally, realizing that she had almost overlooked a damning connection in the case. She put her hands to her heat-pinked cheeks.

At last I had a partner in the girlish art and agony of blushing.

31.

Sins of the Son

He presented a mixture of primordial delirium of persecution (devil, antichrist, persecution, poisoning, persecuting voices) and delusions of grandeur (Christ, redemption of the world) with impulsive, incoherent actions.

—RICHARD VON KRAFFT-EBING, *PSYCHOPATHIA SEXUALIS*

I found him soaked and shivering near the statue of the Virgin.

It was past the early services and before the next. No one was near. The great cathedral pillars soared around us like stalactites and stalagmites the ages had shaped into a vast cavern of frozen wax turned to stone by some poor excuse of a Midas.

I had been nurtured in this world of incense and beeswax candles and sanctimony, but the savagery of the steppes and the sweeping riders of the East is in my veins and my holy water is now blood and not wine.

"What is it?" I crooned, holding him as Mother Church does sinners.

His teeth were chattering, his fabled strength a limp rag. So does the God of Christians magnify weakness.

"I am crucified," he whispered in the language that we share.

It is hard to offer spiritual advice to a demon.

"Tell me your trouble." I care for no one. Well, one. But that is an aberration I will deal with later.

"Tell me your trouble," I crooned. He is a beast, after all, and responds to simple things. Simple sins. Simple falsities, simple lies.

"I am torn! I am torn," the tearer cries. Terror.

"Hush. How?"

"I flew with the hunter. Above the wooden rooftops, over the gilded dome of the church, over the marsh and the firs, the mountains and the spires, over the roof of the world. I see myself suspended over the dome of the Temple, tempted by the Devil to dash myself onto stones and sin. I see myself suspended over domes, great gilt domes in a great gilt city, on my own holy power, dashing the Devil onto stones and eternal fires. Will I be in Heaven, or in Hell? What is holy? What is power?"

"Both. Power is holy. Holy is power."

"And sin?"

"Sin is . . . salvation."

"Yes, yes! We sense that in my village. We must sin to be saved."

I couldn't restrain a shrug. I only recognized the first part of that sentence, to which we all serve life terms. We must sin or be sinned against. The rest is delusion.

He raked his hands—claws—into the tangled wet hair at his temples, his eyes as wild as a stallion's.

"I have come out of the wilderness, walking for months, to seek salvation. I have come to this stone city, and others like it, to find fellow sinners and fellow saints.

"But their wines are weak and their stomachs as well. The horses are fettered and the women . . . the women refuse, or demand pay! It was not like that in my village," he added drunkenly. "No one drank deeper, or rode faster or farther, or sang louder, or danced longer, or cursed harder, or loved more women, willing women, women who couldn't resist. . . ."

My glance lifted to the Virgin's simpering face. She resisted him, too, but he didn't see it.

"This is a foreign city," I consoled him. "You have come to learn about foreign cities, and what you may accomplish in them."

And so have I.

"I will go to a finer foreign city than any. I will be a power higher than any ruler. I will bring myself up so high that I will bring them all down."

He let himself sprawl against the wall, took a long draught from the thick pottery bottle in his hand. He drank as if it were water, when I knew that the slightest swallow was scouring liquid fire.

"I must go to the Gypsies," he said, "and stroke their horses and hear their violins and have their women. My mind screams from the silence of these cities, of these stone blocks, houses of God, and houses of women.

"I have sinned." He buried his shaven boy's face in his huge callused hands, in which he clutched a crude wooden cross. His anguish was genuine. It was most interesting.

He is a very young man with the broad shoulders of a boar, of only medium height but with brute strength that multiplies when fueled by his erratic emotions, or the always reliable liquor. Even he does not know his own age. He thinks he is around twenty, give or take a few years.

Peasants are so refreshing, unspoiled.

32.

Sherlock the Shredder

A. did not show the slightest trace of emotion, and gave no explanation of the motive or circumstances of his horrible deed. He was a psychopathic individual, and occasionally subject to fits of depression. . . .

—RICHARD VON KRAFFT-EBING, *PSYCHOPATHIA SEXUALIS*

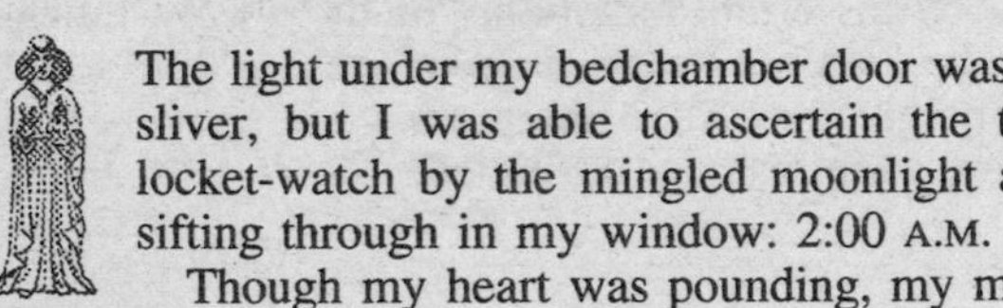

The light under my bedchamber door was the faintest sliver, but I was able to ascertain the time on my locket-watch by the mingled moonlight and gaslight sifting through in my window: 2:00 A.M.

Though my heart was pounding, my mind told me that such a phenomenon must be investigated.

I pushed my feet into my icy slippers and donned my dimity dressing gown, then slowly opened my door.

The heavy hinges did not squeak. I had long moments to examine the scene: Irene, hair down, poring over the Ripper papers and my notes by the light of an oil lamp.

I shuffled into the outer room, and she looked up, her finger already at her lips to demand silence.

The pleasure that filled me was immense. This was something she did not wish Elizabeth to know. Our old equilibrium seemed fully established again as I slipped into the empty chair at her side and raised my eyebrows.

Not only my painstaking list of the Ripper suspects and their specifics lay scattered over the table's surface. So did new pages filled with Irene's large, looping penmanship.

"What are you doing?" I whispered.

She whispered back. "Trying to determine which suspect was Sherlock Holmes."

My toes curled in my slippers. Not only was Irene confiding in me and not that upstart Elizabeth Pink, but she was attempting to implicate Sherlock Holmes in the Whitechapel horrors!

I really could not imagine a more blissful moment, except that Quentin Stanhope would walk through the passage door and join us.

"Height is the key," Irene said. "Except for the last victim, who was attacked in her bed apparently, all of the victims were of short stature. You see what that means?"

"Ah, they were easier to attack."

"On the streets. And," she added to herself, "in the act."

The Act. I was informed enough to know that this was not a portion of a stage play. More than that I did not wish to know, but perhaps it was necessary that I know some small bit more.

"I do not understand, Irene."

"You understand my . . . implications about the bizarre piece of furniture in the *maison de rendezvous*."

I nodded like a student spouting back algebraic formulas. "It was a kind of bed, designed for immoral purposes, so that the . . . gentleman (here I thought of the rotund Bertie and nearly gagged) need not recline. Or could recline on a surface even with the floor, so he should not exert himself. Unduly. For whatever reason."

"Excellent! You have the gist of it anyway. But in Whitechapel, where the likes of the Prince of Wales would not usually set boot toe, the women there most often did not recline. Do you understand what I mean?" She eyed me with some concern.

"Oh! Like sheep, you mean. In Shropshire. Why did you not say so plainly? They always . . . stood up."

"I would not know, but apparently you do. Sheep. Yes. But in Whitechapel the Ripper who went to the slaughter laid them down as he cut their throats. They were dead by the time they touched ground, and felt nothing, thank God, when he went to his real work."

"The mutilations."

She nodded.

"We had people in the country, men, I suppose, who mutilated animals on occasion. The poor beasts would be found in the fields, made evil work of. Were they attacked by these same sort of men who kill women?"

"I don't know, Nell. Krafft-Ebing notes that young boys who torture and kill animals often advance to higher forms of life to destroy."

"I am glad that I do not read German," I said with a shudder.

"But you have lived in Shropshire, and that was apparently enough to glimpse the work of some Jack the Ripper or another."

"True. All things come to Shropshire. So what is your point, Irene, about Sherlock Holmes in Whitechapel?"

"Only that he was at a distinct disadvantage. Like Godfrey, he is a man well above average height."

"As is Quentin," I said complacently.

"But Quentin was not in Whitechapel. Nor Godfrey. We know that Sherlock Holmes was, because he told us so. Why did he do that, do you think?"

"He wished to confound me?"

"He wished to confound me also, and to warn us that he has been active in this case since the beginning. And to tell us that the suspects for the role of Ripper are wider and broader, and taller, than we may think."

"So—?"

"So. I am looking for Sherlock Holmes in Whitechapel. I am sure he went there in disguise. Perhaps several. I suspect it is true that, in disguise, he was identified as a suspect. I 'suspect' that this amused him mightily. I also suspect that if we determine where and when he was identified, however erroneously, we shall know a great deal more about the more likely suspects for the crimes."

"What of the mad upholsterer who fled to France?"

"We should definitely pursue him, but in what way I am not sure."

"So you don't think that Sherlock Holmes really did it?" I

had not intended to sound so disappointed, but I could not prevent it.

She tilted her head to consider the idea with as much dispassion as Sherlock Holmes himself considered the impression of a footprint.

"It is not impossible. Mr. Holmes shows the same unusual lack of emotion that is required to commit such vile acts. He is a man driven by enthusiasm, who may descend into great depths of melancholia. In many ways he is a typical actor, like Henry Irving. Poor Bram! Devoted to that monster of self-pride, brilliant but brutal to all around him. Only Ellen Terry could survive Irving's monstrous self-indulgence, and she does, with grace."

"I do not think that these other theatrical people are involved, although it would cheer me up considerably to implicate Sarah Bernhardt."

Irene laughed, though she choked the sound behind the offices of her palm. "Sarah on the prowl in Whitechapel. Quite the comedy."

"She dresses in male garb, as do you."

"Ah." Irene eyed me again. "A woman dressed as a man could have committed the crimes. And the height would be no problem in that case! Thank goodness that Sarah and I have our whereabouts strictly accounted for during the Autumn of Terror. Did you not see us both then? You are our alibi."

"*Hmmph,*" I said, which I always did when I had nothing more substantial to contribute.

Irene moved her papers around like parts of a puzzle. "No, Nell. However fascinating it is to speculate, I keep coming back to the mathematical facts. And they are very clear. There is only one suspect who could possibly be Sherlock Holmes, and that is in the case of the third victim, Elizabeth Stride."

"She is the one who was only killed."

"Yes, if you can call having your throat slashed being 'only killed.' " Irene shot me a quick, forgiving smile. "In the cases of the Whitechapel Ripper, that was indeed a boon." She searched through the papers until she found and laid two atop each other.

"If you remember, Nell, Liz Stride was the most widely seen victim the night of her death."

"Busy about her disgusting business, you mean."

"Now, Nell. These women had lives aside from the way they earned their pence. In fact, Liz had earned sixpence that day for cleaning some rooms at Flower and Dean Street. The woman who oversaw the lodging house she had cleaned paid her as they shared a drink at the Queen's Head public house."

"Earn an honest sixpence, and she spends it on drink the moment after."

"It was a friendly round with the woman who employed her. Men celebrate such transactions every day in the same way, and are thought no less for it."

"By me they are."

Irene sighed. I was interrupting her declamation. "Anyway, Liz Stride was at the Queen's Head at 6:00 P.M."

"Which queen was that? The head's, I mean? One of Henry VIII's, whom you intend to impersonate?"

"I don't know which beheaded queen the pub is named after! That is not pertinent. What is pertinent is that Liz Stride was next seen by a barber and charwoman of her acquaintance at her common-lodging house on Flower and Dean Street at 7:00 or 8:00 P.M. She borrowed a clothes brush, as she intended to go out, and left a piece of velvet with the charwoman to look after."

"Velvet?"

"Velvet. Mary Ann Nichols had a 'jolly bonnet.' Annie Chapman had two combs, a piece of rough muslin, and a bit of envelope containing two pills in her pocket, which the Ripper slashed open as he did her body. Missing were two or three brass rings she wore on her fingers. They couldn't have been taken for reasons of robbery, having no value. This killer invaded every odd corner of their lives. These women had so very little, but what they had, they treasured. Including life, I would think."

I could say nothing to that. I rustled among the papers, then glanced to the drawn curtains to Elizabeth's sleeping alcove.

"She sleeps like the dead," Irene noted in a spectral whisper. "She suffers from that brittle energy of the young, which collapses upon itself if called upon to do too much."

I nodded. We were not quite so young, so it was we two again on the case, as it had been in London and, I hope, ever shall be.

"Look," I said, resuming my role of sister sleuth. "This journal says that Liz Stride was seen at 11:00 P.M. by two laborers outside the Bricklayer's Arms. She was with a man dressed in a black morning coat with a billycock hat and a thick black mustache. Oh dear. They were hugging and kissing in the rain. Most inappropriate."

"The rain? Or the hugging and kissing?"

"Both." I did not want to appear prejudiced against one over the other.

Irene gave me her most ironic look. "And then there was the fruit seller with the appropriate name of Packer. He sold some of his wares to a woman who looked like Liz Stride and a man of medium height with a dark complexion within the next hour."

"Oh!" I said, having read ahead. "That's right. Liz Stride was the one the man made the odd remark to."

"As overheard by another laborer on Berner Street just before midnight." Irene's forefinger touched the quote as she declaimed in a husky voice eerily masculine. 'The couple kissed,'" she read, "and then he said, 'You would say anything but your prayers.' " Such an odd remark, almost threatening. Very theatrical really."

"The man who spoke," I reminded her, "was about five-foot-six, middle-aged and stout and clean-shaven! I say this was another couple. The man seemed familiar with her, although all these men seemed overfamiliar with all these women . . . I mean, in a personal way."

"But what are we to make of his clerklike attire: small black cutaway coat, dark trousers, and a round cap with a peak?"

"Oh, I don't know! These men who are reported with the soon-to-be-dead women all dress in the oddest fashion, half-gentlemanly and half like a rough worker."

"Within forty-five minutes, a police constable saw a man

and woman in Berner Street, opposite the side where the body was later found. *This* man was five-foot-seven, under thirty, with a dark complexion and small black mustache. He wore a black diagonal cutaway coat, a white collar and tie, and carried a sinister parcel just the right size for a savage assortment of knives. The woman wore a red flower pinned to her jacket."

I put my hands to my head. "It's simple. The Ripper traveled with a medieval torture rack and simply stretched himself taller on every sighting."

Irene smiled. "There was Morris Eagle, who was attending a Jewish man's socialist club on Berner Street at 12:30 A.M. He saw nothing, one of the few witnesses who blessedly had no confusing sightings to report.

"But then came Israel Schwartz. You can see why Baron Rothschild is concerned. The Jewish population of Whitechapel thronged around the scenes of the crime. Now I would love to have Mr. Israel Schwartz sitting at this table with us, for his was the most interesting sighting of all."

I glanced askance at the empty third chair around our table. I did not care to have any odd Whitechapel witnesses in our presence, innocent though they might be of any wrongdoing.

"He saw the woman with the flower with a man five-foot-five, around thirty, dark hair, small mustache, fair complexion, wearing a dark jacket and trousers with a black peaked cap. This is the man who tried to throw her down, and succeeded. She screamed," Irene noted.

"I believe that she was the only Ripper victim to scream."

"I believe that you're right. But here is where it gets astounding. Mr. Schwartz also saw a man across the street watching this scene. He was five feet eleven inches tall and around thirty-five years old, smoking a clay pipe. Fresh complexion, light brown hair and mustache. Dark overcoat and an old black hard felt hat with a wide brim."

"He is the tallest man in the case."

"Indeed. The man who was accosting Liz Stride called out 'Lipski' at him."

"Then he knew him," I concluded.

"That's what Israel Schwartz thought. He took them for

accomplices at robbery and ran away, fearing they wanted no witnesses and that the first man had warned his partner 'Lipski' to take care of Schwartz.

"But no one followed the fleeing laborer, who fled to a nearby railway arch."

"Here it is! Look, Irene!" I cried. "The incident is in the *Police Gazette* for October 19, 1888. But the only description given is of the man who was assaulting Liz Stride. There is no mention of this man across the way he called Lipski. Do you think the papers were suppressing any Jewish connection because they feared attacks on the community?"

"Possibly." Irene's lips pursed. "It's true that within hours Sir Charles Warren would order erased the fascinating assertion that 'The Juwes are the men That Will not be Blamed for nothing,' which was found near the body of the evening's second victim, Catharine Eddowes. She, by the way, lived with a porter named John *Kelly* at Flower and Dean Street.

"But you must understand in what connection the word 'Lipski' was used in that quarter at the time. I remember reading in one of Godfrey's newspapers of a man named Israel Lipski, a Jew who murdered a woman named Miriam Angel in 1887. No doubt it had become an East End taunt to call any Jew, who were often accused of murdering Christians, 'Lipski.' "

"I thought you were above reading news of sensational murders in the newspapers."

"Not above, Nell, simply pleased to be removed from such violence. And the Rothschilds have supplied us with every word."

I let my eyes fall back to my list of suspects. "So the man who was abusing Liz Stride called out the name of the notorious Jewish murderer, and Israel Schwartz ran?"

"He was Jewish. He knew the name was a prelude to further abuse."

"But the man he feared, the second man, did not run."

"No. Was it because he was an accomplice, or because he was not Jewish, and therefore not alarmed? The newspapers did not even bother to put him forth as a suspect, only the first man."

I considered what Irene was saying.

Time	Place	Man's Clothes	Type & Face	Height
11 p.m.	*Bricklayer's Arms*	*smartly dressed, black morning coat, billycock hat*	*thick black mustache*	*5'5"*
11:30 p.m.	*44 Berner Street*		*30–35, dark complexion*	*medium*
11:45 p.m.	*64 Berner Street*	*clerkish, small black cutaway coat, dark trousers, round peaked cap, "You would say anything but your prayers."*	*middle-aged, stout, clean-shaven*	*5'6"*
12:30 p.m.	*36 Berner Street, opposite body site*	*black diagonal cutaway coat, white collar & tie, carrying parcel*	*28, dark complexion and small black mustache*	*5'7"*
12:45 p.m.	*40 Berner Street*	*dark jacket and trousers, black peaked cap*	*30, full face, broad shoulders, dark hair, small brown mustache, fair complexion*	*5'5"*
12:45 p.m.	*40 Berner Street*	*dark overcoat and old black hard felt hat with wide brim, smoking a clay pipe*	*35, fresh complexion, light brown hair & mustache*	*5'11"*
1 a.m.	*40 Berner Street*	*STRIDE FOUND DEAD!*		

"That is because this second fellow was too tall to be the Ripper. All of the witnesses describe a man no taller than five-foot-seven, and considerably less and those seen with Liz Stride averaged five-foot-six."

Irene nodded encouragingly. I know she was giving me rope enough to arrive at my own solution, for hers had been reached even before I came upon the scene. But she enjoyed testing her conclusions against the sounding board of other minds.

Indeed, I found it rather exhilarating to know that I had arrived at the same end as Irene.

I looked at my newest list. "Then you are convinced."

Her finger nailed the almost-six-foot-tall nicotine addict with the clay pipe. "That is Sherlock Holmes. And I must wonder how, if he was there, he was unable to prevent the killing of Liz Stride fifteen minutes later."

"Perhaps he drove off the man who was abusing her and . . ." —well, I never *had* liked the man— *"killed her himself."*

33. With Bated Breath

Women are never to be entirely trusted—
not the best of them.
—SHERLOCK HOLMES, "THE SIGN OF FOUR"

I awoke with shattered memories of a tall, storklike man pursuing me through endless catacombs until we reached the sewers, whose murky waters flowed red.

There I saw a woman's form, elevated above the flood, her hands folded like a Catholic saint's.

When I turned, there was no one behind me but an alleyway of white-marble statues, as in a garden, save their faces had no features.

I was glad to open my eyes and find them gazing upon the overly ornate plasterwork common to French hotels, respectable or not.

The playful putti surrounding the ceiling rosette reminded me of the gantlet of statues in my dream, but these smiling cherubs could hardly be construed as ominous.

I heard the click of breakfast china from the other room and hastened to don my dressing gown.

When I entered our common chamber, Irene and Pink were drinking coffee from an urn, the Paris newspapers spread all around them. Of the Ripper materials there was no sign, and Irene greeted me with a cup lifted as for a toast.

"Welcome, lazybones. There is tea in that china pot that is disguised as a Shropshire sheep and there is a letter from Godfrey for you, not to mention an assortment of pastries."

"A letter from Godfrey? For me? Why?"

"I don't know, Nell. Apparently he felt moved to write you for a change. He has arrived in Prague, at least. I am so glad that I had our post transferred from the country to our city quarters."

"I am amazed the postal service managed to follow our perambulating address," I murmured as I sat down, shook out my serviette, and accepted the cup of tea Elizabeth had charmingly prepared for me.

"Milk?" she asked.

I nodded, and she poured the creamy liquid into my half-filled cup as if she knew my preferences from such slight acquaintance. I added two lumps of sugar and took a soothing sip. From their cups wafted a bitter aroma of coffee that smelled like a poison.

There was indeed a plump envelope at my place, and I was so excited I used the butter knife to open it, after first verifying that Irene's and Elizabeth's eyes were on the papers.

My dear Nell,

It is pleasant to be in Prague again and to recall our

interesting outings in this city of golden spires not long ago.

I will send a letter to Irene in the next post, never fear, but wanted to tend you greetings from this city that has been your only foreign landscape besides Paris and Monaco.

Also, I thought that you would be wildly interested in the fact that some of the folk here believe our friend the Golem has risen yet again.

This time his reputed appearance has stirred even more panic than before, for it is a particularly bloody murder that they attribute to this automaton.

Of course, you and I and a few others know that the Golem's previous appearance was not what everybody assumed it to be, and that it is extremely unlikely that this medieval legend has bestirred itself to spread terror in the residents' hearts once again.

So the city is its charming self, wrapped up in its own legends like an ancient mummy in its winding cloths. We who know better can laugh at their quaint superstitions.

My business meetings will shortly bring me to Prague Castle. I am looking forward to seeing the Queen again, if not the King. And I am sure that Irene will want detailed reports on both, so I will save my hand for a later, more fulsome report more befitting a barrister abroad.

This is merely a note to remind you of our mutual sojourns in Bohemia, and to assure you that all is well, although I greatly miss your valued company.

As always,
Godfrey

"Oh, dear," I said.

"What is it, Nell?"

I could hardly admit how dreadful I felt that Godfrey was so far away, thinking of me, when I was happily ensconced in Paris working to prove that Sherlock Holmes was Jack the Ripper, and missing him not a jot.

"Godfrey has arrived safely."

"So I deduced from the postmark."

"He is sending you a letter in the very next post."

"He had better. What did he say in this one?"

"Only that the poor superstitious residents of Prague are still nattering about the Golem being loose and on the rampage and that he will begin business meetings shortly."

"Not the Golem, I hope. Do they involve the Castle?"

"I . . . gather they do."

"A pity we could not spare you to report from the scene, but you are of far more use here."

"I am?"

"Of course." She smiled and idly wound a long lock of her hair around her forefinger.

Elizabeth watched her as closely as I did. Irene girlish was an Irene to beware of.

"I have decided on a battle plan." Irene pushed away her coffee cup as if realizing its bitter aroma. "You may finish your late breakfast, Nell," she added, eyeing my empty plate. "But as soon as you are done, we will divide our forces and scatter like pigeons among the stones of Paris."

"Scatter?" I asked faintly.

"Pink and I are off to the Eiffel Tower and the international displays at the World Exposition to investigate Red Indians."

"And I?" I asked even more faintly, for it was clear that I was to venture forth alone, on my own, once again unescorted.

"Back to the bordello to investigate the matter of the *siége d'amour* upholstery."

"They will not heed me, or answer any questions I may have."

"Nonsense. I have great faith in your powers of persuasion, Nell. You need only obtain the name of the designer of the . . . couch and the address of his studio. They will understand that you were with me on the previous visits and that I—we—are serving persons too highly placed to ignore."

"They will not remember that I was with you before, Irene! They never do. I shall undergo the humiliation of being driven out of a house of ill repute!"

She considered me for a few silent moments. "If you do not wish to go alone, there is an alternative."

"Yes?"

"I doubt you would find it any more pleasant."

"Anything! Even Inspector le Villard, if he must accompany me. I know you can persuade him, Irene."

"Oh, we need not subject you to anything so unpleasant as that."

"You are thinking of Sarah Bernhardt. You know I detest her even though she is your friend." I sighed and sat up straight enough to pour tea for the Queen. "But I will tolerate her, if she will smooth the way for my awkward questions in that dreadful place."

"No, I would never send you into such a situation in the company of a person you regarded as so scandalous."

"I am relieved, but who is left?"

"No one, really, which is why I am afraid we must draw Sherlock Holmes into our equation again."

"Him! But he may be a—" I glanced at Elizabeth just in time. She had been watching our conversation with the eager snapping glance of a cat engaged in following the short, futile flight of a canary in a cage. "—a rival in our investigation. We do not wish him to know what we do."

"That is why I have already sent a note to his hotel advising him to expect you, with some evidence that might be of interest to him."

"Evidence? What evidence? Only of your insanity and my absolute bewilderment."

"La, Nell, this is simply a small exercise"—the fingers of Irene's right hand rippled off a silent glissando on the immaculate table linens—"in using a rival to our own ends. You will bring him the container with the substance we plucked from the carpet at the, er, *maison de rendezvous*."

She glanced at Elizabeth as she avoided the word "bordello," although the girl had the grace to flush nevertheless. I was beginning to wonder whether Elizabeth pinked so often out of shame, or simply frustration.

"I believe," Irene went on, "that Mr. Holmes is irresistibly fascinated by minuscule bits of evidence, so the contents of your etui should occupy him for some time. And I am sure he is an authority recognized enough to demand cooperation at the *maison* when you question the madam about the provenance of the *siège d'amour.*"

"I am thinking now, Irene, that I would rather carry out this task alone."

She shook her head. "You needn't worry that you will be providing our archrival with ammunition. From what you said of your interview yesterday, he had already admitted that your visit had been of some small use. What else would he have gleaned except the oddity of the *siège d'amour*? Only Mary Jane—once and briefly Marie Jeanne here in Paris, according to her own somewhat suspect testimony—was permitted to die upon her own bed, the only victim the Ripper killed indoors and supine. So were these two women killed in Paris. Indoors and supine. The London Police believe the Ripper is no longer on the loose because the killing of Mary Jane Kelly so far exceeded his previous violence that they think he either killed himself or went so mad he was sent to an institution.

"They underestimate the ability of the monster to be monstrous. I believe that the Kelly murder only whetted his taste for further excess."

She smiled and handed me a buttered roll. "Now eat your breakfast."

Of course I had no appetite at all after this discussion of the murders.

"You will need your strength," she went on, "if you are going to outwit Sherlock Holmes at his own game."

At least I knew the way to the man's hotel, improper as such knowledge and such a journey was. At least I had taken an omnibus by myself before. And how strange it was, as I traveled alone amid the alien chatter and the subtle perfume of horse manure, for I began to be able actually to eavesdrop now and then. Sentence fragments suddenly flashed as clear as stones at the bottom of a shallow stream. Before the words had been obscured by audible murk with only an occasional pair understandable, and by the time I had recognized them and converted them into English, the foreign sentences had bounded into the next paragraph.

I tried not to think of Irene and Elizabeth exploring the exhibitions at the World Exposition, particularly the Wild West Show of Mr. Buffalo Bill.

Buffalo Bill! There you had everything that was immature and ridiculous about America bundled up into two words, into a single name. What kind of name was that for a man whose representations showed long white hair and a snowy goatee, like some skimpy American Santa Claus?

Imagine calling an Englishman . . . Hereford Harry! Or Guernsey Godfrey! The very thought made me burst into solitary laughter, which caused my fellow passengers to stop jabbering and stare at me, instead of me staring at them.

I controlled myself by drawing my handkerchief and pretending to sneeze. And then I thought of the Jersey Lillie, Lillie Langtry, of course, except I'd never pictured her as a cow before!

And off I went again into cyclones of laughter.

I had dressed with almost as much care as Irene normally used. My walking suit of gold velveteen impressed with a piquelike pattern and trimmed in touches of black-satin trim on skirt and jacket announced me as a serious woman of affairs. My shirtwaist was lace-ruffled at bodice and sleeve, but not unduly fussy. I wore the less domestic attachments of my chatelaine clipped to my broad waistband, various elements dangling in plain sight as long as two feet, with my small silver notebook the longest and most prominent.

This time I knew exactly where to go in the hotel, so I took the elevated car from the lobby. The ride was terrifying enough to sober me before I had risen one floor. I knocked on Sherlock Holmes's door, reminding myself that we would use him before he would benefit an iota from any interaction with us.

I must say that Paris agreed with him. Perhaps it was that

his aquiline breed of nose was among its forebears. At any rate, he looked quite civil in a city suit.

"Paris agrees with you, Miss Huxleigh," was his annoying and disconcerting greeting. "I see the omnibus was crowded."

I was not going to gratify his showing off on what he could discern about my journey. It is like dealing with a self-important young lad of twelve who is full of his tutors and believes himself far beyond the schoolroom. Maintain a stiff dignity, and there is nothing he can do to upset you.

"I am not here by my own wishes," I said.

"Nor I mine," he said with a quick smile. "Yet I suggest that we make the best of it, and I do not think that Madam Irene would put us together to no good effect . . . at least not for her purposes."

"Why do you call her that?"

"What did I call her?"

"Madam Irene. It is not even the proper French form, *Madame*, and is rather forward."

"I am an Englishman, Miss Huxleigh, whatever French blood may flow in a forebear's veins, so I use 'Madam.' As for the title, believe me that it is one of respect, rather than of familiarity. As you know only too well, she and I have barely met despite a series of er, unfortunate encounters."

I shrugged, an inelegant gesture I had acquired from Irene, and perhaps from rubbing shoulders with too many Frenchmen on omnibuses. Still, one cannot fault the gesture for sheer economy and the ability to avoid a direct answer.

Besides, it allowed me to sidestep mentioning the times when Irene had encountered Sherlock Holmes and he was not aware of her identity. I studied him, coming to some conclusions that might surprise him.

His height on my entering had struck me as very close to five-foot-eleven. His extreme leanness made him seem taller, perhaps over six feet, but I was sure that a slight stoop would banish two or three inches in an instant.

I noticed his hands, thin but flexible and strong. I had seen pianists' hands with that same tensile power. His complexion was "fresh" and English, or pale. His hair was dark, but it would not take much powder to lighten it, and a mustache—

unwholesome flourish—would disarm the entire angularity of his face, not to mention soften the hawkish sharpness of his nose.

I was certain that he was the man who had stood across the street watching while Liz Stride was hurled to the ground, just as Israel Schwartz had watched.

I was also certain that my calm assessment was something he was not accustomed to. He looked around and went to a pipe on a side table.

"Do you mind, Miss Huxleigh?"

"I most decidedly do, although I am given to understand by those I know that fumes of foul-smelling smoke can aid the cognitive functions."

He pushed some messy shocks of tobacco into the pipe bowl, packed it down, then scratched a lucifer on a striking box and lit the assemblage, drawing on the pipe with the huff and puff of a train leaving the station.

"That's right," he said between puffs, chuffing out steam as regularly as an engine of the Great Western line. "Madam Irene is devoted to small cigars."

"Only when she is deeply puzzled."

"Is she deeply puzzled often?"

"Only when she has inserted herself into the muddled affairs of others."

"Ha!" He gave that strange bark of a laugh I had heard from him before and moved to the window, whether to give me his back or to look down upon the street I could not tell. Either intent was insulting. "How does she survive your disapproval of her habits?"

"Do you mean of smoking or of inserting herself into the muddled affairs of others?"

"Both."

"Very well," I said coolly. "Everybody does."

He barked in laughter again and turned to face me. "I must say I admire one of your own habits."

"My habits? I have none."

"On the contrary, I have never seen a more habit-prone woman. I am referring to that feminine gewgaw you wear. Apparently it has it uses."

It took me a moment to realize he meant my trusty chatelaine. I took its presence so for granted that I had forgotten about it, as a man might a pocket watch and chain.

I suppose this sterling silver assemblage of accessories that dangle from a central piece that clasps onto my belt was actually an elegant female appurtenance. Yet I, who avoid ornament for its own sake, did not regard it so. Perhaps it was from the habit of doing needlework, but I was so used to having my daily tools by my side that they seemed pure practicality, like a man's pocketknife. And indeed, I did carry a small but sharp blade among the many implements upon my chatelaine.

I disconnected one small item from its leash of slim silver chain now: the etched and enameled etui, or Oriental needle case.

"Irene wished me to bring you this," I said, holding it up, knowing that what I held would for him be irresistible.

He strode toward me, his face bright with curiosity. This alien object was from his former adversary, Irene Adler. It was small and hidden. It was being offered by a rival, or an enemy, or perhaps by a colleague. It came to him, a gift, by the command of a beautiful woman he admired above all others of her sex.

He came to me as a fish to a hook, and I knew an intermediary's triumph.

Yes, we all have our all-too-predictable habits. Even, or especially, Mr. Sherlock Holmes.

34.

Buffalo Gals

Buffalo Gals, won't you come out tonight,
And dance by the light of the moon.
—AMERICAN MINSTREL SONG

FROM A JOURNAL

"Too bad that Nell must immerse herself in the affairs of the *maison de rendezvous*," I told Irene as we jolted toward the red-painted iron-lace minaret of the Eiffel Tower on the open second level of a horse omnibus. For a few centimes we could suffer along with the mobs of men of affairs and visitors to Paris. "She might actually enjoy an outing to the World Exposition."

"I doubt it. She has at least confronted the exotic individuals available at the *maison*. Cowboys and Indians and buffalo herds are utterly alien, and might be even more distressing."

Irene gave me an exceptionally level glance, as if she now was talking to a person she perceived behind my current guise. "It is best that we Americans investigate the Wild West Show. Luckily, today is a command performance for the Baroness Rothschild, and we are to be guests in their pavilion."

I nearly choked at this casual information. I had never dreamed to be in spitting distance of a Rothschild.

"After the performance," Irene went on, "I have taken the liberty of arranging for a British 'scout' for our behind-the-scenes tour."

"Really?"

"Bram Stoker."

I blinked quickly. "I've always wondered. Is Bram short for Abraham?"

"Probably. I've never thought about it. He has always been 'Bram.' Wondering otherwise would be like questioning why 'Pink' replaces Elizabeth, or why Elizabeth does not admit to a last name."

I felt myself flushing. It didn't matter the emotion: anger, anxiety, indignation, I always flushed in response. The one thing I never flushed from was shame, because I never felt any. Which fact would astound Miss Penelope Huxleigh.

"Cochrane," I said, bitingly.

"Irish," Irene mused, "the blessed race."

"Blessed into starving by the millions not four decades ago."

She eyed me sharply, as if I had just confessed to something I had meant to keep secret.

"You have a thirst for justice, Elizabeth Cochrane, that is most unusual in the inhabitant of a bordello."

I flushed more, furious but unable to answer her.

"I have a thirst for justice, too," she admitted. "It surprises me, but there it is. I am appalled that the London police have so easily given Jack the Ripper up for dead. If he is not, many more women will die both horribly and uselessly."

"You can understand that the police would hope that the crimes were merely a madman's last gasp."

"And you think—?"

"I have seen the rough side of life's hand. There is much needless suffering and too many who inflict it in every land. Such infamy is not an accident, and it usually doesn't end so conveniently."

Irene nodded. She had dressed for our outing in an ensemble fashioned like a riding habit, but more useful than that lovely but confining English fashion.

There was no trailing train to drape gracefully down from a sidesaddle, for instance, but a street-length skirt that brushed her boot tops and gave the impression of being divided. A veiled derby dipped over her forehead, the veil caught up with a feathered cockade. I also realized that Irene had assembled this ensemble from a skirt, jacket, boots, and hat never meant to commune together.

I was startled, on regarding her dress, to realize that in some inimitably elegant Parisian way it recalled the sharp-shooting rig of Miss Annie Oakley, Sitting Bull's "Little Sure Shot," who performed under her two middle names, in actuality being Miss Phoebe Moses. I smiled at that fact. Women who performed were not always as barefaced in using their private names as Irene Adler.

The sharpshooting ladies of the Wild West Show were much admired, both within the company and beyond it. My companion was subtly appropriating that revered position by mimicking their attire.

I considered my all-purpose checked overcoat, neat and practical. I would pass muster with Nell, surely, and on the necessarily trampled grounds of the Wild West Show, but Irene Adler Norton would seem strangely at home, however much a stranger. She had prepared for this expedition as an actress for a play.

I wondered whether this would be a melodrama or a tragedy. Or merely an exhibition.

⚜ ⚜ ⚜

The domes and spires and mansards and peaked rooftops and pagodas and tent tops gathered around the foundation of the Eiffel tower like gaudy circus wagons surrounding the fiery red central pole of a tent fashioned from the smooth, gray-clouded Parisian sky.

The audacity of Gustave Eiffel's Tower was astounding and the talk of the world. Its broad, arched base stood astride the cream of French architecture, dwarfing everything with its three hundred meters of height topped by a fifty-meter-high all-metal electric light at the very pinnacle.

It was, in short (if such an expression has any business being applied to a temple of modern hubris like the Eiffel Tower), the world's tallest building and an immense lightning rod for all Paris. And this role became literal when they lit the entire structure at night. The tower glowed ember red, with gold lights gleaming around each of the three tiers and the four foundation arches. The great beam at the top flashed up into the clouds and down upon the glittering domes and glass ceilings of the exposition buildings. I had seen it from our hotel room windows when I could not sleep.

The theme of the exposition was Jules Verne and the industrial transformation his stories predicted, mechanical whales in the sea and such.

Irene stood still on the river embankment, gazing at the hurly-burly of the crowds. She was used to the bucolic quiet of the country, I think, and to entering Paris only to visit its grand institutions.

Then the History of Human Habitation display clustered around the tower's base caught her eye.

"That is the great architect Garnier's work," she said brightly, almost wistfully. "He designed the Opéra of Paris, a quite extraordinary building. One feels impelled to sing just to look at it. And that is from the outside! We must see this exhibition."

"What of Mr. Stoker?"

"Oh, he is tall enough to be seen, or to see us. We have time to explore."

She took my arm, and soon we were strolling under imported palm trees gazing into Sudanese huts or, mere moments later, passing stunted Oriental trees beside Chinese and Japanese structures as intricately constructed as paper lanterns.

At one moment we were viewing the crude cubbyhole of a Stone Age arrow-maker, at the next three-dimensional representation we were peering into an elegant Etruscan villa or a Persian mansion.

Beside these architectural adornments squatted the crude skin and hide huts of Lapps, Eskimos, the reed huts of African tribes, and . . .

We stopped to admire the simple towering triangle of a teepee.

"Quite different from a *maison de rendezvous*," Irene murmured as we observed an architecture of sticks and skins that yet radiated a simplicity and strength which rivaled the Eiffel Tower itself.

"This is supposed savagery," she said. "The tower is civilization. Which society would more easily spawn a Ripper, do you think, Pink?"

"You are doing it," I said.

"Doing what."

"What Nell complains of."

"Which is?"

"Rhyming our names. 'Well, Nell.' '. . . think, Pink.' "

"Really, I am doing that?"

I nodded.

"Perhaps I am used to singing in rhyme, or assonance at least. Anyway, what do you think? Does the Ripper's mania spring from too much savagery or too much civility?"

"The answer would seem obvious."

"Yes, but obvious answers are always dangerous. Ah." She lifted her chin like a dainty hound smelling prey. "There is Bram's glorious red head. We will soon have a chance to meet savagery face-to-face."

I trotted obediently after her as she hastened to the side of the very tall, very red-bearded man in a hat and suit who stood gazing over the heads of the crowd looking for someone.

I was free to study him as I had not been in the confines of our hotel room. He was a man of substantial and robust middle age, not portly like the Prince of Wales, yet massive in both height and breadth. Quite handsome in a quiet way, his beard neatly trimmed and his gray eyes lightening with pleasure as he recognized Irene.

Yet there was nothing untoward in his expression or manner, only the easy congeniality so often found in large, secure men who manage to avoid becoming self-satisfied.

He took her hand and brushed his lips against it. "My dear Irene," he murmured happily, then turned politely to me.

And froze in horror.

Instantly I realized that he, too, had taken new stock of me, and that he must have glimpsed me at the *maison de rendezvous,* for there is nothing about me that should strike horror into any man, unless he suspected what I am capable of, and none ever do. I am often called "little," although I stand five-foot-five, but I am slender and pretty enough. Men have always been gallant with me, and I do not mind it, for it is useful.

"You remember meeting this young lady at my hotel, although I neglected to introduce her," Irene said quickly. "Miss Elizabeth Cochrane of Pennsylvania."

"Indeed." Bram Stoker stared hard at me. "I have visited that state during Irving's tours, a fine place."

"And Henry Irving is a very fine actor," I said, "so they are well matched." I extended a hand, which he shook gently. "Are you not his manager?"

He nodded, conveying an air of both pride and modesty that I found charming, as I sensed that all his pride was in Irving and all the modesty was for himself. I could see that the proper introduction that Irene had engineered had dispelled his fear of familiarity. He turned to her, affable again.

"You wish to meet Buffalo Bill, I understand."

"Heavens no, dear Bram! I wish to meet"—Irene visibly consulted her memory, one of her few performances that I found forced—"Red Shirt, is it? Or Mr. Flat Iron?"

Bram Stoker roared with a redhead's unfettered laughter. The blessed race, Irene had called the Irish, and perhaps laughter is our one and only blessing.

I found my lips turned up in company with his, and hers.

"Buffalo Bill is a down-to-earth sort," he went on, "but I imagine that he will be disappointed that two such lovely ladies are more eager to meet a pair of Red Indians than the famous Western scout himself."

Irene put her arm through Bram Stoker's. "If you can find this American marvel, I have no doubt that he will be happy to show us all the exotic elements of his world-famous spectacle."

Mr. Stoker offered me his other arm. He was completely at ease now. I had to wonder how he had seen me during my short time at the *maison de rendezvous*. I certainly had not spied him, which either meant that his presence there was utterly innocent, or appallingly guilty, depending on if he had been behind closed doors the whole time, or not. Few men wander into such a place innocently, but I am always willing to consider an exception to the rule.

"You will indeed meet this 'American marvel,' " Mr. Stoker went on jovially. I could tell he enjoyed having two handsome women on his arm. I am not in Irene's league, but am not to be sniffed at in that line, either. "First I will escort you to the Rothschild box. The show is ending, and you may wish to greet the Baroness and her guests."

I could hear the rapid explosions of firearms and the thunder of hooves followed by applause and hoarse cheers, but by the time Mr. Stoker had escorted us around the grandstands surrounding the vast outdoor performance arena, only a shimmering curtain of dust and a huge expanse of ground churned up by the wheels and hooves of two daily frantic reenactments of war parties and raids was evident.

The baronial box was draped with the flags of America and France as well as velvet swags in both countries' colors: red, white, and blue.

Imagine my surprise when I was introduced to the Baron and Baroness de Rothschild, who then turned to a rather portly gentleman with sleepy spaniel eyes the Baroness introduced as "Edward Albert, Prince of Wales."

Irene apparently knew everyone except the Baroness, whom she had given a deep bow of the head, the gesture of unacquainted equals, which I found interesting. Like me, there was not a servile bone in her body. I could not say as much for Nell.

Yet, for the first time in my life, I simply did not know what to do! At mention of the Prince's name, I found my hand thrusting out, then retracting, then advancing again, not sure if I expected the Prince to kiss it (if a prince could even kiss the hand of a "commoner") or shake it.

"You must be American." His laugh brought a brief spark of life to those heavy-lidded eyes. "All the American sharpshooting ladies when Buffalo Bill's show came to London last year shook hands with Mama, a frightful breach of court etiquette that the Queen and my wife Alex took in gracious spirits. I never thought I should see *that*, Mama dispensing with ceremony, for which I much thank the refreshing American ladies!"

He took and shook my gloved hand rather limply, but his touch was lingering while he consulted Irene behind me. "This is—?"

"Not my usual companion, Miss Huxleigh. This is Miss Elizabeth Cochrane of Pennsylvania."

"Another charming American place name, with as lovely an ambassadoress as New Jersey boasts," he replied with a nod at Irene.

By now my hand was anxious to emigrate from the rule of Britannia, but there was no graceful retreat. So I produced a good old American schoolgirlish curtsy and incidentally retrieved my hand on the pretext of needing it to lift my skirt hem during my exercise.

"It is always a pleasure to see you again, Your Highness," Irene noted during my maneuver.

The Prince nodded complacently. He seemed a man of amiable nature. "Especially with my current visit to Paris proceeding so . . . quietly, thank you, which I can't say about the entertainment we have all enjoyed here today, though there will never be a Wild West Show as thrilling for me as June before last in London. That is when I joined the Kings of Denmark, Belgium, Greece, and Saxony for a thundering ride in the Deadwood Coach during the howling, shooting attack by Red Indians. Quite enthralling.

"Afterward I told Buffalo Bill, 'Colonel, you never held four kings like these, did you?"

" 'I've held four kings,' he replied, 'but four Kings *and* the Prince of Wales make a royal flush, and that is unprecedented."

The Prince chuckled at the showman's swift and flattering response. I confess myself impressed by our American legend's quick wit as well as his ease among the foreign aristocracy.

Irene also exercised that wit and savoir faire. I looked around and saw she had ebbed away for a quick conferral with the Baron, a slight man wearing the white side whiskers of his generation.

By now the Baroness had come to rescue me from the Prince, or perhaps the Prince from me. I exchanged a polite glance with her only to encounter the cool, assessing eyes of a woman who regards other women as rivals, at least on first acquaintance.

It occurred to me that Edward Albert might be a special friend of hers, so I gave him a darling, dimpled smile of farewell just to irritate her before flouncing off to join Irene.

"Your theories are most intriguing," the Baron was saying. "Anything further I can do is yours to command."

Irene murmured thanks as she took me by the elbow and we left the formalities of the box and its occupants.

"What do you think of Bram Stoker now that you have seen him again?" she asked me, as we walked away.

"The nicest Englishman I have ever met, even barring the Prince, who's all right for an heir to the throne."

"You haven't met Godfrey yet," she said with the contented smile of a relatively new wife. I was dubious, having seen my mother's travails in the institution of marriage. "But I was asking if you thought Bram might be a habituée, as the French put it, of brothels?"

I considered my answer for a long time. "If he is, he would be a welcome one."

Irene was still laughing at my response when the gentleman in question, truly as innocent as a lamb on this occasion, rejoined us to lead us behind the arena to the vast area that housed the show.

An entire tent city thrust its homely peaks into the pungent air. People and beasts bustled back and forth in thick array, every one of them out of the ordinary as far as metropolitan life goes, except for the horses.

Outside a massive tent that Mr. Stoker identified as the dining chamber for the company he paused, while Red Indians with faces painted white, black, green, and red passed us, feathers and braids upon their heads. Mr. Stoker excused himself to go in to find the famous Indian fighter and showman.

Now I would have to be truly on my toes! It isn't as if I hadn't seen a Buffalo Bill production a few times. Yet Irene Adler Norton was clearly new to the whole venture. She eyed the massive tent from a distance at first, almost childlike in her amazement and curiosity.

"I was forced to miss attending this spectacle when I lived in London," she said finally.

"Forced? I cannot imagine you being forced into, or away from, anything."

"Oh, my dear Pink! We are all forced one way or another all of our lives. We simply do not notice who is doing the forcing, especially if they are in the four estates."

"The four estates. That means the aristocracy, the clergy, the professions and are the . . . newspapers the fourth estate?"

"I think you deserve high marks for that answer." She eyed me sideways. "Here in Paris the four estates are a bit different, as everything is in Paree: the boulevards or café society; the press; the artists, and the morgue. There you have it: Society, Sensation, Imagination, and Death. You notice that the Paris press is the second estate. The Anglo-Saxon 'old order' of churchman, tradesman, journalist quite literally applies only to England and the United States."

"But we do not have an aristocracy in America," I objected.

Mr. Stoker had returned just in time to overhear my opinion.

"Of course you do, Miss Cochrane. They are called nabobs and captains of industry. They are elevated by virtue of black ink rather than blue blood. Some call it a plutocracy, but I say it's a Midasocracy."

"I like that word," I said.

"That is because there is not much blue blood among us three, or among this company of rough riders," Irene said.

I looked around at what resembled a camp of ragtag soldiers without uniforms. "This is an out-of-doors stage play but it commemorates the shedding of much red blood not too long past."

"How it fascinates me," Mr. Stoker confessed, turning to examine the huge assemblage of tents, with massive animals being led to and fro and numerous handlers rushing between the tents. "I believed the Lyceum had mounted some stupendous spectacles. Act Four of *Faust* alone employed 250 warlocks, demons, imps, and goblins. But this . . . importing a hundred animal actors as well as hundreds of human performers and stagehands across oceans. Amazing! I'm delighted, Irene, that you have given me the opportunity to further my acquaintance with Colonel Cody," he added with a deep bow to her. "Henry Irving and Ellen Terry were among the welcoming committee when his Wild West Show played in London last year, but I fear I was overlooked among the likes of the Oscar Wildes and other notables. So I relish the opportunity to see his operations. I can learn a thing or two from Buffalo Bill about herding actors, props, and supernumeraries at the Lyceum. And here he comes now."

"Stoker," cried a tall extravagant figure that was descending upon us like a poster come to startling life.

The long yellow fringe on his buckskin shirt and trousers fluttered from the energy of his advance. A pale felt hat, extravagantly brimmed, tilted jauntily on his head. And what a proud, maned head it was, almost larger than life, like the shaggy heads of the buffalo he was famous for hunting nigh unto extinction. Though he sported a mustache and goatee, his long, curling hair rippled down his back like the loosened tresses of a woman.

But woe to any who would impugn the virility of the showman known the world over as Buffalo Bill. I'd been hearing and reading about him my entire life, thanks to Ned Buntline's inexhaustible dime novels: wagon train errand boy at twelve, Pony Express rider at fifteen, U.S. Cavalry scout and buffalo hunter at twenty, Winner of the Medal of Honor, hunting guide for Grand Dukes, star of his own stage adventures since the seventies.

This world-renowned Wild West Show merely memorialized a life that had personally reshaped the future of a continent once black with moving clouds of buffalo. In sixteen years the shaggy beasts and their Indian hunters were virtually gone; cattle and the white men have flooded onto the prairie that once knew more wood than steel. The long, bitter, and brutal Indian battles seemed over now, too. It had been almost fifteen years since William F. Cody had killed Chief Yellow Hand and taken his scalp to avenge Custer and the Seventh Cavalry only weeks after that most famous rout of the Indian

Wars. Now Indians were tame entertainers in a traveling show. I had seen Buffalo Bill quoted as saying the Sioux had not massacred Custer, that they were combating skilled fighters for the sakes of their families and their land. The hero had become a healer.

I admit that a thrill went up my spine at the famous scout's approach, akin to the chill that had shaken me when Irene and I had visited the undiscovered catacombs under Notre Dame two nights ago.

But this was a chill of national pride, not of horror. Unlike Irene, I had lived in the States until very recently. Although I had seen his Wild West Show at Madison Square Garden and knew him for a consummate performer and the commanding general of a mighty cast of men, beasts, and a few good women, I had never personally confronted the sheer magnetism of the man. It was considerable. Even Irene stood silent and contemplative in the face of such an apparition.

This was a Prince of the Prairie in the flesh, and more commanding than the fleshly Prince of Wales.

His eyes narrowed as Mr. Stoker introduced him to Irene. "You have a feisty look about you, ma'am. Do you shoot?"

"Only in self-defense." His brows lifted at her dead-serious tone. "But I fence," she added.

"Do you ride?"

"Not much or well or far, but I . . . walk a great deal."

He laughed at that.

"I fear I am a confirmed city dweller, Colonel Cody, but I have worked for the Pinkertons"—at that word the colonel straightened as if either shocked or about to give a salute—"and I come to you in search of information involving heinous crimes."

"You, a Pinkerton agent?"

"Not recently. Now that I live in Europe I handle private inquiries for my own profit and amusement." Irene came closer, touched his buckskin-clad arm. "And for persons of substance. Tiffany has been a client. And the"—for some reason she almost choked on the next name before she dropped it, but drop it she did, like a metal medieval gauntlet—"King of Bohemia. And . . . others whom I dare not name."

The narrowed eyes that had seen entire species and tribes vanish from the American West took her measure. She did not flinch, or worse, flutter.

"Well, ma'am." He doffed his hat with the same panache as he took his final bow at the end of four hours of Wild West Show. "If you are a friend of Bram, and say you need my help, I am at your disposal. For half an hour today, at any rate. I am the toast of Paree, you see, and kept running eighteen hours a day to this soirée and that, not to mention rounding up two daily shows."

"I am most grateful for your valuable time, and your help." She took his arm as if they were strolling into supper together at Kensington Palace. I could see that the veteran Indian scout was in the hands of a veteran herder of *Homo sapiens.*

"Excuse us, Bram," he said to our guide, who nodded and remained behind.

He had not exempted me.

So I slipped into step behind them, like a child content to be seen and not heard, as they moved into the trampled central arena. I noticed that although Irene was in deep conversation with the showman, she managed to avoid treading on the clumps of animal dung littering their path. Buffalo will be buffalo.

I struggled to walk in her pristine footsteps. "I walk a great deal" indeed! No wonder Buffalo Bill had taken a liking to her. She pretended to nothing, but apologized for nothing either.

I must remember that technique in future.

"You must forgive me. I have lived in Europe since I was eighteen," she began.

"Only a fortnight ago, surely, Madame."

"You have been overhearing too many Frenchmen, Colonel."

He laughed, but would not let it go. "I deal in herd animals, but I know each one. Each has a scar, a gait, a shape. A hallmark. Pardon me for putting it so plainly, but you have a hallmark like no other. I have seen you before. Not recently. In the East. Can you swear differently to this old scout?"

She was silent while they walked through the muck as if ambling in a château garden.

"The late 'seventies, do you think, Colonel?"

He nodded. "I was performing in my dime-novel plays on the Eastern seaboard then."

"Perhaps . . . *perhaps* you recall Merlinda the Mermaid and the Treasure of Blackbeard."

They stopped. Buffalo Bill stared at Irene Adler. Then he doffed his hat, made a deep Cavalier bow, and slapped his befringed leg with the brim so a small, astounded cough of dust rose in the air between them. His laugh was as loud as a thundering herd.

"I'll be damned! Held her breath for five minutes in that huge tank of water, hair longer than mine weaving like seaweed, that fancy spangled tail waving like prairie grass in a windstorm. Five minutes underwater, eyes open, in plain view. And hauling up those jeweled gewgaws all the while. I clocked you, Madame Mermaid. It was five minutes. How'd you manage it?"

"How'd you manage scalping Yellow Hand?"

"Battle bloodlust." He sighed. "I don't deny it, but the West was wild then. Men are capable of more than they think."

"Good? Or bad?"

"Both, ma'am. And women, too, I guess."

She nodded, as if he had cleared a hurdle she had set up, and abruptly changed the subject back to the first matter. "I was training to become an opera singer. I needed money for lessons. In opera, breath control is paramount. Merlinda helped me to become one who sang instead of swam for her supper, and the critics have always noted since then that my breath control is peerless."

"Grand opera or Wild West roundup. It's all a show, isn't it?"

"Yes, it is, yet I am now involved in matters that are not a show but all too real. And the bloodlust you mention is being exercised on helpless women."

He stopped again. "You've shot in self-defense?"

She nodded, once.

"Killed anything?"

"Not yet. But we were shot at the other night, near Notre Dame."

He glanced back at me, his eyes unerringly focusing on mine as if hitting a target. He had always known I was there, eavesdropping. He had heard every step and breath I took, I realized. He had never been unaware of me.

"Two women, out alone, at night?" He sounded skeptical.

"I was dressed as a man."

The silence was deafening.

"We had been at the Paris Morgue," Irene added, piling one incongruity atop another.

"Like no other," Buffalo Bill quoted himself at last. "You are going after Yellow Hand."

"In a sense. But I will take justice instead of a scalp."

"Actually, his name was Yellow Hair. The newspapers made it Yellow Hand. Guess they figured an Indian wouldn't be named Yellow Hair. Oddly appropriate name, given Custer was known for his long yellow hair."

I shuddered at the comparison: a dead cavalry colonel known for his yellow hair. The Indian known as Yellow Hair present at the battle, then later killed and scalped by a white scout and buffalo hunter and Indian slayer who now led a world-famous entertainment centered around buffalo and Indians . . .

"I have lived in Europe for a long time," Irene repeated, returning to her circuitous introduction of this topic. "I am ignorant of the ways of the frontier that you know so well, that you forged. I need to ask some ignorant questions. Will you forgive me that?"

"I'll tell you what. I will, if Merlinda the Mermaid will make an appearance at my command performance for the French president next month."

"Colonel Cody, that was a long time ago! I do not even sing opera anymore."

"Old skills never die."

"I have no costume, no tank."

"If I can cart my whole show across the Atlantic, I can come up with a few hundred gallons of water in a glass box." He eyed her as if inspecting a steed. "And I'm willing to bet that your hair is as long and your breath control is as peerless as it ever was. It was the darnedest thing I ever saw."

"Very well," Irene said, "but you won't like my questions."

"Questions never killed a man. But first I've got a thing or two to tell, or ask, you."

"Yes?"

"About that shooting near Notre Dame. At night? What? Gaslights still around there? Not electric lights?"

She nodded.

"Misty, though, fog thick as mohair coming off of the river?"

She nodded again.

"You two were silhouettes in the fog. Not recognizable."

"Unless someone knew who we were. . . ."

"Had followed you from the morgue, you mean. I was taken there. Now that's a show. They think my outfit celebrates death. Hmmph. This morgue's at the rear of the cathedral. Quite a system: church and then the morgue at the back door, so to speak. You see anyone following you?"

Irene shook her head.

"You look?"

"As best I could without being overly obvious."

He grunted. "Didn't shoot with a pistol. Revolver. Would have had to have been close enough to spot, and you were looking, right?"

She nodded, listening hard.

"Rifle. Only possible weapon. You hear the bullets hit?"

"Stone. They scored stone. Perhaps I could find the places in daylight, but it would be difficult."

"It doesn't make sense, Madame Mermaid. Not at all. No one could expect to hit a target under those conditions, not even Miss Annie Oakley."

"A warning?"

"You don't get any warnings on the prairie."

"But here?"

He nodded. "So what kind of critter are you hunting?"

"You performed in England in 1887?"

"A triumph, three command performances for Queen Victoria. It's why we're here at this World Exposition in Paris now."

"And the next year, in 1888?"

He grinned. "Three hundred years after the Spanish Armada tried to take England, and failed, we had knocked them dead on their own turf and were back in the States, playing along the seaboard where the English lost America a bit over a century ago. History is a lesson and an irony. It was another triumphal tour. Why?"

"That was the autumn in which Jack the Ripper was terrorizing Whitechapel in London."

"He was a wild one."

"But he took no scalps."

"Not . . . quite. Took a lot more."

"There have been recent deaths in Paris."

"Pulled up stakes and moved on, hmmm?"

She nodded, watching him as narrowly as an American eagle on a poster. "Mutilations. After death. Less . . . anatomical, more gruesome."

"Aha." He buried his goatee in his hand as he thought. "These Indians of mine come from a talent agency. Some are a bit wild to control, but so are the horses and the buffalo, and the cowboys, too, for that matter."

"Did any Indians leave your show while you were in England?"

"You're following the wrong trail. There's a lot of rot about the Indians been written. They have their ways and they are not ours. But what is ours? How alike are you and me? Or me and that girl? Or a French count and an Indian chief? Whoever shot at you wasn't an Indian."

"Perhaps not, but it takes nerve to use Paris pedestrians for target practice. Or blithe ignorance. Perhaps someone from another culture, from a savage past, is being used by someone quite civilized."

"Wouldn't be the first or last time." He thought again. "Was a couple Indians who deserted, only you can't call absent actors 'deserters.' That's what we all are now. Actors. Like you. Opera. Wild West Shows. A couple Indians didn't go back to the States with us after that England tour in eighty-seven."

"Do you remember their names?"

"Do I remember my own? Crazy Fox and Long Wolf. Long Wolf was quite the celebrity. Wore a black beaver top hat with his regular regalia. The English folk made quite a fuss over him. He said he had never seen a village so large and that he wished to learn its limits. Crazy Fox was another case. He had a taste for alcohol. Can't blame him. I do myself." The veteran scout laughed and shook his head. "You really think Jack the Ripper could be an Indian? What about those letters to the newspapers? They were full of Americanisms, but they weren't written by any Indian."

"The letters may have been from anyone but the Ripper."

"Who?"

"Newspaper writers hoping to sell more papers. There's quite a competition to outdo each other with sensational and sordid stories, in America, England, France."

"These reporters do jostle for something to print. And I can tell you from doing a few hundred interviews that those folks invent up one side and down the other. Usually it's to my benefit, though. Lies only add to your legend. Oscar Wilde found that out when he came to the States. He and his wife received us when we appeared in London. Love the way the English and the French are coming to us now. We have grown up as a country, Missus Norton. We are of consequence."

She smiled. "We are. So you say that the Indians are . . . utterly subdued. They would not revert to their savage ways on foreign soil."

"Their savage ways are not so different from our savage ways. I found that out when I took Yellow Hand's scalp. On the prairie there's only wind and God and what men do, and not all of it's nice. Savagery has its reasons, you must understand that. They worship their gods with their particular sacrifices. And sacrifices are always human, one way or another. We celebrate the torture of a god-man on a cross. That so different from how a Jesuit died at the hands of the Huron two hundred years ago? Some of the Plains Indians mutilate the bodies of dead enemies. We think that's savage. We kil 'em and embalm 'em and bury 'em whole. Much more civil, right? But some Indian tribes think the cuts in dead flesh release the souls to the Great Spirit, keep evil ghosts from walking the land. Savagery? Or spirituality?"

"Spirituality seems an odd concept for Indians."

"Oh, I don't know. Sitting Bull is a warrior, yes, but he is much more of a spiritual leader. Once he stopped a fray by sitting down on open ground between hostile Indian and Army forces. They shot away at each other, but not a bullet touched Sitting Bull. After a while, both sides were surprised enough to sit down with Sitting Bull and talk treaty."

"Impressive," Irene said, "but when I lived in America I heard that women who have fallen into Indian hands—"

"They can be brutal to captives, but so were the Romans. And some whites have become Indian in captivity. The Indian has lost his lands, thanks in part to me. I'd like to see them get some recompense. The ones in my show are chiefs the government would like locked up as 'hostiles' on a reservation, like Sitting Bull. Look at my posters." He gestured at the iron standards everywhere bearing colorful illustrations. "In my programs I say, 'The Former Foe—Present Friend, the American.' Can't make it plainer than that. The Plains Indians are the best light cavalry on the planet. I like working with them. They have been my enemy, but they are fine warriors. I have seen an Indian chief match the dignity of the Queen of England. She saluted our American flag at my command performance for her in London, one of three. Victoria Regina has been Queen longer than I've been on this prairie. Where would an Indian get the hatred to stalk and kill foreign women?"

"These were prostitutes. He might not understand that kind of citified corruption."

"No, the Indians didn't have brothels, but some had slaves, or prisoners of war, and those poor souls could be treated quite savagely, white or red, men or women. And some Indians, like the Apache, would rape as well as kill. But Indian women were also used by the white man. The word 'squaw' came to mean that, like 'Jane' or 'Mandy.' All were words for prostitutes on the frontier."

" 'Jane' or 'Mandy' were used as description for prostitutes in the West?"

"Now don't you go telling Calamity *Jane* that. Could get dangerous."

Irene, however, was thinking aloud. "*Mandy. Jane. Mary Jane. Mary Ann. Annie.* An Indian on his own in London might hear names like those, especially in a district like the East End that was riddled with prostitutes, and think that the white man's privilege was his at last."

"Not likely! Indians don't think tit for tat like that."

"But if one were mad?"

"Insane? I suppose it's possible. Being cut loose in some of these European cities might do that. Or drink. But not likely. They've always stuck to themselves. That's all they've wanted, and that's the only thing we white men couldn't let happen."

"And from what you know of Jack the Ripper's work, it couldn't be Indian mutilations?"

"I was traveling the Eastern seaboard when that Jack fellow was doing his worst, but I read about it in the papers. Some of the women were disemboweled. Apaches'd do that. Have done that. But they like to work on the living, and Saucy Jack was sure to kill first, with a slash to the neck. He butchered the dead. Now the Cheyenne and Sioux, they do their work in battle, or just after. They can be postmortem throat-cutters, I admit. And scalp-takers, but it's all a part of war.

"The truth is the Army and the frontiersmen, they've been as bad about after-death mutilations as anyone, once they got the idea." He glanced quickly at me as if worried about letting me overhear such things. "You've been a Pinkerton, Missus Norton, and this gal here claims sympathy for the thousands of buffalo I've slain. So I'll tell you plain: the white man, soldier or settler, he did as bad or worse. I've heard them brag of 'trophies'—purses made from Indian women's breasts, necklaces strung with toes and fingers, some of them child-size."

I gasped, and he turned to me as fast as a striking snake. "That era's over, thank God. The Indians who've survived have become curiosities, at least around the world. The Queen last year in London and some of her ladies tickled the chins of the Indian babies in our troupe, and the babes laughed, and laughter knows no language. We are ambassadors, and we give the Indians their rightful title back: Americans."

"It seems," said Irene, "as if the late unpleasantries on the frontier are nearly over."

"Oh, we may look like wild men, ma'am, but we are progressive. I am proud to number Theodore Roosevelt as a friend, and we plan to raise some dust together. I've got a town a-growing in Wyoming, but before America paves the plains with streets and tram-cars, I'm looking into plans to preserve some of the land and its creatures for the future. And," he added, looking each one of us in the eye in turn, "the women in my show earn the same as the men. I support the suffragist cause to give each and every one of 'em the vote."

"I applaud you, sir," I said, ashamed of sounding like a civic booster.

"I will believe it when I see it," Irene added, smiling ruefully.

"True, good intentions don't put food upon the widow's table," he rejoined politely, "but the notion of universal suffrage will not pass away like the buffalo. Mark my words.

"I do want to bring the American ideal of independence and enterprise to the whole world," he added. "It's my thought to form a troupe soon of the world's finest horsemen—Arabs, German Cuirassiers, Vaqueros, Cossacks, American Indians and cavalrymen, Cubans, and Pacific Islanders. East, West, or in between, they're superb riders and more alike than different."

"More alike than different," Irene repeated slowly. She waited until Buffalo Bill's full attention had returned to her. "Then the forces that created Jack the Ripper could spring from any culture. East. West. Or in between. Which is where we stand. Europe."

He fidgeted, grinding his bootheels in the muck, but finally nodded.

"Yes, ma'am. If you put it that way."

He took a deep breath. "It's possible your Whitechapel

killer is an insane Indian. Who'd blame 'em for going insane? You have to picture it: them living in the American wilds for centuries. Then a first white man comes, with a few more. And a few horses. The Indian takes the horse and forgets the riders. Then a few decades later more white men. And more horses. Then the horse soldiers. And the settlers. At first they think it's just that few and this few that they can fight. But the buffalo dwindle from the white man's guns, from a blanket of millions to a few thousand. Food, clothing, weapons, all gone. And the white man keeps coming, with his women and children and cattle and horses and guns. Finally, they see that, wide as the land they've always known is, there is other land beyond knowing, filled with other people beyond knowing, and there are not enough warriors to stop the new herd that is swallowing up the land. The folks in Europe must have felt that way when the Huns came from the East. Suddenly, everything they were was not enough. So I suppose an Indian, facing this in his lifetime, could go a little crazy. Anything is possible.

"If you need my further help, let me know. I am not a scout any longer. There is almost no more need for what I was. What I would like to be is someone who builds the future, though I am entombed by my past. I'll help you if you need it." He grinned. "And I'm itching to introduce Merlinda the Mermaid to a European audience."

35.

Of Couches and Corks

The filles who people the maison de prostitution would almost all be incapable of regulating their expenses themselves; they would fall into the most wretched misery if their material life were not governed and ensured by the maitrônes.

—DR. JULIAN JEANNEL, *DE LA PROSTITUTION*

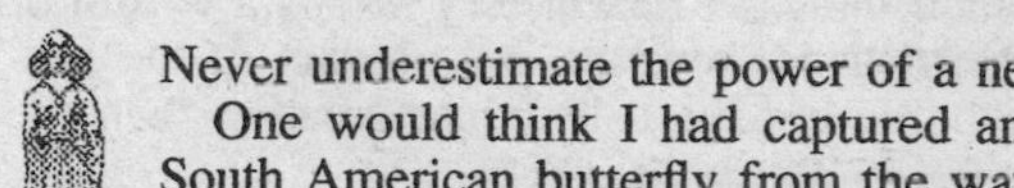

Never underestimate the power of a needle case.

One would think I had captured an ineffably rare South American butterfly from the way that Sherlock Holmes displayed my tiny prize under the lamplight.

He clapped a magnifying glass to his right eye like an oversize monocle while he pricked and stared at and . . . smelled the poor brown crumb I had carried on my person since Irene and I had visited the *maison de rendezvous.*

"If only I had my chemicals and vessels from Baker Street!" he lamented, more to himself than to me. "Or a larger sample. It is cork, of course. The wine was probably Spanish. Are you aware of the many arcane processes necessary for the production of a simple wine-bottle cork, Miss Huxleigh?"

"Thankfully no. I am barely aware of wine, sir, much less the method that lets the evil genie out of the bottle, so to speak."

He ignored my temperance speech, as most people did, but I felt obligated as a parson's daughter to make it now and again.

"I believe I see part of the impress of the letter 's' on this crumb," he went on. Obviously, this was a man used to talking to himself or to some docile associate who would only nod and clear his throat. "It could be from '*bodegas*,' the Spanish word for wine cellar. And you swear that you found this fragment on the death-chamber carpeting? Did you not say you visited the house wine cellar on another occasion?"

"Irene found the crumb of cork. And we descended to the wine cellar the next night."

"For one who avoids spirits, you have certainly frequented the wine cellars of France of late."

"Only because Irene insisted."

"She insists, does she? And you obey?"

"I have found her imperatives to be at least interesting."

"Ha!"

I could not tell if he was reacting to my words or something he had seen in that magnifying glass of his.

"It is a pity you are so incurious about the origin of bottle corks, Miss Huxleigh. Their creation is a long and laborious effort. Like all such things, a rich history means a wealth of information to be gleaned from the end product of the process. A humble bottle cork is a lengthier creation than the wine it entombs."

I murmured my surprise. This revelation was quite astounding to one who, after residing in France, had been cowed into believing that the wine-maker's art was the most ancient and holy of pursuits, eclipsing all others.

"Indeed," he said, warming to his topic, "the cork oak tree, most usually found in the sere, hot plains of Portugal, has been protected since the thirteenth century. It must grow twenty-five years and may be harvested only once every decade. Even then, the tree must have its outer bark stripped away by ax at least twice before the proper layer of cork is bared. The virgin bark is used for boards and tiles. Only the deepest, densest bark is suitable for wine corks."

For some reason I found his depiction of the process rather . . . unsettling. "I thought that the French invented all things having to do with wine," I said rather tartly. Nothing vanquishes an unsettled feeling like a tart retort.

"So do the French, but they use Portuguese cork. Actually, the notorious monk Dom Pérignon was the first to apply cork to wine bottle necks."

I frowned.

"Yes, he was the Frenchman who invented champagne. In that they are correct, but today Portugal is the largest producer of corks."

"Then why do you think the wine is Spanish?"

"Besides the telltale 's'? I can see that you do not put much faith in it, but then you have not studied wine bottles as I have."

I was tempted to comment on the obvious conclusion, but remembered my role as spy and saboteur.

He mistook my silence for acquiescence. Irene was right; he was an infant in the ways of women, particularly in the ways that women have of dealing with male presumption.

"You say the wine cellar was relatively undisturbed?" he asked.

"Yes. I was told that the usual wines were kept upstairs. Only the unusual vintage was brought from below."

"Perhaps for an unusually high-ranking patron?"

This I had not thought of. "You mean Bertie." I had no trouble referring to the Prince of Wales by that childish nickname now that I had learned just what that nasty boy was up to.

"I must see the wine cellar for myself."

"That seems wise."

"And you must accompany me to say if it has been further disturbed since your last visit."

"I? How would I know?"

"My questions will aid your memory. Besides"—he stood, having replaced the crumb of cork in my etui, which he then appropriated by tucking it into his coat pocket—"I will rely upon you to extract the name of the Crown Prince's . . . er, upholsterer from the madam of this place. These sorts of discussions are best left to women."

Also best left to women for longer even than cork had been used to stopper fine wine was . . . silent indignation.

⚜ ⚜ ⚜

Still, there was no denying the satisfaction of sweeping back into the *maison de rendezvous* in the train of Sherlock Holmes.

The doorman greeted him by name and deep bow. We were immediately escorted into the madam's private sitting room and offered sherry.

Neither of us succumbed.

"I am here, Madame," he said without taking the offered seat, "on the business of our mutual honored client."

She eyed me pointedly, clearly having forgotten my visit to her establishment with Irene.

"My, ah, secretary. She will accompany me to the wine cellar, and then I would wish you to make yourself available for any questions she might have. You realize that international matters of great moment hinge on what we do here."

"Wales is likely to see more of himself in the press than he likes," she answered with French frankness, her chins quivering with amusement. "He does so love Paris. It would be *très triste* if this last escape from the wearying rounds of statecraft were denied him. So"—she clapped fat, beringed hands together—"I can deny his emissary nothing. Even"—here she glanced at me with dismay—"if one such emissary dresses like a shopgirl.

"If there is any service of the house you would like after your investigations, Mr. Holmes, I would be happy to provide . . . her. Or them."

His expression tautened to match my inner indignation. "Thank you, no, Madame. My investigations in all cases are reward enough. I will leave you now, but Miss Huxleigh will return shortly."

She sighed her disappointment and fluttered lamp-blacked eyelashes.

Sherlock Holmes observed her as he would a bug twitching under a pin.

"Au revoir," he said, with a curt bow, exiting the room and leaving me to totter after him.

In the passage he stopped to take a deep breath, his hands shifting on the handles of the doctor's bag he had brought with him. "I must apologize, Miss Huxleigh, for exposing you to such shameless sorts as Madame Portiere."

"That is nothing," I said, "for one who has been exposed to such a shameless sort as the Prince of Wales."

He eyed me with one eyebrow raised. "You are obviously a stout-hearted soul. You see that I have a certain authority by virtue of my illustrious client. I advise you to keep your opinion of him to yourself in this place, for I rely upon you to gain the information I require from that corrupt creature. It is not a task for a gentlewoman, but I trust that you see it is necessary."

I nodded, speechless. He had called me a gentlewoman, which bespoke some notion of gentlemanliness on his part, will wonders never cease.

I led him to the back stairs and the route to the wine cellar, well remembering my last descent this way with Irene and Pink. Elizabeth, that is. Though household servants observed us, they offered no challenge. I suspect the detective's tall, spry figure was no stranger to any part of this vast house. In the kitchen he swooped an oil lamp from a table and announced his intent to borrow it. No one objected although all watched like chained mastiffs.

We plunged down the narrow stone stairs to the wine cellar.

"It is difficult to imagine the Prince visiting these lower regions," he remarked, as we entered the damp, dark kingdom of Brother Dom Pérignon.

I was reminded of princes of darkness from Gothic novels, of hooded figures gathering in dungeons, of torture chambers and blasphemous ceremonies. . . .

Nothing stirred, save the occasional rat. Which brought my mind back to Bertie.

"Why would you suppose the Prince had been down here?"

"He is known to go where Princes seldom do . . . the cancan clubs in Montmartre, artists' studios, houses like this. I admit that I wonder if perhaps His Royal Highness did not precede Miss Pink on the death scene. No one would admit it, of course."

"Really? You would dare suspect your own client? Not to mention your future King?"

"I serve my calling and no man. Or woman," he added sternly. "You do not know, and you may not choose to believe, Miss Huxleigh, that I disliked the King of Bohemia from the first, and to the last."

I was not surprised, having read Dr. Watson's account of the affair, but I could not admit it. "Yet you took his commission," I pointed out.

"He seemed to have a grievance."

"You no longer believe so?"

"I believe the note your friend left for me: that he had wronged her, and she only defended herself. The King himself admitted at the end that her word was incontrovertible. That fact alone clashed with his earlier depiction of her as a spurned woman and heartless adventuress. I would have procured the photograph for him if I could have. As it was . . . I am not unhappy with the outcome, and neither was the King."

"She did leave another portrait for the King."

At that his quick eyes ceased darting around the dim cellar. I glimpsed an ironic smile that the lamp in his hand turned slightly sinister.

"That she did, and an appealing portrait it was. Most appealing."

This reminded me of the doctor's words on this artifact, which were branded on my memory (and later onto my diary pages, in case I should ever forget a jot of it): "And when he speaks of Irene Adler, or when he refers to her photograph, it is always under the honorable title of *the* woman." So just how often does Mr. Sherlock Holmes have occasion to refer to this photograph, and why?

"I am sure the King was glad to have some small, tangible remembrance of the woman he could never have," I said stiffly. "Irene can forgive, but she can never forget."

I surprised a strange expression on Sherlock Holmes's angular face. Someone from Shropshire would have called it "sheepish." But it must have been a trick of the flickering lamplight. *The* man was far too self-sufficient to feel sheepish about anything, much less show it.

"Ah!" He knelt on the cold dirt floor, gazing upon the subtle waves in the surface. "Is this much more trampled since your last visit?"

"Not at all, to my eye."

"Here! The French heel from the murder chamber. The American *jeune fille,* I think."

"You need not use French with me, even if the heel is such."

"It is hard to describe Miss Pink," he said, then hesitated. "Very hard indeed. I am aware that certain brutish members of my sex drive some women into desperate actions. I would like to think that Miss Pink is such a young person."

"So would I," I said fervently.

He stared at me.

I had not meant to be in agreement.

"I understand that she is under Madam Irene's wing now," he said.

"Indeed. We both couldn't countenance her remaining in this place of . . . of assignation."

"And death," he added sardonically. "Assignation is not usually fatal, I am given to understand."

"Of course we would not want her in physical danger either."

"Well done," he said, "though I may need to speak to her later. What was her dainty foot doing down here?"

"She called us to the cellar to see the disturbance."

"And what brought her below in the first place?"

"I don't know. She is an enterprising girl. Perhaps she had been sent down to fetch a bottle of wine."

"No mere girl would be called upon to do that. There is a house wine steward. Not only do the distinguished patrons expect to eat and drink well here, but the residents themselves are offered first-class cuisine and spirits. It encourages them to enjoy their work, I'm told."

"Oh! This is such a disgusting subject. I really do not care to know the habits of the house."

"Habits, however, are the undoing of every criminal whose path has crossed mine." He set the leather bag to the side. I wondered whether he had appropriated Dr. Watson's equipage, but there was no monogram on the brass fittings. And then I wondered about the man with the sinister parcel in Whitechapel. Did "Lipski" carry an unseen doctor's bag? Was this it?

"I have work to do here, Huxleigh," he murmured absently.

I started as if stabbed.

"Your task awaits upstairs," he reminded me, unaware that I might take umbrage at being addressed in the brusque, impersonal manner of surname-only that betters use to servants, or men use between men. "Do remember that you have every right to whatever information you wish. You are temporarily my agent, and I am the agent of the Prince of Wales. You will not be intimidated?"

"Indeed not!"

Thus launched, I stomped back up the stairs and through the service areas until I was once again in the elegant portions of the house.

Imagine my horror after knocking on the madam's chamber door again and being invited in to find the room full of fallen women.

Not only fallen, but lounging about the furnishing in hose and corselet and gaping dressing gown, their hair frowsy bird's-nests and their bosoms barely contained.

Momentarily speechless, I could not at first discern Madame Portiere's figure of painted and melted tallow, rather like a burned wax museum piece, among the mob of *demoiselles* in deshabille.

I really had no idea where to look, for everything my eye fell upon was quite improper. I could only imagine what Sherlock Holmes would make of this assemblage. I felt like a new instructress at a bizarre girls' academy. And Madame Portiere was headmistress!

Quel nightmare, as the French would say, if they had a word for nightmare, which perhaps they do, but I don't know it. Fortunately.

"The great detective delves below?" the madam's voice came from somewhere amongst this display of disintegrating lingerie.

She at least used English. I followed the sound to find her

reclining on a chaise longue in a dressing gown with her stays loosened.

Sherlock Holmes had much to answer for by sending me into this den of indecency, but I approached the woman while her collection of coquettes watched and snickered.

"My business is confidential," I told her.

"So is ours." Enough of them knew English to laugh, and I imagine that they were used to English-speaking clients.

"Then sit beside me." The madam patted the foot of the chaise longue.

I had no desire to join this flock of half-attired women, but apparently she would offer me a private interview.

I sat, feeling I was in the midst of a colony of feral cats or chattering pigeons, for the women were both girlish and quite predatory, I suppose.

I also imagined that the gentlemen (I use the word as a courtesy) who came to claim their favors were also subjected to their united and disconcerting summation.

There was such a sense of lazy feminine power in the room. I had never encountered anything like it. Or was it a sense of forbidden knowledge, as if they were sibyls the gods had visited and made mad, and therefore were powerful where before they had no power?

I sensed that they would hold an equal contempt for both the guilty and the innocent. As for themselves.

While I regarded their disheveled hair and slack expressions, their vigilant eyes, I found myself longing for the clean, cutting company of Sherlock Holmes.

Oh, to be scrabbling on my hands and knees on the cold dirt of the deserted wine cellar than to be perched on these upholstered roosts for a flock of vultures in female guise. For the first time I understood the ancient Greeks' concept of the Furies.

"And what do you want, miss?" the madam demanded lazily.

"The name of the designer who constructed the, ah, couch that the two dead women were found upon."

"Crave one for yourself, no doubt," she responded.

I gazed into her slitted, mocking eyes and remembered what this interview was about.

"This is serious business, Madame. No doubt Mr. Holmes could extract this information from you in person, but his patron would be unhappy to hear he had been forced to deal with such minor matters personally."

She tried to push herself up against the chaise back, but she was too corpulent to manage the move with any dignity.

" 'His patron,' " she finally said, "commissioned that particular piece. He might not like that known. Why does not this Mr. Holmes who knows everything ask the Prince?"

"Because royalty will not be troubled with trifles, Madame. Bertie does not care who created this commission, as long as it suits him. He does care that his designated agent should have all possible assistance in stopping these vicious murders before the autumn horrors of Whitechapel become better known as the spring terrors of *le tout Paris*."

I spoke with hauteur, which the French respect above all other attitudes. It did not come naturally to me, but I had been taught by masters: Irene Adler and now, latterly, Sherlock Holmes.

"Durand," she snapped through lips curdled with paint and disdain. "In the rue Caron. Why the great Sherlock Holmes should chase a cabinetmaker, I do not know."

I stood. "That is why he is the great Sherlock Holmes and you are just . . . Madame. Madame."

I nodded and took my leave. The *demoiselles* cooed like pigeons behind me, and I did not dare imagine what they would be doing in the many nights to come, on what examples of the cabinetmaker's art.

36.

Couched in Ambiguity

The manifestly made-up woman is too atrocious a blot on the landscape to even discuss.

—HARRIET HUBBARD AYER

"Very well," said Irene, daubing more soot on her wet eyelashes, "I will take only Pink then."

The room stank of sulphur, as Hell must. A long row of burnt lucifers lay on the dresser next to the pier mirror before which we stood.

Speechless, I wrung my hands.

"I don't know why Sherlock Holmes left you to investigate the cabinetmaker, Nell, but I'm glad that you chose to obscure your information."

"I could not actually lie, of course, not even to him," I admitted (though I could happily avenge myself for that unthinking "Huxleigh"). "I can only say that my French is pitiable and Madame Portiere's English is almost as bad. I cannot help it if Durand in the rue Caron sounded more like Durant in the rue Capron when I reported our conversation to Mr. Holmes."

"Poor man! I hate to mislead him, but I'm certain that I will extract better information from the cabinetmaker than he would. Matters involving the secret personal habits of royalty require a subtle approach."

In illustration of which, she turned from her image in the mirror, hands on hips, confronting me with frizzled hair, a powdered face so pale it looked both ghostly and ghastly, reddened lips and cheeks, and charred eyelashes.

"You are still far more presentable," I pointed out, "than Madame Portiere."

"I dare not look too raddled or I would not be taken for someone who had a refined and wide enough clientele to require, much less pay for, a *siège d'amour*."

"Refined!" I glanced at Elizabeth across the chamber, who was shaking out the flounces on her absinthe green taffeta skirt. Irene had curled and snarled the girl's dark hair into a bird's-nest festooned with too many ribbons, and her face too was a mask of thick whitening paste, rouge, and burnt-lucifer black.

"Please come with us, Nell," the minx pled. "Three would be more convincing than two."

"I would not be convincing at all in the role you two assume."

"You would not need to say anything," Irene suggested. "Just add . . . presence."

"I have no presence."

"You will when I am through with you."

That could be taken as either a threat or a challenge. I was annoyed enough to rise to both, but decided that this was more a matter of duty. While Elizabeth's experience in a house of tolerance was undeniable, Irene, for all her knowledge of princes and prosceniums, was still a respectable barrister's wife. Since the respectable barrister was not here to rein in her whims, I must be there to do it for him. It is amazing into what shocking straits I must continually put myself merely by trying to keep others on the straight and narrow path.

"Very well," I said with a heavy sigh. "Do your worst."

Of course, later, I was rather sorry to have said that.

The only consolation was that I looked quite unlike myself.

After half an hour's labor with the iron, my hair had been tortured into a series of tight curls around my face, which itself resembled a china doll's that had been attacked by a set of rogue watercolors.

My gown was also courtesy of Irene's forays into the Paris street markets, which, she told me, the French call *marchés aux puce, puce* being the enterprising fleas so often found on discarded clothing. She assured me that no fleas inhabited my gown. It was of plaid silk in the colors of poison green—*chartreuse* to the French, who are never too weary to find a new word for decadence and which is taken from the green-colored liqueur that another monk (naturally, France is full of brewer-monks) invented—and pink, for which I already knew the French did not have an exact word, no doubt because of its baby-innocent connotations. The gown's arrangement most resembled those frilly draperies known as Austrian curtains. The bodice neckline was barely suitable for evening, "bare" indeed being the case. I refused the use of powder and rouge upon my bosom, although Irene assured me that the Princess of Wales used all these artifices for evening events.

"The poor woman is married to 'Bertie,' " I spat. "She cannot be expected to have any judgment whatsoever."

"Of course," Irene added, using the rabbit's foot to daub the fruits of the rouge pot lightly at my forehead, nose tip, and chin, "such stratagems are best employed with a much lighter hand. China ink and rosewater for the lashes, for instance, instead of burnt matches or cork. And I have never countenanced drawing blue veins on my skin to imply a translucent complexion. One begins to resemble a road map. But perhaps I am wrong to overlook this 'vein' artifice. We do not wish to be subtle."

"I certainly do not feel subtle."

My neck was already stiff, for the back of my hair had been left down and lay heavy on my shoulders. This fact alone made me feel completely undressed, although I was, in fact, lamentably overdressed. How could that be?

Elizabeth eyed me enviously in the mirror. "Oh, Nell, you make up so deliciously more tawdry than I do." She fitfully jerked her neckline out of order, to little effect. I became aware that I was more generously equipped than she. I was not used to being "more" of anything than anyone, and it was an unsettling discovery. "Perhaps it's because you are usually so much more proper than I. We do make a trio, though, don't we?"

She pranced over to link arms with Irene and me, forward girl! We looked like the Three Musketeers of the Moulin Rouge in the looking glass: feathered and frilled and off for adventure. Still, our grossly frivolous appearance poignantly reminded me of Annie Chapman's "jolly bonnet" and Liz Stride's treasured "piece of velvet" that she had left for safe-keeping with a friend. Forever.

Perhaps that friend was wearing it now in Whitechapel, standing up against some wall like a sheep, hoping for pence to buy a bed for the night . . .

I tore my gaze from our altered images in the mirror. This was a game of pretend. The rest was real.

"Nell! Are you all right?" Irene shook my arm.

"Of course. But you will have to do all of the interrogation."

"*Mais oui, mademoiselle*. You two are just for show. Together we compose an entire house of disrepute, and thus will be taken seriously."

Still, she led us out the back stairs of the hotel. We passed a chambermaid and a footman.

They looked away, but didn't comment or raise an alarm. I realized that they were used to seeing fallen women slinking up and down the back stairs, and perhaps were well paid by the gentlemen guests to hold their tongues.

It was indeed another world into which I walked, or tottered, rather, on Irene's second-best satin dancing slippers. Which pinched.

Although the sun had not yet warmed the late afternoon with its rosé glow, we were still far too flagrantly got up for the hour and won many arched-eyebrow looks on the street. Too many apparent gentlemen tipped their hats.

"Shameless!" Irene hissed to us as a stage direction. "Remember. Our own mothers wouldn't know us."

"I've never known my own mother," I put in.

"Nor I," Irene admitted.

Pink was silent. When I looked at her she shrugged. "As you recall, my mother was widowed twice and then forced to divorce her brute of a third husband. I was the eldest girl and expected to earn my way for the whole family."

"They expected *this* of a young girl!?"

"No. I did some office work first, but the pay was not enough." At this she looked away as though to indicate she would say no more on the subject.

Irene had hailed a cab with a flagrant wave of her gaudily gloved hand. In moments we three were stuffed into the seat meant for two and were jolting toward the cabinetmaker's.

"What kind of establishment will this be?" I wondered.

"Respectable, I presume," Irene said. "The elegance of the piece we saw created for Bertie bespeaks that. Like all businesses that prize royal patronage, it will be discreet and certainly not specific about what the royally commissioned furniture was in this case."

Irene paid our fare after we dismounted the carriage. The blasé driver flicked his horse onward without a backward look.

A dusty gilt sign above the door read Durand Frères. There was no display window, not even a bell above the door to announce us.

"No doubt Durand Frères call upon clients, rather than the clients calling upon them," Irene said, thinking aloud. "Since we are unconventional clients, we will have to brazen it out."

Her gloved hand hesitated above the doorknob, then seized it and wrenched it open.

The door opened on silent hinges, and we walked into the second most enchanting smell in Christendom. The first is freshly baked bread, and I must admit that Paris produces the finest, most fragrant form of this simple staple of life. The second scent is not the perfume any city is renowned for, but, to me at least, the divine odor of freshly cut wood.

Perhaps their attraction is that both odors are common to the kitchens and outbuildings of the humblest cottage and the most magnificent castle or château alike.

We smell them and all think of home.

Odd as it may seem, this was the first time that I considered myself a resident of Paris rather than a refugee and visitor.

A doleful little man in a (gasp) leather apron scuttled to greet us.

His torrent of words became a ripple Irene translated for Elizabeth and me: this was a workshop, not a place of commerce.

Irene loosed her own torrent, all the while the little man blinked to regard each of us in turn. He began to blush and bow, then vanished into the larger room beyond.

Faint light fell through the still-open door, which made chair frames naked of upholstery cast tortured shadows on the floor. I felt as if I was in the lumber room of a favorite house where I had been a governess: the Turnpennys of Berkeley Square, for instance, where I had played blindman's buff with Allegra and her friends, and, unbeknownst to me until much too late, with her very dashing uncle Quentin. . . .

Disturbed dust swirled in the single shaft of daylight, dancing like tiny fairies in a moonbeam. I heard the distant rhythm of a hammer. The entire effect was so soporific that I felt like Alice dozing off before she slipped down the rabbit hole into Wonderland.

At last the gnome reappeared, behind him a figure so like Charles Frederick Worth, the Englishman who gowned women the world over, that I almost clapped my hands and laughed in delight.

He wore a velvet beret, a poet's shirt, a brocade apron.

"I am maestro," he said proudly in French-accented English that for once sounded charming instead of silly. "You wish to compliment me upon a creation?"

"Indeed," Irene said, beaming. The obvious paint melted away under the radiant force of her unabetted personality. "You are an artiste, *monsieur*. I have seen the magnificent *siège d'amour* you made for . . . well, for a man of great prominence in the English-speaking world."

Here the *artiste* laughed and pantomimed a massive stomach. "Prominence indeed, *Mademoiselle*, that is why the *siège* was needed."

"As you say." She dimpled, she fluttered her eyelashes. She did all but wink. She played the perfect coquette, and I reflected what an actress the world had lost when the King of

Bohemia and Sherlock Holmes had conspired to force her fictional death.

"*Monsieur.*" She took his arm; they were old acquaintances from this moment on. I saw Elizabeth staring after them as if watching a scene oddly familiar. They walked a bit away, but Elizabeth and I could still overhear them.

"*Monsieur.* I am . . . ah, an American in Paris. I have a little house, yes?"

"*Une maison. Mais oui, Mademoiselle.* Like Madame Kelly's."

"Not so famous as Madame Kelly's, but perhaps you can help me make mine so." Without uttering one falsehood, Irene was building the impression she wished on the foundation of his own expectations.

"I need . . . such a chair. *Siège. D'amour. Pour ma maison.*"

She could have been requesting a last tumbler of water for her dying mother. The *artiste's* sensitive features quivered. To deny such a charming mademoiselle was against the Parisian code of honor.

"I have heard," she said, most affected. "Of the . . . foul desecration of your magnificent creation at, um . . ." She whispered the name of the house into his ear. "Is it possible you could create another?"

"*Possible! C'est possible. C'est vrai.*" He was so beside himself with triumph that he pushed open a door into the vast workroom behind the sun-dusted foyer, and we all entered.

"Lillian Russell's diamond spider garters!" Elizabeth gasped beside me. "Who would think the world would need so many sieges of love! Or what passes for it."

"The word is *siège*," I corrected her, ever the alert governess. I was, after all, the elder. But I was also astounded by the array of these odd creations.

And still the filtered rays from the skylight high above us played with dust motes, and the rich scent of sawdust filled our nostrils like sandalwood. Again I was struck by the impossibility of describing them, these sort-of brocaded sledges or sleighs with spidery leaf-twined gilt limbs.

Monsieur mistook our bemusement for admiration.

"These are, of course, a very hidden part of my craft. The price is—"

"Princely," Irene said.

He bowed. "Perhaps something in the way of stools?"

"No, we require a chair." She walked around one. "May we . . . inspect, in private?"

"Of course."

He vanished into the dust motes and beyond the door, which hushed shut behind him.

"I had not seen the like, until I got to Paris," Elizabeth said, walking around the nearest *siège*.

I attempted to make sense of its sinuous shape. Although the upper "seat" curved softly back like a chaise longue, below the supporting tendrils of carved wood, at floor level, was a sort of built-in sofa bed, with a small neck roll at one end, a middle section that was double-tufted, where the scored metal footrests protruded with their decorative end cups, and then a curved frontal lip.

Irene saw me studying that apron of upholstery so near the floor. "A kneeler, I suppose."

"This is a Romanish religious artifact?"

"Hardly. Pink, perhaps you could attempt to arrange yourself on the contraption. The draping skirts of the murdered woman above obscured the position of the one below."

It quite cramped my stomach to watch Elizabeth slither onto the bottom tier, pulling her skirts through the cage of struts, lying back, placing her boot soles into the flat metal sheaths. "Stirrups," Irene had called them, and they were oddly similar. Elizabeth's skirted knees jutted into the air in a position that struck a faint memory. As a child I had blundered into a cottage bedroom where a woman was giving birth.

"Such a very odd feeling," Elizabeth exclaimed. "There is a painting on the underside of the upper tier, so the bottom lady has something to look at, I suppose."

"What is the subject of the painting?" Irene inquired.

I shut my eyes.

"I think . . . Zeus raping Europa. You know, the white bull—"

I kept my eyes closed.

Irene walked around the abomination. The lovely smell of sawdust had turned to something wretched. "Women arranged on this 'seat of love' would not be able to move quickly if someone came at them unexpectedly."

"From behind," Elizabeth pointed out, straining to lift her head a trifle from the embroidered upholstery to demonstrate her confinement. She was as helpless as a tortoise on its back.

Irene leaned against the graceful but bizarre upper arms. "This time the Ripper wouldn't have to wait for his victims to fall to the ground, both were down and ready."

"Do you think," I asked, "that he had just happened upon them?"

She nodded, briskly. "I do. They had come early to the assignation with the Prince. Such women like to set the stage, do they not, Pink?"

"Give me a hand up, Nell," she ordered, thrashing to work free of the metal stirrups and the wooden struts that hemmed her in.

I reached down gingerly, not sure those metal appliances wouldn't snap at me like lethal jaws.

She grunted as she finally came upright again. "They would have done as I did. Tried out the new toy. Once they were flat on their backs . . ."

"Their necks were offered to the slaughter." Irene gazed at the empty upholstery. "He could cut their throats in a simple sweep from behind, like a barber turned surgeon. And this is just the weapon to do it."

She held up a flat-edged, wooden-handled chisel, a homely object that suddenly looked sinister.

"He!" I demanded. "Who?"

"I'll ask," she said mysteriously, gliding to the open door.

I heard her talking with the cabinetmaker in the other room. "A *ripping* chisel, you say. Such a . . . descriptive name for a simple tool."

I shuddered at her underlying emphasis. A reciprocal murmur that indicated negotiation came next, softening into purrs, then chirps of utter agreement.

"And I shall expect," she finished, leading the *artiste* like a lamb back to the unlikely sacrificial altar of his creation, "impeccably smooth upholstery. Can you not send someone along to assist with the installation?"

He frowned, bereft of good news and too shattered to transmit the bad. "Alas, *Mademoiselle!* We have just lost our finishing upholsterer and have not hired another."

"Lost? Has he rolled under a sofa, like a thumbtack?"

Monsieur shrugged unhappily. "Such a splendid workman. Such almost surgical precision with the knife and the nail, devoted to his art. That is why I hired a foreigner and allowed him to work on a piece destined for—well, I may tell you, *Mademoiselle*—royalty. Alas, he has disappeared since installing the *siège d'amour.* I cannot explain it. Perhaps the scandalous purpose of the *siège* and the *maison de rendezvous* unnerved him. He was English."

"He was there, then?"

"Supposedly, but he was a strange man, mad about the violin and little else, though a superb upholsterer. He had walked to Paris, he said, from the north. He had been apprenticed in upholstery at the age of fifteen, and I found his work excellent, so entrusted him with the finishing work on the Prince of Wales's *siège*. I hired two men with a cart to deliver it, and sent James along to ensure that the fabric was smooth after transport."

"Smooth," I repeated, repelled by the extraordinary care given to an object of debauchery.

"James?" Irene inquired.

"Kellee," he said, "likc the infamous madam, you know." His tone implied that all we fallen women would know one another. "He had worked with the East London Upholsterer's Trade Society, and we all know how precise the English are about their dress and upholstery."

"Oh, yes," Irene agreed, rolling her eyes toward me. "To the English, good dress *is* upholstery, and they are always agonizingly meticulous. In fact, you could say that fashion makes upholstery of all women.

"I have American and English girls," she added with a glance at me. "It would be useful to have an English-speaking upholsterer. I may provide my own fabric from Worth, if that is satisfactory."

The man's eyes bulged. "You . . . know the great couturier Worth?"

"Indeed. I have been of some service to him in the past."

"But . . . he is devoted to his wife."

"Purely business, *Monsieur*, if anything is purely business in Paris. Now, surely, you must have some idea of where this gifted but nomadic upholsterer dwells. A description would be useful as well."

⚜ ⚜ ⚜

"East London," Irene said tightly as the three of us left Durand Frères.

"We must go there?" I asked, startled.

"No, but James Kelly obviously *was* there. Medium-dark mustache, neat, clerkish appearance, five-foot-five or -seven indeed. How inconsiderate of Saucy Jack to be so annoyingly middling in all his particulars. Half the male population of the known world could be the Ripper!"

We hurried along the cobblestones. The elusive upholsterer's lodgings were only a few streets distant. I was tired of gazing through the veil of lucifer haze on my lashes, so I brushed a forefinger against them. The cream-colored glove came away smeared with soot.

"Oh!"

"Face paints demand constant consideration," Irene agreed, "but they are necessary on the stage."

"They do not look so garish there."

"That's because the limelights wash out the color."

I observed various people we passed. The women gathered their skirts to pull them aside from contact with ours. The men eyed us appreciatively.

"I can't help feeling that someone could recognize me, and then what will I do?"

"We will encounter no one we know in this part of Paris, Nell."

Elizabeth had been uncharacteristically quiet, and suddenly I knew why.

"There," she said, putting a hand on my arm to stop me, for I felt that if I walked fast enough, no one would be able to focus on my disreputable appearance.

"There is the patisserie we were told about, and there . . . number forty-four, that door painted blue-green. The Durand Frère said Kelly kept rooms on the first floor."

Such a plain whitewashed building for frilly Paris, mean almost! Its long French windows were fenced with wrought-iron railings behind a tiny balcony barely wide enough to hold a cat, although one did.

"Not prosperous," Irene noted. "Unfortunately, even for this neighborhood we are not properly dressed to impress the concierge."

While we paused to consider what we could do about this, I heard a sharp whistle behind me. I turned to face the street.

Elizabeth caught my forearm and spun me back toward the building. "Ignore rude whistles, or we shall get ruder attentions."

"How do you know it was a rude whistle meant for us?"

"Have you never had a rude whistle directed at you before?"

I shook my head, trying to brush off another layer of char since my glove was already tainted.

Before we could do more, a snapping crack above us made us stare. One of the first-floor windows was flung open and a man came crashing through, balancing for a moment with one thick work shoe atop the balcony railing, then springing off and down into the street.

The impact almost took our breaths away.

Then his feet were pounding past us. Irene lunged toward him and thrust her booted foot into his path.

He sprawled forward, facedown on the cobblestones so hard I winced.

"Sit on him!" Irene ordered. "Hold him at all costs." I glanced where she was looking, which was back at the window.

An apparition hung there, a man in a priest's long, black,

buttoned cassock, with a shock of snowy white hair.

He vanished as soon as I spied him, so Irene hurried to the small door that led to the building's stairs.

"Nell!" Elizabeth cried. "We must both sit or we will not hold him."

I eyed the moaning figure on the street with distaste. I would really rather arrange myself on a nice clean *siège d'amour* than this filthy lout.

I gave up and let myself sink down upon his back. The air left his lungs with a bellowslike wheeze.

As I looked around I could see that the rude loungers who had whistled at us were now grinning from Gallic ear to Gallic ear.

Irene and the clergyman were speeding to our rescue, however. "May I help you, *Mademoiselles*?" the old man asked in beautifully stentorian French.

With that he bent, snagged the fellow by the back of the collar with stern strength, and dragged him to his feet. "You could have hurt yourself, my son."

The priest was a commanding, wiry man, but perhaps the moral force of his garb quieted the fellow the most, for he became almost obsequious.

"I am sorry, Father. So sorry, Father. Forgive me, Father," he began babbling in English. "I know not what I do."

"*Merci, Mademoiselles,*" the priest said, bowing. "I will help this unfortunate back to his rooms. Apparently he is suffering from dementia."

"We will assist you," Irene said.

I tugged mightily on her gown sleeve. I had no wish to go up to whatever dreary room lay behind that gaping window.

"*Non, non.*" The elderly priest smiled with sweet urbanity. "These young ladies must be about their business and leave this poor soul to me."

He was really quite a commanding figure, despite wearing skirts, and I was beginning to think I spied a glint reminiscent of my parson father's kindly expression behind the spectacles that lay under his thick snowy brows as "eyebrow" windows underline a mansard roof. . . .

Irene spoke again. "I will be about my *father*'s business,

indeed," she said. "This is not my first encounter with elderly clergymen in the street."

His gaze sharpened as he took in her attire. "If that is so, then you are obviously in need of instant shriving, and should seek the nearest church." He drew the man's arm over his neck and began guiding him back into the building.

"We are as wicked as you are saintly, *Père*," Irene called after him in tones I could only call ringing, and when a contralto opera singer wishes her voice to ring, she is a full carillon. "We will accompany you."

Elizabeth and I exchanged quick glances. Irene said "sit," we had sat. Irene said "go," we would go.

We stepped forward as one, or three.

The face of the man named Kelly grew frantic. "No! Keep them away from me! They are tainted. You're a holy priest. You must save me from them!" His words alternated English and French phrases, like one new to a foreign language, and I understood the whole.

Instead of struggling to elude the old man's custody, Kelly now sank to his knees and clutched the cassock folds like a terrified child.

"I will confess anything," he cried, "only keep those fiends of hell from me."

"I think," Irene said to the priest in French, "we will be of good use to you."

His once-sweet old face grew sour.

"Oh, very well," said Sherlock Holmes, in French, not English. I think this was the gist of it: "I suppose you assisted in his capture, although I would have had him secured by the café at the corner. I was about to suggest you would do best sending for le Villard, but I am not ready for him yet."

He gazed at the confused man now down on his knees in the street, clutching his skirt hem, but he spoke to Irene. "Come along, if you must, but the place reeks of boiled tripe and garlic."

37.

We Three Queens

All three had brilliant white teeth, that shone like pearls against the ruby of their voluptuous lips . . . something about them that made me uneasy, some longing and at the same time some deadly fear. I felt in my heart a wicked, burning desire that they would kiss me with those red lips. . . . Faugh! . . . They are devils of the Pit!

—BRAM STOKER, *DRACULA*

These unsavory cooking odors, and others too unpleasant to spend time naming, crowded with us into the small passage, where we confronted the place's guardian.

The concierge was a sharp-faced woman with hair of the same lurid shade as in a poster for some Montmartre establishment of low repute. She ordinarily would not have let even President of the Republic Carnot go unchallenged, I am sure.

Still, she was so taken aback by our cortege—stately priest, distraught lodger, and three painted women—that she let us proceed inside without a word. I heard a series of clicks after we passed. She was either fumbling for her rosary beads or her absinthe bottle. With the French both are props of the soul in times of uncertainty.

We trudged up the dark, narrow stairs, single file, our prisoner first, then Father Holmes, then Irene, Elizabeth, and I.

The hapless Kelly resided in a room on the first floor, just off the stairwell.

Docile, though still apparently unnerved, he led the priest

through a door that was still ajar. We followed until we were fully in a mean little room bare of any but the most necessary furnishings.

While Sherlock Holmes sat Kelly down at an uneven-legged table matched with a pair of rickety stools, I surveyed the cot covered with soiled blankets, a visible night jar near it, and a chair missing its back struts in a corner. There was no fireplace, only the one door, the window over the street, and a smaller window high up on the sidewall.

The upholsterer's room sported not one piece of furniture that was covered with anything more than grime or dust.

Without a word being said by anyone, Irene marched to the long window overlooking the street, whose frame held glass windows split into two in the style known as "French doors."

She swiftly drew the gaping side closed to match its sister, then jerked her head to summon Elizabeth, who sped to take a position before the secured windows.

I was nearest the door. At Irene's nod, I shut it and stationed myself there.

Sherlock Holmes had ignored our movements, concentrating his attention on the prisoner as he pushed him onto one stool.

Irene went to the chair in the corner, and sat.

Kelly's eyes followed our every move as if Mesmerized.

I was not used to inspiring dread in anyone, and was amazed that I could do it only in so debased a guise, though I myself should have shrunk from us three in the streets, not knowing our true characters.

Yet in this room, only one person was in his true character, and that was the suspect.

"You will keep them away from me, Father?" he whined.

How could we harm him, really? Especially if he was upright enough to resist the temptations posed by such women as we impersonated.

But he kept twisting on his stool to assure himself that we remained at the fringes of the room. I sensed that he would rather perish than attempt to cross a threshold we guarded.

"You are James Kelly, the East End upholsterer?" Mr. Holmes asked him, also speaking in English.

Kelly blinked, his muddy hazel gaze sharpening for an instant. "Strange. I am hearing in tongues. That is such sweet heavenly music, a chorus speaking in dozens of tongues. Here there are two tongues anyway. Your holy presence keeps those demons at bay, Father, and I have been permitted to hear your French words in English. Do not leave me, I beg you! They will fly upon me like mad things and force me into lewd acts."

"Rest easy, my son. I can tell that you are not well."

"Not well! I have been tainted by these devilish women! A pox upon them who have given me a pox, innocent lad that I am. It is a foul conspiracy. Can you not make them vanish, Father?"

"Alas"—Sherlock Holmes looked over his shoulder at Irene seated in the corner, glanced at Elizabeth and me standing guard at the window and door—"I have hoped for such deliverance before, but it has not yet been granted. Now."

He drew away, looked down on the man, and his voice assumed an authoritarian certainty. "You are an upholsterer by trade, and that is your most recent pursuit, but I see that you followed the sea for some time. You were born in Liverpool, have been briefly married but descended into drink and debauchery. I see the blood of a murder on your hands."

Irene and I had witnessed Sherlock Holmes's skill at assessing people's pasts from the present testimony of their speech eccentricities, their dress and demeanor, and the telltale marks of professions or pursuits upon their anatomy.

James Kelly had not. His eyes protruded like a puppet's. For a moment he forgot the demonic presence of three fallen women, two of whom were innocent of all wrongdoing.

"Y-you know? But I have seen Him already. The Master came and gathered the flock until the Holy Spirit descended in tongues of flame everywhere, and all we disciples prayed in tongues and drank the blood of Our Lord. Our Lord was a carpenter and I am a mere upholsterer, but still I pounded the bloody nails and must atone, must atone. I have seen the

Master and you are not He. How can you be He who will save me?"

A distinctly uncomfortable expression passed over Sherlock Holmes's disguised features. Although his detective work might have "saved" innumerable clients from disgrace and even death, I suspect that he found the notion of spiritual salvation a repugnant one, at least in relation to himself as either the object or bestower of it.

As Irene had often told me, he relied on evidence and logic and science. Anything other than that earned his disdain, including the finer feelings, I think. In his own way, he was as intent as the cowering man on the stool in keeping us wicked women at a distance.

In my case, I took it as a compliment.

Kelly spread his hands, as if looking for Sherlock Holmes's dramatic blood evidence. "They were to hang me," he said, "but I knew God would not permit it. He had a better plan for me. A mission."

"And why should you be so chosen of God?" Sherlock Holmes demanded.

"I was raised in a religious home, Father, good Catholics all, and was apprenticed by age fifteen to the upholsterer's trade, happy in all things, until I learned one day of my so-called good fortune. I'd inherited a substantial sum, held in trust for me for ten years, but mine through one John Allen, a master mariner and no relation."

"God's fortune did indeed shine upon you, my son."

"No! It was the Devil's own bargain. I was Satan's bastard, born out of wedlock and left for my whoring mother's mother to rear while off my bedamned dam went and later wed this mariner. I was, for my own 'advantage,' taken from my trade and packed off to business school and then to work in a pawnbroker's shop, which is only one step up from the practice of usury, in my opinion. Only four years later did my misery persuade those who held the purse strings on my tainted inheritance to give me the money to resume the upholsterer's trade. I went to London."

"Yes, yes." Mr. Holmes seemed about to say something, then clasped his hands behind his back and strode to and fro in the manner of an agitated cleric. "It is best to confess quickly, in one long rush. Tell me what you did in London."

"Upholstery jobs, Father. It were good work. I liked it. Always did. Pounding the little nail heads nice and neat along the trim. I was a 'finisher.' They don't let just no one be a finisher." He frowned, glanced at the door, the window, at us three silent witnesses.

"I got to having a pint or two after work. Everybody did." His expression darkened. "Then *they* came around. Them painted demons from Hell! What's a young lad to do? I didn't know. The drink fuddled me! I was a good boy 'til then. Then they made me bad. I tried to resist but they were always there, always comin' 'round, teasing, wanting money."

His head jerked around to view each of us, then he clamped his hands to his face so he couldn't see us. "I did the best thing. Took off. Took to sea on a man-o'-war, where they don't have those demon women."

"A man of war? How would you be taken on such a ship?"

He shrugged. "It was American. But I had to come back. 'Twasn't home. Home was . . . Curtain Road."

"Curtain Road?"

"In the East End. Did upholstery work there, then got some casual work around the docks, shipping back and forth from the Continent. I was a seaman now, too. But the pints and the whores was still there, and the Devil had drunk down my spirit, and I couldn't resist. So I thought, like the Book says, 'tis better to marry than to burn. I found Sarah and we started walking out. Nothing nasty now! Nothing your lot do." He glared at us again, then clapped his hands to his ears.

"I can't stand the sight of 'em! But I got to hold my hands to my ears 'stead of my eyes. They hurt so, the pain between them, and sometimes my brain is rotting-like, and the bad smell and pus comes oozing out my ears." He shut his eyes, keening and rocking with apparent pain, or the remembered agony. "Some mates said I'd caught a, a . . . disease from the filthy whores, God damn 'em all for making me go wi' 'em!" He looked up, dull-eyed. "A year later we wed. Sarah an' me."

"When was that?"

"When?"

"What year, man?"

"Ah . . . eighty-three. I think. A bad year."

"You told Sarah nothing about your condition before you wed?"

His head shook. "The moment we became man and wife, I saw she was just another dirty whore. A harlot who'd lured me into sin. All she wanted was my money, like the rest of 'em, only she was smart enough to marry me to get it. She probly'd given me the oozing pox, I told her. And the pain in my head, my ears . . . I took my penknife one day and . . . and I was going to dig out the filth in her ears that she got into my ears. I stuck the blade in under her ear and dug and dug. Her mother went screeching into the street, but the whores wouldn't help her. The copper pulled me off Sarah, but I'd lanced the evil and it ate her up and she died a day or two later. So I was up in the dock for murder, when anyone would know I was the wronged party. Even the jury recommended mercy, but the judge sentenced me to hang, though I told 'em God had forgiven me and had a mission for me."

"You didn't hang," Mr. Holmes noted, with a touch of distaste.

"No, and I won't, for who would blame me for killing whores?"

A mad scrabbling along the wooden floor confused me. Kelly had lurched off the stool and, still crouched like an animal, ran around Mr. Holmes for the door.

I stood before it.

He was there so swiftly, seizing my arm and spinning me around and away from the door. But he didn't release me and flee. Instead, he caught me close and pressed something hard and cold and sharp against my throat.

I could smell his fear through the medium of days-old clothing and nearly gagged.

Had I been wearing proper street clothes, my high collar would have protected my neck, but my slatternly costume afforded no such protection.

"There," he said, breath and spittle spraying my ear. "The

world won't miss one more whore, and I shall be gone about my Master's business in one more moment."

Everyone else in the room had leaped forward at his charge and then frozen in place, in horror.

He had been quick and sure.

I now stood in the same position the victims of Jack the Ripper had faced in Whitechapel instants before their throats shed lifeblood onto the chill cobblestones.

A dagger of fear pierced my heart, but I could not move nor speak. I was as paralyzed as my would-be defenders all too, too far away.

Nothing could beat the swift stroke of a master upholsterer. I found it odd that the hand that had ornamented the Prince of Wales's *siège d'amour* should shortly send me to my Maker.

"You do not want to slay before the eyes of one of God's servants," Mr. Holmes said.

A silence. "God's servants, if they be true, are all down on whores."

We four remained silent, the expression "down on whores" from the supposed Jack the Ripper letters echoing in our pounding ears.

I could hear my blood pulsing, as if eager to escape my skin under the quick glide of the upholsterer's knife.

I put a hand to my left ear to try to shut out that incessant thunder in my veins.

The edge of steel at my throat, thin as a violin string, pressed harder.

Sherlock Holmes was only three steps away. Irene five. Elizabeth ten. They might as well have all been in Afghanistan.

And then I realized that I must be my own salvation.

"All greedy, lying whores must die," the madman Kelly was intoning in my right ear.

I moved the fingers clapping the left side of my head delicately, as if penetrating a sewing basket filled with naked pins and needles.

Practicing the domestic arts develops a fine touch. Blindly, I withdrew the jet head of a hatpin and struck the long steel tine at the rough hand resting where my neck joined my shoulder.

Kelly yowled as three forms converged on us like leaping hounds, and I let myself slide to the floor.

I was not too proud to scrabble away from the fray on hands and knees, despite the filthy condition of the floor.

When I looked up, Sherlock Holmes had wrestled Kelly into firm custody. For a gaunt man he seemed to possess incredible strength. But more than Mr. Holmes was responsible for Kelly's sudden absence of struggle. Irene stood beside him, her pistol barrel pressed against his temple. Even a madmen recognized the futility of arguing with that.

Mr. Holmes slung him back to the stool like a bag of coal.

"Now, my son," he said sternly, "you will answer my questions with no further outbursts, and ignore these women. Do you not recall that in the er, Good Book, sometimes, ah, angels appear in unlikely forms."

I could tell that Mr. Sherlock Holmes was only familiar with the Bible and the usages of the Christian religion in the vaguest of terms.

Kelly's eyes narrowed in calculation. "I see. This is a test. I am to prove myself fit to follow in the Master's footsteps by heeding his priest, no matter what temptations surround me."

He folded his arms and straightened his shoulders. "Yes. I will prove my ability to resist these devils, which you say are angels in disguise."

"Excellent." Mr. Holmes again paused. "You have worked on an elaborate article of furniture for Durand Frères?"

Kelly squirmed on his stool. "A piece of angel's work for the acts of the devil, but I did not know its purpose until I accompanied it to the house of sin and shame."

"Of course you did not," Mr. Holmes soothed the fellow, as if he were indeed a clergyman. "You were the innocent tool. But once there, and once you had realized—"

"I left, Father. As soon as I could."

"You did not dally on the premises?"

"Dally? Who'd want the likes of me at such a place?"

"You did not visit the house's wine cellar?"

Kelly's expression hardened, either with distaste or the effort of appearing not to lie. "Wine? I like my pints too well, I admit, but wine is for the Master and the Mass, not the sort of doings that go on in a place like that. Not for the likes of me."

"So you claim that you left the house as soon as the . . . lounge was delivered?"

"I am a workman, Father. I do the job and then go."

It was not lost upon me that Kelly might consider the elimination of fallen women an occupation or even a calling.

"Hmmmm," said Mr. Holmes, with as much skepticism as I felt. "Now you must tell me what your mission from God is, and how you have gone about it."

Had we not been three, with a celebrated detective between us and him, I am sure none of us would have remained in the chamber with him for the next outpouring. Well, I wouldn't have at any rate, not after endless moments in his homicidal embrace. To judge by the fascinated expressions on Irene's and Elizabeth's faces, fear was the least emotion they were feeling, though my skin crawled as if the man's vitriolic hatred were poisonous spittle that was sprinkling my physical person as well as my senses.

His theme was simple. Women were conniving, vicious, diseased beings who wanted his money and forced him into unwanted relations. God had given him a mission to stop them for the sake of good men everywhere, and when he found an opportunity, he did. He related a horrific number of attacks, but his accounts were so disjointed and confused that it would take hours and hours of questioning to sort out what was true and what a jumble, and he really admitted nothing when it came to the London horrors, although he seemed very familiar with them. But then, what Whitechapel resident would not be?

During this inconclusive recital, I began to see why the London press had assumed the Ripper would soon be dead or confined to an insane asylum.

⚜ ⚜ ⚜

Obviously a formal and longer interrogation was needed. We remained in Kelly's miserable room while Sherlock Holmes delivered the resident to Inspector le Villard and two gendarmes in the street below.

No curtains concealed the window, but Irene flattened herself against the adjacent wall, dingy as it was, and peered down into the street.

"Is that it?" Elizabeth asked breathlessly of no one in particular. "We have witnessed the capture of Jack the Ripper?"

"It would seem so," Irene said. She glanced pointedly at Elizabeth. "But it would be premature to make any announcements to the public."

"And that is . . . was Sherlock Holmes himself?"

"Not quite himself."

"I should like to meet him."

The words were barely out of her mouth when the narrow door to the chamber creaked open to reveal the tall form of the French priest.

We all turned, then converged on him. Perhaps he had absorbed some of Kelly's mania, for he seemed taken aback, and drew away.

"Is he arrested?" Irene wanted to know.

"Is he the Ripper?" Elizabeth demanded.

"Is he mad?" I piped in.

He ignored our questions to present his own. "I recognize the marshal-general tendencies of Madam Irene Adler Norton," he said with a flicking glance at her. "But I cannot discern which fair flower of French womanhood is Miss Nell Huxleigh, and which is Miss Pink from the rue des Moulins."

Elizabeth and I exchanged glances, our gazes resting of the same overpainted female visage. We could have been Siamese twins, and smiled at each other, pleased to have confounded Sherlock Holmes in one small respect.

We extended our hands until they clasped, smiled, and turned to face Sherlock Holmes as one.

"Ha!" A long accusing forefinger isolated me. "I told you our habits betray us, Miss Huxleigh. Now that the lunatic and his howlings are removed from the scene, I hear the unmistakable clink of a pocket chatelaine."

I thrust a hand between the folds of my skirt and deep into the concealed pocket without thinking.

"Thank you." He turned and bowed to Elizabeth. "I have not seen Miss Pink in a week, but must say that she looked far better as a true rather than a false courtesan. It was a pity you knew so little of the murderous incident when first interviewed there. Perhaps you know a bit more now." He glanced to Irene. "You are both American. Is that as far as the acquaintance goes?"

"So far," Irene said. "You haven't answered our questions."

"You will excuse me," he said. "I do not wish to visit the quarters of the Sûreté in my present guise."

He strode to the closed windows and used the reflective surface of one long pane as a mirror while he literally peeled the likeness of the French priest from his features.

Irene was too much at home in the theater to regard the act of removing makeup as an excuse for silence.

She went to hover behind his shoulder like a ghost in the impromptu mirror.

"Kelly was one of the London police's suspects," she declared.

"Indeed. They were most interested in Mr. Kelly, especially when he disappeared right after Mary Jane Kelly's gruesome death. The police became intrigued by his movements, but they had lost him. I did not, finally determining he had walked eighty miles to Dover before taking ship to Dieppe. Since there were other candidates more likely, I pursued them. All such suspects proved unsatisfactory for one reason or another, which is why the official police conclusion is that Jack the Ripper was one Montague John Druitt, a barrister and schoolmaster, quite mad, whose body conveniently surfaced in the Thames on the very last day of 1888, December 31. He was judged to have been waterborne for at least a month. His own family had suspected him of the crimes, for he had long been known to be what is called 'sexually insane.' "

"And you think that Druitt—?" Irene asked.

"Was convenient and dead. That is all." He had by now removed the putty that had enlarged his honest English hawk nose into something that would have plunged Cyrano de Bergerac into even greater despair, the bushy white eyebrows, and head of hair.

Emerging from the imposing clerical guise with his natural dark hair sleeked back, he resembled some clever bird-beaked otter. When he began undoing the long row of cassock buttons that ran from neck to hem as if strange women were not in the room, I looked away.

After no gasps emerged from Irene or Elizabeth, who were made of sterner stuff, I looked back. His street dress had fit under the encompassing black garment. It took him only moments to straighten his cuffs and tie, then fold the cassock into the same Gladstone bag I had seen him carry earlier.

"Mustn't keep the constabulary of any land waiting unduly," he announced, the persona of the French priest now totally in the bag. He turned from his makeshift mirror to face us with satisfaction.

"For your information, ladies, there were two other leading candidates in the London police's estimation, which I found fairly unlikely. One was Kosminsky, a Polish Jew who hated women, particularly prostitutes. The other was Michael Ostrog, a Russian doctor and also a convict, always an intriguing combination in the history of crime. I have long told Watson that a doctor who turns to crime is liable to commit the most fiendish offenses. I believe that once one has abandoned the Hippocratic oath, there is no holding him back."

"What made Ostrog a suspect?" Irene asked.

"Why, he was a homicidal maniac, known to carry surgical knives. And he was cruel to women. I must give the police credit for turning up an admirable number of these misfits, but I believe all these men were more legitimate candidates for the lunatic asylum than the gallows. You see that even such a known murderer as Kelly escaped the gallows for the asylum. Luckily, his escape has ended here, and so, we hope, has the career of Jack the Ripper."

He retrieved a top hat from the bag, donned it, and went to the door like a doctor bidding a healed patient adieu.

"I think that you all may consider your meddlings over. Kelly is a demented man already convicted of murder once.

He may not ever see trial in England for such crimes, but he is sure to be incarcerated in a French madhouse. The Ripper furor has abated in London, the murders in France have been successfully underplayed, and it is now best to let sleeping mad dogs die.

"I do not approve of your efforts in this matter," he added, "but concede that your appearance and presence today was useful in upsetting the suspect and thus revealing his manias. So, in this instance, you have been of accidental aid. I believe that such worldly ladies can find your way back to the Hotel du Louvre without escort, and bid you good-bye."

He stood aside in the hall, so that we could exit through the open door.

Elizabeth was the first to leave. "I should like to speak with you more someday, Mr. Holmes."

"That is extremely unlikely, Miss Pink."

I went next and said nothing.

"I suggest French and possibly geography lessons," he said acidly. "There is a rue Capron but there is no Durant firm of cabinetmakers there, which I soon found out."

Mortified, I skittered into the hall.

Irene came last and paused before him, chin lifted to put her face in whatever dim light seeped into the passage from the uncurtained window through which a madman had leaped to the street not two hours before.

"We were of more than accidental help, Mr. Holmes, which I think you will realize before much time has passed. You may call upon us at the Hotel du Louvre when you are so inclined."

He gazed down at her for a moment. For that one moment I thought he would speak sense instead of superiority, but I was wrong. "Alas, I fear events will not make such a social call possible or necessary. I will return to England soon."

"Oh, it will not be a social call, I fear. I hope that you are as good at anticipating the worst as you are at divining the past." Irene smiled and sailed past him like a ship of the line.

We all clattered down the stairs, past the still-bemused concierge and into the Paris streets.

38.

A Message from Abroad

I think had there been any alternative I should have taken it, instead of prosecuting that unknown night journey.

—JONATHAN HARKER'S JOURNAL, *DRACULA*

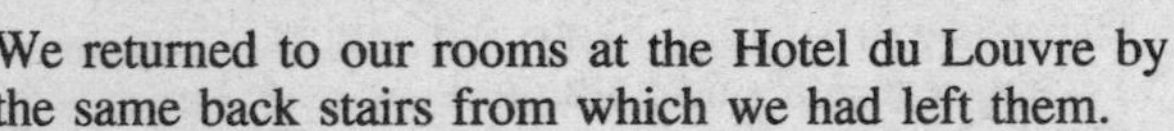

We returned to our rooms at the Hotel du Louvre by the same back stairs from which we had left them.

I believe we passed even the same footman and maid we encountered when we had departed.

We were as taken for granted as before, which was rather disappointing. Looking like a sinner was less exciting than I had thought.

Once the door to our suite had shut on us, we all threw ourselves down on the nearest couch, chair, or—in Elizabeth's case—empty area of carpeting.

"So then he is captured!" Elizabeth leaned back on her elbows, the very image of a hoyden, were one ever made up like a harlot. "There is something about him, something about his name that tickles my memory. But it is gone."

"I felt the same way when we were at the cabinetmaker's," I said. "It is indeed suspicious that he left England just after Mary Jane Kelly's murder. Wait! What about this notorious Madam Kelly? Isn't Mary Jane Kelly the one who had claimed a gentleman had taken her to Paris once? Perhaps she is a relative of Madam Kelly."

"Kelly, as we can see, is as common a name as Smith nowadays," Irene said.

"Especially," Elizabeth added dourly, "since the famine in

Ireland forced Kellys and O'Connors and everybody Irish from their homeland."

"Really, Pink," Irene said, amused. "I cannot decide if you are more indignant about the stamping out of the Irish, the buffalo, or the fallen woman."

"I am equally outraged by all such acts of extermination," she said.

Their exchange, which made little sense to me, especially the part about the buffalo, had at least allowed me to think.

"Now I have it. James Kelly was married, and his first overt crime was against his wife. Perhaps he was no stranger to escaping to Paris, and perhaps he had taken one of the Whitechapel prostitutes he despised to Paris, because she shared his last name, and it was as if they were a man and wife on a honeymoon. After all, Irene, Godfrey took you to Paris for a honeymoon."

"Godfrey has nothing in common with James Kelly," she said sternly, "but that is a very good point, Nell. It might explain much about the progress of the Ripper's crimes, and why they ended abruptly after the savage death of Mary Jane Kelly."

Elizabeth gazed at me with something resembling awe. "Good work, Nell! Of course. He may have killed the other women as he wandered the Whitechapel streets attempting to meet up with Mary Jane Kelly again. In some strange way she was the mirror of his first crime: attacking his actual wife, Sarah. Only with Mary Jane Kelly, he could do everything he had only begun to do to Sarah years before."

"We have gone to all this trouble to find and confront that miserable little man," I complained, "and Sherlock Holmes will get all the credit."

Irene had stripped off her gloves and was untying her heavy taffeta bonnet ribbons. "*Mais certainement*. Sherlock Holmes will get all the credit."

"Where would he have been," I inquired indignantly, "if we had not been there to cow the suspect?"

"Yes," Irene agreed pensively, leaning her chin on her hands, which were braced on her knees, "we were herded like sheep to the perimeter to keep the wolf at bay. Isn't that the reverse of common practice? Usually the shepherdesses don't repel the wolf, but the other way around."

"We are rather lurid shepherdesses," I put in. "Most repellent, really."

"To such a man, yes," Irene said. "Elizabeth, would you fetch our Krafft-Ebing from my room?"

"Oh, that awful book," I complained, as Elizabeth jumped up and darted off with the energy of a twelve-year-old.

"You have not read it, Nell."

"You have not let me read it, Irene, which is how I know it is an awful book."

She looked beyond me to the desk. "What is that?"

I turned slowly to look over my shoulder, past the heavy fall of my undressed hair. Masquerading as a fallen woman was a wearying occupation.

A small white sort of pillow lay upon the desktop's green-leather inset.

"A letter?" I suggested, squinting at it.

"Could you fetch it? It must have been delivered while we were gone."

That is the problem with living in a hotel. People come in and do things while you are out. Of course, our own Sophie was no better.

I pushed myself upright and tottered to the desk. Irene's thin-soled slippers had turned the bottoms of my feet into skates of fire.

"Godfrey's hand!" I cried, thankful to see something familiar and welcome after our immersion into gruesome crime. "And many, many sheets." I seized the brass letter opener and slashed open the flap. Three folded pages of thick foreign vellum practically sprung out. "You will want to read it right away, Irene."

"No, Nell, you read it to me. I am too exhausted."

I returned to my chair, withdrew my pince-nez from its silver case on the chatelaine in my pocket—betraying accessory that it was, but then someone's *clay pipe* had been a clear clue in Whitechapel, too—and unfolded the heavy foreign paper with a sigh.

After all I had been through, holding Godfrey's neat lawyerly script in my hands was a return to sanity.

"*Dearest Irene*—oh, it may be too personal."

She waved a weary hand. After a performance Irene often sank into an almost-drugged state of fatigue, when even holding her head up seemed too great a task.

"I don't care, Nell."

" '*Dearest Irene*'—oh, '*and Nell.*' There I am, in the parentheses. It is a joint letter after all."

I read on. " 'My departure from Prague was so sudden that I had no time to inform you beforehand.' "

Irene stirred on the couch. "Departure?"

" 'Some trifling business that the Rothschilds found too pressing to ignore has been plunged into my hands. Hence I am on the train once more heading eastward into Hungary. I will be traveling as far east again as I have come thus far from the North Sea inland to Prague. I am writing a serial letter, as I do not know when I will be stopped long enough to post it, and as I am not even sure of my destination.

" 'Apparently these millions of acres between Prague and the Black Sea do not reckon locations and distances as precisely as in the more salubrious and civilized parts of Europe.' "

I paused to take breath.

"Poor Godfrey!" Irene exclaimed, hushing Elizabeth as she came rushing into the room with the dreadful book in her hand. Her nod indicated that Elizabeth should sit on the foot of her couch while I continued to read.

I, of course, was familiar with Godfrey's hand from our work in the Temple together and declaimed smoothly with enough skill that Irene should not be ashamed of my performance.

" 'The first leg of the journey retraced our trip to Vienna, Irene.' " I squinted at the page and was forced to interrupt Godfrey's text. "I believe there is a string of Austrian words. Or are they German? What do people speak in Vienna, anyway?"

"Love, music, and pastry," Irene said, smiling nostalgically. "Don't worry about translating that part. It probably describes . . . tortes. Not legal ones, edible ones."

I resumed reading: " 'Our train track weaves near and then away from the broad blue thread of the Danube as if knitting into its curving course. Buda-Pesth is not as imperial a city as Vienna, though quite as picturesque. I am thankful that I have learned a smattering of German from you and from my visits to Bohemia. English is seldom heard as one ventures into the ancient land of the Turk and the Magyars.

" 'I will not follow the Danube into Bukovina and am not bound so near the Black Sea as Bessarabia. Instead, from Buda-Pesth, where I have time for lunch before the train leaves, my route will strike southeast through the Carpathian Mountains into Transylvania. One expects a quantity of wooded terrain from that name. It appears that I now venture farther east than even you, Irene, for Warsaw far to the north is still west of my destination. Were it not for the barrier of Bessarabia, I would soon be adjoining the Ukraine of Russia, imagine that.

" 'I am to call upon some provincial satrap or other. My train chugs into wooded hills between the Tisza and Mures rivers, with a town called Klausenburgh my goal, and from there, who knows what village? An agent of the Countess will meet me there to conduct me to the family seat. The train compartments are mostly empty. No one shares the space to disturb my writing, though the rocking of the train along the tracks gives my hand a slight palsy.

" 'It is reassuring as I forge deeper into forests and foreign territory to know that you and Nell are safe and amusing yourselves at Neuilly. You must not languish in the country, though, but take yourself into Paris to see the World Exposition, perhaps, and marvel at all the foreign displays. I do not doubt that you will be able to tour more interesting parts of the world in Paris these days than I will see on my entire long journey into the backwaters of Europe.' "

We ended up giggling like girls at Godfrey's well-meant but wildly inappropriate visions for our current occupations.

"Is that all, Nell?" Irene asked after we had stopped laughing. The faint frown had returned.

"Only a postscript that he does not know when he will be able to post a letter after this Klausenburgh stop."

"Why are the Rothschilds sending him into this primitive country?"

"Apparently it is such a trifling errand that he forgot to mention the point."

"Trifling errands do not take people hundreds of miles from civilization." Her fingertips rapped the tabletop beside the sofa, mimicking the sound of galloping horses. Perhaps she was playing an imaginary tarantella on her imaginary piano. "I will wire the Rothschild agent in Prague and ask why. And where. And when he will be back. For a barrister Godfrey was annoyingly vague on these crucial points."

"He wrote in haste," I pointed out in his defense.

"Why such haste to hie to nowhere on a trifling errand? I do not like it." Her fingers drummed the scarf-swathed table again. "Any more than I like the fact that we were followed from the upholsterer's lodgings."

"Followed?" Elizabeth demanded, looking quite alarmed as she held the Krafft-Ebing book open on her knees like a schoolroom miss.

"Why do you think I proposed a detour through the street market?"

"You wanted new fabrics, as you said?" I asked, recalling Irene leading us on a lightning raid upon on the crowded stands. She had moved through the jumbled labyrinth with the random force of a whirlwind, tossing up lengths of cloth and leaving without settling on anything. We had emerged from the area like refugees from a foreign bazaar, empty-handed and breathless, and spun in such a totally different direction that we had to circle back the long way around to our hotel.

Oh.

"I wanted to glimpse our pursuer," Irene was explaining to Elizabeth, "and to lose him."

"Him?" Elizabeth asked, even more alarmed. "Perhaps Sherlock Holmes—"

"Why would he bother to follow us at this point? After all, he has James the Ripper in his grasp, doesn't he? He forgot about us the moment he joined le Villard in his carriage to convey James Kelly to the Sûreté."

"I don't believe he had forgotten about you," Elizabeth added slyly.

This charge startled Irene from her reverie. "Nonsense. You cannot view with silly girlish wishfulness a man who is made of mathematics and test tubes. He relishes a mind that will not kowtow easily to his cleverness, that is all."

"But if that dreadful Kelly was maddened by our presence," Elizabeth persisted politely, "Mr. Sherlock Holmes was made nervous. You must allow, Irene, that by the nature of my trade I have special knowledge of men of many temperaments."

"Miss Pink!" I said, forgetting my resolve to eradicate that unsuitable name. "Boasting of the wisdom learned from severe moral failings is not accepted here."

She turned wide hazel eyes upon me. "*You* make him nervous as well, Nell."

"I do not *do* that!" I gritted between my teeth, feeling the headache coming to wrap itself around my temples like one of Sarah Bernhardt's lithe little parlor snakes.

"Oh. I didn't mean to . . . tell. Nell."

I shut my eyes. The headache was a boa constrictor and it wore the Divine Sarah's face.

"I am the only one," she went on, "he took virtually no serious notice of. I choose to consider that a mark of distinction, rather than a snub. And also a mistake. So, Irene, I have been skimming Krafft-Ebing, if one can skim such strong stuff. You are right. If one relaxes and lets a foreign language sink in, you understand more than you thought you could. Case number ten is interesting, given the reaction of James Kelly."

Irene took the book from Elizabeth's hands and laid it open on the table, under the bright halo cast by the oil lamp. Daylight did not far penetrate the heavy draperies and dark furnishing of our rooms.

"An unnamed *journeyman painter, age thirty*," she noted aloud. "Also a lower craftsman, and almost exactly the same age as Kelly," she noted. "No family history." She looked up to nod at Elizabeth. "A hatred of women."

"I do not understand," I put in. "Why should any man hate

women? We are the gentle sex. We are their sisters, wives, mothers, daughters."

Instead of answering me, Irene bent her gaze back on the page, and quoted: "A hatred of women, especially pregnant women, who are responsible for the misery of the world."

"That is ridiculous! I was unfortunate in that my mother died before I was old enough to know her, but surely every son venerates his own mother."

Someone laughed. Elizabeth. "Surely you are an only child, Nell, due to your mother's untimely death. I am far from that, and I can assure you from my brothers' actions that there is a time when young boys resent their mothers very much, especially when her maternal bonds would keep them from getting into mischief."

"It is true some of my boy charges could be most stubborn at times."

Irene's forefinger tapping the open page of *Psychopathia Sexualis* interrupted our discussion. "As a boy this man cut into his own private parts. He was arrested at age thirty for trying to castrate a boy he had caught in the woods. He hated God and mothers for bringing children into a world of misery and poverty. He himself could have nothing to do with women for that reason, in fact he felt no natural satisfaction in any act."

This recital silenced me, even silenced my thoughts. One was not encouraged to think of such matters. Although I realized that country life had given me some knowledge of the raw facts of congress between male and female of lesser species, I had never, never attached such parts and conditions to humans.

If Case Number Ten—dear God, how many like cases were in that book then?—hated women because they bore children, and James Kelly hated them because he felt it wrong to consort with them—even in marriage apparently, else why would he have stabbed his own wife?—yet he could not resist the prostitutes of Whitechapel . . . then Jack the Ripper was disemboweling women *because they were women*, whether they were mothers or whores.

My thoughts staggered like a dipsomaniac's stride. Jack the

Ripper hated bad women because they were not good, and Case Number Ten hated good women because they were good.

"Krafft-Ebing," Irene said, "calls such cases as Jack the Ripper's 'lustmurders.' "

"But isn't the point of lust," I burst out, "satisfying it?" Not that I had known either state, lust or satisfaction. I considered lust a male failing. One could not attribute it to the women of Whitechapel, or even to Pink. Clearly, their deeds were either driven by a need for money for the most basic necessities, or a lust for drink, perhaps, or—in Pink's case—from a perverse intent to experience all sides of life, even its most sordid.

"This is lust that has . . . relocated its satisfaction," Irene said, eyeing me carefully. "If you were to read further in Krafft-Ebing, you would see that such men often have strange reasons for not seeking the ordinary outlets: marriage or prostitution. They block the usual impulse until it finds expression in the unusual impulse, the unusual act. For such men, murder and mutilation are what marriage acts are for normal men."

"And," said Elizabeth, coming to stand by Irene and gaze down upon the open book, "it is as we concluded the other day when we first confronted the subject matter of this book. Such acts are common, not uncommon. We see the dead woman in the illustrated news, we shake our heads, we say who would do such things . . . and all along there have been plenty of clues to who would do such things, only our police have not been able to see them. And those men who have been caught have been shut away as merely mad."

"They are mad!" I said.

"But in a . . . systematic, similar way, Nell," Elizabeth insisted. "If so, is that true madness? There is reason for what they do, that only they know and feel and understand. This book proves that there is as much similarity among the abnormal as there is among the normal."

"This is supposed to be a comfort?"

"No, Nell, but it offers hope of identifying men who may take women's and children's lives. Somehow they need innocents to purge their own guilt." She turned to Irene. "Is it possible they see themselves in their victims?"

"It's possible that they despise weakness in themselves, and seek to disprove it by making other people their victims. Those smaller than themselves, perhaps."

"Mary Jane Kelly was not smaller than the Ripper," I pointed out, "at least not from the majority of Ripper descriptions."

"And," said Irene, "she was the only woman attacked and killed while lying down. He requires a supine, passive woman, this killer. He strikes so fast that the women literally faint from blood loss and sink to the ground. Does he see the mother lying to give birth? The wife reclining in the marital bed? The sister or child asleep and helpless?"

"What does it matter what he sees?" I cried, repulsed by the vampire visions these questions raised as if from the dead.

"If we see what he sees," Irene said, her face transformed by a vision of a solution, thanks to her new insight into the crimes, "we will see who, or what, he is."

My heart was thudding like a Salvation Army drum. Notions and images and insights clashed like cymbals in my head. I stared at Elizabeth, unable to imagine her lying on the harlot's bed, a vague dark figure bending over her, his face . . . any man's.

I saw the child in the wood, cringing away from the blade. I saw the woman on the street, screaming into the curtain of her own blood that fell red and heavy from her throat like a glittering garnet cascade.

And always I saw the gaunt dark figure at the corner of my eye, the crow flying, the raven croaking, the ghost moaning, the monster laughing.

He had always been there, and I had always chosen not to see him.

Now he was looking right at me.

Now he was judging me worthy of notice.

Now I must see him in return, to let him know that I am not afraid.

Now it is he, or I.

39.

Last Tangle in Paris

From his early years [he] fully understood that he was a man with pathologically corrupt tendencies . . . being both coarse and eloquent, hypocritical, fanatical and holy, a sinner and an ascetic . . .

—*PADENIE*

FROM A YELLOW BOOK

It is worse than I thought.

Which of course suits my ultimate purpose all the more.

Yet, even I am shocked.

It is quite amusing to find myself shocked by such a simple and low creature.

Still, he has a crude force of personality, rather like a Gypsy fortune-teller or an assassin. One senses the depth of what he is capable of, great goodness and great evil twined together into an inseparable strand.

Even he cannot see where one begins and the other ends, and thus he justifies them both.

I have always believed more in sinners than in saints, but in my beast I believe that they both meet.

The combination is demonic.

I will allow him some last . . . excesses in this City of Light, and then we must withdraw. I begin to see how to use him in a larger plan of mine. Certainly he has attracted the attention of some I am most interested in . . . annoying.

And he has distracted the attention of those who will pay dearly for that fact.

What more could one ask of a wild beast?

40.

A Map of Murder

The public would find those people who occupied their attention reproduced with a scrupulous respect for nature.
—CATALOGUE-ALMANACH DU MUSÉE GRÉVIN

FROM A JOURNAL

I tossed and turned half the night on the daybed in the alcove off our dining room.

When I dreamed, Indian warriors on horseback pursued me along the Champs-Elysées and then toward the Eiffel Tower on the Champ de Mars. I tried to escape into the catacombs, but followed the winding tunnel down only to find James Kelly laughing maniacally among piles of old bones and skulls as he upholstered the cavern walls where the lone dead woman had been found with a William Morris pattern.

I awoke still hearing the implacable tap-tap-tap of his small metal upholstery hammer.

Then I realized that the sound I heard was far more subtle and was occurring in the waking world.

I parted the heavy tapestry drapes that curtained off my sleeping area. The double doors to the dining room were shut, but a thread of light gleamed under their edges like gilt.

I didn't bother finding my slippers, but tiptoed barefoot over the wood and carpets until I could peer through the tiny space between the two baize-curtained doors.

Someone sat at our round worktable in the main room, tapping a clogged pen point on a thick pad of paper over and over.

I slipped through the doors in my long lawn nightgown, feeling cold, but too fascinated by who was burning the midnight oil to find a shawl.

Irene looked up from the layers of paper basking in lamplight. She glanced at Nell's closed bedroom door and put a finger to her lips.

"Something secret?" I whispered, coming to her side. I saw that a large map of Paris underlay the various scattered top papers.

"Not secret," she whispered back, "but Nell has just gone to sleep. I could hear her tossing her bed linens into knots."

"I have been riding stormy sleepless seas as well," I admitted, quietly drawing out a chair next to her and sitting.

"We have all heard more than we wish to know about these vicious crimes," she said.

"Not I. I wish to know all! I simply can't sleep for wondering what will happen to Kelly now that Sherlock Holmes has escorted him into French custody. I suppose our role in this investigation is done. If the English detective is right, and I do hate the British assumption of lofty rectitude, Kelly will vanish into the madhouse at Charenton and never be heard of again. Certainly the French Sûreté will not allow a public trial that would embarrass Paris's most titled London visitor, the Prince of Wales."

"No. Events and personalities conspire to bury the Ripper as utterly as he has erased his victim's lives. And the concealment is nothing new. I have the impression that this is exactly what the London police would prefer for Jack the Ripper: permanent, anonymous incarceration, so that he remains an unsolved mystery to the world forever."

"Surely they cannot safely ignore the curiosity of the public?"

"The public will be onto another curiosity in half a heartbeat. No one is more fickle than the mob, even when it most screams for justice and vengeance. We are in a city celebrating that very fact as it occurred one hundred years ago."

"That's right. This is the centenary year of the French Revolution. I keep forgetting that."

"The World Exposition manages to overshadow that fact, especially since the Eiffel Tower has replaced the notion of a guillotine of the same height."

I shuddered at the macabre idea. "It is hard to imagine such sophisticated and delightful people as the French being that bloodthirsty," I admitted, curling my toes under the tent of my hem so they'd escape the room's nighttime frostbite.

Irene's fingertips were white against the pen she wielded, but she seemed insensitive to such distractions as cold. She was making a tracing of the map, only marking certain sites.

"What are you drawing?"

"A map of mystery."

"The mystery has been solved."

"No. A murder or two may have been solved, but not the overall mystery."

I must have looked doubtful, for she glanced at me grimly. "Who shot at us near Notre Dame cathedral? A demented upholsterer? I hardly think firearms are likely to be his weapons. Who followed us from this same demented upholsterer's lodgings when he himself was firmly in the custody of Sherlock Holmes and Inspector le Villard? Who watches this hotel, and our windows in particular, now?"

"No!"

"See for yourself, but be as discreet as a peaceful death."

I rose and hastened back to my alcove. The heavy velvet drapes were drawn over my single window, but I could kneel on the daybed's foot to peek out ever so slightly at the side . . . and so I did.

The street below lay knee deep in mist, as if a river of fog had flooded the cobblestones. Streetlights resembled drowned trees in a mere. No vehicles moved at this hour, not on such a sheltered byway.

The row of chic shops opposite were shuttered, the residence windows above them all dark with drawn curtains.

As I stared, uncertain, I saw that the black arch of one doorway was doubly dark. A figure sheltered in its shadow! With the mist-flooded street I couldn't see its feet, nor tell whether it was a trousered man or skirted woman, though why a woman would be out at this hour in such a deserted place beggared explanation. Yet I viewed a cloaked and hooded figure, more womanly than a hatted or capped man . . . more like a monk.

I shivered at the vague and sinister outline. Someone watched, whatever it was.

Now I was shivering not only from the cold floor on my bare feet, but from the icy inner recognition of surveillance, from the fog of mystery that seeped into our cozy suite and restless minds like smoke.

This time I paused to find and don my slippers in the dark. When I returned to the main room, Irene had marked several more sites on her map. I began to discern a pattern.

"The Eiffel Tower." She nodded. I indicated a spot a half an inch away. "The unsuspected catacomb where the third murder victim was found. But what is this mark over here by the Seine?"

"Notre Dame."

"Where we were fired upon! With the Wild West Show in town—"

"That was not lost upon me either," she said. "But what else was—is—at this same spot?"

Being shot at was such a novel experience that I could think of no other to link with the site.

Irene shook her head, her chestnut hair rippling red-gold in the lamplight. She looked no more than twenty, save her expression was older than time.

"The second undiscovered and likely ancient catacomb," she reminded me.

"Under the cathedral, of course. But . . . there was nothing there."

"Spilled spirits, candle wax. Or do you think those bones had held a recent *soirée*?"

"No body was there, I mean."

"No. No body."

"And this mark?" I touched another.

"Your former residence."

The ink had been still wet and my fingertip was blackened. "Two bodies there."

"And a wine cellar with signs of disturbance."

"But minor enough signs that the broken wine bottle could have been dropped by a careless servant, weeks ago even."

"Or Kelly could have waited down there. After installing the Prince's . . . couch." She leaned back, set the pen down, thought visibly. "You found the women at what time?"

"Just after eight. We have our second meal of the day before seven."

"It lasts more than an hour?"

"You think the girls would let anyone rush them? The food is as exquisite as that given to our noble guests. We are expected to work long into the night. It helps if we are plied with viands and wine."

"So the two dead women would have been tipsy?"

I shrugged, hard-pressed to explain the life of serving men's needs to a woman who had only ever served her own, as men themselves do.

"Not so much tipsy," I said, "as indolently mellow. Gay yet somehow removed, complacent."

"I cannot think of a better formula to create the perfect murder victim," Irene said angrily, careful not to raise her voice with ire. "The women of Whitechapel were drunk as well. I can quite understand their need to dull sensation. I cannot have anything but a contempt beyond expressing for a man who would prey upon such helpless victims, however impaired his mind might be."

"But he was clearly mad. Thanks to your book recording such cases, we know more about the methods and motives of such killers than the London police. I don't think even Sherlock Holmes, despite seeing Kelly's mania with his own eyes, fully understands the man's hatred of women as we do."

She met my gaze. "We understand more than we might wish to."

I lowered my eyes. "I am . . . amazed that your contempt does not extend to me."

"For the role you play? Never."

Her answer equaled the ambiguity in her eyes. She regarded me with an intensity I had never encountered in another person, as if she had always seen far more of me than I had ever seen of her.

The words "role" and "play" echoed in my mind with a mockery her overtone had not given them.

I had the distinct sense that she did harbor contempt for me in some way, and it was not for anything obvious. To me, at least. I cannot explain how shocked and ashamed I felt, although I could not say why.

And yet we sat alone in the night, and she confided in me, as I did not in her. And I felt more shame. The worst shame was that I could not admit it.

Irene was bending over her papers again, making marks.

"That is?" I asked.

"We are back near the Eiffel Tower. This spot is the global village and Buffalo Bill Wild West Show. You see the connection?"

"You are drawing a line between the Eiffel Tower and Notre Dame."

"Not Notre Dame, per se, although it is a stop on the journey."

"But this dot is right where Notre Dame is."

"No, it is not. It is a few hundred paces beyond Notre Dame on the Île de la Cité, at the very end of the isle. It is the Paris Morgue."

I gasped. I had forgotten about the morgue. "But that had nothing to do with the crimes. It is merely where all the dead go."

"It is where all Paris goes to see the dead," she corrected me, "as all Paris goes to Notre Dame and the Eiffel Tower and the World Exposition and Buffalo Bill's Wild West Show. Do you see yet?"

"Not yet, but . . . All Paris does not go to the rue des Moulins."

"All Paris that matters does. The men who run the city and the country and the world."

"But the catacombs are not places that draw the public."

"Not yet." Irene smiled bitterly. "Give the Parisians time to realize that these gruesome sites are worthy of exploitation. The Rothschild maps and papers indicate that most of these are not the usual Christian catacombs dating back to Roman days. They contain bones from cemeteries displaced by the city's growing from a few hundred thousand to two millions of people in this century. These dead date back only to the seventeenth century. Still, they are the dead, they are French, and all Paris hastens to morbid occupations during this last decade of our century. Perhaps the taint of fresh blood in the catacombs will finally bring them the public recognition they deserve."

"It's true that the bloody and sensational attract public attention," I admitted. "They always have."

"But the bloody and the sensational have never been so much a part of the public consciousness, thanks to newspapers that trumpet the worst on every corner."

"The newspapers do not invent the atrocities they report."

She eyed me with a glance as challenging as forged steel until I was forced to temper my opinion.

"Some of them do . . . invent, I suppose. Sometimes."

"More likely foment than invent," she conceded. "Were people not so greedy for news of other people's misfortunes, there would not be money to be made in sensational journals."

"The morgue is free," I pointed out.

"Yes, and what began as a plan to aid in identifying unclaimed bodies—often *les inconnus de la Seine*—has become a permanent exhibition of the macabre. At least London has no such tradition."

"I can't imagine the British permitting such a thing. Too many of the bodies are unclothed, though that fact makes the ones which are presented in clothing so much more interesting."

Irene muffled a laugh in the cup of her hand, incidentally warming her writing fingers. "You are right, Pink. When it comes to naked death, the British would object more to the impropriety of the nakedness than the morbidity of gazing at corpses. But the French . . . they would find some wisps of garments even more intriguing. And the Americans . . . well, they would be appalled by both."

"You realize that your summation of the British character, which I find so annoying, has exactly described Nell. She is quite agreeable to gruesome ghost stories, but appalled by the lust for life."

"I admit that I am surprised by how well she handles sheer grue, better than I. Perhaps I have more imagination than she. As for the lust for life, isn't that something that most women are encouraged to forsake?"

"Most ladies," I said disparagingly.

"No doubt that is why you work so hard to be taken for anything but. Yet you are as conventional in your way as Nell."

"How can two women of such vastly different experience and roles in life be in any way similar?" I demanded.

"Because you are both more than you appear to be. But that has always been the weakness, and power, of women. Now. Watch while I draw the final lines on our map."

She did so, effectively ending my arguments because I was so intrigued by her midnight mapmaking session.

I watched the straight, angled line she drew north from the Eiffel Tower, using the edge of Krafft-Ebing's *Psychopathia Sexualis* as a ruler! I frowned at where the line ended, somewhere near the rue Pigalle, beyond the Paris Opéra.

She then lifted her full dressing-gown sleeve and carefully positioned the book at the other side of map. She dipped the pen a last time, shook off the excess ink, and drew a line from the Paris Morgue that met the end of the other angled line.

"You see?"

"I see you have created a triangle with a base between the Eiffel Tower and Notre Dame, or the morgue and somewhere south of Montmartre."

"The mount of the martyrs," she mused, "where all the raucous night life of Paris cavorts until dawn, watching the shocking cancan dancers and drinking absinthe. And where have you been in all this?"

"Where you have gone. And Nell." I blinked. "Nell accompanied you to the tower and the nearby catacombs, and to the morgue. I went with you to the tower and the nearby World Exposition grounds, and to the catacombs near Notre Dame. How odd. There's a symmetry. . . . And why have you taken only one of us to certain locations?"

"I wished to find out if I was being followed, or one of you."

"All along? We have been followed everywhere?"

"Not at first. But later, everywhere. I believe so."

"I cannot believe that anyone would follow Nell. Or me, for that matter. And have you concluded who was being followed?"

She nodded. "I."

I sat back, out of ideas, a rare state for me. I am extremely quick-witted. I have to be in my profession.

"Well. Nell must be right! It must be that Holmes man. He is oddly taken by you. I noticed he kept one eye on you during the entire interrogation of James Kelly."

"You have swallowed Nell's romantic delusion, I see. The man is all brain and no blood. I assure you that if Mr. Sherlock Holmes is keeping one eye on anyone, it is not for reasons of admiration, but of mistrust. He does not tolerate meddlers, as he calls us, and only permitted our presence because our disguise conveniently set off Kelly's mania." She smiled. "He may also realize that he is almost as much out of his depth in this case as Nell is."

She tapped the pen nib on the apex of the triangle. "Is this not where sits the infamous Moulin Rouge with its can-can dancers so beloved of Bertie? Is not the house we all have in common located in the rue des Moulins?"

I leaned over the map, staring. "I am new to Paris. I am not yet acquainted with all the streets and their locale. You are saying that the bordello is near the apex."

She tapped the nib on a site half an inch below the apex. "Here. In the ninth arrondissement. The twenty arrondissements of Paris are laid out so artfully, like the concentric circles of a snail's shell, with the smallest numbers starting at the center of the city, then rotating outwardly in order around that hub. The English would never use such a scheme. But we are interested in the direct geometry of logic, not the circuitous paths of art. And that is what makes the murders and events so interesting. This double murder at the *hôtel de rendezvous* did not have any connection to a catacomb and did not result in a display of the bodies at the Paris Morgue."

"You believe that the display of the bodies is as much a part of the crime as the killing?"

"I believe that there is a ritual behind them, and behind that ritual, however brutal, a reason. Perhaps the first bodies were intended to be displayed elsewhere, but you found them too soon."

I shivered again. "You mean that the killer was still lurking in the house when I opened that door."

She nodded.

"Then it might not have been James Kelly! Yet he is mad and just the sort of man Krafft-Ebing would find a likely candidate."

"For the Ripper. Perhaps this Paris killer is not the Ripper."

I rubbed my aching temples. "Then Sherlock Holmes has Jack the Ripper in custody for the crimes committed by someone entirely different?"

"Perhaps. We have read the Book. We have learned such killers are commonplace, or at least not uncommon. And here is where the jackal press has worked to conceal rather than reveal. On the one hand, any public atrocity gruesome enough is game for trumpeting to the world. On the other, should an Eminence be involved, or the crime be too obscure, it is buried from view like the victims. We get a very select view of things, only what the authorities wish the public to know." She sat back. "We must revisit the scene of a crime. I am convinced that the game is not over yet."

"When?"

"Now."

"Why are you letting me accompany you?"

"Because you will be useful later."

"Is that all?" I felt another chill, not from the night air, but from the implacable intent of this woman. I had only glimpsed that steel of soul in one other person: Sherlock Holmes, oddly enough. One was an artist, one a scientist, and yet they shared the same will and dreadful purity of purpose.

"Is not the chance of saving one life from a horrible death enough?" she asked me now.

"Yes." But I wished to be regarded as an equal in the hunt. Of course, Irene Adler Norton had no more idea than Sherlock Holmes or Buffalo Bill Cody that I was a hunter also, and worthy of their company.

"I will go as well," said a voice behind us.

Penelope Huxleigh stood at the open door of her chamber, already dressed in some plain dark stuff. I realized that she had been awake and listening to us for a long time.

Irene stood up. "Capital, Nell! Bring your chatelaine. I will fetch my pistol and dress at once."

"What will I carry?" I asked.

"Your wits about you," Irene said. "And I will lend you my lead-headed cane for the rest."

41.

The French Connection

Once he said that reading a description of the tortures visited upon their victims by the Red Indians had tempted him to imitate them.

—RICHARD VON KRAFFT-EBING, *PSYCHOPATHIA SEXUALIS*

I was so angry that I had been left to sleep, supposedly, while Irene made maps and Elizabeth made herself a part of our company, that I did not even object when Irene decreed that we all must dress in male garb.

"As long as there is a pocket for my chatelaine," I said stiffly.

"Oh, Nell," Elizabeth said, "men have ever so many more

pockets than women. You could carry three chatelaines."

"One is sufficient."

Our dressing session, and my redressing one, was interesting, to say the least.

Our pantaloons and stockings fit under the coarse, uncomfortable trousers Irene produced, and she permitted us to wear our walking boots, which she said were not that much different from men's shoes.

I kept my corset and camisole on, though she and Elizabeth used only camisoles under . . . well, what can I say? She felt that men's white starched shirt collars would be both too noisy and too visible for our uses, so we were given dark sailors' jerseys to wear, which required pulling over our heads. Hers and Elizabeth's were part of her fencing wardrobe. I thought I recognized mine from Godfrey's long-ago impersonation of a seaman during our Monaco adventure.

We were short a jacket, for Irene owned only one man's suit and the short Eton-style jacket she produced fit Elizabeth and not me. I was permitted to wear a mock-mannish plaid wool jacket from my own walking suit. Mufflers, caps, and hats finished off the ensembles, and a more pitiful trio I have never viewed in a full-length pier glass before.

"It will be darker outside," Irene said, donning black-leather gloves and pulling a peaked cap low over her eyes.

At least all our hair was decently up, though our headgear completely obscured it, contrary to our previous guise of fallen women, where our hair assumed the same condition. Irene adjusted Elizabeth's bowler lower over her ears and jammed down my tweed cap known as a deerstalker while pulling up my muffler, until only my nose tip and eyes peeked between louring barriers of wool plaid.

"Remember," she urged, "stride. Step wide. And do not bunch together like geese, but rather strut like ganders. You fear nothing in the night."

I feared a great deal in the night, but I feared being usurped in my place as Irene's companion in crime-solving even more. How this brash young American girl had wormed her way so deeply into our alliance, presumed Pinkerton or not, I cannot say. If only Godfrey were here to make a trio instead of this immoral upstart! He would provide the strength and sagacity that only a man can offer. And then, well, then I thought of Quentin. Surely a man who had performed government service in the most wild and treacherous outposts of the British Empire, upon which even the sun feared to set, surely he could have provided the aid we might need, not a green girl of uncertain history and proven frailty.

Yet Irene had some reason for including her in our expedition. "Because I can use you," she had said, her voice chilly, as if she felt Elizabeth might be one to use her instead, if she could.

But that must be my imagination! I am much troubled by imagination in one instance only. I always imagine the worst. In this case, I felt Irene was rushing in all directions without a calming influence. Godfrey's, or mine.

James Kelly—debased creature!—was in the hands of the French, who are better at locking up madmen than almost anyone, as they have so many. Jack the Ripper would be Frenchified, a fate worse than death in my opinion.

So this outing was nothing more than a wild-goose chase, Irene's abjurations for us to act like ganders to the contrary.

I scratched the rough wool collar at my neck. Men wore a great deal of coarse wool apparently. This was good for the sheep farmers of Shropshire, no doubt, but not for more tender skin.

I took a step, repelled when the thick fabric between my limbs rubbed together, almost hobbling me. Dreadful! No wonder men like Kelly went insane, walking around garbed like this all day.

Still, if Pink . . . Elizabeth, that is, could do it, so could I!

"Ready?" Irene asked.

We answered together, like soldiers, then glared at each other.

I was pleased to see Elizabeth's shoulders twitch in her woolen jacket. She scratched her nose above the dark muffler, and then at her leg. We were as ready as geese in gander's clothing ever could be. Irene led the way down the back stairs, and tonight we encountered no one.

A service entry opened on an alley-courtyard. The mist lapped at the stoop.

"Careful!" Irene whispered. "There's a high step down, remember?"

The surrounding stonework shone as if sweating in the muted gaslight. It did not so much rain in Paris as drizzle, and the night was a blanket of invisible dampness.

Irene handed me her cane. I recognized the carved amber dragon's head—Godfrey's sword-stick! Even as my gloved hand wrapped around it, I felt faintly ill to think that Godfrey was out in the wild world without this form of defense. Surely we were safer in Paris.

"Do not touch pavement with the sticks until we have passed the watcher on the avenue."

I had forgotten about the sinister figure Irene had pointed out earlier to Elizabeth. She stepped forward at a brisk but silent pace. I felt like a child jumping over puddles when I matched my gait to hers, but our pace was so swift and businesslike that within a minute we were turning into the street onto which the hotel faced. Looking neither right nor left, with Elizabeth and I paired behind Irene's lead, we moved past the hotel's raked five-story wings and into the light of the entry façade, with its flaring exterior side lamps and the glow of chandeliers within.

Here we were able to hail a cab, or Irene was, with a brusque upward signal of her hand.

The clop of the horse's hooves as we wheeled away was as shocking as sudden applause on that empty street.

Irene turned to peer out the tiny, book-sized rear window. "No vehicle follows us. We have eluded our pursuer."

"*Your* pursuer," Elizabeth said, careful not to raise her voice so the driver up top would hear feminine tones issuing from his three masculine passengers.

Irene, of course, could speak in a booming basso if she chose, but neither Elizabeth nor I were equipped to be convincing male impersonators, save by the dark of the moon.

"My pursuer is your pursuer now," Irene observed.

"Where do we go?" I asked.

"Back to the rue des Moulins."

"We would never pass muster as customers there," I objected. "It is too well lit inside."

"I do not intend to go inside," Irene said in her deepest contralto, "I wish to go beyond it a good ways, but on the same axis."

"Why—?" Elizabeth asked in a husky whisper.

"I wish to find another disturbed wine cellar, and perhaps another scene of a crime."

"Why? Jack the Ripper is captured."

Irene was silent as we jostled over damp stones that made a slight sucking sound under our spinning wheels, like sticking plaster being pulled from a wound.

"Baron Rothschild," Irene finally answered, "had said that anything he could provide was at my disposal. I sent for maps of Paris days ago."

"We did not see them arrive," I noted suspiciously.

"I did not wish to be premature, but I have never been satisfied by the condition of the wine cellar beneath the brothel."

"It was dark, damp, dirty, and full of dusty bottles and smoky-smelling wooden casks," I enumerated with some heat. Albeit whispered. "A typical wine cellar."

"Yes . . ." she agreed slowly enough to tacitly disagree.

"It did connect to the sewer," Elizabeth pointed out with gusto. "I have always found that deliciously interesting. Is that what intrigues you, Irene?"

"Yes. Except that I don't think what we glimpsed was part of the infamous sewers of Paris."

"Oh!" Elizabeth sounded bereft. "If Jack the Ripper had been using the sewers of Paris, it would have been so . . . dramatic."

"Jack the Ripper was dramatic enough with his vanishing act in the byways of Whitechapel. But I admit that Paris is as intriguing a city underground as it is above ground. Those who excavate for the new underground train system in London may not like what they dig up. If I have calculated correctly, on a street near the Parc Monceau we will find another oddly altered cellar. I admit that mathematics is not my forte, although I have a certain flair for the merciless logic of music.

If I have not done my sums properly, this expedition is useless. I can only hope that my formula will prove accurate."

The carriage lurched forward, then back, in that time-tested motion that indicates arrival by putting passengers' stomachs into a semblance of seasickness.

Irene hopped down to the street and drew a five-franc coin from her waistcoat pocket, which she tossed up at the driver, who caught it as it flashed into his upraised hand. It was astounding what skills being an opera singer had given Irene. I fully believe she could have become a sharpshooter like Annie Oakley, should she wish to. Perhaps it was all those trouser roles she had played that suited her dark soprano voice.

Even Elizabeth seemed struck mute by her coin trick.

It was, of course, a completely man-about-town gesture. That was why Irene did it, as part of her role, not from any personal need to show off. So few understood that about a consummate performer: the individual is subsumed into the part and then into the whole of the production. Irene only played the prima donna when she was cast—or had cast herself—in the role.

Once the cab had clattered off in search of another fare, and I'm sure it would be a long one, Irene's jaunty air vanished. She eyed the empty street.

"I am hoping for another innocent-looking entry to the lower levels," Irene said. "Let us walk and look high and low. Mostly low. Looking tipsy would be useful, as well."

She lurched into a shambling gait, still in full stride, swaggering from one side of the street to another, stumbling into doorways and testing them for entry.

Tipsy. I watched Elizabeth follow in Irene's footsteps, so to speak, but in another direction. She was most unconvincing and looked disabled rather than drunk.

I attempted no such nonsense. I would be the sober friend hoping to see these two tipplers home.

We were in luck that the traffic on this street was scarce. Residents kept their noses indoors.

One of Elizabeth's more dramatic but pathetic lurches brought her across my path, where I "steadied" her. Him. I clapped him hard upon the back. "Steady, fellow," I grumbled in as low a voice as I could muster. "Do you miss the warmer work inside that *maison*?" I whispered, as she straightened at my command.

"Warmer indeed, Nell," she responded with a disgraceful wink. "I almost hope that Irene doesn't find a path to the chill cellars below."

I pushed her away in disgust, as my role called for. I began to see the attraction of pretending to be someone other than oneself. It excused a purely honest reaction that must be stifled and concealed in polite society.

We heard thc sound of approaching steps.

"Frère Jacques, Frère Jacques," Irene began singing in a tiddly basso.

Elizabeth rushed to the wall she leaned against to prop her up, and hush her up.

An ill-dressed man lurched past us, his unshaven face slack with alcohol poisoning, his working-man's blouse and trousers wrinkled and . . . odiferous.

Irene's song faded at our attentions, and the man's blcary look returned to the cobblestones his feet stuttered over. In a few instants only the small scuffles of his distant boots could be heard.

Irene leaned back against another barred door, frowning. I pushed the annoying deerstalker up on my forehead so I could see more than the checked umbrella edge of its brim, which clashed abominably with the pattern of my jacket.

"I doubt we shall find anything so convenient as a door," I said.

"I would hate to have to take you two through the kitchen to the wine cellar. You would not fool a gnat."

"You mean Elizabeth would not," I said.

"*I* am unbelievable?" she answered. "You cannot even act drunk."

Our raised walking sticks were about to cross like swords, until Irene stepped in between them, and us.

"If you are coming to fisticuffs in the street, please do it in male voices at least."

Irene glanced up at the first-floor level around us to make sure that no shutters or windows had opened.

"Now." She jerked our hats down on our heads and restored our walking sticks to an upright position at our suited sides. "What I seek will look more like a workman's hole than a door, I have concluded. Look for a niche a rat could disappear into."

A rat! The idea was not appetizing.

Elizabeth bent to survey the grilled windows below street level.

"Kitchens and sculleries," I told her.

"Perhaps not all."

So we continued down the deserted street, now crouching instead of lurching, all the better to peer into darkened arches of half windows sunk into the foundation of the buildings.

I heard a rasp of metal, and turned to find Irene kneeling in the filthy gutter. I did not care for her "walking-out" clothes in masculine form, but even they did not deserve what prostration in a gutter of Paris would do to them.

"This cellar is unoccupied," she whispered when we came to her assistance. "Help me with this grille. It is old, rusted, and, best of all, loose."

We applied gloves to metal mesh, then removed our gloves for a better grip. Together we tugged and grunted like dray-wagon drivers. Behind our mufflers and under our hats, threads of perspiration ran unseen. The itching had become torture.

Still, I could feel the grille within my fists wiggle, then jerk, and finally pull loose so abruptly we all fell back on our heels.

We sat and gasped for a while. I must say that I knew the satisfaction that only achieving the impossible imparts.

"Now we must lift the grille out of the way," Irene said at last.

Elizabeth groaned softly, but we all grabbed on to an edge again and thereafter wrestled the piece as large as a fire screen to rest against the stone foundation.

Finished at last, we gazed into the featureless hole we had bared.

Large as it was, it did not promise a dignified entry even for those wearing trousers.

Irene leaped down into the shallow well surrounding it. "I shall go first. I have the pistol. Who will come next?"

"I!" Elizabeth trumped me.

"I don't know how far below the floor is," Irene cautioned, even as she folded herself in the most astoundingly limber way and disappeared through an opening the size of a painting frame.

We heard a thud, an "oof," and a "Hurry!"

Elizabeth shrugged, exchanged a glance with me, and started to go feetfirst through the gap. This proved to be a mistake. She was soon clinging to the well edge, her upper half visible and her nether regions apparently flailing for purchase.

"Oh!" Her eyes grew round and she gazed into mine as if she were drowning. With a great jerk, her hands gave way, and she had been swallowed by the dark hole below.

I hardly thought going facefirst would work any better, but by now I was the lone person left on the street. I heard the click of something approaching and turned in panic.

A lean, mangy dog had paused in trotting past to regard me with hungry yellow eyes.

I jumped down into the well, then crouched against the hole, wondering if I could back into it and thus keep my eyes on the devil dog watching me as if ready to chase a rat into a hole.

I managed to wiggle my posterior somewhat over the waiting gulf, while keeping my hands and feet attached to terra firma.

Now I was wedged width-wise in the hole with no way of advancing or retreating! The dog could chew upon my face and hands at its leisure.

I managed to push a foot over the abyss, but the sense of unanchored suspension nearly made me swoon.

"Nell!" Irene's voice urged from below.

The mongrel began to growl, showing great yellow teeth.

I hunched a shoulder, getting partway through before sticking again.

By now my midsection was folded so upon itself that I could hardly take breath, much less scream for aid.

I was caught fast in the opening, hopelessly jammed. My walking stick was wedged sideways in the well, useless.

Someone seized my loose ankle and pulled. I gritted my teeth shut against a shout of objection. My shoe was pulling off my foot despite the sturdy laces.

The dog edged nearer. I could feel its hot breath on my face. I could also smell it. The huge muzzle pushed toward me. I shut my eyes. A large wet, warm, tongue swabbed my features from north to south, what was visible of them anyway.

My scream of revulsion was cut off when both my ankles were jerked sharply downward, and I popped through the aperture like a cork pried from a bottle neck. My stick whacked the opening as it followed me through.

It was small comfort to be standing upright only because my companions bracketed me, to be facing utter dark, and to have a slimy, wet face that reeked of garbage.

"There was a dog," I managed to pant out.

"Poor Nell," Irene said. "There is always a dog." She dragged me deeper into the dark, then suddenly there came a sharp scratching sound . . . had the fiendish dog—? But no, my friend had merely drawn a lucifer over the striking edge of its box. A will-o'-the-wisp of light danced against the darkness, and then a small stub of candle she also produced took flame and we could see each other again at last.

"All right?" Irene asked.

When we nodded, she immediately turned to let the feeble light play over the room we had entered. A cellar, empty, with a few broken sticks of wood on the floor and not much else.

"Good," Irene said. "Let us go deeper."

I followed, thrusting my walking stick ahead of me in the dark like the blind men one saw on the streets occasionally. The rhythmic tap of its tip on the hard-packed earth and stone was comforting in an inanimate way. I soon heard the echo of Elizabeth's cane as she emulated me, and smiled.

"Will anyone hear us?" I whispered suddenly.

"My hope is that only the dead will," Irene responded cheerfully from ahead.

I could just glimpse her figure edged by a thin halo of candlelight.

A draft at my ankles told me our course angled downward, as the catacomb near the Eiffel Tower had.

I knew that this was a good sign for Irene, though it was most upsetting to me. Delving into dark places should be done by miners. Still, I would rather be part of this adventure than left sleeping at the hotel, which is what I fear would have happened had I not awakened ready to join the expedition.

"Do you smell anything?" Irene asked.

"Must," I said. "Dust. Dirt. Damp. Rats and cats."

"Candle wax," Elizabeth said, "but you are carrying it. And the scent of some liquor, not wine."

"Obviously," I complained. "I have not spent enough time in brothels, where spirits and candles are plentiful and one may develop a 'nose' for the bouquet of corruption."

"Don't mention 'corruption,' Nell," Irene advised me sardonically from ahead. "That is what I most sincerely hope we find scant evidence of at the end of this passage."

"Scant?"

"Well, no traces at all would not do our investigation any good."

I believe that I stopped moving. At least Miss Elizabeth crashed into me from behind, ramming my ribs with her walking stick.

I mewed protest, all the sound I dared make under the circumstances. I would not be the one to bring the gendarmes down on us!

"Feel the fresh, wet air!" Irene sounded like a passenger on a flyboat on the Seine, one of those large double-decked steamers that ferried sightseers and travelers up and down the river's crooked length.

"We near the sewers," I predicted under my breath.

Apparently my comment was not as beneath my breath as I had intended, for Elizabeth rhapsodized the key word after me.

"Sewers. Of course."

Irene led on, foregoing comment.

In an instant the shaft had widened into a cavern, and she stopped, her small candle casting enough light to show the limits of the place.

The stench was an overwhelming bouillabaisse with an underlying most unpleasant fishy odor. Among the unhappy blend my nose recognized blood, sweat, and urine, the worst that one might encounter in scenes of animal husbandry in the country and in the most debased slums of the city.

The "fresh" air of the sewers hung like a fetid blanket over the scene, intensifying the conjoined reeks as toilet water will vivify a sachet of dried rose petals. Only this was the odor of rot.

I squinted at the uneven walls, hoping to see no neat piles of bones, hoping to avoid the vision of any rag piles on the floor.

And I was rewarded on both counts! Unaccountably, I felt a sense of disappointment. If there was nothing, whatever notion of Irene's had brought us here was worthless.

Another lucifer was struck with that peculiar scraping sound that is so oddly animal-like. I suppose it reminds me of rat claws within the walls.

Irene now held two lit candle stubs, and held one out to us.

Elizabeth rushed to claim it.

Now a double light danced off the dimpled stone walls. I was surprised to see odd letters and symbols scribed here and there in charcoal. Such unlettered scrawls! One looked like a "P" with an "X" through it. Another resembled a backwards "R." Most of the marks were nonsensical wavy lines.

"A beggars' refuge, do you think?" Elizabeth asked Irene.

Irene was already advancing on the dark like a duelist, her candle held at arm's length. Parts of the walls were quite bare of anything other than moss and mold, but a swipe of her light revealed something more as a dustcloth will unveil a scratch in the mahogany.

This scrawl was long and wavering, at waist height, and it seemed etched in blood, not char.

Irene went close to inspect it, with Elizabeth and I close behind merely for the comfort of company.

Such was the drawing's length that she ordered Elizabeth to use her candle to trace it to the other end. Elizabeth only stopped five feet away.

"Les juives . . ." Irene whispered in perfect French. ". . . *sont des gens.*"

She straightened from bending to read the roughly drawn letters.

"Mon dieu!" The written words seemed to have marooned her in the French language. "*C'est*—" She bent to read again, walking along crouched toward Elizabeth. *"que l'on ne blâmera,"* she muttered. Then, *"pas pour rien,"* she finished intoning with the solemnity of a religious celebrant as she stood alongside Elizabeth. Perhaps the candle gave me the unlikely religious impression, for Irene was not given to ritual or invoking the Godhead in any language.

"Do you know what this is? What this means?" she asked in an awed hush.

"No," I admitted. "Tell us."

"There was always something foreign about the phrasing," she went on more to herself than us. "And the haste in erasing it—"

The soft grating sound of a step in the passage behind us stopped her like a falling guillotine. I glimpsed her hand thrusting into her jacket pocket as she hissed, "Douse the candles."

Elizabeth pinched her flame out with her fingertips. I blew mine out an instant later.

I had also glimpsed a shadow in the passage.

The broad swath of an unshuttered lantern splashed into the cavern like a barrel of spilled water, suddenly touching parts of all of us.

The figure that held it was stooped like Quasimodo and wore smudged workman's clothing. He was not much above a beggar, from my one glimpse, and the stubble on his face below the usual peaked cap made him look a debased sort indeed. Perhaps we had been discovered by one of the occasional residents of this pest hole.

Irene cocked the pistol.

What a cold, sinister sound that was, yet it did not shake our unwholesome visitor, who stood teetering on the rubble at the passage end.

He reached into his own pocket, half-torn from its mooring on the baggy denim.

Irene lifted the pistol higher, following his gesture.

From that poor excuse of a pocket he pulled a small clay pipe. He began to spout something French about *chiens* and *fumering*. Perhaps he was saying that he would like to have smoked dog for dinner. I have no idea!

Suddenly Irene shrugged in that Gallic manner she had so mastered and stepped back to permit the man entry into our . . . pit.

But he stayed where he stood, lighting the pipe with a lucifer and then sucking on the dreadful thing until the bowl glowed cheerful as an ember. A smoky scent slowly masked the dreadful odors steaming around us.

"Most unpleasant for ladies," said Sherlock Holmes, "but then I see you are attired as lads. A wise precaution."

"You!" said Elizabeth, as indignant as only the young can be. "You were the one who waited outside our hotel and then followed us here."

"If I were watching you, you would not see me. And I would not station myself so obviously near your windows as to be visible. No. I was your coachman. That is a far more practical method. Why follow when one can lead?"

Irene unleashed an impressive arpeggio of laughter. "You were taking quite a chance. Why on earth gamble that we would go out?"

"Because you have been out at hours and in places where ladies of good reputation would never go. And because I saw that the arrest of James Kelly would not satisfy Pinkerton extraordinary Irene Adler."

"Former Pinkerton," she corrected him. "The only 'Pink' we have here is—" She glanced at Elizabeth, who even in the lamplight could be seen to blush a fiery red.

Was Irene hinting to Sherlock Holmes that Elizabeth was the Pinkerton agent now, or did Irene truly not know that she was? Or was Elizabeth not a Pinkerton as I had suspected? While I began to question who I really was the conversation continued without me.

"I must tell you," said Sherlock Holmes, "that the fragment of cork you found in the cellar on the rue des Moulins is exactly the same as smaller fragments embedded in the soles of Kelly's shoes. He obviously never left the establishment after installing the, er, settee, but lurked in the cellar until the dinner hour, when he could prowl the upper stories undetected."

"And there he stumbled across the two women, er, sitting on the settee, and promptly slit their throats and committed other gruesome but compelling atrocities?" Irene sounded dubious.

"You've seen the man. Quite significantly mad. He is also a very likely suspect in the Whitechapel atrocities, even more especially after this outrage."

"And the death near the Eiffel Tower?"

"Likely his work as well. There will be quite a tussle between the French and English authorities and governments for the possession of Mr. James Kelly. Both will vie for the claim to the most pernicious crimes committed on the motherland's soil. Fortunately, that is not part of my responsibilities." He paused, as if about to broach an unpleasant subject. "Despite the evidence, you believe that the Ripper is still at large?" Mr. Holmes asked Irene then.

I believed that asking the question, rather than telling her the answer, took some measure of humility on Sherlock Holmes's part that he was not used to extending to anyone, least of all a woman.

"*Because* of the evidence, I believe that someone, or something is. I am not convinced that a man as easily unhinged by a trio of fallen women as James Kelly is capable of eluding the police as neatly as Jack the Ripper did."

"Eluding the police in Whitechapel was child's play, Madam. It is a tortured labyrinth of interconnecting streets and yards and byways made for swift escapes. Saucy Jack was interrupted once, for certain, and possibly seen many times.

"Besides," he continued with a stern glance at all of us, "once removed from the infuriating feminine presence this Kelly proved a clever fellow under interrogation. He was certainly wriggling valiantly to save himself. Only my judicious mention of his dead wife provoked an outburst that proved his insanity to the French police. My analysis of the cork from his boot sole provided conclusive evidence that he concealed himself in the *maison*'s cellar."

Irene stood aside. "James Kelly may not have been the only one to lurk in cellars, or even that particular cellar. Look."

"I will," he said, "but someone must hold the lantern."

"I will!" Elizabeth, still scarlet, stepped forward to take custody of it.

"Someone must hold my pipe."

"I will not!" I said.

He smiled, bending to lay it on the ground. "Then perhaps you will extract the usual paper and pencil from your far more practical pockets, Miss Huxleigh, and take notes. But stay behind me please. You must not walk in the evidence any more than you have."

Behind him? Well!

"And I, Mr. Holmes?" came Irene's most silken tone.

"You will stand guard by the passage with the pistol at the ready. You are quite right that someone watched you from the hotel. I did my best to lose any pursuit on the cab drive here, but cannot guarantee that the pursuer was turned completely away."

He glanced around at us with an amusement completely out of place on such a sinister scene. "Poor old Watson! What will he say when I tell him that it took three women in men's clothing to make up for his ever-reliable presence."

"He will say," Irene answered, "that you have much underestimated him, and women."

"Yes, Watson has always been too gallant for his own good." His amusement faded. "You will not find that a flaw of mine."

"Why, Mr. Holmes," Irene said, "should we be looking that closely at you? We'd rather seek the flaws in those who violate the bounds of civil conduct."

That comment he did not answer, but began circling the edges of the cavern, Elizabeth holding the lantern over his stooped form as he produced a magnifying glass from another pocket and began examining the scratches on the walls and the—one would think—utterly unimpressionable ground. While he worked and the light was good, I hastily sketched the odd marks on the wall into my notebook.

Beneath the crude symbols and letters, he bent to find bits of singed wood and produced an envelope into which he swept the disintegrating char. "All that is left of a burnt stick, chestnut I should think, that was used to make the wall markings. There was a fire in the center."

Elizabeth swept the lanternlight in that direction, illuminating a coalish glitter, a gouache of charred wood, now that he had mentioned it. She had volunteered for a most arduous task: holding the heavy metal lantern high enough to create a pool of light for the detective to work in, and yet always moving it high and low to accommodate his quick and unpredictable motions.

Meanwhile, I had relit my candle with one of Irene's lucifers and stood near the passageway, trying to jot down notes by its wavering faint light. Chestnut tree stick. Bonfire in center.

"Blood," said Sherlock Holmes as he lay nearly prone on the ground beyond the charcoal markings. "Drops. From the pattern . . . This is not good."

He moved on, at times reminding me of nursery charges playing games on hands and knees. The man seemed to have no regard for his own dignity. I remembered Irene's comment that he looked close in order to see the larger picture, then thought of him as a sort of microscope on human legs, and his actions made perfect sense.

"Wine," he pronounced. "Red, of course, and it accounts for some of these other drops, but they are thin, and the blood has come in gobbets."

I nearly gagged as my pen dutifully recorded: Wine. Blood. Drops. Gobbets.

"Ah!" He rose slowly to his feet, his change in position illuminated by Elizabeth's mirroring of his motion, lantern still in hand, although held up by both hands now.

He had come upon the long string of French words.

"You realize what this means?" Irene commented from the passage mouth. Although she had not much raised her voice, her contralto carried perfectly across the cavern, like a challenge.

"One would almost think," Sherlock Holmes murmured, "that you had put this here yourself to force a tie to the London . . . unpleasantness, except that I do not know where you would get blood."

"It is blood?" I couldn't help asking, much as I hated to ask that man anything.

"Blood indeed, but perhaps not human." He glanced to the floor, then knelt a distance back from the wall. "Or perhaps very human indeed."

Then he began moving back and forth on his knees the length of the writing, leaning to gaze through his magnifying glass close enough to follow the movements of a single ant, then lurching away to survey the larger wall.

Elizabeth tried to keep behind him, her lantern illuminating the ground and wall he studied. She scurried like a servant girl to accommodate his moves, and like a member of a privileged class, he gave no notice to her exceptional efforts to anticipate his every need.

At last he sat back on his heels, dirty worn heels they were, and sighed.

"Madam Norton, you have indeed unearthed a conundrum. I would be most interested in your reasons for coming here and finding this. I confess myself puzzled. But I warn you, this smacks of an attempt at deceit, and it had better not be that of you and your cohorts."

Stern as his voice had become on the last sentence, I felt an unreasonable glow of pride. I had never been called anything so formidable as a "cohort" before. Not even Sarah Bernhardt, bold, shameless woman, could quite qualify as Irene's "cohort."

He turned over his shoulder to regard Elizabeth. "Oh, do set down that lantern, Miss Pink. There, toward the middle of the cavern so it will light your excavation party's find. It is possible that you three have unearthed what corresponds to lost Troy when it comes to the Jack the Ripper saga. Now be quiet and let me think."

As Elizabeth followed his instructions, the swath of the lantern widened to reveal the entire French phrase scrawled across five feet of cavern wall and the silhouetted figure of Sherlock Holmes on his knees before it like a follower of Islam facing the east for his morning prayers.

The lantern, its shutters opened fully, cast a faint glow upon the entire site so we could see each other at last. We exchanged glances both puzzled and awestruck.

After a few moments, Sherlock Holmes spoke again, and I wrote down every word, as was my role.

"A man knelt here, where I do, not twenty-four hours ago. More likely . . . six. He was lashed savagely. And he dipped his right forefinger in the blood from his shoulders and sides and back to write these words. French is not his native language, but he knows it well. He moved along this length of cavern, roughly that of a human body, his blood spattering the rock in a fine spray like salt water in a cove, lashed all the while, until he had written these words."

He paused as if exhausted, as if he himself had made that hellishly painful journey of firelight, blood, and crude penmanship.

Irene spoke, violating his injunction to be silent.

"The Jews," she said, "are the men that will not be blamed for nothing."

Of course I recognized the phrase, though I had not when first-seeing it in French.

I held my breath. Something astounding was about to be thought, realized, understood, yet I could not quite grasp it myself. I wrote the phrase again in my notebook, in English: "The Juwes (who could forget that bizarre, unlettered spelling, or was it?) are the men That Will not be Blamed for nothing." I remembered the odd capitalization, the confusion of negatives so that one was not sure if the Jews were being exonerated by the writer, or indeed blamed. And this was the evidence found not far from Catharine Eddowes's body, that had been forever erased by the English authorities within hours.

"The Rothschilds were right," she said. Then, "Do you see it, Mr. Holmes?"

"Of course I see it," he said icily. "I see almost everything that transpired in this miserable, brutal cavern. There is an evil beyond the insane obsessions of Jack the Ripper, one far older and far more sinister, and it has been at work here. And I am not sure that anyone on earth can stop it!"

I realized then that all his fine and icy anger was really and truly fear.

"It is bad enough to hunt men who rejoice in hurting others," he added. "It is impossible to hunt men who will so injure themselves."

After a long pause, he spoke again. "There was murder done here as well. I have read that in the quantity and pattern of the blood that sprinkles this chamber of horrors like holy water from a Roman priest's aspergillum, just as you, Madam Norton, read your French and realized that the French word for Jews—*juives*—in a handwritten form and missing the dot of the 'i'—would look like 'Juwes' to the English eyes that saw it for brief instants before it was erased for eternity."

For eternity. What had been done here would last for eternity. We were indeed staring at an undeniable link between London Then and Paris Now and the unholy work of Jack the Ripper. There were two links: the Jewish element that Baron de Rothschild had feared and the French connection that indicated the atrocities in Whitechapel had been just the beginning.

In the long, anguished silence that followed, we all paid tribute to the severity of the crimes that had drawn us together. In those moments, the cavern became a dark chapel filled with the incense of sacrifice in its most primitive, fatal forms. In those moments, we became a congregation determined to resist the darkness.

Irene finally spoke.

"I believe I know where the body that bled here has gone. Now, will you follow us, Mr. Sherlock Holmes, and keep quiet and let me think?"

42.

Tableaux Mordants

It had the reality of a newspaper, which most people enjoyed as reality, despite the fact that it was packaged and sensationalized for everyday consumption.

—VANESSA R. SCHWARTZ, *SPECTACULAR REALITIES*

FROM A JOURNAL

My arms ached from holding up the blasted lantern for the Englishman, as if I'd been rowing a boat across Lake Erie for hours, but of course I could say nothing, or risk being left behind.

Still, how thrilling to be on the hunt with Sherlock Holmes and Irene Adler Norton! I could not have dreamed of a better turn of events.

This unspoken (and sometimes almost-spoken) rivalry between them is fascinating. It must long precede my arrival on the scene. I would love to know just how and when it began.

Nell knows, I imagine, but she would not tell the likes of Pink!

I do think that we three women comported ourselves quite well in that stinking cellar. And although I prefer to dress as a lady, roving about in men's garb is such a lark! Will I dare tell anyone later . . . when this is over? It is all very well to be independent but if one goes too far in offending public sensibilities one can go from being considered a darling of the eccentric to a despised pariah.

Anyway, there we were, four men on the town: three semirespectable gentlemen and one loutish laborer.

As we walked the damp, dark streets following Irene's lead and looking around and behind for signs of stalkers, I couldn't help thinking that we three women were a pretty representative sampling of the various heights attributed to Jack the Ripper. None of us was only five feet tall, but rather a few inches over. Just like the Ripper suspects.

And Sherlock Holmes? Well, he topped six feet by at least an inch or two or I'm a mulberry bush! I could see why he assumed a stooped form when in disguise. An exceptionally tall man would not want to stand out any more than he had to.

Imagine if he would wear cowboy boots like a Wild West Show rider!

Well, that is quite a vision.

I tried not to think such wicked thoughts as we proceeded, but I was very tired, and close quarters with rude death tends to make one resort to bravado.

In truth, I was much disturbed by that cellar and the savage events Mr. Holmes divined as happening there. Surely the scrawling man who used his own blood as an inkwell was a prisoner of some kind. Perhaps the writing assignment was a sort of punishment. I am much against corporal punishment for anyone.

And, speaking of corporal punishment, oh, how my arms ached on that walk. Why had I offered to "lift my lamp beside the golden door"? The Statue of Liberty, at least, was made of copper and not frail flesh.

And Miss Liberty rested on a strong base designed by Monsieur Eiffel. It was only a third as tall as his mighty Tower, and an American Revolution centenary gift installed a decade late, only three years ago in 1886. I was glad the French had not elected to observe the hundredth anniversary of our revolution as they had considered marking the centenary of their own revolution: with a giant guillotine. Imagine all those immigrants "yearning to breathe free" steaming into the face of that in New York Harbor!

I was beginning to recognize the streets. We were not far from the Paris Opéra, moving along the Boulevard Montmartre. The Théâtre des Variétés was on our right, its narrow two stories of classical pillars and top pediment gleaming as if phosphorescent in the gaslit mist. The Théâtre du Vaudeville and the Opéra Comique were also in this area where the Boulevard Montmartre begins and the rue de Richelieu crosses it and famous cafés crowd the sidewalk like pigeons—the Café Riche, the Café Anglais, the Maison Dorée, the Café de Paris. Just ahead was the Passage des Panoramas, those marvelous attractions whose circular scenic paintings twisted perspective into the oddest impression of reality.

Despite the early hour of the morning, this was a celebrated section of Paris, and the occasional cab horse trotted past, though pedestrians were thankfully few, making the possibility of following us harder.

We had all adopted a loping, drunken gait, even Sherlock Holmes, who was, in fact, the most convincingly tipsy of us all.

"How far, Madam?" he asked in slurred tones.

"We are there."

We managed to stop and pile into one bewildered clot. "Where?" I asked.

She nodded at a building across the boulevard. "The Musée Grévin."

This announcement brought silence to us all, except to Nell, of course.

"I have never heard of it. What kind of collection does this museum feature?"

"Bodies," said Sherlock Holmes with a certain relish. "Waxen bodies, many of them impersonating the famous and many of them impersonating the famous dead. The place is locked and barred. Why are we here?"

"To get around locks and bars," Irene replied. "I believe that someone has preceded us in that enterprise."

"This is mad!" Nell said.

"It would seem to lack reason," the English detective seconded in milder tones.

I couldn't help agreeing with Sherlock Holmes. The façade of the Musée Grévin befitted one of the city's most popular museums, and even the misty gaslight could not dim its reputation or luster.

Handsome metal standards before it held the Jules Cheret posters of lissome ladies that are so popular in Paris. The arched entryway was surmounted by graceful cutout brass letters reading MUSÉE GRÉVIN.

Although Baker Street in London now housed the wax museum of Madame Tussaud, whose family had escaped revolutionary France to set up business elsewhere, I had read that this establishment had its roots in the same family, though it had only reopened for business seven years earlier.

No one who had lived in or visited Paris could escape its fame. It drew its most spectacular exhibits from the personalities, events, and very newspaper illustrations of its day.

I found this last fact most interesting. If the written journal merged with the visual tableaux—not merely a tableau vivant, with live actors—but with, well, dead personalities cast in wax, surely some strange blending of news, story, and art was in the offing. Something that was not quite journalism or the stage, but a modern hybrid of both that had its own, and offered to its subjects, eternal life.

And death.

And I suppose that was why Irene had led us all here.

"Is it possible to enter?" Irene asked Sherlock Holmes.

"Not without attracting attention."

"No attention seems to be directed our way," she returned, eyeing the empty street.

"I would doubt that," he replied, "but whatever attention we have drawn probably does not wish to draw attention to itself, at the moment."

"We will crowd around," she decreed, "to conceal your actions."

So we three kept convivial if somewhat tilted company before the door while Sherlock Holmes produced a number of small metal tools from another of his disreputable pockets and set to work picking the door lock like a burglar born.

This was even more of a ripping adventure than I could have hoped for! Like Nell after her solo visit to Mr. Holmes, I was madly impatient for an opportunity to write it all down while the events were still fresh in my mind. Since I was not known for my endless note-taking, as she was; the recording angel in my mind would have to hold her horses. I wonder if she wore cowboy boots!

The door opened just a bit, like a dowager taking a very tiny breath before supper. I know I stood there stupefied, for I had never entered anywhere unlawfully before. Oh, I had entered unwanted, or under false pretenses plenty of times, but never . . . criminally.

It was testimony as to who were the seasoned sleuths among us when Irene wasted no time slipping through the widening opening, Sherlock Holmes on her coattails.

I took a last look 'round at the silent street before I followed Nell into the darkness within.

I immediately bumped into Sherlock Holmes, who was waiting to secure the door behind me.

"Patience, Miss Pink," he said wryly. "We are only four foxes in a house with many hundreds of hens."

Although Mr. Holmes's analogy of a henhouse might have suited our company of women and the American birth of two of us, we hardly stood in so humble an outbuilding but rather in a large soaring chamber lined with columns reminiscent of the Temple at Karnak of ancient Egypt.

"The museum is wired throughout for electric light," Irene noted briskly, "to preserve the wax figures from decaying in the warmer glare of other lighting methods. It is the first such building in Paris to boast this modern convenience. Would that the theaters were so equipped! Many an overweight tenor has nearly melted under the stage lights."

"You know a great deal about this place," Nell said a trifle suspiciously. She was very jealous of Irene's comings and goings.

"That is one thing Godfrey and I did during all those carriage outings to Paris. We visited the Musée Grévin."

"Oh. You did not mention it."

"Oh. You did not ask."

"So you know the building," Mr. Holmes put in almost as sharply as Nell. I wondered what *he* was jealous of. "I am not used to being led by female intuition, Madam Norton. I presume you have some unshared knowledge that leads you to this place."

"Just the usual intuition," she replied airily. "I have always found intuition a supreme advantage upon the stage, and see no reason to ignore its advantages in real life."

"I will admit that I detected signs of a previous assault on the front door."

"Are they still here?" Nell whispered, wide eyes shining white in the light of the shuttered lantern I had been given custody of when Mr. Holmes had bent all his attention and both of his hands to the act and art of gaining entry.

"Ask Madam Intuition," he responded huffily.

I imagine that the great detective, used to working alone, much resented the company of this gaggle of false ganders. Yet we had led him to a scene with chilling implications about the Whitechapel murders. For if the same phrase that had been erased so quickly in Goulston Street—I wonder that it was not spelled "Ghoulston Street" after what we had seen tonight—was now appearing in French on the stone walls of catacomb-like cellars in Paris . . . well, what was the world of lustmurder coming to?

"I hope," he was saying further, "that Madam Norton will explain herself to us after our exploration of the world of wax is over."

"And I hope," she said, "that it will no longer be necessary to explain myself after our exploration."

I aimed the lanternlight ahead of us to encourage more movement and less discussion. If we were to meet monsters in this macabre place, I'd prefer to get it over with.

Still, as my meandering light glinted off men in jackboots and braided uniforms, my heart almost stopped. The gendarmes had anticipated us! We would be arrested. Disgraced. Unmasked. I gasped.

A hand grasped mine on the lantern, then trained it upward.

There, floating well above the floor, was a figure in an encrusted gown, surmounting by a high peaked headdress.

"His Holiness," Irene's voice came sardonically, "being carried by the princes of the church. A papal cortege to greet the hoi polloi as they enter the museum."

"Most unbecoming of a churchman," Nell said, sniffing as only the English can. "Pomp and adulation."

"Most like the Archbishop of Canterbury," Irene put in. "France is a Catholic country."

"So I see." Nell sounded as if she wished she hadn't.

I suspected that if Irene's expedition was as successful as she hoped—or feared—we would all confront what we wished we hadn't.

As I cast my lanternlight high and low, I glimpsed the truly impressive element of this entry to the museum. The many columns had waist-high bases surmounted by carved decorations to a height of six feet or more before they soared to the dark ceiling where rococo capitals gleamed like gilt palm-tree fronds.

Behind this double row of columns that acted as a sort of silent honor guard leading to the museum's actual display rooms stretched an arcade of gilt-framed mirrors. So every wax figure, every flesh-and-blood visitor was reflected back and forth until we all mingled into one confusing "crowd scene." Add the shiny marble floor beneath it all dimly reflecting everything wax and genuine, and the effect was of walking through a mirrored box. What is real, what staged, indeed? I have never experienced such a sensation of suspended reality. Even glimpsing my companions distracted me, made me momentarily take them for heart-stopping phantasms. In such an environment a monster, a killer, could slide up behind one in a mirror, could strike and be gone before the blood from his blade even began to flow.

I wished I, too, carried a little pistol, as Irene did, and I was glad to have the eminent consulting detective among our number.

The lanternlight kept picking out rich details—rattan pedestals holding potted palms, velvet-upholstered benches. Really, the effect was more of the lobby of a luxury hotel than that of a museum.

My lantern moved past the base of a pillar to cast a spotlight on a man and woman chatting just beyond it. She sat, hatted and caped, he stood, hat in hand, hand resting on the bench's top rail.

I expected them to turn and berate us for illuminating their private tête-à-tête, but of course they were wax and could not move.

"Oh!" Nell was pressing her hand to her heart, a quite odd gesture when wearing male dress. "They look just like us. I mean, like we would look if we were properly attired."

Sherlock Holmes had already drawn near to examine them. "A pretty trick, to import ordinary anonymous wax figures to deceive the spectators. Such a dodge might be employed in the service of more serious matters. . . ." His hand paused atop the gentleman's bare head as if in secular benediction.

Then he turned to Irene. "Do you have a destination in mind? Or are we to enjoy the entire contents of the museum at our ill-lit leisure?"

"I do," she said, "but I do not exactly recall its location. If you will bear left with me . . ."

She turned and strode into the dark faster than I could keep up and aim the lanternlight ahead of her. Her Sherlockian boldness amazed, both in her assumption that I would keep up and light her way; and her indifference to whether I managed it after all.

I also had to hope that the place was as deserted of the living as it seemed to be. On the hard floors our footsteps were impossible to muffle.

We sped past vignettes and tableaux that ranged from the familiar to the bizarre. Top-hatted and parasol-shaded European travelers shopped along a street in Cairo populated by overburdened donkeys, veiled women, and turbaned natives. This tableau evoked just such a village I had read of on the World Exposition grounds. A moment later we were peeping into the dancers' dressing room at the Paris Opéra, with the ballerina in her satin toe shoes and knee-length tutu receiving a gentleman caller in evening dress. Next came a scene of human sacrifice in Dahomey, with nearly naked African men gathered to behead one of their own, bound and kneeling. The men's skin shone like bootblack. Then it was the death of Marat in his bathtub. And then top-hatted gentlemen visiting the Eiffel Tower under construction, standing with their waistcoats and canes on the piled girders and angled, airy struts that form the structure, only a panorama of vacant sky behind them.

These glimpses, as sudden as the photographic cards that flash through a stereopticon, had the effect of lightning on the senses, and the quick fashion in which we glimpsed and then passed them almost made the wax figures seem to move. Certainly they were eerily lifelike.

"Ah." Irene had stopped.

My light shone into a room, small and disordered.

At our very feet, a waxen man fell from the bed, his legs still under the blanket, his nightshirted torso lying on the floor, bloodied, the dagger haft growing from his heart like a stunted shoot.

His murderer stood behind him by the wardrobe, searching for something.

"How dreadful," said Nell.

"The blood upon the scattered papers would not have fallen in that direction," Sherlock Holmes noted with disdain.

"The exhibit is called 'The History of a Crime,' " Irene said. "I think if we study it, we will discover the history of another crime entirely."

"You have been mysterious long enough," Mr. Holmes declared. "I am used to predicting the impossible. I do not think that is a function of being a retired opera singer."

"It may be a function of being a retired private inquiry agent for the Pinkertons, however," Irene answered. "I will give you all a clue. This exhibit has seven vignettes. It is called 'The History of a Crime.' I will let you imagine what might be the subject of the next six vignettes, and I will let you speculate how one of them would relate to one of the murders that have recently occurred in Paris."

"Only one?" he asked sharply.

"Indirectly to all three—if there are but three, and I think now that there are not—and directly to one."

She moved forward, I trotting after, shedding light on the second vignette. Another room showed the killer held down on the Oriental carpet by caped and capped gendarmes. Maidservants gawked in the background and men dressed remarkably like Inspector le Villard in frock coats, vests, and soft ties looked on.

"The arrest," Sherlock Holmes announced.

Irene had already moved on, so I followed.

And my heart slowed, then sped up as the lanternlight revealed a scene so like one at which I had been present that I thought for an instant that everything since then and now had been a hallucination, and I had never left that pitiful scene.

Behind me Nell drew a breath she did not let out.

I sensed Sherlock Holmes coming to stand behind us all, easily seeing over our heads.

This room was no bigger than the others, but it seemed to swell until it was all I could see: the brick floor, the pale arched stone walls and ceiling, so like a cellar. The high, long, narrow board equipped with hooks that hosted a sad array of clothing—shoes, stockings, vest, singlet, trousers, jacket, hat. All that the victim on the low stone slab had worn.

Two top-hatted men stood on the corpse's left. One pointed an accusing arm. One took frantic notes, reminding me of Nell in the cavern this very night.

On the right, the accused man shrank from the sight of his naked victim while a uniformed gendarme and an inspector in bowler hat and suit stood by to ensure his custody.

The body on the slab lay feetfirst toward us, the living, the spectators. The flesh was pale and slightly gray. A cloth covering all from neck to knee.

We all stood speechless, not at the waxen effigy of death, but at its sex. The dead man from the first chamber was now a dead woman. Of the head all that could be seen was the underside of a chin, the tip of a nose, both delicate and feminine and utterly horrific.

"Remarkable," said Sherlock Holmes. It was the first time I had detected a note of awe in his tone.

He stepped into the tableau and bent over the body, obscuring it from us.

I blinked. He didn't move for a few instants and for that time I thought he had been swallowed by the waxwork tableau never to emerge and move again.

When he finally straightened and stepped back, the lamplight showed him as pale the corpse.

"The woman is dead," he said.

"Of course she's 'dead,' " Nell objected. "That is the entire idea of the scene. This represents a room in the morgue, does it not?"

"It does," Irene said. Her tone was very heavy. "I would be interested in your diagnosis, Mr. Holmes."

"I am sorry to say that your intuition has been alarmingly exonerated, Madam." His tones were harsh, clipped. "This is not the wax figure that previously occupied this place. This woman was killed only hours ago, not here, killed and—or perhaps I should say, killed *after* . . . being horribly mutilated."

My fears were confirmed: cold, false waxen flesh had been replaced by cold, honest human flesh. What kind of fiend would set such a stage for an unsuspecting public? Although the public that flocked daily to the Paris Morgue would no doubt thrill to news of a freshly mutilated corpse appearing in a museum devoted to mimicking life. Thanks to Irene, the public would be defrauded of its excitement, for this discovery would surely be kept secret.

"Now." Mr. Holmes turned to us a face of such granite seriousness that I thought it should crack even as he spoke. "If you would be so kind, please leave me the lantern and to my business. I must collect what evidence remains before I inform the police and permit them to trample the entire museum like a herd of camels from the Cairo tableau. I suggest you join the waxen couple on the benches in the main salon until I am done."

"You want no help?" Irene asked incredulously.

"You can give none that I need, and I must insist on sparing you any more intimate involvement with a case that bears the mark of the Fiend himself upon it. I would even hesitate to ask Dr. Watson to share such a task."

He turned his back as if we no longer existed, as if we had all been frozen into wax figures in a museum and he was the only living being in the Musée Grévin.

43.

Calendar of Crime

Beyond the troubling but fascinating lull of sexual violence that hangs around the murders like Sherlockian fog, the killings remain so intriguing because the suspect was not found. . . .

—MAXIM JAKUBOWSKI AND NATHAN BRAUND, *THE MAMMOTH BOOK OF JACK THE RIPPER*

Dawn brought the merest moderation of light. Paris skies had opened a drizzling mouse-colored umbrella over her boulevards and streets. Everything reflected in the dull sheen that coated cobblestones and buildings.

I peeked from Elizabeth's sleeping alcove window, but could spy only the bowed figures of hurried pedestrians on the street below, no watching figure.

I had changed from the heavy men's clothing into my nightshirt and dressing gown. The voluminous and familiar cottons felt like a feminine cocoon sheltering me from the crude realities of the previous night. My very body had seemed bruised by the welted wools, as my mind had been blasted into some state from which I feared it might never return.

None of us had returned to bed.

Elizabeth, enamored of her alien garb, had kept it on for an hour or two before surrendering to the common comfort of nightwear. Her attire surprised me: a simple cotton flannel white gown edged with factory-made crochetwork and a plaid wool dressing gown.

Irene had retired to her room and emerged in a crackling black-green taffeta dressing gown that covered her like the glittering carapace of an exotic tropical beetle. A Worth creation, of course. I found it odd that she should seek shelter in such a costume after what we had found, after what she had led us all—including the renowned consulting detective—to find.

She occupied an upholstered armchair before the fire Elizabeth had coaxed into predawn life, saying nothing, not even smoking her vile small cigars. She sat like an empress on a throne, as if her court robes were too heavy to permit motion, as if only her mind stirred behind her impassive face. It was as dread and cold as Sherlock Holmes's features had been when he had consigned us to the entry salon of the Musée Grévin last night.

I almost considered her as an actor onstage and in place, waiting for the curtain to open to begin the next, or last, act of the current drama.

And suddenly I understood, not only Irene but, God help me, Sarah Bernhardt. They both had absorbed the conviction and strength of the often larger-than-life women they had so often portrayed on the stage. Judith from the Bible or Theodora the Byzantine Empress. They were not about to step away from such towering roles to flutter and bow and scrape in real life. If they had a tendency to regard life as a drama, at least they would play a leading role, no matter how modestly cast by society and custom. I had never thought before that perhaps the corrupting power of the theater was not upon the emotions of the audience, but in giving the players a taste of lives that had not been ordinary.

Finally, after an hour, Irene bestirred herself. She asked Elizabeth to order breakfast over the internal telephone system. Elizabeth met my eyes as she gave her instructions to the kitchens far below. We neither of us had an appetite, and neither expected to for some time.

But Irene had been right. After the waiter had delivered covered trays of steaming foodstuffs and our round table was laden with plates of porridge and raisins, sausage, fish, omelettes, and pastries, in addition to pots of coffee, tea, and chocolate, it was as if the world had turned a notch and in that motion some order had been restored to a sadly askew universe.

I found myself accepting a cup of bitter coffee while Elizabeth poured cream into it. Certainly more than ordinary remedies were called for this morning.

We each ate what we could in silent concentration. None of us finished whatever we touched.

At last Irene rose and, rustling like a flock of rooks in her taffeta gown, she set the half-empty plates back on the trays and moved them to the desk while I removed the beverage pots.

"Now," she said, sitting at the cleared table, "we must decide our next move."

"Next move!" I repeated. "Irene, we have been surely set aside after this last atrocity. Although you can take secret satisfaction in knowing that you led the great Sherlock Holmes to the scene of the crime, I have never seen a murder more made for the police and such professional investigators as Sherlock Holmes. You say that we are already being watched. It would be wisest to return to Neuilly and leave this series of slaughters to the gendarmes."

"Secret satisfaction is most underrated, Nell," she replied, a deadly gleam in her eye.

"I agree with Nell," Elizabeth said, sounding subdued for once. "I don't understand how you knew to lead us to those two terrible sites last night, but this entire puzzle has multiplied beyond any understanding. Many elements smack of the London horrors of last autumn. Others seem part of their own mysterious pattern."

"Not so puzzling," Irene said. "Like all leaps of logic, my path last night was actually quite forthright once you understand what trail of bread crumbs I was following. Sherlock Holmes may be able to detect and follow actual bread crumbs, or cork crumbs, or drops of blood, in this case. I must use my head rather than my nose, or my eyes, or my magnifying glass." She rose to rustle into the other room and returned with the tracing of the Paris map she had made the previous night.

She spread it out until it covered the table scarf like a great white wrinkled serviette, that strange bare-bones map she had drawn. I couldn't help thinking of some uncharted constellation from the heavens, all dots and connecting lines.

"Not so amazing," Irene insisted. "All three murdered women ended up in the Paris Morgue, though only one, the last, was on actual display. The authorities were too concerned about the prominent persons involved at the *maison de rendezvous* to allow those first victims public exposure, and they already knew their identities. The anonymous young woman from the catacombs near the Eiffel Tower seemed safe to flaunt . . . and thus she was, though her throat had been cut like those of the first two women.

"Yet she was covered to disguise the nature of the mutilations." Irene glanced at me. "Nell, you read the descriptions of Jack the Ripper's rampages?"

I nodded, letting feeble explanations for my morbid curiosity go unsaid. I had grown up reading ghost stories in the dark of country nights. Perhaps that had given me an unaccountable taste for terror.

"Did he not," Irene went on, "this London monster, leave the bodies in plain sight, with no attempt to hide them? Did he not let them lie as he left them, with interior organs drawn out and draped around the corpses?"

I nodded.

"Did he not also on occasion lay out the pitiful belongings of these poor women, delving into their pockets as well as their bodies?"

I nodded again, sorry that I had swallowed more than coffee, sorry even for sampling that searing beverage, which burned my throat and stomach like an unspoken apology.

"Then one might say that display itself is a large part of the killer's need and desire, his pattern?" she went on.

This time Elizabeth joined me in nodding.

"There is one thing Jack the Ripper never did in London. Can you tell me what?"

"He never moved a body," I said slowly, remembering the pale bare corpse of last night, which would have been appalling enough to regard had it merely been made of wax. "That we know of."

"No. He never moved a body, although his last killing was a departure, moving from out of doors to within doors. Perhaps moving a body is only his next . . . refinement. And—?"

I glanced at Elizabeth, who shook her head.

Irene was building her case, like a barrister well satisfied by his witnesses' puzzlement, pacing before us, her hands hidden in her wide, sweeping sleeves.

She stopped in a rasp of whirling taffeta. "One thing the Ripper never did. He never went underground."

"That we know of," Elizabeth said. "He could have escaped the area by some underground means."

"What underground means?" Irene demanded. "London is not noted for an accessible network of sewers, as Paris is. There are no convenient yet mostly forgotten catacombs, and the excavation for the underground trains is too well watched. Especially absent is that subterranean honeycomb of granite tunnels that underlies forty percent of Paris."

"The Ripper is merely using what a new city offers," Elizabeth said.

This gave Irene pause. "Perhaps," she said quietly. "But I find the murders of the women at the bordello out of character for Jack the Ripper. And you notice that the wine cellar there had been disturbed in some fashion. Yet another underground site.

"Now, this disordered cavern we found last night on a line with the bordello. Perhaps it is even connected. We saw in the bordello wine cellar what seemed to be a branch of the sewers. I now believe it to be a flooded granite passage instead. And the symbols found! No symbols decorated the sites of the London crimes."

"Except for the mysterious phrase about the Jews, which has been repeated here in French," Elizabeth said.

"Yes. One wonders why. Especially when one realizes that the *'juives'* phrase that makes sense of the London scrawl 'Juwes' is the feminine form of the plural of 'Jews' in French, so the sentence really indicates that the 'Jewesses are the

Men . . .' Well, Nell, I know you drew those markings last night. Mr. Holmes asked for your notations before he went to find a gendarme to sound the alarm at the Musée Grévin. I assume you managed to copy them somehow as you were extracting the pages before he took them?"

"No—"

Her face lost all expression but horror.

"—but I had begun copying them over in a neater form as we cooled our heels at Mr. Holmes's orders in the *salon des colonnes* for what seemed like hours. I was hardly going to spend my time staring at the papal cortege. So, when he appeared before us in that high-handed manner and demanded my notes, I gave him . . . the first version."

"Oh, Nell!" Irene came and caught me by the elbows as if she would waltz me around the room in jubilation. "Most excellent! I had to bite my tongue almost clear through not to betray my anxiety when you ripped those pages out at his command. Yet I knew I could count on you to somehow resist giving Mr. Holmes what he wanted."

"Well, I gave him only a lesser version of what he wanted. I do not work for him, you know."

"Nor do I. Let's see those scrawls. They could be arcane signs left behind by some beggars' conclave who visited the same cavern, or they could relate directly to this latest killing."

I went to my chamber to fetch the notebook, which I had tossed on a table after removing it from the jacket pocket.

Irene lit the lamp while I was gone so my small drawings would be as visible as possible.

I frowned at the symbols. "This P with the X crossing the upright reminds me of a shepherd's crook for some reason. Why would a chamber with the strange sentence about the 'Juwes' written in blood on its walls bear the sign of a shepherd?"

Irene's head snapped upright as if jerked by a leash instead of a sudden thought. "Why not the sign of the Shepherd?"

Elizabeth had stood to stare down at the symbol. "The papal cortege at the Musée Grévin . . . I saw that very symbol embroidered on one of the official's robes. I remember thinking how the papal crown—it's called a miter, isn't it?—resembled the headpiece of upper and lower Egypt in ancient times and how this"—she tapped the symbol—"struck me as almost a hieroglyph."

"You are saying this is a religious symbol?" I was dubious. "Why would a religious symbol be left in that cavern of blood and likely death? I cannot credit it, not even if it is a Papist symbol."

Irene, ignoring my usual Church of England distaste for things Roman Catholic, was hovering over me now. "The shepherd is an Old Testament figure as well as a New, and might be considered a Jewish symbol as well as a Christian, although that X is reminiscent of a cross, and thus more Christian than Jewish if it represents more than the simple letter X. I have seen it before . . . I know! Near the ossuary in the catacomb where the poor girl was found. Very faint. I took it for some ancient marking, but these Paris catacombs are not ancient, except perhaps that under Notre Dame."

"We must take this drawing to a churchman," Elizabeth said.

At that moment a knock sounded on our door, sharp enough to have been made by a walking stick. Or a policeman's club.

44.

A Confederacy of Paper

I have seen too much not to know that the impression of a woman may be more valuable than the conclusion of an analytical reasoner.

—SHERLOCK HOLMES, "THE MAN WITH THE TWISTED LIP"

After an exchange of startled stares amongst us three, Irene swept forward to swing the door wide.

There, his walking stick raised to rap again, stood Mr. Sherlock Holmes. Attired in frock coat and top hat, he would have almost resembled a boulevardier had his buttonhole sported a carnation, but it was thankfully empty of ornament.

The abrupt answer to his summons seemed to surprise him, or perhaps it was Irene in her dazzling Worth dressing gown (which really more resembled a ball gown, in my opinion).

"It is after noon." Shocked into announcing the obvious, his expression showed instant regret.

"A brilliant deduction," Irene agreed. "I cannot dispute it. None of us wears a timepiece and I have been too busy to consult the mantel clock."

"I meant that you are late to rise."

"As we were late to bed, if you recall the events of last night."

"Forgive my untimely visit. I have perhaps considered too much the imperatives of this case and not enough of the habits of ladies."

"Our 'habits,' " Irene said, spreading her mandarin sleeves like butterfly wings, "as you can plainly see, are domestic.

We have, in fact, been reviewing the elements of the 'case,' as you call it."

He retreated a pace. "I will step down to the lobby and return later."

"There is no time." Irene dropped her tone of ironic banter. "Come in and perhaps you will answer some of our questions, as we may be able to answer some of yours."

"I have only one question, Madam," he said. As usual, in his acerbic tone the English form of the courtesy address seemed more demanding and less respectful than the French. "What is the identity of the confederate who has been feeding you information on this matter?"

"Confederate?" Elizabeth burst out. "Only us."

His cool gray glance swept over us two so swiftly that we might have been barely visible.

"I mean your hidden confederate," he told Irene. "I at first suspected your husband, but from what hasty inquiries I was able to make yesterday, he does seem to be safely established in Prague, or he was, until days ago. Unfortunately he left the city so recently that he could not have returned to Paris without wings."

Irene stepped quickly past him into the hall, glancing sharply both ways. "Such matters are not suitable conversations for a public passage. Come in, Mr. Holmes, and interrogate us as you will."

He hesitated as if crossing our threshold was equivalent to plunging into Caesar's Rubicon. He did not strike me as a man who hesitated often. But then again he must not confront three women in dressing gowns very often.

"You are not attired for company," he began to object.

"And have you not spent many profitable hours at home in your dressing gown, Mr. Holmes? I doubt very seriously that the manner of clothing has much to do with the quality of thinking among those wearing it. As you said, we have no time. Come in. Elizabeth, fetch Mr. Holmes some coffee. I believe it is still hot enough if he is able to take it black. Nell, clear the table of our papers. We will all sit down together peacefully and discuss the arts of slaughter."

I understood at once that she did not wish Mr. Holmes to

see our maps and drawings, so I swept them into Elizabeth's sleeping alcove, letting the curtain fall slowly enough that he would surely see what the space was. No gentleman could violate a woman's sleeping chamber without permission, and in this situation, Sherlock Holmes was clearly ill served by his gentlemanly approach. I do not doubt that he would not stick at returning as a burglar later to see what he wanted, but for now he was cast in the role of caller, no matter how urgent.

He did indeed sip the dreadful black coffee that Elizabeth brought him, and sternly kept his eyes from dwelling on our conjoined state of deshabille.

His manner brought to mind the madman Kelly's utter distress at our presence during his interrogation. I even remembered Bram Stoker's rather anxious diffidence in our presence, and he was both a man of theater used to seeing women in semidressed states, and a married man to boot. When we had been dressed as women of the streets, Sherlock Holmes had uneasily maintained his air of masculine authority, yet here and now, in our mostly respectable selves (I exempt Elizabeth, who however was suspiciously refined for a tart) . . . we had him at a disadvantage merely by wearing dressing gowns and having our hair down. I was struck by the fact that the more scandalously a woman attired herself, the more power she had over men. Most strange.

"Now," said Irene, her gown crackling like raven wings as she settled at the table, "I would be obliged if you would recount for me the latest intelligence on my husband's movements, since I find the post a rather belated source of information."

Sherlock Holmes cleared his throat. "I have, er, Foreign Office connections in Prague. I am told that your husband suddenly left the city three days ago by rail, bound for Vienna."

"This I knew. Is that all that Foreign Office connections can contribute?"

"Usually no, but in this case—" He paused. "I do not wish to alarm you, but neither the Rothschilds' Prague emissaries nor the palace knew why your husband left the city or where he was bound. I realize that the sort of paper pathway a barrister's work entails may require following many unexpected turns."

"Indeed." Irene spun her demitasse spoon in her coffee cup until she had created a creamy whirlpool that I suspected mirrored her mental agitation. "Since Godfrey appears to have removed himself from your suspicion, not to mention our knowledge, who else did you suspect of being our confederate?"

Mr. Holmes brought the cooling brew to his lips and sipped with much the same expression of resigned distaste that I should have, were I ever so foolish as to take cold coffee.

He glanced at me suddenly, with both accusation and, oddly enough, apology.

"I did have reason to remember the interesting British agent that we shall refer to only as 'Cobra.' "

"And—?" I asked, my heart in my throat, as it always was at mention of Quentin Stanhope, even when only I knew his real name. News of him, however scant, would be greatly welcome.

"Cobra appears to have disappeared under a rock. Oh, do not be alarmed, Miss Huxleigh. I only worry about a foreign agent when he is heard of." His unexpectedly encouraging smile, brief as it was, both reassured and embarrassed me. Just how did Sherlock Holmes know that I would want to hear news of Cobra?

"If Godfrey and Cobra are in the clear," Irene asked, "whom then do you suspect of aiding us? Surely not the King?"

"I believe that at this point the King of Bohemia would do whatever you asked of him, which also seems to be the condition to which you have reduced the Prince of Wales. These facts make me extremely grateful that my bloodlines are free of royal taint, Madam. I do not underestimate you, at least not now. You must have some additional aid for you to have dogged my footsteps in this investigation."

"I am not sure who is dogging whose footsteps," Irene answered, "but I see that you will take no denials we could make for an answer."

"I am afraid that I can spare no one the most rigorous interrogation." His features tightened, if that was possible for a face already drawn drumskin-taut across the bones. "I regret to inform you what I myself have just learned: James Kelly escaped from the Paris police while being transferred to a facility for the mad."

"Escaped?" Elizabeth repeated.

"When?" Irene demanded.

"Yesterday. Afternoon."

"Then he was free—"

"He was at large yesterday afternoon and evening, in good time for him to participate in the atrocities in the cellar we discovered, yes."

"How could he escape?" I finally found breath to ask.

Mr. Holmes's quick glance in my direction became uneasy. "Le Villard does not have the influence he deserves. Kelly's mad behavior on arrest, despite his canny responses during questioning, lulled the custodians into thinking him too demented to escape. He did not elude the hangman's rope for no reason. Too absurd. His hands were manacled, but not his feet. When there was an omnibus accident on the route he plunged from the carriage and disappeared into the crowd. Given his adeptness with tools, he certainly slipped the irons shortly after and was as free a man as ever before."

He looked back at Irene. "Now that you see the urgency, Madam, you realize that I must know: who is your unseen confederate in this case?

He leaned back in the chair, sure of an answer.

Irene stood. "I will summon our 'confederate' from the other room."

Satisfaction settled on his features. I daresay they were a trifle smug.

I watched Irene turn and enter her bedchamber, wondering what on earth she had in mind . . . unless Godfrey secretly had been bound here and had somehow overcome time and space to arrive in ungodly time.

When Irene returned Mr. Holmes's eyes focused behind her, intent on identifying the presumed confederate. His conviction was so strong that he never really looked at her, which is always a mistake.

"You are trifling with me," he said in disappointment when no one appeared in her wake. "I had thought you above such coquettish stratagems."

She slapped a book to the tabletop in answer, the volume that had hidden in the folds of her heavy taffeta skirt.

"This is our 'confederate,' Mr. Holmes. You see that he is both discreet and portable, and need not rely on train schedules."

I almost spied a faint flush along the detective's gaunt cheekbones, a phenomenon perhaps unleashed both by Irene's righteous tone and his own grasp of just what book this was.

"Richard von Krafft-Ebing," he muttered. "I have heard of the baron's . . . work, but never came across a copy."

"A pity you do not visit the Beefsteak Club when in London," Irene suggested. "This book was all the talk of the Irving set not long ago."

"Much is the talk of the Irving set that the general run of men would do well to avoid," he said in forbidding tones that I would be proud to produce. "And women," he added, with a piercing look at all three of us. "I am sorry that my assumptions were more general than literal, but I thank you for . . . sharing this most interesting volume, which you feel may have some bearing upon recent events. I take it I may borrow it."

"Why, Mr. Holmes," Irene said in full ironic plumage, "you may keep it. Certainly it is not proper reading material for us."

He eyed it eagerly, yet picked it up as if it were something he had found in the street and did not wish to examine in polite company.

"If this book had been—" he began.

"Take it," she insisted. "It has done us all the ill that it can do, and may be of some good to you."

As he hesitated, I could not help saying "It is, after all, not the first memento you have of . . . us."

Again that faintest of flushes. He did not look at me, but did not dare ask me, or even himself, how I might know that he had kept the cabinet photograph of Irene that she had left for the King of Bohemia. I doubt even he knew that his doctor friend had committed the "case" to script with intentions of publishing it, or that I had found opportunity to peruse the secret manuscript.

"Thank you," was all he said, sounding quite genuine, not sardonic at all. "I bid you good day." He nodded to the room in general, avoiding looking any of us in the eye, or the dressing gown, swooped his hat and cane from the table, and was shortly out the door.

"How could you give it to him?" Elizabeth burst out in a fury as soon as the passage had swallowed him, book and all. "You have thrown away our sole advantage."

Irene rounded on her, like the angry goddess who had confronted the thieving urchin on my behalf years ago.

"What are you saying, Pink? Mr. Holmes is the foremost investigator in Europe. He has been intimate with the inquiry into the murders of Jack the Ripper in London from the beginning, and he is here in Paris at the behest of the same individuals who came to me. First, I admit," she added in less corrosive tones, but her eyes still were as dark as cold coffee with indignation. "What are you thinking of? This is not a race! We seek to stop these horrible deaths, as does he. And I sought the book. It is mine to keep or give."

I must say that I could barely contain myself from marking the end of this remarkable speech with a sturdy round of applause. I had been so mystified by Irene's adoption of Pink, by her sweeping Pink into the bosom of our partnership. I had never understood it. I had consoled myself with the notion that Pink was actually a Pinkerton agent from America, that Irene had somehow discerned this fact and taken her under her wing as an undeclared colleague. Even then it was hard to stomach the constant presence of this upstart. In some ways she had reminded me of a young Irene: so self-confident, far beyond her years and the situation in which we had found her. This same self-confidence now had led her to challenge her benefactor. I knew that Irene would tolerate a good many things, but self-interest was not one of them.

"I'm sorry." Elizabeth glanced at me for support and found

none. "I . . . forgot myself. And Mr. Holmes is most possessive of his investigation."

"He must be," Irene said more easily, mollified by the girl's contrition. "Detection is his profession. We are amateurs at it."

"But doesn't his arrogance, his assumption that women are not worthwhile associates, annoy you?"

"Not so much as these brutal killings offend me. So Kelly is at large again. This is . . . appalling news. Now." Irene nodded to me and Elizabeth's alcove. "Quick, Nell, the maps. We have an appointment this evening at the World Exposition grounds to meet Colonel Cody and a certain Red Tomahawk for a private hunting party."

"You know where the murderer will strike again!" Elizabeth said breathlessly.

"No. I think I know when the murderer will strike again. We must still discover exactly where."

I returned to spread the papers over the tabletop. Irene sighed and stared down at them.

"You have a scheme," I said. "Why not tell us?"

"It is half-formed."

"We may more than half help."

"Indeed you may, Nell, but I hesitate to unveil the directions of my thoughts."

"Why?" I demanded. "I have certainly proved myself able to survive the several shocking directions your investigation has taken so far, including repeated doses of Mr. Sherlock Holmes!"

"Hear, hear, Nell," Elizabeth said approvingly. "The man is quite the lone wolf and irritatingly self-sure."

"Lone wolf," Irene said, fixing on the phrase as only a stage-trained actor would. "And so is Jack the Ripper."

I felt a thrill that was not the least bit nasty. "Then you think it's possible that Sherlock Holmes . . ."

"Anything is possible, Nell. Sherlock Holmes the Ripper? I could say, yes, possibly. I could say that Bram Stoker remains a suspect. Or that Inspector le Villard might be one. As for Sherlock Holmes, if he is guilty of anything in this case, it is of failing to apprehend the Whitechapel Ripper only minutes before another murder, and I believe he well knows it and it haunts him. Also, I find it unlikely that he is ruled by a calendar of crimes as I think our Jack the Ripper is."

"Our Jack the Ripper?" Elizabeth had quickly learned to fasten on Irene's least intonation. "You are convinced that the Paris murders are by another hand?"

"Yes, I think the Paris murders are by other hands."

"More than one Ripper?" I asked, shocked by her use of the plural.

"Then what has happened here has nothing to do with London," Elizabeth said excitedly.

"On the contrary, it has everything to do with London. Nell, what are the dates again of the five Whitechapel murders the officials have attributed to Jack the Ripper?"

"I have made another table," I said, rushing to my bedchamber to fetch my fattening portfolio.

Elizabeth groaned.

"Facts," I told her sternly when I returned to pull my papers onto the table, "are useless when they are scattered all over. They must be marshaled like troops and stood in line so we can see them in relation to each other."

I ran a finger down one column of my smartly marshaled facts.

"August 31, September 8, September 30 for the two murders, Stride and Eddowes, and November 9."

"Nothing in October," Irene mused, "but silence."

"The Ripper was out of the city, or incarcerated during that month?" Elizabeth suggested.

Irene studied my maligned table. "There's a pattern here, not exact, but rough. Nichols is killed the last day of August. Eight days later in September, Chapman dies. Three weeks and a day later on the last day of September, Stride and Eddowes are killed. Then silence for five weeks and five days."

"If there were patterns," I said, "then a woman should have died October 8 and another on October 30. And then another November 8 . . . but Kelly did die on the ninth."

"Only a day out of the pattern," Elizabeth noted. Even she was bent over my despised table, studying the dates. "Disturbing."

Irene went to the desk to retrieve a small packet from the Baron, sent at her request, as the Paris maps had been.

"Isn't it possible," Irene said, "that the double killing on September 30 also accounted for what would have been the October 8 murder? The Ripper obviously went more berserk than usual that night, perhaps because his work with Stride was interrupted. That is also the night the strange sentence about the Juwes appeared."

"But why didn't the fifth murder occur on October 31 then, the last day of that month, as the last days of August and September saw women killed?" Elizabeth asked.

Irene pulled some loose calendar pages out of the packet and fanned them on the table. I first saw the titles at the top: August, September, October, and November of last year, 1888. Then I quickly glanced to the dates in question on each sheet. I gave an involuntary gasp as my eye fell on the box for the day before the Mary Jane Kelly murder on November 9.

"What is Godfrey's name doing on this calendar?" I demanded.

Irene smiled. "Put on your spectacles, Nell. That is indeed 'Godfrey' you see, but in this instance it is 'St. Godfrey.' We all agree that Godfrey is without equal, but I do think that sainthood is still a bit beyond him. This is an ecclesiastical calendar."

"An ecclesiastical calendar, that is a new one for you," I said as I pulled the pince-nez from its tiny case and propped it on my nose.

"I believe," Irene went on, "that the Ripper meant to kill on November 8 but was prevented. From the testimony of witnesses, Mary Jane Kelly was almost constantly in male company all the evening of the eighth and well into the morning of the ninth. In fact, several witnesses testify to seeing and hearing her around and about her Miller's Court rooms long after she had to have been dead.

"What the Ripper seems to have done in October," she added, "is harass the police with a boasting postcard and letter. During that same period, they received dozens of purported messages from the killer, and even charged one woman with writing some that very month."

"But no journalists," Elizabeth suggested, with great interest.

"No. The journalists, if they wrote any fraudulent Ripper missives, would have been sophisticated enough to escape detection. At least during the heat of the investigation. Who knows what time will say about that?"

While they quibbled over note-writers, I studied the ecclesiastical calendar.

"These are not the correct saints."

"Are there any incorrect saints, Nell?" Elizabeth asked with amusement.

"It's a Roman Catholic ecclesiastical calendar," Irene explained, "not Anglican."

I raised my brows. I had not thought about it, but of course the Papists would emphasize an entirely different lot of saints, since they were always canonizing people right and left.

"And the Rothschilds supplied you with these pages?" I asked with some amazement.

"They do business with Catholic ruling families as well as Church of England royalty," Irene explained. "Besides, information is information, and the Rothschilds are situated to provide anything I could ask for. They sponsor the finest spy network in Europe."

"And if a Jew is implicated as Jack the Ripper?"

"I have discussed this with the Baron, and we agree that it is extremely unlikely. In that unlikely event, I imagine that we should find the British authorities and the Prince of Wales and the Rothschilds as eager to hush that up as they would be were someone like, oh, Prince Eddy, found to be guilty."

"You admit that these immensely powerful cabals would hide the truth from the public? And yet you are in their employ?"

"Immensely powerful people have always done that sort of thing. At least the more benign powers believe their role is to protect the public, if not enlighten it. All they want is to get Jack the Ripper off the streets and the killings stopped. They judge the man hopelessly mad anyway, so incarceration would be the answer whether there is a public trial or a private imprisonment."

"You did not like how the Bohemian servant girl was privately imprisoned in Bohemia."

"That is true, but she was not mad, only a rather simple-minded tool of others who were too powerful to punish. In that case I intervened when I could. In the case of the Ripper, not even Sherlock Holmes can obtain justice if the powers that be wish silence rather than a solution."

I shuddered my distaste for the ways of the great and powerful and returned to studying the calendar, listing the facts.

"Mary Ann Nichols was killed on the feast day of St. Aristedes, Annie Chapman on the day celebrating the Birth of the Blessed Virgin Mary, Liz Stride and Catharine Eddowes on St. Jerome's holy day. And Mary Jane Kelly missed the feast of St. Godfrey to die on the day the Papists honor the Dedication of St. John Lateran Basilica in Rome."

"The Anglican Church does not observe any of these saints' days?" Irene asked.

"Certainly not! We did away with all that idol-worshiping folderol with King Henry VIII."

"Who did away with a goodly number of wives. I wonder if any of them are Catholic saints."

"Only two were beheaded," I pointed out, "and neither of those was suitably saintly, since adultery was their crime."

"And so was failing to bear sons," Irene added, "which I believe was the truer and greater flaw."

"Listen, ladies," Elizabeth put in. "We are not here to argue religious history. Will someone tell me what this saint feast-day calendar means?"

"I'm thinking of the religious symbol scribbled on the catacomb wall," Irene said.

I immediately produced my drawing of the strange letter P overwritten with an X.

To my surprise, Irene drew a much finer representation from the Rothschild packet.

"This image is near-Eastern and it is ancient," she said. "It's known as the Constantine Cross. This early Christian sign was used in the catacombs in Rome, and it was adopted by the first Holy Roman Emperor, Constantine, in the fourth century, when he saw a flaming cross in the sky and converted to Christianity. It is formed of the first two Greek letters that spell the name of Christ, the Chi-rho. This was the form he described."

"So—" Elizabeth turned the calendar pages to face her. "You're saying there's good reason to suspect a religious link to these crimes, and to attribute that link to Christians rather than Jews."

"Or to the rituals of the Christian rather than of the Jewish faith."

"Christian rituals do not involve killing!" I pointed out indignantly. "Not even of animal sacrifices."

"What of the body and blood of Christ that is drunk and eaten as wine and host?"

"That is Papist doctrine. Heresy! Our Church does not accept the literal consuming of the Savior's body and blood. That is . . . disgusting."

Irene nodded. "I know the Anglican Church broke with traditional Roman Catholic doctrine on many issues, but Christianity is the only world religion whose chief deity became human and was horribly tortured and killed, as well as His disciples and many of His followers through the centuries. Church history is a saga of martyrs and saints, no matter how many are struck from the ecclesiastical calendar by the religious revisionism of maritally troubled monarchs on one small island in the north Atlantic sea."

"This is the most I have ever heard you say of religion in our long association, Irene, and it is a terribly unjust summation."

She shrugged. "I'm no theologian, Nell. I would ask you to turn to the calendar for the month of May for this year and look up the saint honored on the thirtieth, which is tomorrow. I believe this is one Papist saint you will instantly recognize."

I did so, with Elizabeth hanging over my shoulder in a most annoying way.

I shuffled through the sheets of winter and early spring before May showed its face, a richly gilded medieval illustration of a hunting party from the Duc de Berry's Book of Hours.

Elizabeth rudely jabbed her fingertip onto the month's last day.

"Joan of Arc! Warrior maid and martyr and as French as they come!"

45.

WORLDS FAIR AND FOUL

Jules Verne dreamed of travelling around the world in eighty days. At the Esplanade and the Champ de Mars you can do it in six hours.

—*BULLETIN OFFICIEL DE L'EXPOSITION UNIVERSELLE DE* 1889, 22 DECEMBER 1888

"A pity Mr. Holmes cannot join the hunt," Irene noted the next afternoon, "but I believe he will still be occupied today with some most absorbing reading, particularly if German is not his long suit in languages."

"Ha!" Elizabeth burst out in a most hoydenish manner, clapping her hands. She finally saw Irene's surrender of the book yesterday for the clever diversion it was.

"Long suit?" I asked Irene.

"An American expression, Nell, referring to holding almost all the cards of a particular suit in a game."

"You said this was not a game."

"True, but it is for whoever has been watching these atrocities and our pursuit unfold."

"You believe that this . . . butcher regards these murders as entertainment?"

"No, but such murders involve an element of perverse gamesmanship with the forces of order and law. If Jack the Ripper really wrote those notes to the papers in London, then he relished taunting the police. Here it is different. Here the police are not being taunted, but the unofficial investigators."

"Us? You believe so?"

"I would swear to it. The killer may not see beyond the unexplored needs that drive him to these acts, as Krafft-Ebing made clear, but someone else is watching."

"Watching us?"

She nodded. "And probably Mr. Holmes as well, which is why I'd like him someplace far away today and tonight."

"And today and tonight we will—?"

Irene pulled the map of Paris to the top of our papers. The first thing one saw now was the triangle of lines that she had drawn, the Paris Morgue to the *maison* to the catacomb near the Eiffel Tower.

With a few swift strokes and the ruler she etched an upside-down triangle above it, beginning at the *maison* in the rue des Moulins near the Paris Opéra. Her new lines extended the bottom triangle's sides up to the Musée Grévin on the right, and the bloody cellar of last night on the left near the Parc Monceau.

"You see the pattern?" she asked.

"Triangles," Elizabeth burst out too quickly.

Before the dawning look of disappointment could settle on Irene's features, I put my hands to my face, covering my eyes. "Wait! I see something I have vaguely seen before." I took away my hands so that the new lines on the map should strike my eyes with a fresh impact.

"It's . . . the bodies we viewed were seen on the left of the map, at the morgue and the wax museum, which are almost directly above each other. And the places we saw where the bodies were dead, or killed, are on the left, with the cellar almost directly above the Eiffel Tower.

"And the rue des Moulins is in the precise middle. This pattern is maddeningly familiar . . . but what!"

"I am sure you would perceive it in time, Nell," Irene said, beaming upon me as if I were a prize pupil. Elizabeth looked particularly exasperated.

"But we have no time," Irene concluded.

Her fingertip touched the Eiffel Tower, the Paris Morgue, the Musée Grévin above it and finally the park.

"It's a box waltz," I blurted out as I followed the pattern.

"Or," she corrected, "if you see lines that begin and end instead of an enclosure like a box. . . ."

I would not be denied my prize, but quickly sketched a figure over the streetmap. "The four sites are the end points of the X on the Chi-rho."

Irene applauded. I was not aware of Elizabeth doing anything but sulking.

"But where, and what," I wondered, "does the *maison* on the rue des Moulins have to do with it?"

"If you were to draw the P behind the X, Nell, you would find that the *maison de rendezvous* is located on the P's central staff, just below where the curve begins."

"Someone has been playing games of geography and calendars with us?" Elizabeth asked indignantly.

"Oh, it's not a game," Irene said quickly. "It is a serious and revolting ritual."

"And from this pattern," I asked, after adding the P, "you know where to begin a hunting party for the next atrocity? Where shall that be?

"Where else? The catacomb was near but not exactly at the Eiffel Tower, which is on the side where deaths occur. The Tour Eiffel is an unfulfilled site. But don't call it a hunting party, Nell. First must come 'scouting' the wilderness. We will merely be out enjoying the *l'Exposition universelle* with *le tout Paris*."

Even I had to admit that *l'Exposition universelle* was nothing short of a fairyland of a world's fair, filled with exotic food, music, and sights so vast and varied that one became quite dizzy just to look at it all.

Not to mention getting a crick in the neck, for everything loomed above the milling throngs, most especially the Eiffel Tower, tarted up in a coat of scarlet paint.

The Esplanade des Invalides stretched along the glittering Seine, which had become a mirror for the exposition's frenetic lights and motion, presenting all the jumbled sights of the French colonial pavilions with their air of an Oriental fairyland, not to mention the displays of various countries and cities.

The entire scene, darkened only by the flood of visitors snaking among the kiosks and fountains and pavilions, gave me the odd impression of a collision between Mount Olympus and the Tower of Babel.

No one regarded our trio as we wove through the jumble of people and noise. Besides boulevardiers in their frock coats and top hats, there were many men in the shorter-jacketed lounge suits that were becoming popular city wear, and women in walking suits and skirts and shirtwaists, as well as boys and girls in short pants and skirts.

We were all dressed as ourselves at last! I wore my favorite checked coat-dress, which was a feminine fitted version of a gentleman's country ulster, I suppose, and most practical for city sight-seeing.

Irene could never forgo being smart unless she was in disguise, and then she reveled in wearing the most tawdry, unflattering costumes possible.

Today her dark buffalo red gown was subdued except for a puff of sleeve from shoulder to elbow and a central design from neck to hem of widening black passementerie cord design. It was only on the exposition grounds that I realized that the gown's lacy vertical design exactly mimicked the pierced cast-iron shape of the Eiffel Tower itself!

The artistic soul ever seeks points of reference in even the most common things. And, of course, the fashionable new French color paid tribute to Buffalo Bill!

Elizabeth's dress was charmingly reminiscent of an English riding habit with a bodice buttoning to the side and a mannish green silk tie over the white-linen collar and chemisette. When I mentioned this fact before we left the hotel, she got on her high horse. The style, she stated, more resembled fashions at the time of the French Revolution and nothing English at all.

Well! I hated to tell her that English riding habits of today are descended from women's dress during the aftermath of the French Revolution early in the present century, which is more importantly known to world history as the English Regency period. I hated to tell her, but I did.

I was the only one of our trio to wear a small-billed cap that resembled the long-enduring bonnet. Irene and Elizabeth both wore the new wide-brimmed hats, which required dagger-length hatpins to stay put. It only struck me later that this may not have been a matter of fashion, but of prescient self-defense.

I only mention our attire to point out that we in no way

stood out among the many similarly garbed women who walked the same aisles, sidewalks, and parklands that day and night, except for the contents of our cleverly concealed skirt pockets.

I carried my larger notebook and pencil in one pocket, and my chatelaine muffled in cotton flannel in the other. (Sherlock Holmes's odiously impolite comment that my rattling chatelaine announced my presence had not fallen on deaf ears.) Irene's right pocket held her small pistol. She also carried Godfrey's sword-stick. Why he left it at home I shall never know. Elizabeth carried a smart ladies's walking stick that was also sturdy enough to crack craniums as well as knuckles.

These were the only accessories that hinted at our true purpose in visiting these hurly-burly surroundings.

At first, our wanderings were solely instructional. We took the moving sidewalk to the machinery building. This was much more pleasant than a ride in an elevated car, for it was entirely open and utterly horizontal. I predicted to my companions a far more universal future for this step-saving device than for the box that plummets people down in small enclosed cages.

Impressive as the machinery building was with its arched glass ceiling higher than even Notre Dame's soaring stone nave, I called my American companions' attention to the fact that the entire fashion for airy metal-supported roofs on everything from this behemoth of a building, the world's largest, to French department stores and train stations in every world capital, stemmed from the marvelous Crystal Palace designed for London's 1851 World Exposition almost forty years earlier.

This was all incontestably true, but they did not seem properly impressed.

Elizabeth, like an overgrown child, was eager to forsake the educational exhibits for the louder, more crowded, and infinitely more lurid features of the global villages and the food and souvenir kiosks.

Hence it was that we all three bought rather atrocious silk scarves in a sepia tone that pictured the Tour Awful amid a rather busy design of the various exposition erections.

We also suffered the scents of delicacies from many lands wafting from stands and braziers, along with the pungent contributions of the exotic beasts brought to the civilized world's doorstep, if one can consider Paris truly civilized.

"Oh!" I declared in some distress as we rounded a corner to confront a sadly familiar scene.

"Oh indeed," Irene said. "The Musée Grévin made a superb effort to reproduce this scene."

Granted, and at least the original didn't involve dead bodies, for which I was supremely grateful. The Cairo market scene before our eyes was complete with European travelers, draped natives, and overburdened donkeys, only all were live.

Elizabeth laughed with delight. "Now I see it. The Europeans in the *tableau vivant* at the Musée Grévin weren't part of the original scene, but exposition-goers. If we were to walk into that bazaar, we would become a real part of the false scene as well. This is more than theater, more than reenactment of reality in a far part of the globe, this is reality and more distant reality meeting in a fictional setting. I admit I am confused."

Irene contemplated the scene, her walking stick planted dead center of her still figure, like a sword she rested point down after—or before—a duel or fencing match.

"So too the actions of Jack the Ripper may be a blending of two separate realities into one puzzling and disturbing appearance of absolute reality. Is it coincidence only that the murders appear to have moved from the crude stage setting of Whitechapel to the more sophisticated yet equally corruptible environs of Paris?"

I was pleased to hear her admit the many corruptions of Paris. I was tired of hearing the City of Light hailed as the quintessential modern capital when too much of it was yet the City of Dark.

Still, that afternoon all was festive and bright.

The infectious oompah-pah of German orchestras vied with the delicate bells and strange thin melodies of the Javanese Temple music and French sailors in striped uniforms singing "*Auprès de ma blonde*" as they lurched merrily among the crowds.

We ambled toward the Eiffel Tower to find at its base a mammoth kiosk in praise of American invention. There is no doubt that the *Exposition Tricolore*, the fair's informal title, celebrated the red, white, and blue of America as well as the French flag.

In fact, the French and the Americans have been very cozy all along, much to poor England's disadvantage. I suppose it is a result of both countries having stirred up revolutions against God-given kingships in the last quarter of the previous century. In fact, France's insistence on marking the centenary of its bloody revolution had made several countries withdraw as official sponsors of pavilions, including Great Britain, Italy, and Russia!

Of course America had no such scruples as these great world powers. It was there with a Telephone Pavilion, with maps showing the invention's tentacles of lines radiating from Paris to the outlying provinces. Along one wall an entire row of telephones with two earpieces were connected to ten telephone receivers at the Opéra and the Comédie-Française. For fifty centimes, one could listen to both theater and opera, though why one would wish to blend two such different performances, both in foreign languages, I cannot imagine.

Elizabeth and Irene were like children competing for toys, both wanting to try the devices. I accompanied them in line, but refused all their pleadings to put the alien instruments to my ears.

"But, Nell," Irene cajoled, "you remember how I first heard sound from a distant stage at Gilbert's house years ago, when Bertie heard a murder committed over a telephone line to the Savoy Theater? This is the same, but much better. Please try it. You can even sense the actors moving from side to side of the stage as they speak, and the singing is remarkably good."

"I'll take your word for it, Irene. I also recall that the dinner at Gilbert's was the occasion on which you allowed a Certain Personage to gain a Very Wrong Impression about you, and I have no desire to be reminded of that sad situation."

Irene rolled her eyes and clamped the devices to her temples like a set of mechanical earmuffs, moving her head in time to the music only she heard and looking like an utter idiot, as did Elizabeth and every one else in the long row of other fools who had paid fifty centimes for the privilege.

After this exhibition in which my companions were actual performers, nothing would do but that they would see the rest of the American exhibition area.

Thus it was that I was treated to such cultural landmarks of the land over the ocean as the heads of every American president, including the current model, Grover Cleveland, carved into the bowls of meerschaum pipes! I can well imagine that these presidential heads would flush with shame when the lit pipe bowls burned cherry red.

Not only that, but the pipes were so huge one couldn't even picture a man as large as Bram Stoker smoking one. And one pipe in particular was most strange.

"Which president is that?" I asked. "The one with the huge bushy head and beard?"

Irene burst into an aria of laughter that made heads in the room all turn our way. "La, Nell! That isn't a president's head. It's a buffalo head. Get out your spectacles, quickly!"

While I was thus engaged, thinking to myself that a buffalo as president probably would have done the Republic good, a woman joined our party.

"Isn't it a marvel?" she demanded. "That pipe has been promised to Buffalo Bill after the exposition is over. He rode over here from the show grounds to see the exhibit and tied his mount to the Eiffel Tower, can you imagine?"

I could imagine many fair-goers stepping around the horse droppings later and not being at all impressed that the souvenir was courtesy of Buffalo Bill's horse.

"A pity," Irene said with mock sincerity. "I was thinking what a fine gift this pipe would make for Sherlock Holmes."

"Sherlock who?" asked the attendant, thus making my day surpassingly brighter.

While the American pavilion boasted exhibits on such modern marvels as the telephone, the telegraph, and the phonograph, the native gift for vulgar exaggeration was also in full flower, especially a larger-than-life-size representation of the *Venus de Milo* weighing over a ton and a half and executed in solid chocolate.

Whatever the medium, she was shockingly undressed and still missing significant limbs.

At last I was allowed to leave the shadow of the tower and tour the other buildings, although I did not see anything to equal the sheer nerve of American invention.

Irene was happy to see that Louis Comfort Tiffany, the son of our sometime client and benefactor, the international jeweler Charles Tiffany, had won grand prize in silver crafting. I was pleased to see that lad's skills had advanced in the several years since Irene had been presented an example of his jewelry work by the proud but misguided father. The brooch was in the odious shape of a sinuous squid ornamented with irregularly shaped pearls, amber, and aquamarine . . . quite obviously worthless save in its maker's eyes.

The sunlight was slanting and growing cool by the time we finished the grand tour of the major buildings and paused near an awning-shaded kiosk dispensing beverages and food.

"The cafés are crowded and noisy," Irene declared. "Let us picnic here and we shall be set for the night."

"Oh, Irene, I am already fatigued," I said. "How much longer are we to stay?"

"Until the hunting is right. After dark."

"What has this outing accomplished?"

Elizabeth made a face. "It has been fun, Nell. We are allowed to have fun!"

"Not when we are on a mission. We are on a mission?" I asked Irene anxiously, for my feet were tired and I had a headache from the close-fitting cap.

"Yes, but first I wanted to survey the fairgrounds. Buffalo Bill has suggested that we arrange to be in the Esplanade des Invalides before they light up the tower for the evening. He can't join us until after his show ends and is tucked away for the night."

"How will he find us in this mob?" I asked.

"I suspect that it will be easier for us to find him, but . . . don't worry. He said he would send a 'scout' to locate us as long as we stayed in the entry area to the colonial section."

"Hmmph," I said as we walked another long way toward the riverbank. "There is only one exhibit I should like to see."

"And what is that," Elizabeth asked.

"The panorama building that is shaped like a ship."

"Well, there it lies at anchor, dead ahead," Irene said in a voice like Long John Silver, pointing. Everyone on the exposition grounds gawked and pointed and shouted to each other like sailors on shore leave.

I made out the interesting shape of the ship at the very edge of the Seine, and also a long line of people waiting to pay their entry fee and snake into the attraction. I was fated instead to view more of the usual vulgarities.

We stood in line at the entrance kiosk until our coins were taken, and I must confess that as we passed beyond the entry gate we found ourselves in an Arabian Nights environment where each few steps whisked us like a magic carpet to different distant and exotic sites. Representing the width and breadth of France's colonial empire, the exhibit surprised at every turn with its sights, sounds, and, unfortunately, smells.

"I had no idea," I found myself murmuring.

"No idea of what, Nell?" Elizabeth inquired.

"That France had a foot in so many regions of the world, on so many continents."

"It's not just the British who have marched in jackboots over the face of the Earth."

"Well, no, but I thought that after we defeated Napoleon . . ."

"I am grateful that you did not defeat Washington," she said with a smile. "This is quite a picture, though, scenes from the Americas to the Congo to Algeria to Java."

"And smells," I added, waving a gloved hand in front of my face as odors of fried rice and saffron wafted past us.

"This section," Irene said, "is quite popular for those who tire of the French cuisine in the cafés that dot the exposition. The food is sure to be genuine, as the performers and workers live on these grounds."

I noted that as the daylight ebbed, people from the panoramic ship were ambling from the riverside to the many foreign restaurants interspersing the exotic theater buildings.

Already the swooping and soaring and notched and curved rooflines were becoming profiles against the pale sky, and the air was tinged with the chill of dusk. At the Tunisian café, crowds huddled to wait for coffee so thick and black as it poured into ornate cups that its odor clung to the scene forty feet around like a rich scented Oriental ointment to a wound.

Sound was as powerful as smell in the darkening dusk. I winced at the whining and percussive tones of Egypt and Algiers and the tinkling bells of Java.

At that moment I became aware of a European threnody amid the uproar, an off-tune screeching and eerie wailing. I looked around.

Irene, too, had lifted her head to hear better, picking out the wild yet somehow familiar discordance from among the strains of foreign music wafting around the buildings, gardens, and cafés.

"You recognize that, too. What is it, Nell?"

"Violins, badly played. I am sorry to say that the sleuth of Baker Street apparently murders that instrument when he is not on the trail of more punishable offenses."

"The violin? Sherlock Holmes plays the violin?"

"I would not call it playing, sawing rather. And I did not see the crime while it was being committed, but he was the only person visible in his rooms . . . unless his physician friend has secretly accompanied him and was the culprit in torturing horsehair and catgut."

"Nell!" Elizabeth remonstrated. "Please don't put the poor honest fiddle in those terms. I prefer not to know how many creatures have suffered to bring music to the ages."

"Music!"

By now we had followed the sound to its source between the theater of Cairo and an edifice as delicate yet towering as an Oriental headdress.

"Gypsies!" Irene exclaimed, delighted to have diagnosed the source of the sounds.

Indeed. We viewed a Gypsy encampment complete with surging campfire, circled wagons, and a poor swaybacked horse.

A crowd had gathered around the heat generated by the

huge bonfire and were tapping toes and clapping hands to encourage the swarthy-skinned Romanies cavorting around the roaring fire, men and women together, while lean wolfish dogs nipped at flying hems from the fringes.

The fiddlers were three middle-aged men with dark curling hair and beards and sweat streaming down from one nest of unkempt hair into the other, and finally onto the checkered varnished surfaces of their instruments.

A most unappetizing display.

"Surely the Gypsies are not a colonial holding of France," I shouted into Irene's ear.

"Surely not. But they are chronic trespassers, and I think they have squatted here in more ways than one," she shouted back. With the noise and the crowd I doubt anyone heard us, or that anyone cared if the Gypsies came here uninvited. What else did Gypsies do after all, and there were plenty of coins to be had here, even now spinning in amongst the flashing boots.

This appeared only to encourage the dancers, who whirled ever faster, the women's many-petticoated skirts spinning wide despite their bulk to show grimy bare legs and feet, some with gold rings on their toes!

The men were even more unfettered, squatting like dogs into crouches, only keeping themselves upright by the swift kicks of their legs. One came kicking in this energetic yet repugnant fashion toward our group, his fiery gaze fixed upon us.

I had never seen a more primitive display until I sensed a presence behind me and turned around.

Oh, goodness. A figure loomed behind me in the dimming light like a statue, a vest of bones visible upon its chest, its dark, firelit visage framed by grease-slicked black hair and topped by a single feather, like a quill inserted into a plum pudding.

My frozen horror had communicated itself to my companions without my uttering a word. Irene and Elizabeth turned as one to view our new "shadow." Neither seemed appalled.

"Red Tomahawk, I presume?" Irene inquired with her typical sang-froid, a French phrase for unshakable calm. "How did you find us?"

Red Tomahawk. No doubt Buffalo Bill's "scout." The names of the American Wild West are unmistakable. The Indian turned to gaze up at the Eiffel Tower. "I climbed a hill and looked down upon the multitude. Three white women I was to find." He shrugged.

Three white women he had found. And his "hill" had been one of elevator cars whose cramped quarters I loathed. Amazing that an inhabitant of the endless open should adapt to such a device better than a city dweller like me.

"There are multitudes of white women here," Irene said, adapting his expression.

"There were once many more multitudes of buffalo on the prairie. I mark my one, or two, or three and find them."

"The buffalo have vanished," Irene pointed out.

Red Tomahawk shook his head. "Multitudes are everywhere I go now. Many white people. I can still look. Find. Among the multitudes."

"Is there an exhibit of an Indian village?" Elizabeth asked eagerly. As she had explained to me long ago, Americans from Pennsylvania were as bewitched by frontier tales as gullible Europeans. England, of course, is not part of Europe proper, or improper.

He grunted, assent I assume, to Elizabeth's question, but stood for a moment frowning at the Gypsy encampment, the wild dancing, the circling curs, the discordant music.

"Not here. Next to the Persian mansion by the tower."

It struck me that perhaps this Gypsy scene presented elements of Indian life, from what I have read of their activities before going on a "warpath."

"Have you seen Gypsies before?" I asked, struck by the intent way he stared at their wild activities.

Instead of answering, he sniffed the air with the disdain of a drawing-room fop and declared the cryptic phrase, "much firewater."

At that he turned and walked away, leaving us to do nothing but follow after..

"Firewater?" I asked my companions when we were far

enough away from the Gypsy cacophony to hear each other.

"Raw hard liquor, Nell," Elizabeth answered with zest. "That's what the Indians named it when the frontiersmen first offered it to them in trade. I fear the red man is as likely as the white man to overdrink."

"Don't forget," Irene said, "that James Kelly was driven by drink."

I blanched, regarding this as a warning that a Red Indian was still a suspect for the role of Ripper. This Red Indian?

"How do they get their names?" I asked nervously.

Elizabeth grinned in the light of flickering torch. "I think it has something to do with deeds."

"And I am right in thinking that a tomahawk is a sort of hatchet?"

"Exactly."

"Oh."

At least the figure of our guide was hard to lose even in these milling masses of people. He was not particularly tall—more ominous proof that a Red Indian could indeed have prowled Whitechapel—but his fringed shirt and trousers and quilled head ornament would hardly give him the nondescript appearance that the Ripper had taken such advantage of.

I mentioned this to my companions.

"Oh, pooh, Nell," Elizabeth answered in that unmannerly way of hers. "Buffalo Bill has them all dress up in full ceremonial regalia for the Wild West Show, but many have adopted citified dress while traveling. Long Eagle, who left the show to stay in England last year, was known all over London for his tall beaver hat. Don't believe everything you see at an exposition. It's all show."

Red Tomahawk stopped near the river's edge and turned to face the length of the colonial exhibit. The Gypsy fire glowed like an ember far enough away that only the occasional whine of violins drifted to our ears, but the line of exotic buildings had darkened into a ragged escarpment.

I noticed then that people were streaming out of the area toward the Eiffel Tower.

"Ceremony starts," our guide said. "Buffalo Bill will come soon."

I gathered we were to wait here until the famous scout climbed a hill and found us.

Suddenly the sound of hooves came pounding from the far end of the Esplanade. Ranks of mounted soldiers were galloping up the now-deserted walkway, a fearsome sight in the dusk.

Then, as if the sky had split like a theatrical curtain, a red-and-yellow glow like a great celestial bonfire cast a lurid light on everything around us.

Red Tomahawk gave a long, low sound of admiration as these coursers pranced past us, ridden by black men in colorful plumed uniform, all illuminated by the unearthly glow.

I looked to the left to see the Eiffel Tower's tall scarlet silhouette glaring like a sunset. Strings of electric lights like gilt braid circled its tiers and outlined its huge foundation arches.

Above it all shot bright white heavenly rays from the great lamp atop the tower, a lamp as powerful as a lighthouse beam, which reflected on the many islands of heroic sculpture and fountains dotting the grounds. Its man-made lightning glanced off the glass domes and crystal roofs of the mammoth buildings also erected for the occasion, the machinery pavilion and the various pavilions devoted to art as well as industry. We stood in the midst of an electric fairyland.

The colonial area, however, only basked in the reflection of the exposition lighting. The passageway was still darkish and felt miles away from the crowds and illumination surrounding the tower and extending far back from the river.

Before us, still on parade now that the mounted vanguard had passed us, came Indian, Chinese, and Arab foot soldiers in their colorful, exotic garb, marching in unnerving order.

Before this display of military might could make me uneasy, along came a troupe of planned disorder, the theatrical performers displaying their wares . . . themselves.

Robed figures in frightening masks dashed from side to side to confront the watchers. Algerian dancers, women veiled everywhere but their torsos, performed lascivious motions and managed to progress forward at the same time. The Javanese dancers who followed were clothed completely in stiff, jeweled robes, masks, and whole pagodas of headdresses that rose perhaps two feet above them. The music changed with each company that danced past, so the cacophony was ear-splitting.

Palanquins were carried past, drums beat as black people from the Congo in wildly clashing figured robes danced past us, and finally came a lurching group of people waving banners and paper parasols and lanterns, banging on gongs until I thought my head would split open down the center as if from a tomahawk blow.

Behind them all came the endlessly long, undulating, gaudy form of a huge dragon, a kind of gigantic puppet/kite carried and manipulated by a band of puppeteers beneath the writhing silk construction, their churning legs like those of a centipede.

As the parade passed, the watching crowd flowed into its wake, laughing and running, skipping and dancing, all heading to the fount from which all light and noise flowed, the Eiffel Tower.

We three—four, of course; I was forgetting our silent, stoic scout—remained to watch a few stragglers pass. The scene of such recent hectic merriment grew dim again, and quiet.

"Magnificent," said a voice behind us. "I'd give my eyeteeth to have that Senegalese cavalry in my show, eh, Red Tomahawk?"

"Good horses," Red Tomahawk agreed. I gather he was not as impressed by the riders.

Of course I had turned to view the last exotic foreign visitor on my menu that night: Buffalo Bill.

His light-colored hat and fringed shirt and trousers, accoutered with a wide, studded belt and other strange accessories, reflected highlights of pink from the inescapable Eiffel Tower, which made me think of water-thinned blood.

"I am glad you could join us," Irene said.

"When I got your message day before yesterday, you saw I answered 'yes' in Pony Express time," he answered. "A manhunt on a World Exposition ground is too intriguing to resist. And who is the third of your party? I don't believe we've met."

The famous scout's attention to the courtesies surprised me, but Irene introduced me as if we were at a tea party.

"My pleasure, Miss Huxleigh," said the man Irene had addressed as Colonel Cody, much to my relief. Apparently Red Tomahawk had no more formal name, and I would have to avoid addressing him completely. "I salute you. We are not surprised to see so many doughty women on the frontier, but here in the Old World there are few with the true grit to face off a villain the likes of Jack the Ripper."

There was nothing I could do in answer except smile politely.

I had no intention of facing off the likes of Jack the Ripper and had all the hopes in the world that such plainsmen as Buffalo Bill and Red Tomahawk could do it for me. I was here only as a chaperone, really, and because I could not bear the anxiety of not knowing what was happening with Irene when she thrust herself onto such treacherous and terrible ground.

"Now, don't you worry, Miss Huxleigh," he consoled me quite unasked. "If I thought we were really facing any danger, I'd have asked Miss Annie Oakley along. And Madam Irene is not relying on us old Wild West hands alone." He turned to her. "When are the reinforcements coming?"

"Anytime now," she assured him. "I thought it best they not be seen by the parade viewers."

"The police will be here?" I asked in relief.

Irene was silent a moment too long. "I thought it best to call in the police only if we are successful in finding the culprit."

"Then who are our reinforcements?" I asked.

She nodded beyond me, and we all turned. A party of men in dark lounge suits was moving through the dusk toward us. I glanced back at Irene.

She lowered her voice and spoke only to me. "The Rothschilds still have the greatest interest in catching this man, and this ensures that these murders are not used to foment political unrest."

Much as I was pleased to have armed men among us, I was surprised by their number, perhaps seven or eight.

I glanced around. The area was deserted except for our

company. I noticed with a pang that the ship-shaped panorama was outlined by the same gold strings of electric lights as decorated the Eiffel Tower and cast a glittering reflection of itself on the Seine's fluttering waters.

It looked so festive, and what we were about to do was so grim.

The Indian suddenly uttered some unintelligible words to Buffalo Bill, who nodded, then spoke softly to Irene and whoever stood close enough to hear.

"Red Tomahawk and I have paid a visit to the site near here where the young woman was killed, and also to the cellar you told me of. He has seen signs, and tells me he wishes to start by visiting the camp you just saw. I will have to explain Gypsies to him."

Gypsies! Now that was an idea. They were everywhere, after all, and wild, unreliable people. And terrible violin players as well. Why should not a Jack the Ripper hide among their nomadic tribes?

Red Tomahawk took the lead, and we all moved quietly in his wake, not speaking.

I was surprised to notice that the Gypsy bonfire was no longer visible. When we reached the site everyone and everything was gone, even the charred wood from the fire.

All that remained to testify to the Gypsy camp's passage was a dark burnt circle on the bare ground.

46.

An Exhibition in Terror

He who is possessed of the spirit belongs not to himself, but to the spirit who controls him and who is responsible for all his actions and for any sins he may commit.

—PRINCE YUSUPOV

While Irene conferred with the Rothschild agents, Elizabeth pestered me with questions.

"Who are those men with Irene? Are they French detectives? They speak the language, but they look more like Pinkertons."

You should know, I thought uncharitably. I only wished the girl would honor us with some honesty at last. Yet I could not ascribe much frankness to Irene, not that I blamed her. Her work with the Rothschilds had replaced her Pinkerton assignments in America, and being active in a larger enterprise was something her performer's soul craved as deeply as Sherlock Holmes evidently craved puzzles and pipes as well as other less benign things.

I well understood that my presence here was due solely to Elizabeth. Like a relentless kitten, she always insisted on going everywhere and getting into everything. She would never have permitted Irene to escape unaccompanied on this bizarre scouting expedition, and for some strange reason Irene felt far less protective of Elizabeth than she did of me.

In turn, Irene knew she would never hear the end of it if I had been left behind while Elizabeth accompanied her. At least Buffalo Bill had no qualms about a female presence. Apparently the harsh life of the frontier had forced women to rely more upon themselves and had made men less aware of their duty to protect them from all unseemliness. If the Rothschild agents objected to women, it did not show. They seemed to regard their role as a rear guard, ceding the night's action to the odd commanding trio of Irene, the famed Indian fighter, and his exotic former foe turned employee.

The rest of us stood at a respectful distance as the two plainsmen scoured the area with lanterns, eyes, and noses.

Although I found the process distasteful to watch, they managed to produce evidence where I would have sworn there was none. While Red Tomahawk circled in the empty space like a dog (for good reason I was to learn later), Buffalo Bill made similar circles widening out from what had been the fringes of the camp.

He returned with a pottery bottle that could have been as old as the Romans or as new as last week.

This he first showed to Red Tomahawk, who sniffed it at great length and with an almost-snobbish seriousness, like a Frenchman judging a new wine, then nodded and pronounced a judgment the onlookers could not hear.

Buffalo Bill moved to the fringes again and, lantern bobbing in his hand, carefully made his way back to us women.

"Red Tomahawk says this held firewater," he noted on arrival, "though I can't smell whiskey and he admits that he has never smelled or tasted a spirit like this before. He says the same odd odor was present in the cavern near here where the murdered woman was found and in the bloodied cellar you explored near the Parc Monceau. You ladies care to see if you have a better nose for liquor than an old scout?"

I certainly did not wish to play human bloodhound, but Elizabeth nodded eagerly. First Irene took the crude bottle and lifted its small mouth to her nose.

She nodded at last. "I smell something faintly caustic, but can't identify it. It could be spirits, it could be poison."

"Some say they are one and the same thing," I pointed out.

Buffalo Bill laughed as if I had committed a great witticism. "Truly spoken, Miss H. I'd guess it's some crude homemade variety of pure alcohol, so unmannered it bears no odor of any aging process or wooden cask. I have sampled the products of England and France, but must admit they were all of splendid vintage, and all released a telltale and most persuasive perfume."

Elizabeth sniffed eagerly at the rude lip, but was unable to add anything to the speculations, as if a green girl could.

I waved away the bottle in her offering hand. "I know so little of spirits that the only liquid I can recognize by aroma is good English tea," I said.

In the meantime, Red Tomahawk had returned to us. He turned to point out areas of the site. "Wagon left, loaded, with many people and dogs on foot beside it. I will follow."

At that he trotted off along the parade route, lantern in hand, pausing frequently to study the frequent horse droppings and to sniff at the foundations of buildings along the route.

"What is he tracking?" Irene asked Buffalo Bill as we followed at a respectful twenty paces behind the Red Man. "Surely no footprints can be traced on this ground."

"I agree that the exposition grounds look like they've been trampled by a buffalo stampede, but even then a good tracker can find a sign or two. Red Tomahawk doesn't have to do that. He's following the most reliable trail markers on the planet: the Gypsies' dogs. They are sure to mark any spot where another dog has left its scent. Dogs being dogs, that's every few feet or so."

"You mean," I said, "that we have an inadvertent pack of bloodhounds working for us."

"Exactly. And our own bloodhound to trail them."

The Indian had stopped and held up a hand to halt our party. Then he nodded to Colonel Cody.

"Only we four should go scout what Red Tomahawk has found," he declared, as if reading the Indian's mind.

Irene turned and instructed the men behind us to wait.

We approached the area diffidently, Buffalo Bill in the lead, then Irene, with Elizabeth and I bringing up the rear in tandem, neither wanting the other to be the first to see and hear.

Indian and scout conferred in a blend of English and some native tongue, with Buffalo Bill translating by pointing to what—to me—were meaningless marks in the trampled turf.

"The wagon stopped here. See the deep heel marks? A man leaped out."

"How can he tell the marks weren't made earlier by someone else?" Elizabeth asked.

"Because the parade had already passed when the Gypsy wagon left by a reverse route. They made the latest spoor and thus the freshest impressions. Besides, Red Tomahawk detects a scent of the same spilled liquid here. The boots move onto less-trod-upon ground, toward the river beyond the promenades. And, he says, other feet have gone in that direction recently, perhaps two or three hours ago."

"You are saying," Irene mused, "that one man from the Gypsy troupe left them here to join other men who had been gathering somewhere below on the river embankment."

Buffalo Bill consulted Red Tomahawk in the same guttural language, then turned back to us.

"People, yes, but Red Tomahawk says several were women."

"Women!" I hadn't intended to insert myself into the discussion, but was too shocked to keep quiet. "If women are meeting men below the promenades for some lascivious end, and if the man who left the Gypsy wagon is following them, he will have victims for the picking."

"It is indeed possible," Elizabeth said. "Jack the Ripper frequented the one area of London where prostitutes were in profuse, open evidence. If there is a clandestine meeting place here at the exposition for such activities, he would naturally hunt those grounds, and that is why the woman was found in the nearby catacombs."

"Perhaps," Irene said, sounding doubtful, "but I suspect it's not nearly as simple as that. Colonel Cody, can you ask Red Tomahawk to lead us where this man has gone, but quietly so we do not lose our ability to spy upon him?"

The scout chuckled. "You are talking about a war party sneaking up on an encampment. Red Tomahawk could do that in his sleep. But tell those city fellows to stay well behind us, and only to come forward if called."

Irene went back to the cluster of confused men to do just

that. While she conversed in French with them, I shook my head.

"What is the matter, Nell?" Elizabeth inquired, shivering with chill and excitement and stamping her numbing feet on the ground like an impatient horse.

"French to the back of us, Pony or Sue or whatever breed of wild Red Indian I have heard of to the front of us. Was there ever such an odd hunting party?"

"Pawnee," Elizabeth corrected me. "And you forget to include the Romany language of the Gypsies. I find it hard to believe that Jack the Ripper is a Gypsy, though. You saw the women dancing; some were girls of barely twelve or thirteen. Plenty of women are freely available to Gypsy men; they have no inhibitions about that sort of thing, men or women. The book by Krafft-Ebing points to a killer who has little access to women, or who hates himself for wishing to consort with them."

"You are saying that Jack the Ripper has a conscience."

"That is one way to put it, I suppose. I would rather say that Jack the Ripper has a very confused conscience."

"That is exactly it, Pink." Irene had come up during our discussion. "A man with a seriously confused conscience is a danger to himself and others. But, look, Red Tomahawk has shuttered his lantern and is moving down the embankment behind the Javanese temple building. It will be darker and steeper if we follow. Let us hold hands."

The ghostly outline of the panorama ship's strings of electric lights lay along the waterline only a hundred feet from the Esplanade, and lent the area some slight illumination. With shock I recognized the moving panorama attraction that had earlier been too crowded to see, now shut up and illuminated for the night.

The ship's faint glow made Buffalo Bill's buff-colored fringed suit into a kind of will-o'-the-wisp to follow. Soon our bootheels were digging into soft dirt, and our downward progress developed an impetus of its own we were unable to slow, only our clasped hands keeping all three upright.

We were forced to check our breakneck progress as we came abreast of the plainsmen on level ground. We glanced behind to see the bristled silhouettes of the Rothschild agents on the brow of the embankment above us.

Red Tomahawk was squatting on the ground, the dimmed lantern beside him, shaking his feathered head from side to side.

"Rock," Buffalo Bill whispered to us. "No tracks."

"Not rock," Irene answered in a hushed though triumphant tone, "but granite." She nodded to the foundation of the Javanese temple's elaborate upper stories. It was a cellar wall of hard stone. "There is a way beyond that wall," she said, "and probably a natural cavern beyond that."

Buffalo Bill conveyed that conviction to Red Tomahawk, who leaped up and on silent moccasins approached the wall and began running his hands over it like a blind man feeling a door for the entry knob.

He eventually moved to the wild bushes springing from the embankment base and suddenly stood upright, brandishing a trophy high in one hand.

For a wild moment I feared a scalp, but it was only another of the crude pottery bottles he had found at the Gypsy camp.

When we tiptoed nearer to see, he pulled aside the shrubbery to reveal a gaping natural opening in the rock perhaps four feet high.

Without a word, Buffalo Bill sprang back up the embankment and brought the agents to our sides.

Whispered consultation produced a plan: the plainsmen would lead, the women follow, the agents bring up the rear, weapons at the ready.

No one said it, but we women were obviously to be sheltered in the middle of a front and a rear guard.

Red Tomahawk bowed so low that even his penultimate feather would not brush stone and entered the tunnel.

Buffalo Bill doffed his hat to follow suit.

Irene and Elizabeth exchanged glances. Their broad-brimmed hats were affixed 'til death did them part with foot-long pins and would only be a nuisance in their hands. They bent over deeply to enter the yawning hole.

My cap was no problem and the Rothschild men wore bowlers, so we all made appropriate obeisance and instantly found ourselves in a dark passage. Both Red Tomahawk and Buffalo Bill (somehow I was finding it easier to use those astonishing names than I ever had been able to accept "Pink," even now when I knew the nickname was a clue and not simply an affront to convention) had darkened their lanterns.

Our first impression of the tunnel was a warm exhalation of air that implied it led deep into the earth. Then came the eerie thrum of sound, of distant chanting. A single voice droned for a few instants. Many voices responded.

It sounded like nothing so much as a Roman High Mass.

This sound paralyzed us all, perhaps for different reasons.

Whatever we had expected, it was not ceremony, although Irene, perhaps, was the least surprised of us all.

Nor had we expected the scent that wafted along on the warm air: candle wax.

Yet again, this was not truly surprising. We had seen candle stumps and candle droppings on other sites, but had thought them necessary for light. Now we had to wonder.

Of course we could not consult, bowed over as we were in the narrow tunnel, so we simply crept forward one by one, lost in our own speculations and worries.

I wondered what the Indian warrior thought, if these sounds and mission were reminiscent of conflict-filled life on the frontier . . . if Buffalo Bill relished this return to his early scouting days . . . if the Rothschild men, city dwellers all who no doubt knew mob violence and secret cabals, could countenance the pursuit of people who retreated to caves for whatever Godless purposes they might have.

Our path led upward and finally leveled out. Here the tunnel grew higher if not much wider, and we were able to walk upright, all but Buffalo Bill.

A light was visible ahead: a bright yellow-white light. No one in our party by now could resist the pull of that unearthly vision so deep under the exposition grounds. Now the path led downward again, as if to Hell, and we walked until the light swelled to loom before us like an insubstantial door.

Beyond it the chanting had stopped to be replaced by wild screams and cries, by the sound of people contending madly.

Red Tomahawk assumed a crouch deep enough to follow

dog markings and crept into the light, dodging quickly to the right of the opening. A moment later his left arm appeared, beckoning.

Buffalo Bill replicated his beastlike posture and crept after him.

Again a fringed arm appeared, also beckoning.

Irene dropped to hands and knees and crawled after them, then Elizabeth.

I hesitated. The cries and moans had reached a hellish pitch. I suspected that people so forgetful of all civilization would hardly notice our stealthy approach, especially if they were all murdering each other, as I feared.

No arms beckoned further. I glanced back at the Rothschild agents. One stepped up beside me.

"What next?" he asked me in French.

I didn't know what to answer, and realized I shouldn't know until I followed the others. I told him to wait. *"Arrêtez,"* I said in desperation, but he understood my meaning and held back.

I dropped to my knees, pretending I was in the nursery and playing bear with the youngest children. Then I shambled into the light and heat awaiting beyond the opening.

At first my dark-accustomed eyes could only water and blink. Noise filled the cavern and echoed back and forth until it sounded like all the souls of the damned were confined in this one space.

I saw the others, still crouched, peering over a natural barrier of rocks into the scene below.

I crawled near to Elizabeth and cautiously leaned over to view the cavern floor.

Candles sat everywhere, the floor, on scattered rocks, in niches in the walls, spangling the dark stone with light. A blazing fire in the center provided the fiery furnace that lit even the cavern roof.

Beside it stood a single robed figure, babbling in some foreign language, perhaps even a language not of this earth, hands and head lifted to . . . I hesitate to say Heaven . . . lifted to the ceiling of that devil's cave.

Around it danced and screamed a dozen naked figures,

trampling their dark cast-off robes, more than half of them women, I am ashamed to say, the light cast by the flames licking at their writhing, glistening bodies.

One naked man stood on the fringe with a whip, lashing anyone who lagged in the wild dance. Rivulets of blood as well as sweat streaked the quivering flesh, but some dancers collapsed to the cavern floor despite the lash. Then others fell atop them and they writhed and screamed until the vision of Hell was even more vivid than any Renaissance master could paint.

The only ones untouched by the madness were a trio in monks' robes who stood watching by the far cavern wall like an Inquisition panel of judges.

The frantic motion, heat, noise made it hard to absorb the scene, what was happening besides utter madness.

The leader had ripped open his shirt and trousers and hurled himself onto the writhing figures on the ground, a bed of naked abandoned women. One woman screamed as if being murdered at the bottom of a pile of three men, then two pulled her by her arms from the ground and laid her over a large rock. The third man drew a knife from the tangle of discarded clothes and bent over her.

I couldn't believe what I saw. Even as I write this now, many days later in my own desperate circumstances, my pen stops and fails to follow the will of my mind and my hand, my resolve to record all that I saw, however awful.

The man took the knife and cut off her breast.

I couldn't help myself. I stood and screamed, my sound lost in the shriek from the mutilated woman. The entire world seemed to be screaming as everyone around me stood.

An ungodly whoop beside me, a blood-chillingly long, savage howl overcame even the din below.

The man below with the knife lifted his bloody trophy, then stood paralyzed as a hatchet blade bloomed in the middle of his back. He fell, but the writhing, moaning, gabbling masses on the cavern floor were lost to everything around them, even when Buffalo Bill hurled a lantern into the middle of the fire, sending wood shards and sparks flying like fireworks.

A pistol discharged, Irene's, shot into the air. The Rothschild men pounded into the cavern, then stopped in horror.

I noticed that the observers along the wall had vanished.

Red Tomahawk, still howling, leaped over the barrier of rocks to the floor some fifteen feet below. Buffalo Bill followed him, and the Rothschild agents finally gathered their wits and ran down the ramp leading below, pistols pointed but yet unfired.

The leader pushed himself free of the twining limbs of three wild-eyed women and started upright, looking like the only one who would give fight.

"We must help that woman," Irene muttered, starting after the men.

Another wild man was charging from the fray, pupils lost in the rolling whites you see on a terrified horse, running toward us.

Despite the half-clothed form and wild eyes and hair, I recognized James Kelly!

And he seemed to recognize me!

I saw the child in the wood, cringing away from the blade. I saw the woman on the street, screaming into the curtain of her own blood that fell red and heavy from her throat like a glittering garnet cascade.

And always I saw the gaunt dark figure at the corner of my eye, the crow flying, the raven croaking, the ghost moaning, the monster laughing.

He had always been there, and I had always chosen not to see him.

Now he was looking right at me.

Now he was judging me worthy of notice.

Now I must see him in return to let him know that I am not afraid.

Now it is he, or I.

Irene saw Kelly, saw our converging paths, the danger.

She seized and spun me to face the tunnel. "Run, Nell! Run out and do not look back, do not come back until we emerge safely. And we will. Don't question me!" She thrust a stick, probably Elizabeth's, into my hand. "Warn the authorities if you can. It is far worse than even I thought. For the love of God, go now!"

She shoved me so hard down the tunnel that I stumbled and nearly fell.

"Go! As you love me, go! Run!"

I cannot describe the imperative in her words, the utter conviction, the utter command.

I scrambled forward, still stumbling, my hands scraping along the rough stone ground until I could get my balance and run half-upright. I stumbled into first one side of the tunnel wall, then the other, only darkness ahead of me, shouts and confusion and occasional pistol shots behind me.

I must warn. Get out. Not look back. Not like Lot's wife. Not a pillar of salt. Not me. Run. Go. Not look back. Not think. Not decipher what I had seen. Run. Run.

47.

Paranoia

We are entering panoramania. . . .
—THE VOLTAIRE, 1881

The longer I obeyed and ran, the less I could bear to leave Irene to the fray and condemn myself to learning the outcome later from a safe distance.

I let my pounding steps slow, even as my heartbeat accelerated. I paused in the darkness still lit by flashes from the conflagration behind me. I had the stick. Who knows if one blow might not make all the difference?

None of us had expected to encounter devil-worshipers at their evil rituals. The implications of this scene straight from an illustration of Hell on the history and identity of Jack the Ripper were too massive to contemplate. What I had glimpsed was branded on my brain, but without the clarity of meaning that would let the full horror penetrate.

All I knew is that our party had uncovered a nest of vipers far too numerous and venomous to handle and that my presence was a hindrance. I only could pray that Elizabeth, too, would heed Irene's directive, but I doubted it. I could only pray, as my feet pounded the packed dirt, that Irene would escape the carnage herself.

I could only take comfort in the brave way Buffalo Bill and Red Tomahawk had waded into the maddened creatures, unabashed by blood and frenzy, themselves figures of a fearsome and exotic force. A gathering of such prime evil required a foe that had practiced primitive warfare far from the rank and file of European battlefields.

The Rothschild agents on the cavern's fringes, even with their pistols drawn, seemed like lapdogs at a bear-baiting match. Irene, too, had been reduced to armed observer. I prayed she stayed that way, but suspected that James Kelly would not pass her to pursue me.

Yet I heard no more shots as I reached the level section of the tunnel and began the descent to the entrance. I did hear the feeble beat of running footsteps behind me. Irene and Elizabeth come to join me in retreat, like sensible women? Yes!

I turned as the pulsing steps pounded nearer. No! The footsteps rang too loud for women's shoes. They were boots. I spun to run forward again, pressing ahead harder, and finally went gasping out into the night air, hearing the distant roar of the fairground crowd as a tiny buzz on the glittering horizon of lights that now seemed as far away as any sunset.

Onward the running footsteps came, in escape or pursuit, neither one boding well for me, alone and undefended as I was.

The Seine sparkled like a ribbon of spangled velvet. Some barrier darkened the view ahead of me, but rows of electric lights traced its outline.

The waterborne panorama building! I was on the level below the gangway that brought sightseers aboard. Heavy footsteps behind me impelled me forward into the dark passage and through a door-size opening. Dim light from above sprinkled an assemblage of bulky mechanisms. I felt as if I were in the lumber room beneath the stage of a theater, where *deus ex machina* gears lay momentarily idle and stage furnishings stood jumbled in piles.

I felt my way among the alien shapes, thinking that a panorama was a sort of stage in round form, hoping for some means to reach the main floor of the attraction. What had Irene called the trapdoor in the stage floor designed for the appearance and disappearance of ghosts and monsters . . . ? Ah, the vampire box. I had to hope there was a vampire box here that would allow me to enter the panorama's main floor and then exit into the peaceful night.

I still did not hear the report of shots, and the running footsteps had gone silent.

Nevertheless, I trod as softly as I could in the narrow aisles between wood-and-metal barriers and finally banged my toe on something sharp and metal on the floor.

I swallowed cries of fierce pain. Rejoicing outweighed momentary agony as my patting hands traced the shape of metal steps coiling upward.

I could hear the Seine lapping gently at the ship's exterior. Nothing moved here but the water, for this ship was a building.

I began to climb the tight steep staircase, trying to keep my stick on the curving handrail.

At last I came onto level wooden flooring . . . no vampire box to break free of, just the shadowy environs of the panorama display boxing me into a huge room shaped like the interior of a drum.

Faint electric lights cast fitful light on the painted scenes and figures filling the walls all around. These were not the bright lights of display, but night-lights left on to secure the premises while closed.

My heart beat faster at the notion that a guard might visit this echoing space from time to time. Was I more in danger of being taken for an intruder than seen as a lost soul in need of rescue?

The panoramas I had heard of since my arrival in Paris had

been like the main salon wax tableaux at the Musée Grévin: scenes of real-life pomp like the Czar's coronation or the French President's visit to the Russian fleet. These were huge paintings done in the round and populated with famous figures of the day as well as mobs of nobodies, yet reconstructions in front of the painting, like the exhibits on the exposition grounds, used waxen figures.

So I was not startled to glimpse standing and sitting figures posted all around the room, and even to vaguely recognize a few silhouettes.

A new site honoring the French Revolution's hundredth year on the site of the former Bastille featured a panorama of the storming of the famous prison and a re-creation of the building itself, an eighteenth-century Breton village, and a Historical and Patriotic Museum with a panorama of the life of Joan of Arc! She whose bloody feast day this was. The *Histoire du siècle* panorama continued the theme by presenting the celebrities of each era.

Granted, these many displays repeated themselves, but the French are not a people to blow their own horn only once or twice, and certainly there were patrons enough for each new lavish and self-congratulatory display.

Why I had especially wished to see, that is, "board" this particular panorama on the exposition grounds is because it was the first actually to simulate motion, and very convincingly, too, to hear tell. The clever part is that motion is only of the painted views and not of the so-called ship, so there is none of the lurching that leads to sickness for the passengers.

I could indeed testify now to the admirable stability of the good ship Panorama.

I began walking across the "deck," wincing at every creak of the planking beneath my feet. I had no reason to suspect that my unseen pursuers had followed me into the attraction, but no reason to assume they hadn't either.

I could not help noticing the agreeable representation of Le Havre harbor filled with painted ships on a painted sea, nor the feeling of security I felt with waxen ship's officers dressed in the smart uniforms of the steamship company that sponsored the attraction.

I had entered by the back and from below. I need only find the front entrance to debark, then seek help. Meanwhile, I prowled the captain's deck in the "open air," the sole moving person among the wax effigies.

A sudden clang from below ended my luxurious solo tour of the scene. Hard boots hit the metal steps in quick succession, more than one pair to judge by the rat-a-tat-tat of oncoming footsteps.

Desperate, I looked around. I had not yet discovered the entrance area and was therefore trapped, with only moments to act. . . .

My mind and heart galloped, but in different directions. What would Irene do? What would she do! She would . . . act.

In two of the longest and quietest strides I had ever managed I stepped next to the wax figure of the ship's captain pointing out sights to a female passenger.

I planted my walking stick on the deck so that I had some support and tucked my hand into the crook of the waxen woman's elbow for further stability. Then I tilted my head politely to gaze with rapt attention at the captain's wax face.

The boots bounded onto the wooden deck behind me and stopped.

I dared not look anywhere but at the captain's bland waxen features beyond the "woman" next to me, on which my far-sighted eyes could focus perfectly. His cheeks were as rosy as ripening pears, and there was even a fleck of tobacco from the pipe in his gesticulating hand on his lip!

Behind me the boots began taking long, deliberately noisy steps around the scene.

I was thankful that my wool-check coat-dress not only had the look of a deckside garment, but that the sturdy material had no generous folds to be still settling from my last, hasty motion.

The boots, perhaps two pair, continued their lordly, leisurely stroll around the scene.

A sudden crack! Wood on wood. My startled heart nearly leaped out of my chest and undid the pin of my lapel watch.

But my desperate caution had made me visibly immune to such a trick. I moved not a muscle.

The steps circled to my right now and then in front of me. I sensed motion between me and the panoramic painting, but my farsightedness protected me from a clear view of the man entering my line of sight. He was just a vague blur, like the people in the painting, and I had no trouble keeping my gaze frozen upon the captain.

My performance may have been "wooden" in theatrical terms, but that was just what the situation called for.

I heard one set of boots clattering down the rear circular staircase. The other prowler had paused somewhere before me. Then he moved toward me, pausing behind the captain's shoulder. I forced myself not to blink, and suspended breathing.

A hand reached out. I resisted the urge to avoid it. It dusted off the captain's shoulder. Then it struck the pipe from his hand.

The sound of the piece clattering across the floor could have taken place on another planet for all the attention I paid it.

Keep utterly still, I ordered myself. You are a statue. You cannot move.

Another vaguely seen blow, and the walking stick sailed from under my hand to go spinning across the wooden deck.

My hand remained clutched on empty air. I forced all the will in my body to keep each finger motionless.

The strain was intense.

The man sighed, and I could feel his warm breath on my eyelashes.

Then he spun on his heel and suddenly approached a couple in deck chairs, spinning the woman around. The waxen figure slumped, then slowly fell to the floor.

He made a sound like an inarticulate curse, then was stalking away. Again the metal stairs reverberated with descending steps.

I slowly let my breath depress, then inflate, my bosom.

Still I did not move.

Why were they bothering with me? I wondered. I was of

no threat to them. Didn't their vile companions below need their defense? Yet the man I could not quite see had been looking for a woman among the mannequins. Did they think I was Irene?

I waited a long time, wishing I dared disturb the chatelaine in my pocket to get out my pince-nez. But I had been warned by the Master that it was too noisy on certain occasions. I wished I still wore Irene's borrowed satin slippers of several days ago, for I could have slipped surreptitiously out of them and stolen away over the wooden floor, but I wore high-button boots too complicated to shed without wasting time or making a betraying sound.

The entrance had to lie ahead, and it had to involve stairs down to the level of the quai.

After what seemed like an eternity, but was probably only ten minutes by the faithful watch affixed to my bosom, I eased my position and took a soft step forward, then another.

A third. A fourth. The building remained silent. Another. In between steps, I breathed.

And then the walls began moving. Just a blurred sense of the painted ships bobbling in the breeze. I blinked like mad, but the impression only intensified. I heard the creak and thrum of underlying equipment in motion. I could see just enough to feel dizzy, and began running, my steps tapping like one of the wild Congo drums in the street parade.

I seemed to see an aperture, a curtained opening of the kind that blocks light from the seating area of a theater.

I reached it, felt the heavy velvet in my hands, rushed through.

And was suddenly jerked back by someone waiting behind the curtain. I tried to tear loose and bolt back into the panorama room and head for the back steps, but then I could hear boots springing up the metal steps two at a time.

A horridly strong grip had me around the shoulders while a hand clapped a thick, sickly-sweet-smelling cloth over my face.

I struggled like a drowning person, only my eyes above the noxious fumes that were suffocating my senses. I reached up, but my arm only reached as far as the small oval brooch of my watch before it flailed and fell limply away, a waxen appendage that did not quite belong to me.

A massive blur was thundering toward me like an ogre from a fairy tale. As the image neared and resolved into that of a man, I could smell the reek of liquor and vomit, could see red streaks upon his coarse, loose shirt, see finally and clearly his demented staring eyes, pale as the water that was rising over my head on a nauseous tide. . . .

He was laughing as he neared, a wild man. James Kelly came for me at last. I could sense rough hands pawing at the front buttons of my gown, but thankfully could no longer feel, nor think, nor know anything but darkness.

48. No Quarter

I saw around us a ring of wolves, with white teeth and lolling red tongues, with long, sinewy limbs and shaggy hair.

—BRAM STOKER, *DRACULA*

FROM A JOURNAL

Three of the Rothschilds' men had Irene and me pinned against the rough granite wall, presenting a defensive bulwark to any who would rush us.

We both struggled, in vain, to elude this misguided protective border.

The other five had run to aid the two plainsmen as they tried to herd the dozen or so drunken, moaning wild men and women into one corner of the cavern, away from the bonfire and the crude altar-cum–operating table.

A few of the group were too wounded to resist. Others

were so drunkenly in awe of the oddly attired Americans that they fell on their knees and clutched at the men's fringed trousers. Still, they were mad, drunken brutes who had surrendered to every bestial urge that the mind of man can imagine in the past couple hours and were not about to be subdued by only two men, however legendary.

Even I could see that neither plainsman was inclined to slaughter such inebriated and pathetic prey, for all their demonic deeds. I imagine they'd both seen, and perhaps done, worse in the Indian Wars.

I did think that the taking and flourishing of one scalp would have ended the resistance immediately, and this did not seem too bloody an act to perform given what we'd seen them do to one of their own, or on the hundredth anniversary of the French Revolution and the offices of the guillotine, but do not think it would have done the reputation of the Wild West Show much good for future engagements.

While we were at this impasse, I heard a slight stir down the tunnel.

"Has Nell come back?" I asked Irene.

"I hope not, and I wish you had gone when you had a chance," she said, trying once again to thrust her personal guardian aside, with little success. "The worst have gotten away," she shouted in French at her defender. "Let me go after them!"

But their prime assignment was obviously protection, not capture, and we were the prisoners of their damned French chivalry!

Then a new figure ran onto the scene. At first I thought one of the fiends' number had returned because of his simple workman's trousers and shirt, but this man was taller than any of the fleeing figures.

He paused, observed our tableau against the wall and the other Rothschild agents standing uncertainly behind the contesting figures, their pistols aimed but unfired.

He called some French words. *Vite!* for hurry, then some I didn't recognize.

The Frenchmen's actions soon revealed his orders. The three men left off impeding Irene and me to join the others in forming a human line that drove the remaining people into so tight a knot that they could no longer fight.

He picked a bloody petticoat from the stones and, with a tremendous, heedless show of strength, ripped the cloth lengthwise into rags, tossing them to the agents to use as bonds.

Irene rushed to seize some ruffles from the petticoat hem and went to wind them around the chest of the moaning woman, who still lay by the obscene "altar."

"Was she meant to survive this barbaric rite?" I asked as I knelt beside Irene to assist in the binding.

"If she didn't bleed to death or become so infected that her festering wounds would kill her. I don't think they thought beyond their frenzy."

"What is the purpose behind it all? And has the Ripper sprung from this cult, or is he someone quite separate?"

"Ask Sherlock Holmes," she said with a sardonic glance to the lean form that was bent over binding hands as we bound wounds. "I imagine that it will take even him some time to decipher the riddle of these lethal ceremonies. It is enough that we have stopped it for tonight, although I fear that—"

The woman we tended had become unconscious, and her release from pain seemed to permit Irene to think beyond the scene at hand.

"Buffalo Bill!" she called out, and he stepped from the mass of fallen men.

"We've got them hog-tied," he announced. "Danger's over."

"But . . . did you see? Where is Nell?"

Before he could answer her eyes had sought and found Sherlock Holmes, who suddenly stopped tying knots as if sensing her attention. He turned to face us.

"You must know," she told him. "You came in last. You must have seen Nell leaving, or outside."

"I saw no one." He stood.

"How are you here?" she asked.

"I suddenly realized that once again I was at home waiting until the morning to act, this time reading the chilling casebook of Krafft-Ebing. I also realized that waiting to act is a fatal mistake with you, Madam. I arose at once, went out, and inquired at your hotel. Your party's manner of dress suggested the exposition. That you attempted to divert me again with the gift of a parting puzzle made me realize you expected to find some evil work afoot here. I've spent the afternoon and evening an hour behind you, interrogating sightseers and ultimately Gypsies. The trail led here."

"Trail! In all the footsteps and hoofprints that have trampled these parade grounds?"

Sherlock Holmes pointed to Red Tomahawk's feet. "Only one set of moccasins to follow."

The Red Man nodded, a slight relaxation of his features the only hint that he was amused, and even pleased. "I came to follow, not to have one follow me. You would not have seen moccasins otherwise."

"No doubt," said Sherlock Holmes. He turned again to Irene. "But where and when did Miss Huxleigh go? She should be collected before she gets into trouble."

"I know that!" Irene was standing. "I will search the grounds. I meant only to protect her from the worst of this ghastly scene. Where can she have gone?"

By now two of the Rothschild agents had picked up the swooning woman between them and were preparing to return up the tunnel with her. Others had preceded them out, seeking medical attention and the gendarmes, I suppose.

I wanted very badly to ask Irene what she believed had happened here, but she was looking around in a distracted state. "Nell must have gone out as I asked. We will have to follow her path and decide what she would have done."

"She'll be waiting for us," I assured Irene. "Now that the police will be coming and going, she will feel safer about showing herself."

"Quite likely," Sherlock Holmes said, endorsing my explanation. "We will find her in no time."

And he took the lead in conducting us out of that dreadful place of pain and terror.

49.

Lost Innocence

My age is fourteen years . . . I was present when my mother was married to J. J. Ford . . . The first time I seen Ford take hold of mother, he attempted to choke her.

—PINKEY E. J. COCHRANE, ARMSTRONG COUNTY COURT, APOLLO, PENNSYLVANIA, 1878

FROM A JOURNAL

There is a grief one sees only in madhouses, a grief so dark and deep that one possessed by it is immured beyond reach in a realm even lower than the pit of Hell itself.

I have been among such lost souls, and shall never forget it.

So shall I never forget those dreadful hours when Irene Adler Norton joined that forsaken company.

An hour's search of the area outside the cavern found no trace of Nell Huxleigh. At first Irene was intent on the search, suggesting other places, other paths. For another two hours we ranged as far as the crowds still milling around the Eiffel Tower, interrogating the kiosk tenders, ambling fairgoers, the ever-present gendarmes.

Then she grew wild, wild with anxiety and fury at our helplessness in the face of Nell's utter disappearance.

Only after a two-hour search did she bow to the conjoined urging of Sherlock Holmes, Colonel Cody, and Inspector le Villard, who had come along later, that she and I return to the hotel. There we would await the result of their united efforts to search the exposition grounds in the night's wee hours with all the crowds gone.

Perhaps the last, laconic grunt of agreement from the Sioux tracker, Red Tomahawk, finally swayed her. And his comment, "Less feet better trail."

Perhaps she also realized that, though she was far from hysterical, her personal terror would infect what must be a cool, impersonal process, a scientific process, in fact, tailored in Heaven for the likes of Sherlock Holmes.

"You have done the right thing," I told her again and again in the carriage en route to the hotel. "Were I the worst and most elusive villain on Earth, I would still shudder to have three such superb hunters upon my trail. Not only Sherlock Holmes and the famous frontiersman Buffalo Bill, but an Indian tracker! The whole world knows the Indian for the finest reader of minute physical evidence. The entire prairie has been their hunting grounds. These few hundred acres of parkland and buildings are child's play to such a one."

"This is not child's play," she replied, and said no more.

How could I answer? When a man has gone missing there is always the possibility that it is voluntary. He may have gone to sea or the Army, or to another town to escape a burdensome personal or business life. When a woman or child has gone missing, there is scant such chance. If the missing person is not found swiftly and nearby, the odds increase with every passing minute that she will not be found, or will only be found far away long after, and no longer living.

Inspector le Villard exchanged a glance with me and shrugged as we jolted along in uneasy silence. I know that he ached to be back on the grounds with the trackers, but understood Sherlock Holmes's insistence that he see us to the hotel.

Only an escort could ensure that Irene would follow the course she had so reluctantly agreed upon. Certainly I could do nothing to stop her if she wished to go back.

But, as with any course, the farther you follow it, the harder it becomes to reverse its momentum.

By the time the inspector had seen us to our rooms and

bowed out, Irene's agitation was ready to burst into uncivil unrest.

She began to pace back and forth. "I should have stayed. Why did I listen to them? Men are always trying to exclude women. In the name of protecting us, they actually protect their own domination of events."

"This was hardly the case here, Irene. We were present for the capture of that fiendish cabal. Nothing of that atrocious scene was spared us."

"They believe because my emotions are involved in Nell's disappearance that I cannot think! I can think, only too well!"

My own thoughts returned to the bloody ceremonies our party had interrupted. If Nell had been kidnapped by anyone involved in those obscenities . . . dear God, the mind could not imagine possibilities dire enough. I could only consider them with my imagination averted, like a face half–turned away from a nauseating sight.

Irene was still pacing, back and forth like a great lion in a zoo cage. I could never stand to see such animals contained, pacing endlessly, rage and loss in their eyes and something even more alien for these once-free wild beasts: the first bewildering glint of fear in creatures who had never felt it before.

I could only keep watch. I loathed my feeling of helplessness, the lengthening absence of Nell, the fact that Irene and I were consigned to the ignorant fringes of events.

"You know why they wanted us away," she said after long silence, during one lashing turn before she began pacing in the other direction. "They don't expect to find her. Why? What led her away from us? Why would the fleeing madmen take her?"

"As a hostage, perhaps? But, Irene, we don't know that the people from the cavern took her. She might have fallen in the confusion after she fled, might have hit her head and been carried to safety by someone meaning to assist her. I'm sure they will search the hospitals tomorrow." I glanced at the windows, which were slowly turning the odd lavender-gray color of half-mourning clothes. "Today."

I suggested we change from our walking clothes, and she

vanished into her bedchamber. I offered to assist her, as Nell would have, but before I could even phrase my suggestion her face froze, and she refused.

Standing alone in the main room, I wondered if I could trust her. She was not beyond going out the hotel window.

But I heard encouraging rustling noises through the door, so slipped into my alcove speedily to don my own dressing gown. I rushed back to the parlor to find Irene's bedroom door open.

She herself stood just outside it, to my relief, obliviously as resplendent as a Byzantine empress in her green-taffeta dressing gown, frozen like a tragic heroine in an opera, staring at an envelope in her hand.

"Irene—?"

She neither moved nor answered. I approached with the caution one reserves for things likc coiled snakes. Only when I reached her did she extend the envelope to me.

"It was on my pillow."

I lifted the heavy flap, which was unsealed, expecting God knows what momentous communication . . . a ransom note for Nell, perhaps, though it was hard to suppose that her disappearance had been planned.

The envelope was empty. I looked again and found a thick dark comma of hair in one corner.

"Nell's hair isn't—"

"It's Godfrey's."

Her tone had been oddly flat. I looked into her eyes, and that is when I saw those empty hellish depths you find in madhouses.

I can't explain it, though I've tried more than once. It's as if all of a being's energy has been drained deep into the earth. Only the physical shell of a person remains in the here and now. To see Irene Adler Norton reduced to such a state was horrifying.

She allowed me to guide her to our round table, to sit her on one of the chairs. A ghost sat there with us. Nell's. I had never met Godfrey Norton, so he could not haunt me, but I saw his presence in the dull gaze Irene focused on some distant point only she could see.

How long we remained like that, I cannot say.

My mind tried to churn in speculation—her friend and companion, gone in an instant last night. Her husband, far away and now brought to mind and memory by the sinister token of a lock of hair left, intimately, on a pillow.

Someone had entered our rooms while we were out to leave this mute message, to imply danger at a distance as well as at hand. Were the incidents related, or oddly coincidental? How could I know? Only Irene would have the faintest notion, and she had retreated into shock.

Daylight crept into our dark night of the soul, gradually allowing the so-familiar furnishings of the room to take visible shape around us. Every object that became clear brought with it a memory of Nell passing behind it, or touching it. I almost felt I could reach out and make the memory solid, bring her back.

But there was only Irene sitting at the table, the envelope beneath her slack hands.

A knock at the door startled me, but not her.

I stood, hesitant, but she did not move.

So I went to answer it and admitted Sherlock Holmes.

He was dressed for business in striped trousers, frock coat, and top hat. Having last seen him only hours before on the exposition grounds in workman's clothing, I found his current attire too reminiscent of a funeral director's.

His face was gaunt, and his eyes had fastened on Irene at the table.

"News?" I asked.

He shook his head quickly, slightly, and came fully into the room.

She looked up slowly, and that look stopped him.

He reached into his waistcoat pocket and withdrew something gold.

When Irene neither moved nor spoke, he went near, and laid the object on the table scarf near her hand.

"We found her watch in the panorama building, near the entrance way. Colonel Cody is convinced it was lost during a struggle. I believe that she managed to unfasten it herself, and let it drop as a sign. There is a bend in the shaft that could confirm either conclusion."

He paused, as if the next words were hard to say.

"Red Tomahawk," he resumed a bit self-consciously, as what Englishman wouldn't, given the name, "has quite amazing tracking abilities. We were able to discern three sets of footprints besides Miss Huxleigh's. Only the three left the panorama building, but there were . . . drag marks. Also traces of chloroform on the velvet curtain near the exit. We assume she was made unconscious and abducted, which bodes well for her immediate survival. Red, er, Tomahawk believes he can identify the hoofprints of the carriage horse, but of course a search for hired vehicles will take some time, and the carriage may have been private. I confess that I cannot imagine why Miss Huxleigh should have been abducted."

When Irene did not speak, or even look up, he set his hat and cane on the table.

"I have called on a royal personage this morning, despite the hour. He, too, was in his dressing gown. He is well aware of your significant efforts on his behalf in the instance of these murders, and that . . . our investigations have also managed to maintain his privacy in what could have been an unparalleled scandal to the throne. It is in his power and interest to see that every resource, both French and English, is used to find and pursue those who abducted Miss Huxleigh. Unfortunately, last night's events demand that I return to London. This puts an entire new complexion on the Ripper murders. I must be there to reinvestigate in light of what I have learned here. You may rest assured that I will lend any aid I can to the search for Miss Huxleigh. If only you could give us some indication of why she was abducted—"

Irene remained as still as a statue carved of salt.

He paused and looked at me in utter frustration.

I nodded at the envelope on the table.

He frowned at its bland face, marked only by the initials I. A.

Suddenly his features sharpened with interest, perhaps even suspicion. He placed his fingers on the envelope, watching Irene as he would a snake he feared might strike.

When she didn't move, he delicately slid the envelope from the loose custody of her hands and held it up before his face.

"German paper," he announced to whoever would care to hear. "Handmade. Very fine. Dusseldorf. It has been carried in a velvet-lined pocket or case. Red velvet. Some tiny threads have snagged on the deckle edge of the flap. The ink is . . . problematical without analysis. And—"

He opened the envelope, peered inside. His gazed hardened as he looked at me again.

"And it appears that we are dealing with someone bold but reckless. A formidable opponent, but not omnipotent. They never are. My own casual inquiries indicated that Mr. Norton was traveling beyond Vienna. My brother is of some influence in the Foreign Office. In fact, in many respects, he *is* the Foreign Office. I shall wire him immediately. If I may dare suggest, the Rothschild family should be notified of this second . . . mystery at once. Their network of agents in all the capitals of Europe is unsurpassed."

Irene said nothing, did nothing.

He slapped the envelope back down on the table. I jumped, but Irene did not.

"Madam," he commanded.

He moved behind her, then pulled the chair out, with her on it, a feat of amazing strength. His hand on her elbow brought her upright. He turned her to face him, but her eyes never lifted from staring straight ahead, through him as if he were a featureless wall.

I had never seen him more remote, more the stern lecturer devoted to science and stoicism.

"Madam," he said, "fives times you eluded the King of Bohemia's best agents during your flight from Bohemia."

She roused enough to stare sideways. "He is a minor king, and his agents are not very good."

"I am very good," Sherlock Holmes said, "yet you saw through my clergyman's guise in short order in the Serpentine Mews when I started the house fire to force you to reveal where you had hidden the photograph the King so feared."

Her head shook slightly, like some dumb beast's reacting to gnats buzzing about its ears.

"You had stolen the idea from Edgar Allan Poe's C. Auguste Dupin in 'The Purloined Letter,' " she said listlessly. "Those stories have been popular in America, England, and France for decades. It was no great feat to see through the stratagem."

"You further had the audacity, the unparalleled audacity, to don men's dress and shortly after accost me on the steps to 221B Baker Street, wishing me good night by name."

"No feat for an actress, and you were not aware of my suspicions."

"Further, you arranged to marry Norton and escape England within hours, before the King and I returned the following day to collect the now-missing photo."

She shrugged.

"You are the only woman ever to outwit me."

"You have not had many dealings with women."

"You fought a duel with a French viscount, and won."

"I was trained to duel for trouser roles in the opera."

"You saved the King of Bohemia's throne—twice!"

"An insignificant little throne, not worth ruling from and not worth saving."

Mr. Holmes appeared to have exhausted his repertoire of bracing reminders of past triumphs.

While he paused, defeated, she slowly raised her eyes to his. "That woman, last night—"

"She is in good care. A Frenchwoman, of all things. A 'reformed' prostitute, she calls herself. She had some demented notion that she was sacrificing the source of her sin and that of the many men who used her to the Master."

Irene's eyes dropped again, look aslant, saw scenes that we could not.

After a long pause, Mr. Holmes moved as silently as a performing mime to collect his hat and stick and go to the door. I followed, but Irene never seemed to notice our defection.

"If it had been Watson . . ." he whispered to me on the threshold, then shook his head. "I can do nothing more here."

"Why is the past in London more key than the present here in Paris?" I asked quickly.

For this I received a glance of irritation mixed with surprise.

"Because I perceive for the first time a keen and twisted intelligence behind the brutal murders in both these great cities, despite the crude and perplexing nature of the atrocities." His gaze fastened on me with reluctant curiosity. "I trust that I am not so opinionated a man that I cannot admire the courage of a woman as well as that of another man. I grant that in the past few days you three women have found and faced such dark crimes as would drive the majority of your sex mad."

At this he glanced to Irene, who again sat slumped at the table, lost in her torment like some absinthe drinker enslaved by "the Green Fairy" of delusion. The crude artists who sell their wares in Montmartre often depict these abandoned souls. I had not seen her react to anything around her since Sherlock Holmes had left her side.

He lowered his voice. "You see the results of meddling in matters of such a debased nature." Dark brows lowered over piercing eyes. "I have no time to waste speculating on your purpose here, but do not doubt that you have one. That matters nothing now. You must attend to her, as no one else is able to do so. While I can sympathize with the loss of a trusted companion, I have no closer ties, although my friend Dr. Watson, the married man, could no doubt tell me of the deeper agonies of an endangered spouse. I suspect that the disappearance of an only brother is not quite the same thing, and frankly, my brother is better equipped to defend himself in dire circumstances than I myself." He regarded me as sternly as a parent. "I have no doubt that a young American adventuress like yourself may be convinced that you can weather any corruption, as *she* was once convinced. Now you see what her actions have brought upon her: the attention of forces far beyond the normal."

"You believe there is a supernatural—"

He muffled a snort of dissent and resumed his low tone. It was as if we conferred in a sickroom about a patient beyond all reaching.

"Please, Miss Cochrane! If there is any dimension to the

case that smacks of the unearthly, it is a variety of spiritual, rather than occult ill. Yes, I have ascertained your surname. I am far more aware of the movements of you all, and of those around you, than you suspect, which is as it should be."

His smile at my surprise was wan. "I cannot claim to see the extent of the connections as yet. Yet be of good courage. I am convinced that there are connections. I would almost suspect that Napoleon of crime, who is the one man who may have more influence in London than Whitehall or Windsor, save that he is too rational for the elements loosened on us in this case. I sense the same evil spiderweb trembling beneath our feet, with a hidden source at an unsuspected center. Have you studied the habits of spiders, Miss Cochrane?"

"No," I said. "I am more interested in the human variety."

"You should not neglect the humble arachnid, a varied and ingenious tribe in the world of terrestrial invertebrates, often vilified but seldom credited. While a spider will spend a long, patient night weaving a web many thousandths its own size, it can in the blink of an eye disassemble the lot and vanish. This is what I have seen in Paris."

"Like the Gypsies," I said, remembering the odd band from the exposition grounds.

"Better than Gypsies. They left tracks. A spider leaves no trace. Unless you search for such with a magnifying lens."

"What of those demented people in the cavern? They are 'traces.' "

He shook his head. "A sorry collection of lost souls. The barely human offal of Janus-faced superstition and self-gratification, dredged from the lowest streets. Some are religious zealots turned half-mad, like Kelly. A pity he escaped. So did far too many others. I should have been involved in the matter from the first." He glanced at Irene, as if torn between blaming and pitying her. Then he shook himself back into a brusque analysis of the situation.

"The Paris police are sorting through a tangle of languages . . . Polish, Russian, Portuguese, but are disgusted to number some of their fellow citizens among the congregation, as well as petty thieves and prostitutes. Yet even in their dementia, these benighted beings prate of some god, some "master" who approves their debaucheries in the name of faith, mind you!"

"I have often seen wrongdoers justify their acts by imagining that they do good, Mr. Holmes, but . . . what could justify what we saw last night?"

"Madness, yet within it or behind it the same kernel of method that makes it doubly dangerous. The wellspring lies in London and the crimes attributed to that darling of the sensationalist presses, Jack the Ripper."

"Oh, but how I wish I could accompany you to London!" The words had burst out unbidden. "I—I . . . worked in the London houses, you know, before this, and not long after the Ripper crimes. I might have some insight—"

"Insight is not needed there. Detection is. And you are needed here. You would abandon the woman who has taken you under her wing? Now, at her darkest hour? Are you Americans all enterprise, and no heart?"

"Is it odd to hear a man of supreme rationality arguing the supremacy of the heart."

"Follow me to London, young Miss Cochrane," he said with such icy conviction that I was completely tongue-tied, "and I shall have you arrested for your sins. Prostitution is not legal there, as it is here."

He glowered at me one last time, then clapped his hat upon his head. "Good day."

What an arrogant, priggish *Englishman*! I closed the door behind Sherlock Holmes with mixed feelings. Part of me longed to pursue him and the investigations that he would refine and renew in Whitechapel. Yet beneath my impatience lay a heavy heart. Who could have anticipated this tragedy? I realized with a chill that so easily I instead of Nell could have been missing. I wondered how that would have affected Irene's degree of shock, or Sherlock Holmes's promises of aid.

Irene wasn't looking at the door, either to watch Sherlock Holmes depart or my return to her side.

Instead, she was staring toward my sleeping alcove. "What is that?" she asked in a dead, dazed tone.

I looked to see what she meant. "Oh. My trunk."

In the silence Irene stared at my trunk as if trying to see through it, as if she thought it contained Nell.

"I forgot I'd asked the steward to get it ready," I recalled as much as explained. So much had happened since that moment, so terribly much.

"Ready?" Her tone still held a heart-wrenching note of vague confusion.

"I, I'm sailing tomorrow"—I glanced at my locket-watch, ashamed that mine was still pinned to my bosom while Nell's . . . it was better not to dwell on details. I could as easily take the boat train to London now if I wished to disobey Sherlock Holmes, and I obey no man. Time had already slipped away like a thief, turning midnight to dawn. "I'm sailing . . . today at 6:00 P.M. on the *Persian Queen*. For America. Going home. I'd bought the tickets weeks ago and forgot to mention it in all the—"

I could say no more, for Irene Adler had sprung at me like a panther, bridging the six feet between us in an instant, her hands hard on my wrists, her face and voice as sharp as edged steel.

"No, you are not," she said. "You are not sailing anywhere while Nell is missing, and Godfrey. Not while I need you. We are going to find them."

"But Sherlock Holmes—"

"Sherlock Holmes has other matters to attend to, and I do not want him involved."

"You were a broken woman only moments ago—"

"Let him think so. I do not want him meddling in this. It is too important."

"I can't see how I can be of any help—"

"Don't worry about it. I can."

Her grip had never lessened. For the first time I feared her.

"But I have obligations—"

"Yes, you do! You are obliged to Nell and me. You have ridden on me long enough. Now I will ride on you, Nellie Bly, daredevil reporter, and you will have by far the better story for it, believe me, if that is what it takes to get you to own up to who and what you are."

Stunned, I found myself on the brink of sobs, like a child

who has been caught in a terrible misdeed and knows it. I had not allowed myself even near such a state since I was ten years old and Jack Ford had first torn our house apart and attacked my mother and called her bitch and whore. I felt racked by guilt. Shock. Fear. And a certain dull, dawning sense of . . . excitement.

"How did you know? No one else guessed. Not even Sherlock Holmes. Have you always known?"

"That doesn't matter now. Our next step does. The greater mystery lies not back in London, but here in Paris and . . . beyond."

I nodded. Once. Hard. And shook loose a few large, humiliating tears.

Irene Adler Norton at last eased her grip on my aching wrists. She seemed well satisfied.

50.
Resolution

She has the face of the most beautiful of women, and the mind of the most resolute of men . . . there are no lengths to which she would not go–none.

—THE KING OF BOHEMIA, "A SCANDAL IN BOHEMIA"

She was resolute, set on doing "something that no other girl had ever done."

—BROOKE KROEGER

FROM A JOURNAL

"I cannot allow," Irene said, seated once again at the table across from me, "my anxiety about Nell and Godfrey to distract us from the clues still to be uncovered here in Paris.

"I have thought and thought upon the events of the past two weeks," she continued in a soft monotone. "Yet the horrors we witnessed last night intervene, like scenes from some opera set in Hell itself. My mind struggles to populate the grotesque scenario with my nearest and dearest in the sacrificial roles. This is death to the investigator. I begin to understand why Sherlock Holmes is so aloof from all emotional entanglements. In this matter I must rely upon your reporter's cold-blooded instincts."

"I am very warm-blooded, I assure you! No one cares more about the downtrodden than I. But when I am playing a role during one of my 'stunts,' which is what the American press calls my 'detective' investigations in various false roles, I am used to suppressing my natural sympathies. How did you know who I really was? Did I say or do something to give away the game?"

Her lips twitched in what would have been a weary smile had she been capable of producing one now. Pushing herself upright by the heels of her hands like an old woman, she left the table for her bedchamber. She soon returned bearing a bundle of letters and a small volume that she slapped to the tabletop.

"How did I know? The sprightly little book on your voluntary incarceration."

I blinked to recognize the garlanded and blossom-strewn cover before me, *Ten Days in a Mad-House*, priced at twenty-five cents and with the author's name etched in my most flourished script, "Nellie Bly."

"Your photograph is within," she said, "along with details of ice-cold baths and sitting fourteen hours a day on hard benches with no occupation and forbidden to talk. The Pinkertons apprise me of undercover work in America. In fact, the agency noticed your discreet departure for Paris and alerted me to keep an eye out for you, on the certainty that you would unearth something sensational."

"I expected to be writing *Ten Days in a Paris Brothel*. I didn't expect anything like the double murders there."

"Nor did I anticipate a double abduction."

This silenced me, though little does. I picked at the embroidery knots on the table scarf, unsure what to say next, a rare state with me.

My every nerve wished to be dogging the footsteps of Sherlock Holmes back to Jack the Ripper's home ground in London. The events in Paris were too scattered, too confusing for me to grasp. I doubted that even Irene Adler Norton, for all her gifts and her desperate stake in the outcome, could make them lead her to any conclusion worth having.

Yet . . . Sherlock Holmes was right. For me to desert this woman now would be inexcusable. I was not used to letting others' circumstances curtail my freedom.

"You *will* get a better story with me, you know," Irene said softly.

I looked up, blushing furiously. "That's not my only concern."

"Oh, you are a relentless little bloodhound in the guise of a well-mannered spaniel, and I wouldn't have you any other way right now, Miss Pink. That is the name you use most, isn't it? The best lie is always the truth presented like a glorious gem in a false setting. I know the American 'Girl Reporters of Derring-Do' use pseudonyms. What is your real name?"

"Pink," I conceded. "I've always been called Pink and have always called myself Pink. It is Pink . . . Elizabeth . . . Jane . . . Cochrane."

She nodded and began shuffling through the letters she had fetched, laying them out as if they were tarot cards with omens written on them. Godfrey's letters, I noticed with a wince.

"There is the question," Irene said, "of whether this cult or a similar one was meeting in Whitechapel last autumn. The question of whether Kelly or any other Ripper suspects attended their orgies."

"Those lunatics in Whitechapel? The English don't go in for bizarre religious cults."

"No, they exported all such people to America two centuries ago."

This glimmer of Irene's usual sharp commentary encouraged me.

"Religious maniacs are common to every race," she went on, "even the British. Besides, the London authorities suspected someone like Kelly from the first. Whitechapel teems with poor foreigners practicing odd beliefs."

"Paris is not London."

"No. The city also is not itself these days."

"Not itself?" I feared her mind was still somewhat unanchored, and who could blame her?

"No. Think! The exposition has brought thousands of people from far lands to the heart of the city, people with customs most Parisians would consider savage. Do you believe that the brutal copulation and mutilation we witnessed in the cavern last night, that Jack the Ripper's butchery of women in

Whitechapel, is unprecedented? Ask me to detail for you the Arab bride's wedding night sometime when your stomach is particularly strong, as reported by that intrepid explorer, Sir Richard Burton. The women's bodies we saw bore evidence of similar ritual mutilations. Remember Krafft-Ebing: lust-murder occurs in all places and times and may destroy children as well as women, and sometimes even men."

While I did as she said and sat silent in thought, Irene pulled the letters from their envelopes, slowly, softly, as if handling spun glass. It occurred to me that her husband might be dead, not merely missing. I could be watching a widow mourning her memories.

Certainly she was lost exploring her own personal world again, skimming one page, then another. I dared not speak.

"Here," she said suddenly. "I knew I had read something. It was in his letter to Nell. . . ."

Her voice and attention faded away again. I waited.

All of a sudden she began reading, in a strong, steady voice, as if performing.

> Also, I thought that you would be wildly interested in the fact that some of the folk here believe our friend the Golem has risen yet again.
>
> This time his reputed appearance has stirred even more panic than before, for it is a particularly bloody murder that they attribute to this automaton.
>
> Of course, you and I and a few others know that the Golem's previous appearance was not what everybody assumed it to be, and that it is extremely unlikely that this medieval legend has bestirred itself to spread terror in the residents' hearts once again.

"Now that is significant," she said.

"I'm not familiar with this 'Golem.' "

"You would not want to be. It is a giant clay man, an automaton, conjured by a desperate rabbi to protect his people from assault, an ancient Jewish legend of Prague. Like all monsters summoned for good purposes, it went berserk and threatened those it was to protect until the rabbi removed the spelling paper from its mouth and it 'died.'

"I wonder if we have something similar at work here," she mused in her new and eerily distractable way.

Despite glimpses of her usual wit, she was still a woman scorched to the bone by lightning.

"The letter mentions 'a particularly bloody murder.' "

"Exactly. And Godfrey was lured away from Prague. Obviously, Prague bears investigation. I do have . . . acquaintances in high places there. There we must go."

"Prague! That is half a world away from London and Paris. On the mention of a single murder you would go there?"

"I also have enemies there. Sherlock Holmes is correct: my activities here in Paris have caught the attention of someone operating in a larger context than a mere murderer, no matter how notorious. Obviously, the message left about Godfrey was direct and personal. Nell's disappearance is less clear."

"She could have been abducted by Kelly. He escaped last night, as did several other cult members."

"She could have been taken by somebody completely unrelated to the cult," Irene said. "That section of the exposition was dark and deserted."

"She could have been taken by . . . Gypsies." I was grasping at straws from a melodrama.

"Yes, she could have," Irene agreed seriously. "They roam far and wide, and I sense this matter has sunk its roots in many places and times. I also think that we have been 'shepherded' for some time. Whoever shot at us outside Notre Dame cathedral, was he frightening us away from the catacomb and the evidence of cult meetings below, or toward it?"

"He?"

"I doubt that Annie Oakley has been drafted for this conspiracy, though I know of a certain heavy-game hunter who would have the nerve to fire a rifle at night in Paris. Whoever shot could have hit us if he wished to."

"Well, I don't like that!"

"Let Sherlock Holmes head west into the alleyways of Whitechapel. I smell the Baltic salt of an east wind blowing,

Pink." Irene faltered for a moment. "It is best that I not call you 'Nellie' and betray your public identity."

It was best that she not call me "Nellie" because every instance would recall her missing friend. I nodded and saw a haunting darkness at the back of her eyes draw away.

"We must have Buffalo Bill examine the site of the shot," Irene said, "and find out if Red Tomahawk has yet traced the shoe print of the horse he discovered. Inspector le Villard will assist us, and the Rothschilds. We are not without our resources. No doubt I will think of others. And you will be a hardy ally, I am sure."

She mustered a pale smile. "I suppose I can rely upon you to record the matters that need recording."

I nodded, sick at heart.

This wind of conspiracy sounded like a child's hope of a happy ending. But what was I to do?

I opened my notebook and listed the things she had ticked off.

There the matter stood. I could follow Sherlock Holmes to London despite his and Irene Adler Norton's express wishes and risk arrest as a prostitute, or I could chaperone Irene on a quest across half of Europe to redeem her losses. I thought the outcome of that course all too certain: both Godfrey and Nell were already dead. We would be heading utterly away from any criminal who could ever answer to the name Jack the Ripper in a court of law.

Coda: The Vampire Box

As there were only the big wooden boxes, there were no odd corners where a man could hide.

—CAPTAIN'S LOG OF THE *DEMETER, DRACULA*

Dark.

Motion.

Seasick.

I am sailing on the panorama ship.

And the boots are coming—!

No.

I reach up. Out. Pound wood.

Dark. Utterly dark.

Box.

I am in a box. Oh, dear God . . . !

I will go mad.

If I do not die of retching first.

My hands reach out.

Find limits again. I lie on some thick fabric. The dark is the shape of a box the length and width of my body and not much more.

A coffin.

I will go mad.

If I do not die smothering.

But I breathe.

Calm. I must keep calm.

Pockets.

The fabric is rolled around me like a rug, perhaps so I do not rattle in my box.

I manage to pat the checked wool at my sides where my arms are confined.

My right hand feels the thorny bulk of my chatelaine, my left the wad of a notebook.

They have left me unmolested, despite my memory of the madman with the eyes of a dead devil and the groping hands.

My stomach spasms. Sick.

I will go mad.

If I do not die in my own vomit.

Perhaps I can move a finger to find the slit of my pocket.

There!

Perhaps I can work out the small knife on the chatelaine, cut a hole in this wood box and let some of the darkness out. In time.

I will go mad, cannot breathe in the dark, the close . . . !

My box is moving, taking me somewhere. Someone has seen to it.

Irene! She will be frantic.

She will look for me.

But I am moving, in a box, on land, over water? Far away.

I will go mad if they do not let me out soon.

But . . . sleep is coming. Unnatural sleep. I fear it. Welcome it. I cannot go mad while I sleep.

My left hand finds the pocket slit and two fingers slip within after exhausting effort.

I will go mad, but I will write it all down at the first opportunity.

Afterword

Now it should be obvious why I delayed in releasing what now lies before the reader, scholarly and popular alike.

I could plead the massive amount of material. A daily diary, begun early and recording a preternaturally long life (also composed in the leisurely and convoluted sentences so popular in the nineteenth century), occupies numerous volumes, all written by hand. (And a painstakingly spidery hand Miss Huxleigh used, too. No wonder she needed spectacles, although I suspect that the needing of spectacles is what created the penmanship.)

I could point out that a scholar like me charts an undiscovered country and must first make maps before she pens travelogues. I have not only had the heretofore unknown Huxleigh material to study and present in a logical manner, but newly discovered fragments from the Pink journals and remnants from the anonymous "Watcher."

Enormous as the task was, that alone did not cause the delay. I must admit to reading and researching the Huxleigh diaries in chronological order. I am as surprised as my readers with what the advancing years bring and, given Miss Huxleigh's volubility, they bring a good deal.

After much research I have determined that all of the details about the well-known individuals mentioned in this account tally with what is known of their lives and habits. True, their exact whereabouts during the second half of May of 1889 is not always possible to confirm.

A record does exist, however, that the Prince of Wales used at Madame Kelly's noted Paris establishment an elaborate *siège d'amour* made for him by an M. Soubrier in 1890. Such would be needed to replace a previous model defaced by the events described in Miss Huxleigh's diary. Apparently the Prince changed both his cabinetmaker and his favored brothel after the events of 1889.

Nellie Bly's account tallies with documented events of her family life and reporting career. Although she was busily publishing stories for the *World* of New York City in the spring of 1889, she had sufficient energy and enterprise (and telegraph communications were sophisticated enough then) that she could have slipped away to Europe on the trail of sensational subject matter, such as the legal brothels of Paris. She could have also briefly visited London during the previous autumn when Jack the Ripper was active.

The Prince of Wales formally opened *l'Exposition universelle* May 16, 1889, along with Buffalo Bill and his Wild West Show. Only Red Tomahawk has left little evidence; in that period the doings of native individuals were seldom recorded, sad to say.

Naturally, or unnaturally, details relating to the Jack the Ripper murders and suspects have been documented and analyzed to infinity. The upholsterer Kelly was indeed a suspect and did indeed escape to France and Paris just after the last Whitechapel killing.

Given the extraordinary events and theories of these remarkable testimonies, I stand back, braced and ready, to take and return the fire of all who read this account and the one that follows and still dare to disbelieve. *Castle Rouge*, to be published in fall, 2002, will offer even more astounding revelations. The demands of research and verification, not to mention the quantity of the materials, prevent the presentation of these astonishing events in one volume.

It is only fitting that I finish my labors for the first portion of this duology on the brink of the millennium, although about even that exact year the scholars can, and do, argue. At least they will be silent on that issue for another thousand years.

I suspect, however, that the Jack the Ripper debate will still be raging then.

*Fiona Witherspoon, Ph.D., A.I.A.**
November 5, 2000

*Advocates of Irene Adler

Chapel Noir

A Reader's Guide

Perhaps it has taken until the end of this century for an author like Douglas to be able to imagine a female protagonist who could be called "the" woman by Sherlock Holmes.
—*GROUNDS FOR MURDER*, 1991

About this Reader's Group Guide

To encourage the reading and discussion of Carole Nelson Douglas's acclaimed novels examining the Victorian world from the viewpoint of one of the most mysterious women in literature, the following descriptions and discussion topics are offered. The author interview, biography, and bibliography at the end will aid discussion as well.

Set in the period of 1880–1890 in London, Paris, Prague, and Monaco, the Irene Adler novels reinvent the only woman to have outwitted Sherlock Holmes as a complex and compelling protagonist. Douglas's portrayal of what the *New York Times* called "this remarkable heroine and her keen perspective on the male society in which she must make her independent way," recasts her "not as a loose-living adventuress but a woman ahead of her time." In Douglas's hands, the fascinating but sketchy American prima donna from "A Scandal in Bohemia" becomes an aspiring opera singer moonlighting as a private inquiry agent. When events force her from the stage into the art of detection, Adler's exploits rival those of Sherlock Holmes himself as she crosses paths and swords with the day's leading creative and political figures while sleuthing among the Bad and the Beautiful of Belle Epoque Europe.

Critics praise the novels' rich period detail, numerous historical and "semihistorical" characters, original perspective, wit, and "welcome window on things Victorian."

"The private and public escapades of Irene Adler Norton [are] as erratic and unexpected and brilliant as the character herself," noted *Mystery Scene* concerning *Another Scandal in Bohemia* (formerly *Irene's Last Waltz*), "a long and complex *jeu d'esprit*, simultaneously modeling itself on and critiquing Doyle-esque novels of ratiocination coupled with emotional distancing. Here is Sherlock Holmes in skirts; but as a detective with an artistic temperament and the passion to match, with the intellect to penetrate to the heart of a crime and the heart to show compassion for the intellect behind it."

About This Book

Chapel Noir, the fifth Irene Adler novel, opens in the Paris spring of 1889 as the controversial Eiffel tower is unveiled as the centerpiece of an elaborate world's fair. Irene Adler's barrister husband, Godfrey Norton, is away on secret business for their patron, Baron de Rothschild. Irene's longtime companion, proper parson's daughter Penelope "Nell" Huxleigh, is shocked when the Baron asks Irene to investigate the brutal murders of two courtesans in a bordello patronized by aristocrats. The savagery recalls London's Whitechapel killings of autumn, 1888. Is Jacques the Ripper now terrorizing Paris?

For Discussion

⊰ RELATED TO *CHAPEL NOIR* ⊱

1. A theme of this novel is the double standard of sexual behavior expected of, or tolerated in, men and women then, and by implication, now. How do the moral codes, or lack of them, of various men and women in this book reveal character? How do they compare to modern times?
2. If Nell is a "Watsonette" and Irene Adler takes the leading Sherlockian role, how does this pairing illuminate the mores of the times? Would this interplay be possible if Nell were not such an innocent? Is innocence a handicap for a woman in any time period? Do you think that the "moral watchdog" role, as taken on by Nell and treated with some satire by the author, could be a much more pernicious trait than it is portrayed as here? Where is the middle ground for moral women in society today?
3. Masquerade is a key element in the novel and the series, which features several unrevealed characters, many of whom keep secrets from each other. Is mystery fiction a pretext for revealing the mysteries of character as well as of crime? The Pink Cochrane sections tell the literal truth of an actual woman's life, yet would also explain how she became the "fallen woman" she seems to be. What attributes of the character made her take a pioneering path?
4. The character of Pink blends the worldly experience of Irene Adler with the innocence of Nell Huxleigh. Both Irene Adler and Sherlock Holmes are knowing of the world, but apparently have not been corrupted by it. Do you think Holmes is a virgin? If not, what is his sexual

history, and why? Does it matter, other than spawning decades of speculation and wishful thinking about Sherlock Holmes's sex life? How does Mr. Spock of *Star Trek* fit into this literary mythos? Are women intrigued by logical, unemotional male figures, and, if so, why? How would this reflect inequality in society?

5. In the nineteenth century, Paris hosted several impressive world's fairs and was known as a city of light and dark. Were you surprised by the city's numerous tourist attractions and by the appetite for sensationalism in the displays of the wax museum and the Paris Morgue? How do these trends compare to the tabloid journalism and sex and violence in electronic media—novels, films, music videos—of today?

6. This novel shows women pursuing the killer of women. Does it differ from other novels featuring the Ripper murders you may have read? Were you surprised that the Irving/Stoker theatrical circle knew about the lustmurder studies of Krafft-Ebing? Did such knowledge influence Stoker's Gothic fiction, particularly *Dracula*? How does the double sexual standard play into the notion of the supernaturally powerful man preying on women's bodies and blood? Do you see parallels to the *Dracula* story and characters in this novel? Why has *Dracula* become such a popular cultural touchstone, along with Jack the Ripper? How does this novel reference scenes and characters from *Dracula*, such as the madman Renfield and the three brides of Dracula? Do you see a difference in the fictional way a woman author and women characters approach the violence of the Ripper case? Does the participation of Buffalo Bill and Red Tomahawk contrast or parallel the history of human savagery in New World and Old?

7. This story takes place on the brink of the 1890s, called the Mauve Decade, the Yellow Nineties, and the Decadent Nineties because of a cultural climate that was both artistically fruitful and yet celebrated evil and darkness. What elements of decadence appear in this novel, besides actions relating to the murders? Is our own culture experiencing an end-of-century/end-of-millennium appetite for dark entertainment? Is Hannibal Lecter the new Dracula?

8. Retellings of the Jack the Ripper crimes have made him into something of a heroic figure like Hannibal Lecter: cold, clever, and invincible, the center of endless fascination and even a kind of admiration for the very brutality of his deeds. Does this reflect an underlying misogynism in society? If the Ripper had butchered a series of men, would the crimes still be as famous?

RELATED TO THE IRENE ADLER SERIES

1. Douglas mentions other authors, many of them women, who have reinvented major female characters or minor characters from classic literary or genre novels that reevaluate culture then and now. Can you think of such works in the field of fantasy or historical novels? General literature? What about the recent copyright contest over *The Wind Done Gone*, Alice Randall's reimagining of *Gone with the Wind*'s events and characters from the African-American slaves' viewpoints? Could the novel's important social points have been made as effectively without referencing the classic work generally familiar to most people? What other works have attained the mythic status that might make possible such socially conscious reinventions? Which would you rewrite?
2. Religion and morality are underlying issues in the novels, including the time's anti-Semitism. This is an element absent from the Holmes stories. How is this issue brought out and how do Nell's strictly conventional views affect those around her? Why does she remain both disapproving and fascinated by Irene's pragmatic philosophy? Why is Irene (and also most readers) so fond of her despite her limited opinions?
3. Why did Douglas choose to blend humor with the adventurous plots? Do comic characters and situations satirize the times, or soften them? Is humor a more effective form of social criticism than rhetoric? What other writers and novelists use this technique, besides George Bernard Shaw and Mark Twain?

4. The novels also present a continuing tension between New World and Old World, America and England and the Continent, artist/tradesman and aristocrat, as well as woman and man. Which characters reflect which camps? How does the tension show itself?
5. *Chapel Noir* makes several references to *Dracula* through the presence of Bram Stoker some six years before the novel actually was published. Stoker is also a continuing character in other Adler novels. Various literary figures appear in the Adler novels, including Oscar Wilde, and most of these historical characters knew each other. Why was this period so rich in writers who founded much modern genre fiction, like Doyle and Stoker? Why did this period produce not only *Dracula* and Doyle's Holmes stories and the surviving dinosaurs of *The Lost World*, but also *Trilby* and Svengali, *The Phantom of the Opera, The Prisoner of Zenda*, and *Dr. Jekyll and Mr. Hyde*, among the earliest and most lasting works of science fiction, political intrigue, mystery, and horror? How does Douglas pay homage to this tradition in the plots, characters, and details of the Adler novels?

An Interview with Carole Nelson Douglas

Q: *You were the first woman to write about the Sherlock Holmes world from the viewpoint of one of Arthur Conan Doyle's women characters, and only the second woman to write a Holmes-related novel at all. Why?*

A: Most of my fiction ideas stem from my role as social observer in my first career, journalism. One day I looked at the mystery field and realized that all post-Doyle Sherlockian novels were written by men. I had loved the stories as a child and thought it was high time for a woman to examine the subject from a female point of view.

Q: *So there was* "the *woman,*" *Irene Adler, the only woman to outwit Holmes, waiting for you.*

A: She seems the most obvious candidate, but I bypassed her for that very reason to look at other women in what is called the Holmes Canon. Eventually I came back to "A Scandal in Bohemia." Rereading it, I realized that male writers had all taken Irene Adler at face value as the King of Bohemia's jilted mistress, but the story doesn't support that. As the only woman in the Canon who stirred a hint of romantic interest in the aloof Holmes, Irene Adler had to be more than this beautiful but amoral "Victorian vamp." Once I saw that I could validly interpret her as a gifted and serious performing artist, I had my protagonist.

Q: *It was that simple?*

A: It was that complex. Any deeper psychological exploration of this character still had to adhere to Doyle's story, both literally and in regard to the author's own feeling toward the character. That's how I ended up having to explain that operatic impossibility, a contralto prima donna. It's been great fun justifying Doyle's error by finding operatic roles Irene could conceivably sing. My Irene Adler is as intelligent, self-sufficient, and serious about her professional and personal integrity as Sherlock Holmes, and far too independent to be anyone's mistress but her own. She also moonlights as an inquiry agent while building her performing career. In many ways they are flip sides of the same coin: her profession, music, is his hobby. His profession, detection, is her secondary career. Her adventures intertwine with Holmes's, but she is definitely her own woman in these novels.

Q: *How did Doyle feel toward the character of Irene Adler?*

A: I believe that Holmes and Watson expressed two sides of Dr. Doyle: Watson the medical and scientific man, also the staunch upholder of British convention; Holmes the creative and bohemian writer, fascinated by the criminal and the bizarre. Doyle wrote classic stories of horror and science fiction as well as hefty historical novels set in the age of chivalry. His mixed feelings of attraction and fear toward a liberated, artistic woman like Irene Adler led him to "kill" her as soon as he created her. Watson states she is dead at the beginning of the story that introduces her. Irene was literally too hot for Doyle as well as Holmes to handle. She also debuted (and exited) in the first Holmes/Watson story Doyle ever wrote. Perhaps Doyle wanted to establish an unattainable woman to excuse Holmes remaining a bachelor and aloof from matters of the heart. What he did was to create a fascinatingly unrealized character for generations of readers.

Q: *Do your protagonists represent a split personality as well?*

A: Yes, one even more sociologically interesting than the Holmes/Watson split because it embodies the evolving roles of women in the late nineteenth century. As a larger-than-life heroine, Irene is "up to anything." Her biographer, Penelope "Nell" Huxleigh, however, is the very model of traditional Victorian womanhood. Together they provide a seriocomic point-counterpoint on women's restricted roles then and now. Narrator Nell is the character who "grows" most during the series as the unconventional Irene forces her to see herself and her times in a broader perspective. This is something women writers have been doing in the past two decades: revisiting classic literary terrains and bringing the sketchy women characters into full-bodied prominence.

Q: *What of "the husband," Godfrey Norton?*

A: In my novels, Irene's husband, Godfrey Norton, is more than the "tall, dark, and dashing barrister" Doyle gave her. I made him the son of a woman wronged by England's then female-punitive divorce law, so he is a "supporting" character in every sense of the word. These novels are that rare bird in literature: female "buddy" books. Godfrey fulfills the useful, decorative, and faithful role so often played by women and wives in fiction and real life. Sherlockians anxious to unite Adler and Holmes have tried to oust Godfrey. William S. Baring-Gould even depicted him as a wife-beater in order to promote a later assignation with Holmes that produced Nero Wolfe! That is such an unbelievable violation of a strong female character's psychology. That scenario would make Irene Adler a two-time loser in her choice of men and a masochist to boot. My protagonist is a world away from that notion and a wonderful vehicle for subtle but sharp feminist comment.

Q: *Did you give her any attributes not found in the Doyle story?*

A: I gave her one of Holmes's bad habits. She smokes "little cigars." Smoking was an act of rebellion for women then. And because Doyle shows her sometimes donning male dress to go unhampered into public places, I gave her "a wicked little revolver" to carry. When Doyle put her in male disguise at the end of his story, I doubt he was thinking of the modern psychosexual ramifications of cross-dressing.

Q: *Essentially, you have changed Irene Adler from an ornamental woman to a working woman.*

A: My Irene is more a rival than a romantic interest for Holmes. She is not a logical detective in the same mold as he, but is as gifted in her intuitive way. Nor is her opera singing a convenient profession for a beauty of the day, but a passionate vocation that was taken from her by the King of Bohemia's autocratic attitude toward women, forcing her to occupy herself with detection. Although Doyle's Irene is beautiful, well-dressed, and clever, my Irene demands that she be taken seriously despite these feminine attributes. Now we call it "Grrrrl Power."

I like to write "against" conventions that are no longer true, or were never true. This is the thread that runs through all my fiction: my dissatisfaction with the portrayal of women in literary and popular fiction—then and even now. This begins with *Amberleigh*—my postfeminist mainstream version of the Gothic revival popular novels of the 1960s and 1970s—and continues with Irene Adler today. I'm interested in women as survivors. Men also interest me of necessity, men strong enough to escape cultural blinders to become equal partners to strong women.

Q: *How do you research these books?*

A: From a lifetime of reading English literature and a theatrical background that educated me on the clothing, culture, customs, and speech of various historical periods. I was reading Oscar Wilde plays when I was eight years old. My mother's book club meant that I cut my teeth on Eliot, Balzac, Kipling, Poe, poetry, Greek mythology, Hawthorne, the Brontës, Dumas, and Dickens.

In doing research, I have a fortunate facility of using every nugget I find, or of finding that every little fascinating nugget works itself into the story. Perhaps that's because good journalists must be ingenious in using every fact available to make a story as complete and accurate as possible under deadline conditions. Often the smallest mustard seed of research swells into an entire tree of plot. The corpse on the dining-room table of Bram Stoker, author of *Dracula*, was too macabre to resist and spurred the entire plot of the second Adler novel, *The Adventuress*(formerly *Good Morning, Irene*). Stoker rescued a drowning man from the Thames and carried him home for revival efforts, but it was too late.

Besides using my own extensive library on this period, I've borrowed from my local library all sorts of arcane books they don't even know they have because no one ever checks them out. The Internet aids greatly with the specific fact. I've also visited London and Paris to research the books, a great hardship, but worth it. I also must visit Las Vegas periodically for my contemporary-set Midnight Louie mystery series. No sacrifice is too great.

Q: You've written fantasy and science fiction novels, why did you turn to mystery?

A: All novels are fantasy and all novels are mystery in the largest sense. Although mystery was often an element in my early novels, when I evolved the Irene Adler idea, I just considered it a novel. *Good Night, Mr. Holmes* was almost published before I realized it would be "categorized" as a mystery. So Irene is utterly a product of my mind and times, not of the marketplace, though I always believed that the concept was timely and necessary.

Because of my own extensive library on the period, I've [illegible] my local library, all sorts of [illegible] [illegible] the Internet [illegible] with the [illegible] [illegible] and [illegible] to research the books a [illegible], but [illegible] I also [illegible] Las Vegas [illegible] for my contemporary [illegible] [illegible]

Q: [illegible]

A: [illegible]

Selected Bibliography

Bassermann, Lujo. *The Oldest Profession: A History of Prostitution*. USA: Dorset Press, 1993.

Belford, Barbara. *Bram Stoker*. New York, NY: Alfred A. Knopf, 1996.

Brook-Shepherd, Gordon. *Uncle of Europe: The Social and Diplomatic Life of Edward VII*. New York, NY: Harcourt, Brace, Jovanovich, 1975.

Coleman, Elizabeth Ann. *The Opulent Era*. New York, NY: The Brooklyn Museum, 1989.

Harsin, Jill. *Policing Prostitution in Nineteenth-Century Paris*. Princeton, NJ: Princeton University Press, 1985.

Hibbert, Christopher. *The Royal Victorians*. New York, NY: Lippincott, 1976.

Hovey, Tamara. *Paris Underground*. New York, NY: Orchard Books/Scholastic, Inc., 1991.

Jakubowski, Maxim and Braund, Nathan. *The Mammoth Book of Jack the Ripper*. London: Constable & Robinson Ltd., 1999.

Knowles, Thomas W. and Lansdale, Joe. *The West That Was*. New York, NY: Wings Books, 1993.

Krafft-Ebing, Richard von. *Psychopathia Sexualis*. Various editions.

Lottman, Herbert R. *The French Rothschilds*. New York, NY: Crown, 1995.

National Gallery of Australia. *Paris in the Late 19th Century*. Publications Department, National Gallery of Australia: Canberra, Australia, 1996.

Newman, Bruce M. *Fantasy Furniture*. New York, NY: Rizzoli, 1989.

Pearson, John. *Edward the Rake*. New York, NY: Harcourt, Brace, Jovanovich, 1975.

Russell, John. *Paris*. New York, NY: Abradale Press/Harry N. Abrams, Inc., 1983.

Schwartz, Vanessa R. *Spectacular Realities: Early Mass Culture in Fin-de-Siècle Paris*. Berkeley and Los Angeles, CA: University of California Press, 1999.

Stoker, Bram. *Dracula*. Various editions.

Wetmore, Helen Cody. *Last of the Great Scouts*. Harrisburg, PA: The National Historical Society, 1899/1994.

1.

Evening in Paris

She suffered the penalty paid by all sensation-writers of being compelled to hazard more and more theatric feats.

—WALT MCDOUGALL, *NEW YORK WORLD* ILLUSTRATOR, 1889

FROM A JOURNAL

I was born Elizabeth, but they call me Pink.

I have had to steel myself often in life.

First against my stepfather, Jack Ford, a drunken brute. Then against the men who said I had no right to exist as I was, who would patronize me.

Now against a woman who would appeal to my conscience.

I am an exposer and righter of wrongs. An undercover investigator. My mission is above conscience. My mission is my conscience.

She would divert me.

I do not like it, not even when she assembles Bertie, Prince of Wales; Baron de Rothschild; Bram Stoker; and Sarah Bernhardt into one room in Paris.

Hers.

The only person of interest in this convocation of capitol B's who is missing is Sherlock Holmes, the renowned English consulting detective. She has sent him away. And he went. Like a lamb.

I should perhaps figure her into this scene: Irene Adler Norton, ex-diva, ex-American, ex-Pinkerton agent.

She is now also a woman deprived of the two personal

props in life: her husband Godfrey Norton, and her friend and supporter Nell Huxleigh, both English, both taken in mysterious ways by mysterious enemies.

I think of women in Greek tragedies: Hecuba in *The Trojan Women*, Medea mourning her faithless man and sacrificing her children, Electra murdering her mother. Women who like Samson shake the pillars they are bound to and make the known world tremble.

She is very dangerous right now, Irene Adler Norton, and I don't care to be here for the catastrophe.

She has blackmailed me, this woman, this implacable Fury. She has reached into me like the stage artist she was and captured my attention. She has sunk her tiny, precise teeth into my soul, found my aching vulnerabilities and bound me with silken fibers of steel.

She has offered me a story to end all stories. She has promised me Jack the Ripper.

I am proud of her and I do not trust her and I will serve my own purpose, not hers. Meanwhile, here I sit among some of the Great of our Age, and listen to them flounder in the face of one irrational killer.

"My dear Irene," says Bram Stoker, the first to arrive. "I am . . . speechless. Godfrey. Nell. Gone. I think of Irving. It would be as if God had died."

Bram Stoker. Manager of the finest actor in England (the world to hear him tell it), Henry Irving. An auld acquaintance of Irene Adler Norton. He is not so much of an old friend that she has not ruled him out as a new suspect in the recent Ripperlike murders of Paris. In the London Ripper crimes of last autumn as well? Possibly. My special system of notes that only I can read records it all.

Nell had used to "take notes" for Irene when she solved cases the Pinkertons sent her way. Now I take notes. But they are my property, for publication later, when I, Elizabeth Jane Cochrane, am released from my vow of silence and fully free to be the daredevil girl reporter who has made my reputation: Nellie Bly, who will go anywhere to expose any wrong. That suits her.

"Bram. Thank you for coming." Irene takes his big hands

in hers. They gaze at each other, people in a common profession feeling loss as it happens in the real world, not on a stage.

He is still a suspect in her cast of characters, a theatrical man married to an icy beauty, devoted to a domineering actor who both employs and uses him. Sweet-tempered Bram Stoker, free after midnight in any capital of the world, loving women or loathing them? Jack the Ripper? After what we have learned, she and I, it could be.

"It slays me," he says now, "to think of dear, sweet Miss Huxleigh in villainous hands." He delivers the line with conviction.

Such a big, bluff, hearty soul. Even I who detest the Englishman's sense of superiority adore him. He is Irish, after all, and they are battering my own country into submission with their energy and optimism despite the most shattering prejudice. Big red-haired bear, genial, social, interested in such dark topics as bubble up in his short stories . . . Iron Maidens and vengeance and blood, always blood.

His huge hands tighten on Irene's delicate ones. His are bone and muscle, masculine force. Hers are steel in velvet, feminine survival.

If Bram Stoker is Jack the Ripper, he is lost.

Baron de Rothschild arrives next. An older man, refined, powerful, quiet in that power. He too takes her hands. I am struck by the image of courtiers coming to pay respects to a bereaved queen. She has won hearts as well as minds.

Not mine.

He kisses the back of each hand. "Any agent, any amount of money, they are yours to command."

"Thank you," she murmurs, and shows him to a chair.

It is a seat no better or worse than any other in the room. This is a war council of equals and she is Madam Chairman.

Sarah Bernhardt wafts in on a perfumed zephyr of ostrich boa and red hair as frothy, all fabric-swathed whipcord figure with a leopard on a leash.

"Irene! My darling! My adorable Nell and Godfrey missing! I have traveled all over the world. If you need the aid of any person of power anywhere, just let me know."

The leopard paces back and forth between the two women's skirts, purring.

The Divine Sarah bows to the Baron, nods at Bram Stoker, and arranges herself on a sofa between them.

The leopard watches Irene Adler Norton with bright predatory eyes, its vertical pupils black stab wounds in the glory of jungle-green iris.

Next comes the first of all of them: portly, blustering Bertie.

I cannot stand the man, though he is Prince of Wales now and will become King of England . . . if his black-bombazine-clad pincushion of a Mama ever dies. She has made mourning into an industry for thirty years. Bertie, christened Edward Albert, is fat, self-indulgent, and British. But then, aren't all the English fat and blustering? Well, except for Sherlock Holmes, who is not fat, and Godfrey Norton, who is apparently not only not fat, but also not self-indulgent, a rare quality in an Englishman and in any man for that matter. At least in my limited experience. Actually, more than one man has been my mentor, but they are exceptions.

So is she, Irene Adler Norton, and that is why she is so dangerous, even to me, who am used to being dangerous to others.

Inspector François le Villard comes last, hat in hand, waxed mustaches gleaming like very pointed India ink calligraphy. He accepts a solitary chair.

I wonder if Sherlock Holmes has assembled a similar company of high and low and in-between in London to serve his purposes as he returns to put Whitechapel upside down in a search for a new motive that will unmask the Ripper at last?

But I think that Mr. Holmes is a mostly solitary creature, like the web-weaving spider, and works and waits alone. Certainly he was appalled by the idea that I wanted to return to London. He claimed I had a duty to accompany the bereaved Madam Norton. I have no duty but to my higher purpose.

Still, I find it most agreeable to sit here in this Paris hotel room, among the Mostly Great and Merely Interesting, taking notes as is my wont, and as was requested specifically by our hostess.

It is the actress who makes the opening speech.

"My dear Irene, I speak for all of us, I believe, when I beg to know what we may do to assist you? This sudden disappearance of Miss Penelope, not to mention your dearly beloved spouse, is what you call in English heart-rendering, I think. You play a scene more tragic than any written for me on the stage. Ask anything of us you will. Your wish is our necessity."

A grand sentiment, but the Prince and the Baron stir uneasily, no matter how slightly. "Anything" is not a word the high and mighty toss around like a head of cabbage. Not in America and not here.

"I thank you for your good will," Irene says quietly.

I had not looked closely at her, being busy memorizing the appearance and address of the famous folk in the room. And, I did not like to stare Loss in the face, either.

She is bearing up remarkably well to scrutiny, this woman who had learned scant hours ago that her husband and her long-time companion had both vanished from the earth as if plucked up by eagles, the husband in forgotten reaches of eastern Europe, the companion vanished in the vast wilderness of the gigantic *l'Exposition Universelle* at the heart of Parisian civility in the Champ de Mars under the Eiffel Tower.

She wears a steel-gray taffeta gown as resolute as autumn rain, though it is summer.

Nothing could dampen the drive of her spirit, but her demeanor is still and serious this afternoon. Her calculated calm, however, makes everyone else restive. In their edgy rustle I detect the odor of unwilling overcommitment. She makes them nervous and had intended to.

"My dear friends," she says finally in a low tone that trembles like the finest cello strings, "if I may call so many who are mighty in the world that."

They stutter, murmur, shout that she indeed may.

"You have already put your world-wide spy network at my service, Baron de Rothschild. I can ask no more. Your Highness," she nods at the Prince, "has already offered that 'anything' I might wish for."

So Bertie was not forthcoming with any solid support. What a hypocritical prig! The talk is that he is always hard up for money. Mama keeps her knuckles on the purse strings.

"Sarah, you have your network of not so much spies as devoted admirers, and I may indeed need to call upon some of them in time.

"Inspector le Villard. I know the Paris police are doing all they can and more than many metropolitan forces ever would, including welcoming the activities of our advance American scouting party, Buffalo Bill Cody and Red Tomahawk."

She turns last to the husky Irishman. "And Bram, I have high hopes for you and your wandering soul. I am hoping you will serve as European scout for Pink and myself, for I fear this trial will lead us far from Paris."

The Baron and the Prince look relieved. The inspector appalled. The actress smug. And Bram Stoker looks both pleased and shocked.

I realized that Madam Irene has divided and conquered once again, as she had finessed me not hours ago. The two richest men in the room will be eager to offer whatever small requests she makes, having seen the specter of truly draining ambition. The actress will leave feeling useful, an emotion not common to the profession, and will consider that a contribution of great worth in itself.

The inspector will be grateful if, and when, Irene removes herself from his jurisdiction, and I am convinced that she soon will.

And Bram Stoker, poor Bram Stoker, the poorest and least famous personality, has just been named Knight Errant, the only one present she intends to lean upon in any major way whatsoever.

I wonder if it is because, next to the inspector, he is the least important of the persons gathered together. Excepting me, of course, who is a nobody and happy to live in a land where nobodies can become somebodies. The thought makes me homesick for New York, but I suppose it will be a while before I snag a big enough story to telegraph home and follow fast on its heels for the resulting sensation and acclaim.

Then Irene seizes the moment and turns the joint call of

condolence into something quite different. It is enough to make me sit up and take notes even faster.

"You realize, my friends," she says, eyeing each person in turn, "that we have gathered together in this room the world's most eminent collection of experts on the murderer known as Jack the Ripper."

Protesting waves of demurs in English and French wash against her stone-gray figure to no avail. They had come here to say what they could do for her. Now she is telling them what they can do for the world.

"It is true," she goes on. "What we knew of Jack the Ripper before these recent murders in Paris is now virtually useless. Even Sherlock Holmes has scurried back to London to reinvestigate the events there from the new perspective these Paris atrocities demand."

I doubt that the man I have met "scurries," but I know the description pleases Irene, who had perhaps hoped for his more direct assistance.

"I do not think," she adds, turning her attention to Inspector le Villard, "that our esteemed colleagues are aware of James Kelly's history and actions here in Paris."

"James Kelly!" The Prince of Wales grows immediately interested. "A very English name. I know at least one. Who is this particular man?"

"He may well be the Ripper, Your Highness," Le Villard admits with a bob to the Prince. "I regret to say that he was in the custody of the Paris police after being found and confronted by Sherlock Holmes—"

"And by," Irene interjects, "Miss Pink, myself, and, of course, our dear Nell."

A pause holds while all present acknowledge Nell's alarming absence with respectful silence.

"Indeed," Inspector le Villard says, nervously tweaking his waxed mustaches into sharper points. "I am told that the presence of all you ladies had a very disturbing effect upon him."

(*Not to mention upon Sherlock Holmes*, I jot down in my notes.)

"We were gowned," Irene explains to the room at large, "as ladies of ill repute."

"Now I wish I had been there to see that!" the Prince exclaims.

"I as well," says Sarah.

"And I." Bram Stoker.

The Baron de Rothschild expresses no such desire, which makes him the only true gentleman in the group in my estimation.

"The point is," Irene says, "James Kelly had a history of both despising and consorting with fallen women. His behavior when confronted by Sherlock Holmes in the guise of a French priest, and by we three dressed as women of the street, was odd. He alternated between cowering in fear from our very presence . . . and leaping up to put a knife blade to poor Nell's throat."

"Ah!" Sarah clutches for her own scrawny neck with an actress's instant empathy. "Poor Nell! Of all the ones least bold, the one most . . . mild."

Theatrics do not impress an ex-diva like Irene Adler. "Nell was bold enough to unsheath her hatpin and stab what might be Jack the Ripper in the wrist."

"Might be?" the Baron asks.

Irene turns to the inspector, politely waiting for his opinion.

He preens his mustaches again. "This James Kelly indeed has a sinister history. An upholsterer by trade, he came into some money from a man he had never known to be his father. Instead of enjoying his good fortune, he denounced his long-suffering mother as a whore and moved to London. There he had killed his own wife several years ago, very near the debased district called Whitechapel, by screwing a clasp-knife into her ear during an angry fit. He accused her of being a whore merely for marrying him. Convicted of murder, he obtained release from a madhouse a few years later. I cannot imagine that English madhouses release such fellows, but there it is. He certainly was at large in Whitechapel during the Ripper crimes and, what is most damning, just after the unthinkable slaughter of Marie Jeanne Kelly, he walked eighty miles to Dover and then sailed to Dieppe. From Belgium he came to France, thence making his way to Paris."

"Where," Irene notes, "he managed to forge a link between

himself and a member of the British royal family."

"Oh, I say now!" Bertie assumes full royal pout, pulling his embroidered waistcoat down over his substantial belly. "I have heard enough of these foul rumors trying to connect the Royal family to this Ripper fellow. That is the sort of outrageous gossip the sensational papers revel in. I can assure you that no member of my family would consort with the sort of persons to be found in Whitechapel."

"But Paris is not Whitechapel," Irene says, "and the connection is not a rumor, as unsuspected as it might be to Your Highness. The inspector mentioned that Kelly was an upholsterer. He was apparently a good enough one to find finishing work with a reputable firm here in Paris, one that was creating a unique and exquisite piece of furniture for Your Highness, that was in fact, the structure upon which the two murdered residents of the *maison de rendezvous* were discovered."

The Prince is almost moved enough to bound up from his sofa seat. Almost, but not quite. It is too soon after lunch, which no doubt had been twelve courses.

"No! The scoundrel! You are saying he had a hand in my, er, custom-appointed couch? This is revolting."

"Your Highness must have known the events that occurred upon the object in question during your absence."

"I was told that the piece was ruined and, of course, I would never reclaim anything that had played a part in a scene so opposite to the refined and joyous purpose for which it was intended."

Here I nearly snort my disbelief and contempt. This *siege d'amour* was a spoiled nobleman's toy for cavorting with two bought women at once. To consider this a "refined" use was more than an upright and plain-spoken American could stand.

Fortunately, Irene has lived in Europe long enough avoid plain-speaking when irony will do.

Instead of launching the lecture I would have at this prince of lechery, she merely remarks, "Your Highness has put your finger on the most interesting feature of some of these latter-day Paris slayings: the choice of a refined scene of the crime, and of refined victims. Yes, one could simply say that James Kelly strayed onto the scene in the course of installing the furniture. Certainly, judging from the encounter we three women had with him later, he was unable to restrain himself from violence when in the presence of women of a certain type."

"Whores," Sarah announces in her most ringing, stagy tones, and in English. "Oh, don't frown at me, Bertie. You know you adore the female in every incarnation, from maid to mistress."

"So I was within moments of encountering this monster?" Bertie notes with a shiver.

"So was Bram," Irene adds.

The heavy-set Irishman, who'd been content to cede his usual role as raconteur to Irene during this macabre discussion, finds himself the sudden center of attention. His cheeks pink above his bushy red beard. For all his hearty manner, he is a sensitive soul.

"I had accompanied Irving to the *maison* on previous visits to Paris," he says quickly. "Now that I am in Paris alone, I went only to pay my respects to the, er, madame."

He always refers to Irving as a demigod, presumably recognizable to all by his last name alone. Perhaps that is the role of a manager.

This all-consuming position includes accompanying the Great Man from Paris scenes as scandalous as the cancan clubs and various *maisons de rendezvous*. When Englishmen come to Paris there is only one thing they want to do, apparently. Except for Sherlock Holmes, which raises other, equally interesting speculations in my reportorial mind. Also raising speculation is the more macabre outings of Irving and Stoker along with hundreds of daily gawkers: the public display case of unidentified corpses at the infamous Paris Morgue.

I realize how cleverly Irene has turned a condolence call into an interrogation, for two of the four men in this room had been present at the scene of the first two Paris murders and a third, the Baron de Rothschild, spirited both the Prince and later Irene and Nell from that very *maison*.

I can see by the drooping of the inspector's very disciplined mustaches that he had not known of the Prince's presence in the house of sin and death, nor the fact that the . . . device upon which two women died had been commissioned especially for him. Being French and worldly, he would not condemn the perverse intention, only the murderous turn its use had taken.

"Kelly possessed a certain religious mania," Irene muses for the benefit of her friends and suspects.

I began to wonder if even the inspector and I are excepted from the suspect category, for of course I, too, had been present that night and had found the butchered bodies. Probably we are not. I am beginning to see that, like Sherlock Holmes, Irene is relentless in the pursuit of truth, though her approach is far less direct than his.

I also begin to see that she arranges scenes like a playwright. First she assembles the dramatis personae, then she lets them speak among each other and thus speak the truth to her, all unknowing.

It is a theatrical approach and requires much patience and rehearsal before any denouement can be expected.

"Nothing in Jack the Ripper's London murders indicated a religious mania," the prince says finally, after long mulling over Irene's comment.

The inspector answers for her. "Allow me, Your Highness. I have studied the case most avidly. In all such murders of fallen women a religious mania is suspected. As the purported billet-doux from the Ripper said, 'I am down on whores.' Usually such reactions are moral. I believe that it is the frustration of the natural instincts that creates such madmen. In Paris, in France, we have made houses of prostitution legal for decades and inspect the women to ensure good health. It has eliminated much unnecessary disease and is the only reasonable approach to the situation. England and London are not so enlightened. Men who have contracted foul diseases from whores become murderously infuriated. It is no wonder that these Ripper slayings, and others that frequently occur in this Whitechapel district, are more common to England than to France."

"Until now," Irene notes.

The inspector flashes her an impatient look. "What? Two women at a reputable house?"

I shudder to think what Nell would have to say about the very French notion of a "reputable" whorehouse were she here to ride scout on the discussion.

The inspector natters on. "The third woman was either an unlucky laundress or one of the lone unfortunates, *femmes isloée,* who plies the streets themselves."

"You have not addressed," Irene says, "the strange subterranean aspect of these Paris killings. That is another aspect purely Parisian: cellars, sewers, catacombs. Even the Morgue and the wax museum were used to display the bodies in some bizarre manner."

The inspector shrugs, a classic French response to the mystery of life.

"The *Musée Grévin,*" he says grandly, "is far more than a wax museum, especially during *L'Exposition universelle* and the inauguration of *La tour Eiffel*, is a landmark of Paris. Might not even a madman wish to pay tribute to the attractions of the City of Light in planning his crimes?"

"The Ripper managed to keep to obscure and hidden ways in London," Irene points out.

"London!" The inspector barely restrains himself from spitting. "Whitechapel. Paris has no such sinkhole as this. It is no mystery that the Paris murders involve a finer sort of victim."

"Then the Ripper has moved to Paris and grown nice."

Bram Stoker speaks up at long last. "The bloody rites I heard of in the cavern beneath the fairgrounds don't sound very refined. Were I to write such a scene, I'd be accused of sensation-mongering. I agree with what the man in the street said during the Ripper attacks last autumn. No Englishman would do it."

"Nor any Frenchman!" the inspector shouts, his mustaches twitching like cockroach feelers.

Amazing how no nationality on earth would spawn a Ripper so long as any man of that race is present.

"The Jews," the Baron says quietly, "are often accused, and falsely, of atrocities toward Christians. Oddly enough, the facts prove the atrocities are inevitably committed against them. Us," he adds.

"That is the trouble!" When Prince of Wales finally speaks, he does so passionately. "There are all sorts of political scapegoats abounding that one faction or the other would like to accuse of the Ripper's crimes, including members of England's royal family! I have been repeatedly criticized for consorting with Jews and merchants and jockeys and, er, women."

"And does Your Highness deny any of it?" Irene asks, a trifle archly.

The Prince, like any pampered aristocrat, responds to the coy like a cat to a whisker-tickle. That is one thing I grant Sherlock Holmes. He is not pampered and he is not an aristocrat.

"Well, no," Bertie says, demonstrating the disarming honesty that makes him tolerated if not beloved. "Drat the fellow! He has caused endless trouble and I wish they would lock him away."

" 'They' is always us, Your Highness," Irene says. "And that is why 'we' must do something about Jack the Ripper. I take it I have your permission to try."

The inspector snorts delicately, being French.

Irene needs no one's permission, but she wishes some of the people in this room to see that she has a royal mandate.

"I would be delighted," the Prince says, smiling a bow in her direction. Bertie has always enjoyed deferring to women, except his mother. Irene has never underestimated official approval.

She smiles back. Like a privateer of old, she has won the royal letter of mark.

She is free to hoist the Jolly Roger and to board and commandeer any ships she chooses.

Lord help us, she already has the U.S.S. Nellie Bly in her fleet and I shudder to think what freebooters she will add to her armada.

About the Author

CAROLE NELSON DOUGLAS is journalist-turned-novelist whose writing in both fields has received dozens of awards. A literary chameleon, she has always explored the roles of women in society, first in nonfiction reporting and then in numerous novels ranging from fantasy and science fiction to mainstream fiction. She currently writes two mystery series. The Victorian Irene Adler series examines the role of women in the late nineteenth century through the eyes of the only woman to outwit Sherlock Holmes, an American diva/detective. The contemporary-yet-Runyon-esque Midnight Louie series contrasts the realistic crime-solving activities and personal issues of four main human characters with the interjected first-person feline viewpoint of a black alley cat, P. I., who satirizes the role of the rogue male in crime and popular fiction.

Douglas, born in Everett, Washington, grew up in St. Paul, Minnesota, but emigrated with her husband to Fort Worth, Texas, trading Snowbelt for Sunbelt and journalism for fiction. In college she was a finalist in *Vogue* magazine's *Prix de Paris* writing competition (won earlier by Jacqueline Bouvier Kennedy Onassis) and earned degrees in English literature and speech and theater, with a minor in philosophy. She collects books, vintage clothing, and homeless animals.

Chapel Noir resumes the enormously well-received Irene Adler series after a seven-year hiatus and will be followed by a sequel, *Castle Rouge*. The first Adler novel, *Good Night, Mr. Holmes*, won American Mystery and *Romantic Times* magazine awards and was a *New York Times* Notable Book.

Website: www.catwriter.com
E-mail: IreneAdler@catwriter.com